eternity is temporary

BILL BROADY is the author of the novella *Swimmer* (Flamingo, 2000) and *In This Block There Lives a Slag... and Other Yorkshire Fables* (Flamingo, 2001) and the editor of *You Are Here*, the Redbeck book of contemporary short fiction (Redbeck Press, 2006). This is his first novel.

From the reviews of *Eternity is Temporary*

'Ingeniously comic, bitingly perceptive and endowed with a spaced-out, hyper-real atmosphere all of its own, Bill Broady's first full length work of fiction ranks as the perfect read for the dying days for a long, hot and fractious summer... Both ribald and romantic, *Eternity is Temporary* enjoys the vintage gear but never feels confined by it... This is a novel about dreaming and hoping and waiting for the weather of life to break; about the secret sense shared by young and old that they may stand "just one step away from something remarkable."... Through a series of glorious set pieces, Broady conjures up a summer when rules and boundaries melt like tarmac in the seething streets... Broady counts as a true original, a writer who keeps our judgements nicely suspended and our senses keenly primed... Broady excels at evoking the sort of musical moment that hovers between time and eternity... His novel, too, hits the poised, expectant note that defines these lives, in that summer, and holds it through a bittersweet spell of gently twisted time... writing that glows with uplifting, not belittling, wit on every page.' **Boyd Tonkin, *Independent***

'Bill Broady's original new novel is a teen romance played out in an old people's home... this novel is refreshingly free of motive. We are rarely party to anyone deciding anything, as if the eternity Broady describes is the lull between moments of having to do so... Just when everyone seems stuck in this eternal summer, there is a series of detonations and the drama intensifies. This is not a novel about the 70s or punk rock. It is, much more interestingly, about what happens while you wait for something to happen.' **Lavina Greenlaw, *Guardian***

D1460190

'How do you carry on living – and loving – in the face of the certain knowledge that your days are numbered from the start?... as the novel moves towards a climax, Broady choreographs his imagery and themes with dexterity and verve; his grand finale is inevitable once you reach it, unpredictable before, and infuses this book with an unusual kind of grace.' *Time Out*

'*Eternity is Temporary* slowly gathers momentum as Evan and Adrea screw themselves into the grip of a consuming lassitude, copulating and smoking dope up in the home's attic flat. Broady playfully introduces a surreal fluidity to normal boundaries which, he implies, could be heat induced or the fringes of "psychic commotion". Broady enjoys such frivolous ambiguities. Together with the subtle contrariness of duty and carelessness which underpin this engaging novel, they give his dallying youngsters occasional touches of a Kunderan lightness of being.' **James Urquhart**, *Independent on Sunday*

'Broady allows the plot to unfurl languorously... his chosen form suits his story, in which time and memory, youth and age intermingle until they become almost indistinguishable.' *Metro*

'A pin-sharp depiction of the sex, sherry and shackles in a care home.' ***Independent on Sunday* Critics' Choice**

'Part magic realism, part humorous polemic on the consequences of caring and the experience of ageing, *Eternity is Temporary* is packed with characters of extraordinary potential. This is a story where the everyday and the spectacular merge seamlessly.' **New Books Magazine**

'A fluid and easy read. Broady uses his mastery of the language to tease out his characters' personalities in a languid sweat drenched plot... The dramatic finish burns itself on to your memory very much like the searing after-image you get on the back of your eyelids after gazing a few seconds too long at the fearsome summer sun.' *Bradford Telegraph & Argus*

'Bill Broady pits a poignant yet surreal love story against the unlikely backdrop of a North London old people's home. *Eternity is Temporary* vividly recalls 1976's long, hot summer of Pistols and pogo-ing.' *InStyle Magazine*

eternity is temporary

Bill Broady

Portobello
BOOKS

First published by Portobello Books Ltd 2006
This paperback edition published 2007

Portobello Books Ltd
Eardley House
4 Uxbridge Street
Notting Hill Gate
London w8 7sy, UK

A CIP catalogue record is available from the British Library

9 8 7 6 5 4 3 2 1 ·

ISBN 978 1 84627 036 9

www.portobellobooks.com

Designed by Richard Marston
Typeset in Sabon by Avon DataSet Ltd, Bidford on Avon, Warwickshire B50 4JH
Printed and bound in Great Britain by Bookmarque Ltd, Croydon, Surrey

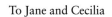
To Jane and Cecilia

'O König, Das
Kann ich dir nicht sagen;
Und was du fragst
Das kannst du nie erfahren'

Wagner, *Tristan und Isolde*, Act II, Scene III

'... Man, if you gotta ask, you'll never know'

Louis Armstrong

one

All through the bank holiday the temperature had far exceeded the seasonal average until on Tuesday, at noon, it hit eighty-two. In the cobalt blue, unEnglish sky, the sun appeared to have swollen to several times its usual size. Shoppers on Camden High Street could feel its rays beating out a steady rhythm on their bowed heads, as if it were requesting admittance. Sweat-drenched, dazzled, assailed by swarms of early wasps, they shuffled through the thickening air, lamenting the perpetual drizzle that they'd groused about all winter. An even fiercer heat seemed to be issuing from the cracks in the pavement: perhaps, far below, Hell itself was burning? At the vegetable market, fresh produce rotted before their eyes like time-lapse photographs. Everything smelt of fish.

The shop fronts glared and throbbed with colour except for a large old dark public house. Its metal, stone and glass looked to have been tarred by the perpetual cortèges of traffic that crept into and out of Central London. Its signboard – of an eagle hovering over a sleeping baby – had long since been reduced to a black triangle above a white oblong on a greyish field.

Although it was relatively cool inside, the six regulars at the bar were even more laconic than usual, intently watching their halves of mild evaporate. In the far corner, part-hidden by ramparts of empty glasses, a man and woman were having their customary lunchtime argument. Any variations were minor – they'd long since perfected it. The landlord yawned and spat. Still, he reflected, the great thing about pub work – especially in London – was that at any moment just about anyone could walk in: Elton John, Ronnie Biggs, the Queen Mum – possibly all three, arm-in-arm.

The landlord's name was Terry but nobody ever called him that. Since he'd taken on the Eagle and Child it had been known locally as 'The Midget' or 'Midge's'. Although he was only four feet seven, he had never considered himself to be a freak: on the contrary, he felt that he had once been an ordinary person who had managed, through sheer hard work, to effect a wonderful metamorphosis.

The punters weren't drawn in by thirst or loneliness: they came to see Midge, hugging themselves with delight like elderly parents who have just produced a late, miraculous child. His novelty never wore off. They cherished his simplest actions, chortling at those tiny fingers on the pumps. Unlike many midgets, his head was in reasonable proportion to his neck and shoulders, and his sharply-cleft chin jutted out six inches above the counter, like an economy version of Kirk Douglas. There were endless speculations about his cock: was it really true that midgets' displaced flesh and bone was packed down between their legs? Women who enquired further always felt the need to keep the legend alive. Mary the barmaid would roll her eyes and trill, 'You can run him off batteries or the mains.'

Midge was quite tall enough to wield the full-size Slazenger cricket bat that he kept under the counter. Not even Brian Close – whose signature endorsed the blade – could have linseed-oiled it more assiduously. When drunks began to flail about or to whistle 'Hi-Ho, Hi-Ho', it would leap to his hand like Excalibur. He'd come at them fast and low, from unfamiliar angles. If they stooped, it needed the merest tap on a knee to floor them; if they leaned back to kick him, their groins were left unprotected. Sometimes, while he was playing scales on their ribs, Midge would feel displaced air fanning his brow as his victims punched at an imaginary face level with their own.

He wasn't in the best of humours that afternoon. The brewery had once again refused his request to change the name of the pub or at least to replace that faded signboard with a portrait of himself. It made no sense: Camden Town wasn't celebrated for its eagles or even its children. 'It's historical,' they told him. Why couldn't they see that he himself might be historical, too? And why had they turned down his suggested compromises: designs of a soaring beaked and taloned midget or himself disguised in swaddling clothes, waiting for unwary raptors to flap within reach of his trusty willow?

If Midge wasn't historical – perhaps you had to be dead to qualify? – he was certainly famous. Everyone remembered him: pinned behind the bar were postcards from all over the world. There were no views of Niagara, the Acropolis or the Pyramids, just a mass of naked female flesh – black, white, yellow, brown – punctuated by saucy McGills from engineers in the Gulf. A reporter from *Where to Go* had even written him up: 'A dingy, dodgy pub notable for its resident violent and swearing midget.' Unfortunately this had been mistranscribed as 'violet and sweating', and the new faces that subsequently appeared had evinced obvious disappointment when he remained chalk-white and bone-dry. This had been Midge's first taste of the downside of celebrity.

'I've had a basinful of them,' the drunken woman shouted, 'and a basinful of you!' About now, thought Midge, would be a good time for Lord Lucan and Mary Poppins to show. He glared hopefully towards the door which, right on cue, began to creak open. A saffron ray sliced across the darkness, reaching halfway to the bar before abruptly disappearing with a crash, as the tightened door hinges snapped back like a mousetrap, ejecting the unsuspecting stranger. People usually interpreted this as a warning and fled, but now the door was slowly opening again. A tall narrow figure, exerting steady pressure of forearm and hip, appeared to be dissolving in the cascades of light until it took a step over the threshold and the door silently closed behind it. The six drinkers simultaneously drew in their breath to create a silence of palpable hostility. They savoured such moments, awaiting the interloper's opening words – 'Which is the way to Castle Dracula?' perhaps, or 'I'm looking for the Ringo Kid.' They leaned back, narrowing their eyes, fingering imaginary six-guns and cruci-fixes.

Midge, having ducked below the bar, was now lying flat on his back, watching the stranger's progress via the tilted mirror above the optics. How he loved those shocked expressions when his pallid face suddenly came popping up between the pump-handles! The steamed-up ones were the best, like that bearded clown who had cleaned his glasses with a canary-yellow cloth, put them back on, taken one look, then run straight out. Midge noticed that today's victim was trying to adjust to the gloom by shaking his head like a scrambled boxer. It was a shame that he'd somehow negotiated the concealed riser at the bottom of the ramp. A tall, unsuspecting stranger: just the ticket for a bad, bold midget! Although Midge was effectively grovelling at the man's feet, he seemed to be looking down at him from an eagle's perch. He took in the straight nose, deep-set eyes, long jaw and left-parted hair: a white star at the crown revealed that he'd be bald by middle age, but Midge suspected that he would have had a pretty good time by then.

Usually he liked to leap up to the newcomer's eye level before crashing back to earth but now he decided to come up slowly, sway-ing like a sleepy cobra, while rumbling in an Arthur Mullard bass, 'YUS?'

The man didn't move a muscle. His expression was neutral, as if it would only have been surprising if Midge *hadn't* been there, as if he'd encountered a thousand midget barmen and hadn't been particularly impressed by even the first. It was hard to put an age to him: some-where between sixteen and thirty. His hair, glossy as a bird's wing, falling raggedly across his forehead, was too short for a hippy but way too long for a skinhead. He wore faded straight-leg denims and a black cap-sleeve T-shirt with a cartoon of a spaniel in a beret blowing on a baritone saxophone, with crotchets and minims flowing out of its bell – unplayable notes, except perhaps by dogs. Midge's hands were gripping the counter, as if to prevent himself sinking into the ground or floating up to the ceiling. He felt himself diminishing under that grey stare, in ways that had nothing to do with feet and inches.

'A pint of bitter, please.' The accent was unplaceable but certainly not local. Midge, finding himself jumping to it like an eager flunkey, had to force himself to slow down. He picked his nose with a crooking little finger before reaching for a half-pint glass.

'*Pint*, please,' said a voice behind him. Ostentatiously scratching his backside with his free hand, Midge moved towards the lager pump.

'*Bitter*, please,' said the voice.

Midge filled the glass and then held it out six inches above the bar top. The man's expression didn't change but a strange ripple, like a subcutaneous pulsing, started at the jaw and slowly progressed up his face, finally disappearing into the hairline. Although Midge slammed the pint down, not a drop was spilt.

'And a packet of cashews,' said the man, with considerable emphasis, as if giving a password, some momentous cue that the midget could never take.

Midge watched him move down the room; he disliked the back view even more than the front. All the tables were covered with burns and sticky with glass-rings; every seat was ripped, leaking sawdust and rusty springs; every ashtray was filled with last night's dog-ends. The man finally settled next to the jukebox, opposite the still bickering couple. Something about the way he ate the cashews – one at a time, periodically licking the salt and dust off his fingers – indicated that this was his lunch, or even breakfast. Midge saw that he kept looking at his own feet, lifting first one cracked monkey-boot then the other. He was obviously high on something. Drugs, Midge imagined, would make the humdrum – even feet – seem exciting, while allowing the really special things in life – roses, rainbows, eagles, midgets – to pass unremarked.

In fact, Evan was thinking about a pair of snakeskin boots. Standing by themselves in the greasy display window of the shoemaker's by the Lock they'd had an ominous fairytale aura, as if anyone who wore them would end up marrying a princess or dancing themselves to death. The thick dust around them had been disturbed – perhaps they sometimes went marching, left and right, on sentry-go? The cobbler, his bald head dotted with angry red patches, never looked up from his bench. Evan had wondered whether he alone was able to see this shop.

They weren't stacks or wedges but had Cuban heels of pale, grained wood and up-tilting winkle-picker toes. He knew that they'd fit, that they were made for him. They looked familiar, as if he'd long been dreaming of them, and he felt that they somehow recognized him, too, as though, in its jungle, the snake had been experiencing its own vague presentiments. He'd watched the scale-patterns teem and shift: the creature's eyes seemed to be mesmerizing him from some hidden folds. His own faithful boots suddenly looked stupid – the metal toecaps bursting through the thinning leather, the eyelets fuzzed and frayed – and began resentfully to pinch and bite. Half-closing his eyes, he could still see the snakeskin shimmering, could feel its cold, wet clasp and hear a faint, welcoming hiss. He couldn't afford them: whatever they cost it would be more than nothing. At that moment he would have given his soul for them, even though he knew that in a few weeks' time their magic would be gone and he'd just be throwing them in the corner along with everything else.

Evan finished the nuts and then took a sip of his beer, which contrived to be at once flat and fizzy, both too sour and too sweet.

What instinct, he wondered, had made him carry his thirst past four pubs and into this indistinguishable fifth? All eyes were still on him, except for those of the couple opposite. They'd been shouting when he came in and although they'd now quietened down, their whispers were still clearly audible.

'I've had a basinful of them,' the woman was saying, 'I've had them up to here.' Her face in profile looked like a crudely-carved, salt-weathered ship's figurehead.

'They think the world of you, though, Mum,' said her companion sententiously, in a Black Country accent. At least twenty years younger than her, he wore a tartan Budgie jacket with tan suede panels, through which his brawny arms and barrel chest were bursting, like the Incredible Hulk.

'No, no, no. They don't know the meaning of the word gratitude.' She was one of those people who can drink and talk at the same time, without too much distortion. 'Swanning around as if they've got some divine right to be alive.' The level of the purple liquid in her glass was dropping at an alarming rate.

'We should burn the whole place down!' yelled the man, in a dramatic change of tone. 'That'd show 'em!'

He rotated his huge hands anti-clockwise when he spoke and then clockwise when she replied: 'No. They'd only rebuild it and send us a new lot' – she dabbed her upper lip into her drink – 'probably even worse.'

Why was it, Evan wondered, that overheard conversations always sounded so sinister and fascinating but when you got to know the people involved they rapidly turned out to be as boring as everyone else? It was just a bitter old woman and her stay-at-home son talking big on drink. As he watched, they simultaneously took great drags on their cigarettes, then extinguished them and stuck their tongues out at each other. His was ash-grey, matching the carpet, while hers was magenta with a black stripe. They came closer until their sharp, waggling tips touched, then rammed into each other's mouths. Most of the man's left arm disappeared up her skirt while her right fist closed in his bulging groin, as if gripping the collar of a savage dog. It was pretty impressive but then, as Evan reflected, incest or murder – in themselves, when you got right down to it – were probably no more exciting than bingo or the telly. At length they broke off, with a sound like a released suction cup, blowing out great mouthfuls of each other's smoke.

'Spring is the worst,' said the woman. 'The sun shines. The little flowers bloom. The birdies sing. And that lot over there start to stink.'

'I didn't think they'd all make it through the winter,' said the man, lighting a fresh cigarette with a repro Zippo lighter. 'I thought that snow would have taken some of them off.'

'I've had a basinful of them,' she said emphatically. 'They've no gratitude. And I've had a basinful of you.'

It was time for music to come to the rescue. The jukebox was in the old-fashioned cabinet style. Along its illuminated side-panels a succession of top-hatted gentlemen and bonneted ladies rode penny-farthing bicycles, while inside the raised wooden lid was a brightly-painted Egyptian mummy-case, flanked by scarabs, ibises and Horus-eyes. Evan sent his last fifty pence rattling into the slot before even checking the selections. The cards weren't printed but hand-written in shaky red capitals. There were no artists listed, only strange titles, that he didn't recognize: 'I'm Randy, Fuck Me', 'Shits in the Night', 'Band with the Runs'. He had apparently stumbled upon a secret world of music that had dispensed with euphemism in favour of the downright scatological and obscene.

He pressed A12 at random: 'Piss, Come and Underpants'. The sound was so distorted that it was some time before he recognized the voice of Nick Lowe:

> As I walk through this wicked world
> Searching for light in the darkness of insanity

I ask myself is all hope lost?
Is there only pain and hatred and misery?
And each time I feel like this inside
There's only one thing I wanna know:
What's so funny 'bout peace, love and understanding?

It felt strange to be so disappointed at hearing one of his favourite songs. A ragged descant – 'Piss, Come and Underpants' – wafted over from the bar. The barman was jabbing his finger at him and jumping up and down like a monkey: it appeared that lack of height was the least of his problems.

Everything became clear. The songs were Ducks De Luxe's 'Ships in the Night', 10CC's 'I'm Mandy' and, appositely enough, the 'Band with the Runs' was McCartney and his bloody Wings. Evan doubted that the current joint number ones – Abba's 'Spermando' and Brotherhood of Man's 'Shave Your Pussy For Me' – would sound any better for being re-titled. Still, at least the good old Who – with 'I Can't See for Piles', '(Talkin' 'Bout) My Genital Inflammation' and 'Cunt, Explain' – were properly represented.

Just one title eluded him, but when Nick Lowe had finished, after a changeover operation entailing twelve discrete and deafening clicks, the mysterious 'Brownhattin' turned out to be poor innocent Ella Fitzgerald's tender transformation of Manhattan Island into a second Eden.

He opened his copy of *Melody Maker*. If 1975 had been a bad year then 1976 was shaping up to be even worse. There were five re-issued Beatles singles in the top thirty. Schumann and Phil Spector had been right: England truly was a land without music. He saw that the huge man opposite was making for the bar, leaning sideways as if into a gale, the massive flares of his grubby white trousers entirely enveloping his feet. His companion seemed to have vanished.

Evan's scalp prickled as the zick-zack-zick opening of War's 'Low Rider' – or 'Loo Roller', as the jukebox styled it – scraped right along his nerve-ends. It was the one good song of the moment: totally original, coming out of nowhere from Eric Burdon's old backing band, of all the unlikely sources. The bass rose and swooped, the banshee guitar played peek-a-boo behind those funny little Tijuana horn-figures, while the vocalist muttered incomprehensibly – about drugs, presumably, and sex and revolution and the great dark spaces between them. Maybe there'd be just one great record every year or maybe 'Low Rider' was the last that anyone, anywhere, would ever make. Coincidentally, the paper featured an interview with Burdon. 'My Five Year Acid Trip', it was headed. 'I talked with Buddha,' said Eric. 'I talked with God. I talked with Hendrix after he was dead. I saw myself at the age of 103.' It was so sad: recalling the rasp and edge of his voice on those great Animals singles, he seemed just about the last person likely to have ended up like that.

Over at the bar they were teasing Midge by sending him up on to the shelf for obscure liqueurs and then changing their minds. Finally he just hung off his ladder like King Kong on the Empire State, roaring defiance, brandishing not Fay Wray but a bottle of Blue Bols. As 'Low Rider' roared into the sax break, Evan felt a draft of chilly air playing over his right cheek. He turned to see that the woman from the table opposite was now seated next to him. Her head swayed as if she were trying to keep him in focus. Her breath smelled of Dettol. 'Horrible racket!' she yelled. Evan nodded vigorously, as if she had expressed the greatest possible approval. She grabbed his hand and gave it a fierce squeeze. She was a formidable creature: her fingers were like little arms. He couldn't catch her name, which sounded Japanese, although her accent was London-Irish. Only at the third try did he realize that she was saying 'Mrs Allen' – elided into one word, with an extremely elongated 'A'. Evan's face did its rippling thing again. Mrs Allen shook her head vigorously and then took another gulp of purple, as if it might be at once the cause and cure. War's trumpet drowned out her next words but he saw the lips forming an all-too-familiar pattern: 'You're not from round here, are you?' Evan was sure that he could summon up a primal memory of midwife, doctor and mother all throwing up their hands and chorusing those very words.

'Just arrived,' he said, pointing in what was probably the wrong direction. 'Tolmers Square.'

'I knew it.' She punched his arm delightedly and winked. 'The moment you walked in I knew you were a squatter.'

Again, despite his best efforts, Evan felt the ripple pass up his face: it was starting to be painful. He'd been trying to stop smiling ever since a girl on yesterday's train – before she'd given him a phone number that he wouldn't be ringing – had ticked him off for smirking. It looked as if his mouth were unzipping itself, she said. Mrs Allen winked again and again: each time he choked off his smile. They fenced like this for a while. Evan's jaws ached. He saw that over at the bar the head of Mrs Allen's lover-son had twisted on its shoulders and was glowering back at them.

She moved her chair closer. 'Do you like old people?'

In all fairness, Evan felt that this was taking self-deprecation a little too far. He saw that she was younger than he'd thought. Despite the slack skin depending from the chin and elbows, or the seams and ridges under her thick, old-fashioned make-up, she couldn't have been much over forty. He wasn't very good at ages, simply dividing the human race into two categories: those he liked to look at and those he didn't. Most of the former relegated themselves to the latter in a very short time.

'It depends,' he finally replied, judiciously.

'On whether they're boiled or fried?' she asked, in a passable impersonation of W.C. Fields. She winked again but this time Evan didn't have to grapple with a smile.

The man at the bar, without waiting for the beer to settle, snatched up his drinks and returned to their table, at a crouching run. 'There's a good boy,' said Mrs Allen. He picked up his chair by its front legs, carefully examined the seat as if instructions for what to do in such circumstances might have been taped there, then carried it over, raised high, as though contemplating braining one or both of them.

'This is Billy,' said Mrs Allen, from inside her fresh glass.

'Evan,' said Evan.

The man sat down and joined his hands, as if in prayer. 'Looks more like 'Ell to me,' he grumbled. He looked older close to, with deep laughter lines around his mouth and eyes, although Evan couldn't imagine him ever cracking a smile, except perhaps with a hammer.

'I think I'm going to make this young man an offer he can't refuse,' said Mrs Allen.

Billy groaned and put his head in his hands: they enveloped it.

She turned back to Evan. 'Would you answer a few questions?'

He shook his head, which she apparently took as assent.

'Are you reliable and trustworthy?'

'No,' said Evan.

'That's all right, dear. Nobody is really. Can you read?'

He indicated *Melody Maker*.

'Can you write?'

With her Biro he drew a large cross on the forehead of 'the latest New Dylan', Bruce Springsteen, then, as she frowned, inscribed 'Hello' in fancy italics.

'How do you get on with your grandparents?'

Evan almost replied that he'd never had any but then, with some thought, managed to summon up some hazy images. 'OK, I think.'

Billy's fingers loosened their grip to allow him to breathe: an unblinking eye observed Evan through the chink.

'I am the matron,' announced Mrs Allen, in a suddenly authoritative tone, 'of a residential home for the elderly. We have vacancies for dedicated, professional care assistants. I knew as soon as I saw you that you were perfect for the job.'

'When do I start?' said Evan.

'Fuck me,' said Billy, his voice resonating in the cave of his palms. 'He's not even going to think about it.' In that split second, however, it had felt to Evan that every conceivable possibility had flashed through his head, like a computer sucking in a thousand negatives and then spitting them out resolved into a resounding yes.

'Tomorrow. Eight ack emma,' said Mrs Allen. 'I'll draw you a map.' At lightning speed, Bruce and The E-Street Band were obliter-ated by an elaborate maze of streets, all of which, for some reason, had been named after birds. Interesting local landmarks – bus-stop, lock-up garage, telephone box – were highlighted, and an enormous rocket marked 'No. 43' appeared to be homing in on a cul de sac called Heron Close.

'Is it far?' asked Evan.

'Why, it's just over the road.' She added NSEW arrows at the bottom right-hand corner, a few stick men and women, something that was either an avenue of trees or an exploding bomb-cluster, and a strange round object with a mane and a smiling face.

'Is that a lion's head?'

She looked indignant. 'No! It's the sun.'

Evan became aware of flurries of movement under the table. Mrs Allen and Billy were kicking each other, although neither face regis-tered the least flicker of pain or pleasure at the impact.

'The money's good,' said Mrs Allen. 'Time-and-a-half for week-ends, double for holidays. Seven-day fortnights – two weeks of early shifts, two of lates. There's nothing to it: just remind them when it's time to get up, eat or go to bed. Stop them falling over and if they do, just pick them up again. It's a bit boring but nice and peaceful. The ressies are as good as gold: not a bad egg in the whole bunch.'

'You sounded as if you were planning to kill them just now,' said Evan.

Mrs Allen ignored Billy's snigger. 'Oh no! We were only relieving the tension. Graveyard humour – like in the Blitz. I think the world of them really.'

'Didn't you say you'd had a basinful?'

'Well' – she gave him a very slow wink – 'it all depends on what's in the basin, doesn't it? There can be nice things as well as nasty.'

Although Evan's final jukebox selection – The Carpenters' novocaine version of 'A Kind of Tush' – had come to an end, Mrs Allen continued to shout.

'You'll learn a lot from them: history, poverty, the war. One of our ladies even saw Queen Victoria. Mind you, it *was* last Thursday.'

Billy's shoulders were shaking but less with laughter than as a warning of imminent eruption.

'We've got to make the most of them. Soon there won't be any left.'

Evan was bemused. 'Any what?'

'People.'

'Aren't we people?'

'Yes,' said Mrs Allen, 'but a different sort.' Using Evan's right shoulder, she levered herself to her feet. 'And now I'm off to powder my nose. If I'm not back in ten minutes, come in and get me.'

'Do you often recruit staff like this?' asked Evan.

'All the time, dear.' She stumped away, legs wide apart, falling off her heels at every third step, like Dick Emery in drag. Evan realized that she hadn't even asked his surname: he felt rather piqued that she hadn't entertained the possibility that he might be a thief or a pervert with a taste for ancient flesh.

Billy's hands dropped from his face to his untouched glass, raising it like a chalice to be drained in one ruthless gulp. The two men sat in silence for a while until Evan became aware of a low bear-like growl, issuing not from Billy's mouth or throat but from his chest. The tendons in his neck throbbed and corded, and his eyes bulged as his face gradually turned the colour of Mrs Allen's drink. Evan felt that he ought to say something.

'Do you two work together, then?'

The growling gave way to a high-pitched whine which finally burst out into an outraged squeak. 'I'm a fucking *SAILOR*!'

As if it should have been somehow obvious, as if Brum – a hundred miles from any coast, without even a decent river – were synonymous with dauntless, world-roving tars. Billy ripped open his shirt, sending buttons rattling across the table, as though his multi-coloured tattoos of anchors, dripping daggers and big-breasted women provided incontrovertible proof.

'You must have been to some interesting places,' said Evan, but Billy was not to be mollified.

'Places that you've never heard of. Places that you've never dreamed of, that you couldn't even imagine.'

He leaned over and took Evan's half-empty glass, grimacing at the first sip, as if its taste had been contaminated.

'Don't go getting any ideas,' he said, his lips hardly moving. 'Keep your hands off. It's mine.' He obviously liked this because he repeated it, slowly. 'Muh-eye-nuh!' It wasn't clear whether he meant Mrs Allen, his Kensitas and Zippo, the pub, North London or something even more general.

'You're welcome to it,' said Evan, 'whatever it is.'

'You're all right,' said Billy. 'I'll let you know when I've finished with it.'

He stood up, drained the last of Evan's beer and, crossing the room as if it were a storm-lashed deck, disappeared into the ladies' toilets.

Evan sat and wondered. What the hell was he doing in this place? Why had he sat just here? Why had he talked to these idiots? Why had he said yes to the last job on earth that he wanted to do? And why did this feel – for no discernible reason – to be the right thing, the only thing, to do? Although he'd been waiting for fate to take a hand, he'd expected it to happen at night and somehow to involve a beautiful, fair-haired, red-lipped woman, preferably wearing dark glasses. It was an unlikely beginning to an adventure, but then, hadn't *Treasure Island* started in an inn?

The sailor reappeared, carrying Mrs Allen in his arms. He looked extremely serious – half proud, half humble, like a mounted knight who has just swept a distressed damsel up to the safety of his saddle, as if, back in the ladies' toilets, some ogre or dragon lay twitching in its own smoking blood. Her skin glowed like a young bride's and she was laughing, oblivious to the dark stain that spread from the crotch to the hem of her dress. This was something new for him to consider; that even people you can hardly bear to look at could, if you kept watching them, suddenly turn beautiful.

As they passed his table, Mrs Allen swung her arm in extravagant farewell, sending a tier of empties crashing to the floor. Midge bustled out from behind the bar: not to sweep up but to stamp the glass fragments into the carpet. As the sailor reached the door, it swung open, knowing better than to get in his way.

'One last thing,' called Mrs Allen from out of the blast of heat: 'Do you have any problems with shit?'

'He looks like he eats it,' said Billy.

Midge felt the kid's smile – huge, closed-eyed, ecstatic – pass like a splinter of ice right through his body, squeezing through the crack of the closing door to follow Billy the Sailor as he bore Mrs Allen across the blaring traffic of Chalk Farm Road.

two

Twenty-three hours later, Evan was in the enormous dining room of the residential home at Heron Close, laying out fifty-two places: four on each round Formica-topped table and twelve on the long trestle. The blunted knives and forks were almost weightless and the plastic crockery felt sticky to his touch. The plates were terracotta brown, the cups and beakers baby blue.

The two electric clocks gave a loud click, announcing the arrival of each new minute. Such clocks occupied every empty space on the walls, and Evan had counted seventeen in all, synchronized, as if every second mattered, as if time were of the essence. He felt disorientated. While the first hour of the shift had seemed interminable, the next three had flown by, but now those gaps between the clicks were getting longer again. The room seemed to be swaying slightly, like a becalmed ship, its voyage – to places Evan had never heard of, never even dreamed of – halted, in the doldrums.

He had arrived late. Mrs Allen's map had borne no relation to reality. Where were the bus-stops, the trees, the rocket? Even the sun, blazing from the wrong direction, had looked nothing like a lion. Evan had wandered, lost, ringed by anonymous wedges of glass and concrete. All the doors were unnumbered, all the curtains closed: whoever lived behind them was sleeping late. The balconies were lined with metal spikes and chicken wire, as if to repel siege ladders. A solitary ragged lawn was weirdly tilted, as though the earth's crust had buckled, but the shrubs, twisting their roots, still pointed upwards. Although there were no signs of life – no stick-people, no birds, not even any wasps – Evan had felt himself being malevolently observed. Perhaps they suspected he was out to steal the secrets of old age?

Then, out of nowhere, a man appeared, moving briskly, turning his hips – half marching, half sidling. He wore a white linen safari suit and carried a large tan briefcase, locked to his wrist by a gold chain. His head was large, his shoulders narrow, his legs too short or perhaps too long: everything was out of proportion. If the midget in the pub had been like a tiny man, thought Evan, then this creature resembled a giant midget. The pale skin had been Coppertoned to orange. The scanty hair was brick-red but the sideburns were black: which bits were dyed? And why on earth had he bothered?

Evan took a step to meet him. 'Excuse me, can you tell me which—'

The man merely redoubled his pace, ducking his head away, but, as if against its owner's will, the left arm shot out, a jabbing forefinger indicating the narrow passageway between two blocks.

On the far side, Evan found himself in a crumbling concrete maze, being turned left and right before he was finally thrown up against a chain-link fence. Through the mesh he could see a group of cowed-looking infants huddling in the shade of their school porch: perhaps 'second childhood' was a literal description?

He retraced his steps, then continued in the opposite direction. In the next courtyard he saw before him a low two-storey block with many windows but only a single door, painted one-coat white over what must have previously been hunting-pink. There was no letter-box or bell. Evan stood and listened, although he wasn't sure what he should be listening for. Snoring? Maniacal cackling? 'String of Pearls' played at high volume? Then the door swung open, revealing a bright face under a mass of dark curls.

'We've been watching you,' said a soft Irish voice. 'I'm Bridie. You're late.'

Now, laying the final place, the plate slipped from his hand but he caught it with the other before it could hit the floor. Bridie, straightening the chairs at the far end of the room, applauded mockingly. Evan smiled and bowed. After an evening in front of the mirror he had made the decision to start smiling again. Keeping his lips pressed together pretty much did the trick – his ears stopped wiggling at least. Bridie, however, did not smile back.

From the glass door behind her, leading to the matron's flat, a terrible racket had been issuing all morning. The same record played over and over: perhaps unsurprisingly it was 'A Glass of Champagne' by Sailor. The louder the music, though, the louder Mrs Allen and Billy shouted. Bridie turned and knocked again. 'Mrs Allen's supposed to be on duty,' she said. 'Perhaps she's in conference or something.'

'It's OK,' said Evan, 'I've met Billy the Sailor.'

'Sailor!' Bridie actually snorted, much to his delight. 'The nearest he's ever got to the sea is pissing in Hawley Lock.' She sighed. 'It looks like it's just you and me and Dracula.'

'Dracula?'

'Mr Price. Vincent. The Deputy Matron. Don't worry: he only comes out of his coffin at mealtimes.'

Evan didn't like to tell her that Crazy Vince had never played a vampire in any of his films.

Most of the morning had been spent on domestic chores. As far as Evan could recall, it was the first time he had ever made a bed with a woman. It was an oddly tender, intimate feeling. Bridie had demonstrated that even the simplest of activities could become an art. At her command, the limp, grubby sheets became crisp and dazzling white; with a flick of her thumbs even ironed-in creases vanished. She could change pillow cases with only one hand. The blankets cracked like whips as she whirled them round her head. She threatened to show him the hospital tuck: Evan imagined this as a deadly wrestling hold or a particularly promising piece of rhyming slang.

The exertions forced open her overall's top two buttons to reveal, as she leaned forward, small, slippery-looking breasts. The sweat on her upper lip brought out a faint Zorro moustache. Evan liked the way she kept tossing her curls for no obvious reason. She was probably about Mrs Allen's age but free from the ravages of drink and landlocked sailors. Perhaps she was going to change his life – take it, shake it, re-make it, like a fusty bed.

Three very thin old women – who looked like sisters but were, according to Bridie, unrelated – kept peeping round the doors, while scribbling with biro pens on their inner arms. 'The Three Stooges,' said Bridie, contemptuously, 'preparing their reports.'

'For who?' Evan asked.

'Mr Snow, the Assistant Matron. He likes to keep in touch with everything. Watch out for Snowy.' She tapped the side of her nose, twice. 'He's not as nice as he looks.'

The final bedroom was windowless and unfurnished except for three beds and two chairs piled high with crumpled yellowish clothing. A huge grey and white cat dashed past them, its claws scrabbling on the lino. Bridie's thrown left shoe just missed it.

'Don't you like cats?'

'I love 'em,' she said, hopping after her shoe. 'But not that nasty sort.'

Losing her balance, she staggered against him. He put an arm around her shoulders: for a few moments their bodies pressed together in soft, warm, hard contact. She was not so much trembling, Evan felt, as vibrating. Then Bridie pulled away to the far side of the bed. Biting her lower lip, staring fiercely into his eyes, she threw back the covers and Evan discovered the answer to Mrs Allen's final question… no, he didn't have any problems with shit but at this particular moment he didn't exactly welcome it.

Although all three beds were heavily soiled and sodden, there was hardly any smell.

'Typical,' said Bridie, 'just cover it up and leave it for Bridie.'

They took the sheets down to the laundry room where Evan insisted on washing them himself.

'At least *you* don't mind getting your hands dirty,' she said. 'Unlike some people.'

All shift she had been muttering about 'a person who shall remain nameless' or 'a certain someone I could mention'. Evan hadn't asked her to elaborate. The intensity seemed to indicate that she was talking about another woman. Bridie seemed to be ageing in front of his eyes, becoming a bossy, nondescript housewife with a wilting perm, full of obscure grievances, increasingly irked when he didn't know where something was kept or what everyone was called. It looked as if their moment had passed. Now, as she approached, he was disconcerted by her expression of utter distaste until he realized that it was directed at something behind him.

'Bloody Dracula,' she whispered.

Although he was dressed predominantly in black, the man coming towards them was surely too portly to be a vampire. Behind thick dark glasses, the face looked to have been moulded out of white bread by a child with grubby hands. He resembled Roy Orbison. Incongruously, a large tray hung from a strap round his neck, as if he were selling Kia-Ora and choc-ices during a cinema intermission. He appeared to be gliding, as though on well-oiled castors.

'I'm off to fetch the Babies,' said Bridie, giving Price a parting glare. Evan observed that he was wearing rope-soled espadrilles with no socks. His paunch canted the tray slightly upwards.

'I know who you are,' he boomed in an actorly voice, extending a be-ringed hand. 'And I'm sure Bridie's told you all about me. Deputy Matron Price.'

The tray was crammed with medicines and pills: he picked out a bottle and rattled it next to Evan's ear.

'Nothing much in our pharmacy, I'm afraid. No uppers or downers, just things to take you sideways, and only a couple of inches at that.'

He began to lay out the pills at each place-setting, smacking them down hard, like a dominoes player.

'Iron... B12... Serenace... Phenergan... and I'm not sure what these are.' He sniffed at a handful of large yellow boluses and then swallowed them.

'What would happen if you gave them the wrong pills?' asked Evan.

'They'd rise up,' Price said, his voice echoing round the room, 'and rape and crucify the staff. Then they'd march to Downing Street, seize control of the key utilities and sack the city.'

A soft, shuffling sound heralded Bridie's returning with the three Babies. Their ankle-length quilted dressing gowns worn back to front were held closed by stockings, tightly knotted at the waist, and their slippers, laced above the ankles, were a couple of sizes too large, presumably to slow them down. Bridie had made fifty-two introductions that morning but their names – Molly, Polly and Dolly – were the only ones that Evan could now remember. Doubly incontinent – the room of filthy linen had been theirs – with matted hair, wide, dead eyes in which the pupils seemed to float and faces dripping with drool and snot, they were hard to forget. They followed Bridie in a line – gentle, grey and wrinkled, holding on to each other's trailing stocking ends, like circus elephants. Second childhood didn't cover this, Evan thought. They were off somewhere else, unimaginably distant but all too close.

Price was watching him intently. He opened his mouth, then snapped it shut and turned away. Evan hated it when people nearly said things: he always felt like taking them by the throat and shaking the words out of them. It wasn't that he felt in need of enlightenment, more as if he had a head full of answers to questions that nobody had asked him yet.

The main body of residents entered the dining room. Until now, there had never been much reason for old people even to register in Evan's visual field. All morning they had floated around him, silent and insubstantial. He was sure that he had seen the wallpaper through the spectral figure of Frances/Francis, who was either a man in a dress or a bearded lady. Seen in a group, though, they were a very different matter. A mass of wood, glass and metal advanced on him. The wheelchairs spun in sync, the sticks and Zimmer frames rose and then struck the ground together. The faces were grim, the eyes were suddenly avid for more than food. It was as if they were congregating for some momentous event, like a coronation or an execution. Perhaps Price's words had not been altogether a joke.

One of the old men paused in the centre of the room to scratch at his arse cleft. 'Butter will be cheap this year!' Bridie called. She said it whenever anyone touched their backsides. Evan asked if this was a reference to *Last Tango in Paris* but she didn't get it. 'It's just one of my mum's sayings.'

Evan saw Price's dark bulk, moving away against the flow. He didn't acknowledge the old people and they seemed to shrink away from him.

'He'll be having his in his room.' Bridie tilted her head in a quaffing mime. 'Four bloody Marys and two Our Fathers. We won't be seeing him again today.'

For Evan the next half-hour was like being back at school six – or was it sixty? – years ago. There, penalty dinner servings had been – beyond lines, detentions, beatings with shoes or sticks – the ultimate humiliation: for a public school man must never serve or wait, except, perhaps, upon the Queen. He had loved it, though: dashing in and out of the heat and clamour, putting red-hot spoons in the beaks' tureens, bringing them custard instead of gravy, dripping food on to the prefects' Brylcreemed heads. It had been the only time his education had made any sense.

The kitchen lay in the bowels of Heron Close: the food was sent up in a dumb-waiter. The door to the stairs was locked. Far below, Evan could hear the clash of metal, as if armoured knights were fighting with maces, counter-pointed by the yappings of a dog. The steel shutters opened to reveal three vast tureens, brimming with blue-green liquid. As he stirred them with a discoloured wooden ladle, something felt to be moving in the sludgy depths, like a giant eel. A few grainy yellow cubes and white filaments came bobbing to the surface. Evan chanced a sip: it was odourless, tasteless and lukewarm. The residents, however, did not complain when their bowls were put before them. On the contrary, most showed unmistakable signs of approval. One old man even clapped his hands in delight, as if at a conjuring trick. 'It's soup!' he exclaimed.

'You serve,' Bridie ordered, 'while I help the Babies.' Once again, Evan admired her patience and expertise: she reminded him of a grandmaster playing simultaneous games of speed-chess. At first, Molly, Polly and Dolly had appeared more interested in talking to the soup, then, turning their heads, in listening to its reply. When Bridie grew more insistent, gently prising at their teeth with the tip of the spoon, they fought as if they were being fed their own children. At length, she shut her eyes, loudly slurped a spoonful herself and pronounced the verdict – 'Yum, yum!' – after which their mouths meekly opened and closed, although, unlike Bridie, they didn't appear to be swallowing.

The main course arrived. Three slices of luncheon meat adhered like Elastoplasts to each plate, next to a green slick of mushy peas, topped by two mysterious white rubbery triangles that proved, on investigation, to be slices of Dairylea. Bridie momentarily left the Babies to dash about with a tub of piccalilli, adding an action painter's yellow splash to every plate. Once again, the residents' reactions surprised Evan: They were laughing – but without irony, as if at the unexpected reappearance of some much-loved old friends.

'Don't touch that!' Bridie yelled. Evan had, without enthusiasm, taken up a spare plate for himself. 'We have ours afterwards. Come over and help Terry.'

Terry's wheelchair was opposite the Babies' places. That morning, when Evan had first glimpsed the bobbing head of hair, as thick and black as his own, he'd wondered whether this could be his predecessor, all cracked up and drained of life.

'He's Parkinsonian,' Bridie had said. 'Terry. Short for Terrible. They sent him to us by mistake but we kept him because he loves it here.'

Evan regarded the twitching, tormented figure. 'How can you tell?'

She smiled. 'By looking in his eyes.'

Evan had never seen eyes like them. They were not so much hypnotic as enveloping: the irises seemed to shift from brown to purple to black. Love, hate, rage, resignation, despair, hope were all present at once, held in suspension by a glint of mockery like a flash of tinder. The rest of the face was gnarled like wood, the nose resembling a recently-lopped branch. The voice – a mixture of deep groans and plosives – seemed to issue from somewhere just behind him, and to the left.

'Dra-dra-dra-dra-dra,' Terry kept saying, as the spoon chased his mouth around his face. 'Dra-dra-dra-dra?' It had an unmistakably interrogative note. What could he want? Evan wondered. Water, salt, toilet? 'Dra-dra-dra!' The voice demanded, then pleaded: 'Dra-dra-dra!' Terry's hands were twisting back on themselves, the fingers sticking out at impossible angles: his head was almost ripping itself off his neck. 'Dra-dra-dra!' At length, exhausted, he gave up. The light in the eyes was extinguished; the mouth chewed the last of the bright pink meat.

Pudding was pineapple hoops. The congealed custard descended on to them with a sound like melting snow sliding off a roof. Terry raised his eyes upwards, like a pained el Greco saint. Evan took the plate away. The bulkier residents didn't seem to eat much, whereas the skeletons were insatiable, as if food were the only thing that kept them in the realm of the visible. Bumpers of tea appeared in the dumb-waiter. There was no milk or sugar on the tables: they had already been admixed in the kitchen below. Everyone took it the same way: sweet, milky and very weak.

Terry was becoming agitated again. Despite the restraining strap, he had managed, by wedging his feet against the table legs, to turn his body sideways. Forcing his head down on to his left shoulder, he raised his right elbow, drew it back and then, like a fisherman making a cast, threw his extending arm towards the table. It narrowly missed his plastic drinking cup. Evan watched as he slowly, agonizingly, realigned himself and then swung again. This time, Evan moved the cup into the arm's path, so that the index finger, which looked as if it had been broken thousands of times, caught the funnel, setting it rocking, then toppling. The tea spilled out to form a four-fingered hand, pale-brown and flecked with cracked milk. It crawled over the Formica and would have plunged itself into Bridie's lap if she hadn't seen it coming and leapt away with a squeal.

'Naughty, naughty!' she laughed, looking at Evan with something like her earlier flirtatiousness. Terry was thrashing about in wild triumph: his left eye, rolling ecstatically, appeared to have worked its way to his ear, while his lips drew back in a rictus grin to reveal alternately black and yellow teeth. It somehow reminded Evan of that moment in his childhood when, hands lacerated from vaulting a barbed-wire fence, he had looked back into the face of the bull that had just chased him across two fields.

Bridie began to push Terry's wheelchair out of the dining room. She leaned forward, so that the top of his head was cushioned against her breasts. The Babies, unchewed food falling from their mouths, went shuffling after her. With surprising speed, the room emptied. As he cleared the tables, Evan became aware of a crunching sound. The floor was thick with discarded pills – yellow, red, brown and blue.

Red and trembling, wearing a bulging peignoir covered with enormous rosebuds, Mrs Allen emerged from the matron's flat. She pretended not to know who Evan was. 'I didn't recognize you in uniform,' she finally said. They had given him a navy-blue nylon overall, which made a sad, whistling sound whenever he moved. 'A Glass of Champagne' had now given way to 'Convoy'. Evan had been disappointed to discover that this song, far from being a drug-addled nightmare of ducks fighting with flying bears, was merely about cops chasing lorry drivers with CB radios. She handed Evan a crumpled job application form. 'Fill this in,' she said. 'And put me and Price as references. We sent them over to the Council yesterday.' He wondered what these testimonials – from a dead-drunk woman and a man he hadn't then met – could possibly have been like. Perhaps they knew more about him than he did himself – like those Tibetan monks who inform a toddler playing in the dust that he is the latest incarnation of Avalokitesvara.

Mrs Allen banged three times on the dumb-waiter's steel hatch: far below, the dog redoubled its barking. As if in response, audible even over 'Convoy's final chorus, a Brummie lion had begun to roar. 'I've had a basinful,' said Mrs Allen. 'All I do is look after him and all he does is treat me like dirt. He's not in the least bit grateful. Mind you' – she gave a smug, private smile – 'I'd probably think the less of him if he was.' She looked hopefully at Evan: 'You don't want looking after, do you?' When he didn't reply she answered for him: 'No, you're the kind that does the looking-after, like me.' Her mottled arms made a flapping, all-encompassing gesture, as if indicating an infinity of looked- and lookers-after. 'I don't know what you're smirking at,' she said indignantly. 'We all need looking after in the end.'

The dog barked and the dumb-waiter groaned. Mrs Allen prised open the shutters and seized the two steaming plates. Flotillas of lamb chops floated on a bay of gravy and mint sauce, by a shore of baby carrots and mangetout peas, under the shadows of twin mountains of mash. She returned to Billy at a run. Evan hoped that he would never come to understand what all that looking-after stuff had been about.

Two similar but half-sized portions subsequently appeared. 'The ressies couldn't manage this,' Bridie said, seeing his expression. 'Even if they could chew it, they'd never digest it. It'd only be torturing them.'

Evan put his plate back in the hatch.

'I should have known you'd be a vegetarian,' she sneered.

Actually, Evan didn't feel as if he'd ever be wanting to eat anything again.

Time speeded up again for the second half of the shift. For a while the Babies were agitated, pinballing in slow motion around the corridors until Bridie calmed them by first brushing their wild hair and then weaving it into long elaborate plaits. Although they chortled and cooed, their eyes remained teary and wet: if they ever were truly unhappy, Evan reflected, no one would notice.

'They never get sick,' said Bridie, her fingers magically working through Molly's knotted mane. 'They're the only ones that take any exercise. Some people I could mention try to stop them running around: they say they'd hurt themselves but when they do fall there's not even a mark. They're like those Indians who walk on hot coals – perfectly relaxed. A harsh voice is the only thing that can harm them.'

Evan had noticed, however, that the Babies all seemed to have bruises or burns on their wrists. Now he could see that there was a similar mark around Molly's throat.

He drifted between the sitting rooms. The residents kept looking towards the door as if expecting someone, whether in hope or dread wasn't clear. 'What does *your* watch say?' they kept asking him, as though they suspected they were being fobbed off with an inferior quality of time and hoped that he, as a newcomer, could be tricked into letting something slip. Perhaps he might give them access to a different time, one that would lengthen or shorten their days?

The men – outnumbered by the women by about four to one – clustered silently around the strobing television set. They seemed to have a tacit agreement to share each other's misery while never acknowledging each other's presence. Only Bridie perked them up: they took it in turns, whenever she appeared, to lever themselves to their feet and scratch their arses. 'Butter will be cheap this year': the more she said it, the happier they became. Given the chance, Evan suspected, they would have filled their waking hours with it.

The heat was getting worse. All the windows were steamed up: with difficulty – the catches had all been painted over – he managed to force one open a few inches.

'There's a terrible draft,' one of the men quavered accusingly, although outside it was dead calm.

'The wasps are coming in,' said another, although there was no sign of any.

The residents huddled deeper into their heavy sweaters, lagging any gaps with scarves and wraps: one even produced a woolly hat. Frances the bearded woman, sitting in the farthest corner, was shivering and turning blue before Evan's very eyes. Even Polly and Dolly had begun to wail. It was as if the window had been admitting unbreathable air from another planet: he slammed it shut.

Facing each other on opposite sides of the room, Mrs Barker and Mrs Parker sat knitting. While all the other residents were addressed by their Christian names, their relative mental and physical robustness had allowed them to retain their surnames and prefixes. Although Mrs Barker was apparently stone-deaf and mute, and was said periodically to fall over, she maintained, by the monumental set of her head alone, considerable presence and dignity. Mrs Parker, whose gleaming false teeth thrust out beyond her lips in a permanent smile, held up her knitting, which resembled a red and white headless toggled sheep. The cat jumped on to her lap, its treadling paws unravelling her wool.

'What is its name?' Evan asked.

Mrs Parker placed a hand on the animal's head, as if to ascertain whether it would authorize such a revelation. 'Stormy,' she said finally.

Evan regarded the mass of fur. There was room for three or four cats in there. 'Why is it called that?'

The old woman's swimming eyes focused in a hard stare. 'Have you ever been to Salisbury, dear?'

'No,' replied Evan, taken aback. 'Why?'

With a deep sigh, Mrs Parker returned to her knitting. Apparently, no further explanation would be forthcoming.

Bridie's manner towards Evan had changed yet again. It was as if a complete relationship had run its course – from attraction to passion to mistrust to antagonism to indifference – in these few hours. At the end of the shift she sent him round the building to do the count. The three Stooges followed him. For the first time he realized that every bedroom contained a professional-looking black and white photograph of its occupant, in a polished rosewood frame. In the triple room – which, strangely, had only begun to smell after they had cleaned it – he saw the Babies posed in half-profile, hands clasped in their laps, twinkling like grandes dames of the British theatre. They seemed to have dropped their senility for the camera.

Perhaps this had distracted him from the counting, because he was two short, at fifty. He went round again. The three Stooges were well-versed in surveillance techniques: one retreated into an alcove only for her partner to observe, while the third waited further along the corridor, ready to slip into position. Evan emptied the rubbish bins. They were all full of milk chocolate bar wrappers. This time there were fifty-four. Something told him that ending his shift with more residents than he had started with would be even less acceptable than losing a few. He returned to the main sitting room.

'All present and correct,' he told Bridie. Another old man arose to do the scratching routine. 'Butter will be cheap this year,' Evan said. Every head in the room – even Bridie's, even Stormy's – turned and regarded him with silent horror.

As the clock hands clicked on to six, Bridie and Evan went off to change. Evan felt exhausted: his knee joints ached, his vision swam, his hands were trembling slightly. It was a different order of tiredness to that following sex, football, dancing or amphetamine jags. They shared the staff room with a stack of zinc buckets and a row of mops, gravely inclining their green and white dreadlocks. Without self-consciousness, Bridie was rolling on her stockings: her inner thighs were shockingly flabby. Evan choked on her geranium-like perfume. Outside, a car horn sounded 'The Battle Hymn of the Republic'. 'It's my better half,' Bridie explained, smiling at Evan as if sentimentally recalling their long-extinguished passion. 'See you tomorrow, then.'

'So you think I'm coming back?' he asked.

She look puzzled. 'Of course.'

As the echoes of her stilettos faded, he realized that she was right. Not returning the next morning seemed unthinkable: it was as if he had signed on for the voyage. He took down his salt-rimed denim jacket. A long, dark gabardine was now hanging on the neighbouring peg. Here was someone who didn't trust the weather forecasters. A school name-tag had been sewn inside its neck: 'MASON A. (U6H)'.

A pall of black smoke lingered outside but the General Lee had burnt rubber. Evan opened the front door and then froze – at the far end of the corridor he had seen a familiar figure. It was the marching man who had misdirected him that morning. He had changed into a short white jacket, like a steward's, and shiny aquamarine trousers with knife-edge creases. Depending from his belt was a heavy sporran of brass and iron keys, which looked as if they could open every lock in the world. Two women were talking to him, their backs turned towards Evan. He recalled the sailor's words, 'I thought that Snow would have taken some of them off', and Bridie's 'He's not as nice as he looks.' What crimes could the man commit, Evan wondered, that could possibly be worse than walking around with that face?

Then Snow saw him. His lips stopped moving as their eyes locked.

Evan gave him a little wave but Snow didn't respond. The women swivelled round: the short one's face was a featureless blur, while the other was the strangest – no, the most beautiful – girl that he had ever seen. The light, mercilessly glaring on Snow's bumpy forehead, melted around her to a golden haze. The sleeves of her overall were folded back to the elbow, and Evan could see the down on her forearms, the long line of the ulna, the shadow of that hollow at the base of the thumb. He didn't dare to look into her face again. Realizing that his hand was still raised foolishly, he turned back to the door.

As he was stepping into the sunshine he heard Snow's voice, exactly as he had imagined it, as if speech were merely a means of clearing slime from the bronchial tract: 'Sweep the terrace, please. I will check the clocks and tie those Babies down.'

three

The morning of his forty-seventh birthday – just past eleven o'clock – found Deputy Matron Price shaving the densely-lathered face of an 83-year-old woman. This was *not* how he had expected things to turn out. He should have been reclining on a marble terrace, overlooking a wine-dark sea, checking the proofs of his latest book – a philosophical romance at once as light as a feather and as heavy as lead – drinking something sweet yet sharp, under a cloudless sky. At least the clothes he was wearing – silk shirt, linen suit, espadrilles – passed muster, but they had been packed with thick, solid flesh that could surely have nothing to do with him. He had always dreaded forty-seven– the two ugliest numbers in alignment, like a cripple groping for his cane – although he suspected that seventy-four – the cane belabouring its master's back – was going to be even worse.

In fact, these shavings were the highlight of his working week. Up and down, left to right, right to left – the simplicity and purity of the action recalled long-vanished pleasures such as haymaking or tree-felling. He dreamed of achieving the perfect, transcendental shave, when just the blue light flaring off the blade would send the hairs retracting into their follicles, like rabbits down a burrow. While not exactly paradise, perpetual shaving might provide a perfectly acceptable Purgatory. Perhaps, in a corner that Dante and Virgil had skipped, there was a windowless attic where old women were being shaved by fat men in over-expensive suits – forty-seven for all eternity.

When Frances had arrived at Heron Close she had been a dead ringer for George Bernard Shaw. On the referral form, Price had changed her 'e' to 'i' and crossed the 's' off Mrs. Only when they manoeuvred her into the bath did they realize their mistake. He had wanted to leave her a Dali moustache but Mrs Allen had put her foot down.

Every fifth day he shaved her. Frances always hid away behind her bedroom door and looked flabbergasted on being discovered. Now she sat twitching in his chair, white-knuckled fingers gripping the arm-rests, as if high voltage were passing through her body. 'Your whiskers are better than mine,' Price muttered under his breath, 'but my breasts are bigger than yours.' Now he was forty-seven he seemed to be laughing a lot without being particularly amused, whereas in the carefree days of his youth he had been celebrated for never having been seen to smile.

He favoured the cut-throat razor: he liked to strop. The blade's downdraft took the dandelion fluff off Frances' large, crinkled earlobes. Bending his knees, like Compton late-cutting, he severed the four black hairs that sprang from the bulb of her nose, then tilted it with his left forefinger to flick round the nostrils' rims. On release, the nose remained stubbornly *retroussé*: he had to mould it back into position. Three hundred years ago she would have gone to the stake for that convergence of nose and chin, never mind the beard.

As usual, a bluebottle was zinging round the room. He had taped picture postcards over the ventilation grilles but perhaps it had crawled up through the plughole. Bigger and faster than normal, he was sure that it was always the same one: he kept killing it over and over, the ghost of a ghost of a ghost. Teasingly, it minced along the razor's edge.

The internal phone rang. Although he had heard it thousands of times, Price was always struck with fear for a few seconds until he registered what it was.

'That Evan boy is leaving the residents so dirty.' Snow's voice sounded as if it were coming from the other side of the world rather than two floors below. 'And he and Bridie have been doing' – Price plainly heard a sucking noise – 'things.'

The fly was slaloming down Frances' cheek. 'What sort of things?'

'Bad things,' came the reply. Or had it been 'bed things'? However had Snow – Cricklewood born and bred – contrived to speak like a villainous Mexican in a B-Western?

'You haven't even worked a shift with him yet,' said Price.

'He opens the windows! The old people freeze!'

'There's a heatwave.' Price checked his broken thermometer. 'It's three below zero!'

'The Babies will get out! Burglars will come in!'

Snow had spent the whole week complaining about Evan. How he breezed in late and sneaked out early, but also contrived to be there when he shouldn't; how he never left the TV room but somehow nobody ever knew where he was; how he wasn't interested in anything but was always snooping; how he ate like a horse but had insulted the cook by refusing all food. And now he had almost certainly stolen Nobby Clark's false teeth!

Price yawned. Snow was like this with anyone new: unfortunately, he never got used to them subsequently. The sole exception had been the young girl who was filling in her time between school and university: Adrea. Snow liked her well enough. In fact, he was pathetically obsessed with her, although no more pathetically than Price himself. Often, while dogging Adrea's footsteps, he had encountered Snow doing the same. He hoped he didn't mirror that frozen simper, that cringing, wraithlike air. At such times, by unspoken assent, they turned and crept away.

'That boy is bad,' Snow concluded. 'His eyes are different colours! There are bite marks on his neck!'

'Talk to Matron,' Price suggested. Mrs Allen had totally ignored Snow for the last three years.

'He has a knife in his jacket!' The voice cracked. 'And a mouth organ!'

'Put all your complaints in writing,' said Price. 'Four copies.' They hung up simultaneously. By the time Snow – hilariously semi-literate – had finished spelling it out, Evan would be long gone: he was not the type to stay around.

Price had to admit that he didn't like the look of him any more than Snow did. He was probably a perfectly ordinary lad whose only faults were being young and being here, but there was undeniably something off-kilter about that big dazed grin. Snow was clearly in a frenzy about what might happen when Evan and Adrea's paths crossed. There was no point in worrying about it, Price reflected. Things would take their inevitable course because the young – bless them! – always believe that copulation will serve as a magic charm against decay and death. He imagined them together: Adrea's calm features gurning and twisting, her long neck pulsing with Evan's python-thick tongue, their flat bellies slapping together like claves, those tobacco-stained fingers clutching at her bottom. This picture was neither upsetting nor arousing: it was as if it had nothing to do with him. Maybe he was picking up Snow's brain frequency.

The blade had dulled, the lather had crusted, the water in the bowl had cooled. Frances was snoring gently, her chin on her chest, but her grip on the chair had not relaxed. While Price was chopping through the grey fronds wreathing her neck, she awoke: the razor, riding the agitated flesh, moved on. In all his years of shaving, he had never shed a drop of residents' blood, although he had often cut himself. Price wondered why he had never seriously contemplated suicide: he was not a physical coward. Perhaps, like dear old Schopenhauer, he knew that it couldn't be that easy.

He towelled the soap off Frances' ears, doused her in aftershave, then floured her with talc. Taking the oval mirror from the wall, he presented her with her reflection. Frances tittered, as if at a joke she didn't get. She didn't even recognize it as being a face, let alone her own. Taking her arm, he guided her to the door. A stronger smell was fighting through the Givenchy. After eighty, Price reflected, Havergal Brian wrote twenty-one symphonies, Titian painted *The Flaying of Marsyas* and Methuselah begat and begat and begat: history did not record whether they regularly pissed themselves in the process.

The stairwell sucked at him like a vortex: he could sense Adrea's presence below. He resisted: during her shifts he was trying to ration himself to two brief extra descents. On reaching the first landing, Frances had left off stumbling: believing herself to be unobserved, her movements became markedly brisker and more certain. Perhaps, as his old dad used to say, senility was all an act – swinging the lead, malingering. Beneath the scanty hair, Frances' scalp bore a line of scabs, as if tiny creatures had been tunnelling into or out of her brain.

Price had always considered that there was something innately repulsive about the top of the human head. It wasn't just Frances: that of the V&A's marvellous Canova bust of Helen of Troy – even though she was still cauled by the swan's egg from which she had hatched – was equally vile. Tops of heads didn't care about beauty or ugliness, youth or age: whatever the face or the body might be doing. They remained blank and aloof. Who could blame the birds, as they watched the lords of creation strutting and fretting below, for so often losing control of their sphincter muscles? His hands explored his own scalp: it felt like a shelf from which something had been removed. A few flecks of dandruff came floating peacefully down. Although he knew that he was being a little unfair, all he could remember about his ex-wife were those great clumps of badly-dyed hair on the pillow, like a Van Gogh cornfield without the crows. He had deliberately avoided seeing the top of Adrea's head: forty-seven was obviously a sentimental age.

Back in his room he cleaned the razor and replaced it in its green morocco sheath. Then he put his latest acquisition – Mahler's Tenth Symphony – on the gramophone, poured a slug of Powers, lit a birthday Havana and, after sponging away Frances' puddle, sat back in his chair. No one seemed to appreciate the demands of his job. Being on-call you had to achieve and then maintain the state of permanent suspension, at once alert and totally relaxed. Whenever he was unexpectedly summoned – for accidents, fires, floods or unremarkable deaths – his serenity remained absolute. None of these, it appeared, had been the call that he had been awaiting. On his nominal days off, he still made his rounds at the usual time. This was taken by those who sought some redeeming quality in everyone to be evidence of his essential good-heartedness, while the rest suggested that he was merely too mean and lazy to cook for himself. Price could not account for the real reason: simply, he was afraid of missing something. But what on earth was ever going to happen in Heron Close?

'I never take holidays,' Cartier-Bresson always replied when asked why he didn't use colour film. A few hours in the British Museum was holiday enough for Price. Just fifteen minutes on the number 24 bus and he could be everywhere and anywhere, able to move backwards and forwards across the centuries, creating from the myriad civilizations his own private synthesis. His preference for the quieter upstairs rooms had led him to a passion for Celtic La Tene and Sumerian lapis lazuli and brass. He had even made some new friends – German tourists, mostly. Having previously picked up their language through listening to Schubert Lieder, he would try to steer the conversation away from Keegan's transfer to Hamburg and the deficiencies of British beer to enquire about the recent doings of the miller's beautiful daughter and the erlking. Price surveyed the familiar postcard images that covered his walls: the lion-headed bird grasping two stags in its talons, the gold falcon with mirrored wings, the roaring six-armed demon vigorously stamping on a skinny elephant's head. He regarded them as his own family album.

In pride of place, over his bed, was an etching, *Eternity is Temporary,* by the seventeenth-century Italian artist Giovanni Castiglione. Price had happened upon it in an apparently unthemed exhibition in the Museum's Print Room. It was hanging between a crude anti-Popery broadsheet and a Gillray cartoon of William Pitt as a toadstool. He had stood in front of it for a full ten minutes and kept returning thereafter. Something about it fascinated him although he had no idea of its meaning. No postcard was available so they charged him a fiver for a photograph and gave him a form to fill in. 'For What Purpose Do You Require This Item?' it enquired. Price wrote, 'For the purpose of understanding it' but the man said that wouldn't do. They finally settled on 'Study'.

No matter how much he had subsequently studied it, however, the work remained impenetrable. The scene appeared to be of a ruined temple, at the centre of which a group of people were clustered around a cracked stone plaque which bore the inscription '*Temporalis Aeternitas*' – 'Eternity is Temporary'. A bearded man was on his knees before it, his finger tracing some faint numbers below – presumably a date, possibly 1645. A muffled female form crouched next to him, inscribing something in a thick-leaved book. Above her, a third figure with strangely furred or leprous hands and feet was leaning forward to read or perhaps to retch. Next to him was a heroically-proportioned satyr, struggling with voluminous drapes, one foot on what could have been a broken sundial. The last figure was standing slightly apart: a hooded child or dwarf with a long knife at his belt, his back turned towards the viewer. It was impossible to tell what emotions these characters might be feeling at their discovery or even whether they had been searching for this place or merely happened upon it. Huge birds seemed to be hovering above them but Price realized that what he had taken for wings were the branches of hardy trees and bushes growing out of the crumbling walls. Suspended in the air, next to the dwarf's left foot, was a second inscription: '*Nec Sepulcra Legens Uereor Ne Perdam Memoriam*'. Price's little Latin was long-forgotten but it seemed to translate as 'And By Not Reading the Tomb I Fear That I Lose the Memory', which left him none the wiser. Even the British Library had little on Castiglione and only Sir Anthony Blunt mentioned this particular work. 'A mysterious allegory' was how he described it, which indicated that he didn't know what the hell it was about either.

Price had noticed that whenever he played Mahler, that damned cat would come scratching and yowling at his door, except when it was this unfinished, recently restored Tenth Symphony. Despite all the musicological endeavours of Deryck Cooke, Stormy obviously did not consider it to be an authentic work. The fly alighted on a sticky drop of spilt whisky: Price took up a copy of Goethe's *Maxims and Reflections* and, with a backhand flick, splattered it against the table. He opened the book. 'The classical is health,' he read. 'The romantic sickness.' You couldn't beat Goethe: The weight and heft were just right for swatting flies. Recently, to save wear and tear, he had switched to another 176-page paperback – Kingsley Amis's *Ending Up* – but it had been useless, its downdraft blowing the intended victim halfway across the room. The cover claimed that 'Amis stretches himself to the full limit of his formidable powers' but when it came to reducing a bluebottle to an asterisk of blood and yolk, then the Sage of Weimar was your only man.

He fished his limp penis out of his trousers and, wrapping it in a red spotted handkerchief, began to think about Adrea. On her very first coffee break he had, half-deliberately, got off on the wrong foot.

'You don't look like an Andrea,' he had said.

'That's because I'm not,' she muttered. 'It's A-D-R-E-A.'

'You've taken the "N" out.'

'No' – she still didn't look up from her heavily-annotated *Jane Eyre* – 'it was never there in the first place.'

She had read thirty-two pages in the next ten minutes: Price obviously wasn't going to cut it as Mr Rochester. In fact, he liked her name: perhaps it was a shortened form of Andromeda or even – a dream, a dread – an unfinished threat or promise? Her voice was a Home Counties' whine with a slight catch in it, like that of Virginia Wade, the tennis player, which had always set his teeth on edge – in Adrea, of course, he found it charming.

Through two-inch eyelashes – which Bridie insisted must be false – Adrea watched the world. Her long hair was yanked back and held at the nape by two rubber bands. From behind it looked as if a tawny animal had clambered up and hooked its claws on to her shoulder blades. What would it look like when she shook it loose? What would it smell like, sound like? Would panicked small birds fly out? The face was pale, not chalky like Evan's but subtly glazed in blue, rose and nacre, setting off her startlingly crimson mouth – not lipsticked, whatever Bridie claimed. In her loose cotton trousers and smock she reminded him of a Shakespearean heroine who disguises herself to roam the woods but fools no one, being so obviously neither a boy nor a girl but an angel.

Like most tall adolescents she mooched around with her head bowed and didn't know where to put her hands. Price loved it when she occasionally forgot to be self-conscious: she would shake herself, as if emerging from water, then rack up to her full height before letting her body fall – right hip jutting, head cocked – into the tribhanga, the flowing, classical Parvati posture. Her eyes, widening, would boldly rake the room: at such moments she would meet his gaze unflinchingly, or rather, look right through him. Suddenly she would recollect herself and her limbs would retract into their former posture, but there wasn't much that she could do about the glow that was still coming off her skin.

Price's cock still lay inertly across his palm. For the last few months he had been palping and prodding it to no effect: it just didn't work any more. How long had it been that glaucous hue? What had happened to all those purple veins? It looked as if Bridie – one wet lunchtime last spring – might be the last woman he would ever go to bed with. He felt more relief than regret. 'A man without desire is no longer a man,' Baron d'Holbach had written, but Price suspected that this was being wildly over-optimistic.

During the Purgatorio, the symphony's short third movement, he noticed, for the first time, an insistent four-beat tapping. Only when the sound persisted, at the end of the side, did he realize that this spectral *con legno* had, in fact, been someone knocking at his door. He re-knotted his tie, put on his jacket, and then, snatching up a Courvoisier miniature, dabbed a little brandy behind each ear. It provided the world with a satisfyingly simple explanation of his unsociability. He was a whisky alcoholic pretending to be a brandy alcoholic: well, everybody needed to have *some* secrets.

The door, opening, revealed Frances' right fist silently belabouring the air. Someone had cleaned her up and changed her clothes.

'Shave,' she said. 'Shave.'

'But, my dear lady,' said Price, 'I have only just accommodated you.'

'Shave,' Frances repeated, with unexpectedly heavy emphasis. 'Shave!'

When she needed a shave she avoided it: when she didn't, she demanded it. Perhaps this was like a Zen master's direct pointing?

Maybe she was trying to show him that we run from the thing we desire and pursue the thing we fear and that, at the last, they are one and the same?

'How can I shave what isn't there?'

In reply, Frances rubbed her chin with the back of her hand, producing a distinct rasping noise. Price could actually see the white stippling along the jaw-line and two black antennae that were extruding from a cheek mole. The perfect shave had lasted for less than an hour. Taking her in his arms, he gently waltzed her to the head of the stairs. He thought of the dolgothiteli, a fabled gerontocracy out in the Caucasus: it had to be admitted that a world ruled by Frances would at least be a peaceful one. 'See you next Tuesday,' he called after her. He realized that his cock had been hanging out the whole time but she hadn't seemed to notice.

Back in the attic, he put on the scherzo, turned up the volume, lay back on the bed and, with a sigh, knowing what was awaiting him, closed his eyes. For a few seconds he thought that he was safe but then that inescapable image came once again into his mind's eye, as if it were being projected on to the screen of his eyelids. It had first appeared – a dark outline against the vermilion field – just after Adrea's arrival at Heron Close. Every time he shut his eyes or even blinked, there it was. After a few days it had begun to gain definition and he realized that it was a human head, but when it gradually came into focus it was not, as he had been anticipating, Adrea's face.

It was like an advertisement for shampoo, milk chocolate or high-fibre breakfast cereal: a smiling woman with blonde centre-parted hair – young, pretty, healthy and utterly devoid of mystery or threat. Unlike Adrea's, her eyelashes were unquestionably false. She was also well-lipsticked and rouged although, south-west of her cute little nose, a cold sore's fiery tip was breaking through the powder. While Adrea's teeth were tiny and tight like a closed zip, these were large, even and shiny, like a row of shields. The tongue could be seen lolling behind, as if ready to be rolled out like a red carpet. This was not a still image, however: the woman's lips were trembling slightly. The smile never became a rictus, but somehow always remained, vacantly radiant, at the moment of breaking. There was a faint shadow along the upper lip: perhaps, in sixty years' time, she would be knocking at his door for a shave?

It had taken some weeks for him to remember – or admit to himself – who this woman was. She had been a policewoman he had encountered briefly eleven – or was it twelve? – years ago. The image showed only her head and shoulders, so that it was unclear whether she was still wearing her uniform: probably not, with all that slap. It had been a ridiculous, almost humiliating episode: he hadn't thought about it since, couldn't even remember her name.

The persistence of this image was annoying rather than disturbing. Nothing could shift it. He sank her in a lake of pitch but she immediately bobbed back to the surface, still spotless and shining. He invoked Adrea, only to find that he could not picture her at all: weak projections of Branwell Brontë's portrait of Emily flickered across the policewoman's domed forehead. Not even the heroes of his childhood – Hector, Sir Lancelot, Hereward the Wake – could displace her, although Mr Toad had put up a surprisingly good fight. Using his postcards, he tried to fix powerful archetypes in his mind. An Inca smoking mirror, Vishnu in his moustachioed fish incarnation, a Xhosa witchdoctor's leering mask. The moment he shut his eyes, that soppy smile obliterated them all. He had summoned up almost everyone he had ever known – residents, past and present, even Mrs Allen, even Snow – but their flesh just fell away to reveal not a skull but an adorable cutie in coral pink lipstick. At the moment he was attempting to stare her out but so far she hadn't blinked.

Once again, Price became aware of sounds outside his door. Was it Frances, her face now a mass of sprouting hair? Or Billy the Sailor on the Scrounge? Or the Mahlerian Stormy, having revised his judgement? He let them wait until the finale's final sigh – 'to live for you, to die for you!' – then, having re-anointed himself with brandy and buttoned his flies, he threw open the door. No cats, women or sailors. The greasy planes of Snow's face were gleaming in the shadows. Although Price knew that he could be there for only one reason he waited for the man to say the words out loud.

'Death, Deputy Matron.' Fear always turned Snowy counter-tenor. 'We have a death. Mr Clark.'

Who was this Mr Clark? Price wondered. In Heron Close he had always answered to Nobby or 'You old fool': now, after years of mild ignominy, death had, for a few moments, restored his dignity.

'A sad loss,' said Snow, joining his hands as if in prayer. 'A sad, sad loss.'

Price was always delighted by these frenzied posthumous appeasements. He suspected that Snow believed that dying might give his victims some capability – directly or indirectly – to exact revenge.

Returning to his flat, he fished out, with priestly solemnity, the black knitted tie with its curly pink Cardin 'C'. In the mirror he could see Snow on the threshold, twitching like a punchy boxer.

'We must hurry,' he fluted.

'I don't think he's going anywhere,' said Price, carefully adjusting his collar and then knotting and re-knotting the tie.

'I didn't tell the girl.' Snow's voice plunged alarmingly down to its usual register. 'I didn't want to frighten her.'

Price wondered why, during these past five years, he had never done something about Snow. Or about Mrs Allen and Billy. Or about that vile cook. But then again, why hadn't they done something about him? Snow, although regrettable, seemed somehow necessary, like a worm-riddled leg on a chair. All he could do, he felt, was work with what had been given to him, slowly and subtly altering its alignment. At least now some new elements – Evan and Adrea – had come along and things were becoming, if only for a while, a little more interesting.

'Happy birthday,' said Snow, even more dolefully, as Price deliberated over his cufflinks. He was holding out his right palm as if a microscopic present rested on it. Price mischievously seized it between his paws, pressing it hard, savouring Snow's grimace of pain and disgust.

'You go ahead,' he said, releasing him at last. 'I'll be down in a minute.'

He could not resist going to the stairwell for a glimpse of the top of Snow's head. It was a beauty: red and boiling like a relief map of Hell, lacking only a few Bosch demons with big forks and scourges. Back in his room he discovered that the bluebottle, having reincarnated, was once again dashing itself against the walls. Deputy Matron Price picked up the telephone. He was amused to observe that his hand was unsteady. For the first time in over a year he dialled an external number.

four

'The bells of Hell go ting-a-ling-a-ling, / For you but not for me... '

Mrs Parker sighed: she knew that once a tune became lodged in her head nothing was going to shift it. The clash of her knitting needles, Stormy's purring, Frances' snores from across the sitting room, Mr Snow's footsteps pattering up and down the corridor – all took up the rhythm: 'O Death where is thy sting-a-ling-a-ling, / O Grave thy victory?'

For their few happy months together, Joseph, her first husband, had greeted every day by standing half-dressed and saluting at the open window, singing this strange little song. She had warned him not to tempt fate but he wouldn't be told, just sang – or rather shouted –

louder. He had made it through Verdun and Cambrai unscathed, except for the shrapnel that pebble-dashed his shoulders, only for the 1919 influenza epidemic to carry him off. The Grave's victory was in Willesden Cemetery, under the most raggedly lopped yew. And this morning, she reflected, death's sting-a-ling-a-ling was in Nobby Clark.

No one had thought to tell the residents yet but somehow she already knew, even before she saw the stricken expression on Mr Snow's face. It wasn't so much that Nobby's chair was empty – he often had a lie-down before meals – more that it seemed to be empty in a different way. She could plainly see the impression of his body on the fabric as if, now invisible, he still sat there. It even seemed to be moving slightly, as though the spirit Nobby still fumbled in his pockets for his elusive matches. She didn't think that she would be missing him much. He had only shown any animation when he was scratching his bottom for Bridie or when the food arrived, which had been odd because he ate hardly any of it. She had been trying to think of something nice to say about him that you could put on his gravestone. 'He was a very clean man' was the best she could come up with, and she wasn't even sure what she meant by this, because the floor under his chair was thick with biscuit crumbs and ash.

She felt reasonably sure that Nobby was not in Hell but found it hard to imagine him in Heaven either. Perhaps he was in Purgatory, which she pictured as being something like Victoria Coach Station, where most of the people she had known – neither good, nor evil, nor anything else in particular – would end up. Heaven might be rather lonely. Joseph and Stanley would be the only people she would know and she was worried that they might not get on. She knew of one certainty for damnation, though: Mrs You Know Who. She couldn't bring herself even to *think* the name of the woman knitting opposite. Yu-No-Hu suited her, like an inscrutable oriental plotting to take over the world. Sometimes she would see her light a match and just stare at it as if preparing herself for the eternal fires. Mrs Parker imagined all the devils running out of Hell at her approach, their tails between their legs. She wouldn't wish Mrs Yu-No-Hu on Satan himself.

'Sting-a-ling-a-ling,' Mrs Parker sang under her breath. The words tasted fresh and tangy in her mouth, like gin once had but no longer did. Stormy looked up and blinked at her. It was his way of showing affection, so much better than smiling as he only showed his teeth when he was prepared to use them. She could tell that he was pleased with his new collar: blue was his favourite colour. If cats were colour-blind then why did he always get so excited when she took down a can of chicken? How else could he know that it wasn't beef or heart? Unless, of course, he could read the labels. Stormy loved his bell, too: you could hear him coming from a long way off, jingling like Santa's sleigh bells: 'Ting-a-ling-a-ling.'

Stormy didn't really want to kill: his instincts made him. He never ate those birds and mice, and when his victim stopped moving you could see the bewilderment and shame in his eyes. Why ever have I done this? they asked. He no longer needed to hunt: the bell was saving him from himself, giving evolution a helping hand. As she watched, the cat, with a wonderful fluid movement, sprang up on to Nobby's empty chair. There was no doubt that animals knew a thing or two about death.

From across the room Mrs Barker watched Stormy scratching at his neck. The collar was obviously chafing him and the bell was making his ears ring. And that bright blue clashed with the grey and ruined the line of the fur. The first chance she got she was going to snip it off and throw it in the bin, and she would go on doing so until Mrs Parker gave up or the world ran out of collars. Cats were cats: there was no point in trying to make them nice. Killing was in their nature: if God had wanted a peaceful world he would have filled Noah's Ark with doves. Whenever Mrs Parker began that horrible crooning – 'pusspusspusspusspuss' – it was all Mrs Barker could do to prevent herself from stuffing the woman's knitting into her mouth and ramming the needles deep into her stupid heart.

Before Heron Close Mrs Barker had never had much to do with cats, thinking of them as vermin, like pigeons or rats. But when she saw Stormy she literally could not believe her eyes. He wasn't really like a cat at all – more like a lynx crossed with a Shetland pony, with the proud eyes and terrible talons of an eagle. Now, two years later, she still hadn't got used to him. Whenever he was out of her sight she was terrified that he had gone for ever. And when he reappeared, her awe and delight were just as intense as on that first morning. He belonged in the sky, really: he was far too beautiful for this world.

'I love her so much I could eat her.' That was what her father used to say when she was a little girl. He would crush her face into his chest, the horizontal bars of his ribs biting into her cheek. He seemed to be made of wood and iron. At last, just when she was giving up the fight for breath, he would let her go. It always seemed a long time before her flat feet hit the ground, with a jolt that went right up her spine and neck, then out of the top of her head. Now, at last, she understood him because that was just the way she felt about Stormy. She wanted to scoop him up and squeeze him, squeezing and squeezing until he had passed right through her body and come out the other side.

The one thing that Mrs Barker was going to miss about Nobby was his smoking. His hands shook so much that he sometimes needed to strike a dozen matches before his cigarette caught. She had tried to light them for him but he had always – accidentally on purpose – blown out her flame. He used to drag almost as loudly as Ron, sucking the smoke first down to his lungs and then beyond, to the very tips of his fingers and toes. He never seemed to exhale: it was as if the smoke emanated from his pores. A lovely blue-grey haze still wreathed his chair, like incense round an altar.

Mrs Barker was knitting a sweater for Terry, with thick, scratchy, Herdwick wool: That would really give him something to twitch about. Mrs Parker had been working for a month on a pink and lilac scarf: perhaps the sight of it inching across the floor towards him had done for Nobby? Simultaneously, they both unpicked the morning's rows: what was the point in hurrying when you would only have to buy more wool?

To keep going was the most important thing. Each of them felt that she was knitting for good while the other was knitting for evil: it was as if their needles were fencing. Dolly awoke and, with a great whinnying sigh, gargoyled her mouth to allow a stream of drool to cascade into her lap. Polly and Molly followed suit. The two knitters redoubled their efforts: each congratulated herself when the three mouths slowly closed. Mrs Barker had beaten Mrs Parker. No, Mrs Parker had beaten Mrs Yu-No-Hu.

That new care assistant, Adrea, appeared and began to move anti-clockwise around the room, saying a few words to everyone in turn. Who did she think she was, Mrs Barker wondered, the Queen? She was very kind but it was a sort of cold kindness that made everyone feel uncomfortable. Whenever anyone tried to thank or praise her, the girl would just back away, mumbling incomprehensibly. These days, you obviously needed to be an idiot to get to university. Her great goggling eyes, sloping shoulders and rubbery-looking limbs drove Mrs Parker to distraction. As she watched, Adrea's neck elongated like a periscope and the small head darted about, as if alert to the slightest sound or movement. A goose crossed with a jelly, that was what she was like. Either she didn't know that Nobby was dead, or more likely, had no idea what death meant.

Seated in the office, filling out the seven forms that Nobby's demise required, Price became aware of a hammering at the front door. When he emerged, he found Snow frozen there, facing the wall. Price unlocked the door and Evan stumbled inside. His eyes were swollen, their pupils shrunk to pinpricks and he smelt like a burning compost heap. Ignoring Price and Snow, he peered into the sitting room but Adrea, having suddenly decided to realign Terry's feet on the flaps of his wheelchair, had just ducked out of the line of sight.

Although he was a full nineteen hours early for his shift, Mrs Parker – who didn't usually like surprises – was pleased to see Evan. At least he was clean-shaven, without even the usual horrible side-whiskers, and his hair was nice and short, although she suspected that it had once been long until he had cut it for some nefarious purpose. He had told her that he came from somewhere unpronounceable in Wales: she was sure that it must have a perfectly acceptable English name which he could have used. Perhaps young people these days were having it so easy that they were having it hard? They had too much time to brood, too much time to be bored: what this boy and the goose-girl needed was another war or a Great Depression to take their minds off themselves.

Evan, having finished smoking the last of that lethal temple ball, had been on his way to bed when the phone rang. As soon as Price told him that he had been authorized by the Wages Department to advance him a cash sub, he had run straight out of the house. He had just twenty pence left in his pocket, so he chased the bus and caught it at the Varndell Street lights. Although the flat grey clouds had returned, it still felt oppressively hot. The red leather seats were sticky, apparently beginning to melt. From the upper deck he had checked that the snakeskin boots were still in their window: the High Street crowd had a worrying proportion of coolish-looking blokes, all with obviously size nine feet.

'Do you have a last employer's P45?' asked Price, leading him into the office.

'No,' said Evan, with that annoying smile. 'I didn't fancy going back for it.'

'What were you doing?' Price counted out eight crumpled fivers.

Evan folded them up as small as possible and crammed them into the safety pocket of his jeans. 'Oh, I was sort of working with animals.'

'You need to sign this,' said Price, handing him a sheaf of papers. 'Don't bother reading it. It's just the usual stuff: all your earthly desires are granted and then you forfeit your immortal soul.'

Evan didn't so much sign it as make his mark. He threw the Biro back on the table and, without thanks or farewell, turned to go.

'Not so fast, young feller me lad,' said Price. 'You have appeared at the perfect moment. A chance to kill two birds with one stone. If you could spare a few minutes of your valuable time, it will be to your advantage.'

'What is it?' Evan asked suspiciously.

'You could call it an initiation into the mysteries.'

Evan wasn't sure that he liked the sound of this. It reminded him of his first ever job, at a crisps factory, where the salt women and the bag women were always trying to pull his trousers down. For some reason, though, the more the fat man declared his bad intentions – sneering, cackling and flashing a cloven hoof – the more inclined he felt to trust him.

'Won't you join us, my dear?' Price called into the sitting room. Adrea was still kneeling next to Terry, whispering something in his ear. As she rose to her feet, the Parkinson sufferer's reaction was spectacular – it was as if he had been simultaneously hooked by half a dozen fishing-lines – but nobody noticed. They were all watching Adrea. As she crossed the floor her chin dropped on to her chest three times: it was unclear whether she was trying to force it up or down. Evan felt an impulse to flee and an impulse to move towards her: they cancelled each other out, so he remained motionless. His expression didn't change. Women really went for that stone-faced look, Price reflected. Buster Keaton apparently needed to fight them off.

The moment that Evan saw Adrea on that first day he had realized why he had said yes to Mrs Allen: here was a beautiful princess, guarded by an ogre and a magician. He would probably have to slay Snow and then all the old people would become young again while Adrea – even as he took her in his arms – withered and died. He had arrived early for his last shift and lingered afterwards but Adrea had proved remarkably elusive: she had seemed suddenly to materialize in the midst of the residents. When he asked Bridie about her she had clammed up. The narrowing eyes and tightened mouth revealed that when she had talked of 'certain people I could mention' it had been Adrea that she meant.

'Have you two met?' Price asked. 'Evan, Andrea. Sorry – Adrea! Adrea, Evan.' Neither of them spoke: after the briefest of glances they both looked away but Price wasn't fooled. He resisted the temptation to declaim Prospero's stage aside on the meeting of Miranda and Ferdinand – 'At the first sight they have changed eyes' – to the audience of droolers, knitters and twitchers. Poor old Snowy still hadn't moved and continued to examine his wall.

'Have either of you ever seen' – Price's voice dropped to a whisper – 'a corpse?'

Adrea shook her lowered head.

'Not that I can remember,' said Evan.

This was going to be interesting, thought Price. The casual ones, in his experience, usually had the most adverse reactions.

'Nobby Clark has gone to meet his maker,' he boomed. 'A sad, sad loss. I am going to take you to his body and I want you to touch it. Not just to help you overcome your grief for this beloved resident but because afterwards you will find that you are no longer afraid of death. You will have entered man's estate' – he bowed to Adrea – 'or woman's.'

As they approached Nobby's bedroom, Price realized that Adrea, as women can, was observing Evan without seeming to look at him: it was as if all the surrounding surfaces had suddenly become reflecting.

The inevitable was about to take its course but if he could make them believe that he had facilitated or even caused it, then fascinating possibilities of subsequent manipulation opened up. The wise man must anticipate events: if you got advance notice that a rabbit was about to emerge from a hat then you contrived to be there to point at it, thereby establishing your credentials as a conjuror. The trick was to interpose yourself – looking benevolent or stern, making some hieratic gesture – while whatever happened that would have happened anyway. This was probably about as much as most of the Gods had ever needed to do.

Nobby Clark was laid out on the bed, draped by the spotless white linen sheet that was reserved for this purpose. Evan moved cautiously to the far side, ready lest the corpse, on Price's signal, should jump up and chase him round the room. He had expected it to be cold but it was even stuffier in here, as if the dead man were the source of all this heat. Evan felt a tightness across his chest. The shape under the cover looked all wrong – too bumpy, too jagged, not the anticipated smooth sweep from brow to turned-up toes.

Price opened the mildewed wallet on the bedside table: it was empty. He knew without having to look that Nobby's wrist-watch, cuff-links and medal cases were no longer in the top drawer. 'You're a lucky lad,' he said to Evan, 'getting a nice stiff in your very first week.'

Adrea gasped and rubbed at her left forearm as if she had just been stung. Suddenly Evan sprang forward, grabbed the top of the sheet with both hands and, sweeping it off the bed, flung it into the farthest corner of the room.

The undraped corpse was naked. It was saffron coloured except for the head, which had a blue-ish tinge. The lips, drawn back, revealed that Nobby's false teeth had, at the last, returned from their wanderings. The face wore an expression of wonder and delight, as if death had kindly assumed the form of a particularly tasty meal. The cheeks were dotted with dried blood, while the neck was a tarry mass of black and silver bristles. Nobby would never allow Price's razor anywhere near him, insisting on dry-shaving himself, but whenever he had ventured below the chin he would begin to tremble uncontrollably, as if struck by the vulnerability of his own throat. The rest of the body was remarkably smooth except for a few wisps of pubic hair, like grey smoke that wreathed the base of an enormous penis, doleful and redundant like a pestle without a mortar, hanging almost to the knees.

Now Price realized that the nickname had not been merely the regulation bestowal on all Clarks but also purely descriptive, with the 'k' being silent. It was hard to imagine Nobby, with his teary eyes and bleating voice, as having had a particularly priapic past. The glans was red and shiny: it looked unused, still waiting patiently for the call. Perhaps, in tumescence, it just shrank away to nothing? To his horror he saw that Adrea's right hand was moving towards it, thumb and forefinger poised as if to pinch, but then it passed on to settle, palm flat, above where the heart used to beat. Evan's right thumb pressed into the bulb of Nobby's black-pored nose. For the first time, across the body, their eyes met.

Retrieving the sheet, Price draped it back over Nobby. Evan and Adrea's casualness or callousness had startled him. He had been expecting to be able to gibe at their fear or awkwardness but not for the first time he found himself having to do other people's feelings for them. It felt as if this were *his* maiden corpse, not his 282nd. He was afraid that he would repeat what he had done then and flee snivelling to the toilet. Waves of pity for Nobby, helpless under those merciless eyes, overcame him, even as he admitted – feeling the waistband of his trousers sawing at his gut – that it was really himself he felt sorry for.

'What time did he die?' Adrea asked. Her voice sounded just as Evan knew it would.

'Mr Snow found him half an hour ago,' said Price, 'so perhaps an hour before that.'

'I must have been the last to see him alive,' she said. 'I came into the room and a voice said, "Who's there?" He was just lying on the bed, with his eyes open, staring at the ceiling. I told him I'd brought him a fresh towel. Then, just as I was leaving, he said it again: "Who's there?" They must have been his last words.'

'That's what Billy the Kid said.' Price was repositioning Nobby's feet. 'Although, of course, he didn't know that they *were* his last words, that he was about to be shot down from out of the darkness by his oldest friend. And they were in Spanish because he was in Mexico at the time. "*Quien es*?" If he'd known what was about to happen he'd have said what dying men usually say.' He put on a George Formby voice: 'Oooh, Mother!'

'What do most women say?' asked Adrea.

'Nothing, as a rule,' Price said dreamily. 'They usually go silent a long while beforehand.'

Evan was aware that Price was watching him from behind his shades, smirking as if he could read his mind. Apart from that initial apprehension he had felt nothing at all. He wondered what the correct reaction to death was supposed to be. If it was a test, how did you know whether you'd passed? He recalled the terrified lambs and calves in the slaughterhouse in which he had previously worked, how the black and white bullock that he had released had trampled four people in the shopping centre before a police marksman had shot it. Perhaps a bloodless death was less upsetting? Perhaps he would have felt differently if Nobby was to be cut up and eaten afterwards? He continued to stare at the draped figure. All the residents in Heron Close, he had noticed, had one thing in common – large noses. It was natural selection in action: the best breathers survived, ruthlessly sucking the air out of the lungs of Keats, Mozart or Brian Jones. On that basis, he reflected, Price was going to live for ever.

'*Voilà*,' said Price. 'Next time it won't bother you at all – unless, of course, it's someone you care about.' Actually, he was finding it hard to imagine Evan being bothered about anyone or anything. He turned to Adrea. 'Don't worry. I'll break it to the residents. We'll be taking the body out of the fire exit so as not to upset them.'

Back in the corridor Adrea immediately broke into a half-run, then disappeared once again into the main lounge. Evan showed no surprise at this abrupt exit: he strode past the entrance without even turning his head. Price saw that Snow was still hovering by the front door, as if ready to make a dash for it should Nobby's vengeful ghost come howling down the corridor.

This was the closest Evan had yet been to Snow. He was truly a remarkable sight. The face seemed to have been moulded out of ridged cardboard, while the hair was a baroque marvel of waves and spirals that seemed to be hanging in the air while Snow positioned himself underneath. So there were worse things than baldness, then. You couldn't even say that he had let himself go: he was quite agonizingly *dapper*. He smelt overwhelmingly of jasmine but Evan held his breath, fearful of the smell that it might be overlaying.

'Hi,' said Evan, as he reached him. Snow turned away again, tossing his head in a way horribly reminiscent of Bridie, as if Evan were a hundred times uglier than himself and smelled a thousand times worse. Price watched as Evan froze on the threshold and then, like a film in reverse, stepped back into the hall and brought his face close to Snow's.

'Why did you point me in the wrong direction that first morning?' he asked, mildly.

'I never did anything,' Snow spluttered. 'It wasn't me who met you, mister.'

His indignation seemed genuine. Evan almost found himself believing him. Perhaps there was a Snow twin that was even more repulsive.

Price's slab-like head inserted itself between them. 'Off you go,' he said to Evan, 'and buy yourself some food.'

Evan smiled again. 'Not food' – he eased through the door – 'boots.' His voice was low and solemn, as if the word were a spell of immense power.

'He pushed me,' Snow was whining. 'That boy pushed me.'

'No, he didn't,' said Price, shouldering him back against the wall. 'I did. Whatever do you think happened to all those medals that Nobby was so proud of?'

Snow did not reply. Price could clearly see the shapes of the crosses, roundels and stars pushing against the material of Snow's inside pocket.

'Some of them could be quite valuable,' he said. 'Did you know that Nobby also fought for the Republic in Spain?'

'Why?' asked Snow. 'He wasn't even Spanish.'

It was admittedly even harder to imagine the dead man as a war hero than as a demon lover. Perhaps this rheumy-eyed Nobby, crooning over his fags and food, had – with bayonet, rifle and grenade – killed more men than the fabled William Bonney? *Quien es?* indeed.

'Get along with you, Snowy,' he said at last, prodding him hard in the region of his heart – or rather Nobby's medals. 'You've earned them.'

The Babies, feeling that a sufficient period of mourning had elapsed, had risen from their seats and were revolving in a slow circle, cooing and wonderingly touching each other's faces. They reminded Price of the Three Graces, Aglaia, Euphrosyne and Thalia – Pleasure, Chastity and Beauty, or Piss, Shit and Drool. Molly's sudden pratfall rather spoiled the effect until Adrea, in one lithe movement, scooped her up and returned her to the vertical.

Mrs Parker was wondering what Nobby's funeral would be like. She could remember his family visiting just once. Her own father had left full instructions: oak brass-handled coffin, black-plumed horses and a minimum of three attendant mutes. She remembered how shocked she had been at the wake, when these mutes – nondescript men in shabby suits – had begun drunkenly to sing.

Lunch was a depressing occasion. Nobby's absence took away what little savour the food might have had. Afterwards, Adrea stole back down to his bedroom. She wanted to touch the corpse again, in cold blood as it were, to reassure herself that she had not just been putting on a brave front for Price. She knew that he had been hoping for her to faint or scream but, in fact, she had long been awaiting such a moment. Her heroine, Lady Day – the jazz singer, Billie Holiday – after having been raped at ten, had been put in an orphanage where the nuns, to break her rebellious spirit, had locked her up overnight with the body of a girl who had just committed suicide. But the nuns had got it all wrong: she was still spitting at them the next morning and laughing twice as loudly. Adrea had always imagined the dead girl sitting up and telling Billie not to be afraid, letting her in on all the secrets of life and death, some mysterious knowledge that was to make her the greatest of all jazz singers.

Nobby's door was ajar: she pushed it open very slowly, as if frightened of disturbing him. The covering sheet had gone and the figure on the bed was now not only fully clothed but had apparently swollen to twice its previous size. It took a few seconds before she registered that it was Price. He had taken off his shoes and shades but his eyes were closed: he did not appear to be breathing. She tiptoed out: Price alive was far more frightening than Nobby dead.

When, an hour later, she got up the courage to return, the room was empty. All the bedding, even the plastic groundsheet, had been stripped to reveal the bare mattress, rent and ripped and covered with large dark stains like the map of an unfamiliar world.

five

A week later the weather still hadn't broken. After an almost sleepless night, Adrea, arriving for her shift, saw from across the courtyard the strangest figure disappearing into the basement of Heron Close. Perhaps it was now hot enough for hallucinations or mirages? It had appeared to be a half-naked hunchback, its skin horribly flayed to reveal the muscles and tendons beneath.

She knocked at the door. Why wouldn't they give care assistants their own keys? It was always an age before anyone appeared. She hated having to wait. She imagined hideous faces at the windows opposite, laughing: look at that stupid girl, waiting. She felt like Little Red Riding Hood on Granny's doorstep. From below there was a crash and a curse as someone fell up the steep concrete steps. As Adrea watched, a thickset sandy-haired man in a bloodstained brown coat reeled through the sunlight towards a white van that had been pulled up on the scorched verge. The letters on its side – 'Graham Frizley: Family Butcher' – were formed out of sausage links. He certainly looked like the man to call if you ever wanted your family butchering.

The front door remained closed, although she could see stealthy movement through the frosted glass. The butcher returned, bowed under a second side of beef. Catching sight of her he paused, looked her up and down, then spoke: 'Cheer up, darlin'. It might never happen!' Adrea didn't even bother to glare. At least the residents appeared finally to be getting some decent food. Snow and Price must have been listening to her after all. She was only sorry that Nobby Clark wasn't around to see it.

The door flew back and a small motherly-looking woman emerged: she would have shut it behind her if Adrea had not stepped smartly forward. Neither of them spoke.

Adrea had no idea why Bridie had obviously hated her at first sight. 'Why are you wearing all that make-up in here?' had been her opening words. When Adrea had insisted that she wasn't, Bridie had licked her finger-ends and then rubbed them all over her cheeks and lips. This confirmation, however, had only seemed to make her angrier. Why, Adrea wondered, couldn't people accept that it was just the way she looked?

Having confirmed that the hall was empty, she leapt into the air so that her outstretched fingers brushed the ceiling, then, zigzagging to touch each wall in turn, ran down the corridor to the staff room. She felt better for this. The tension that had knotted her stomach now tingled like electricity in her feet and hands.

The day had started well enough but had then gone sour. While working here she was staying at her elder sister's flat in Edgware, a few stops up the Northern Line: it was easier than trailing in from her parents' home in Datchett. This morning Sally and her boyfriend Trevor – who styled himself a professional gambler but was really a traveller for Metal Box – had left early for Newmarket Races, giving her the run of the place. She had turned *The Billie Holiday Story* up to full volume but had never got beyond the fourth track. Each time 'My Man' finished she put the needle back to the start.

'Oh my man, I love him so… ' The song was about a woman who keeps crawling back to a lover who humiliates and uses her. 'He isn't true. He beats me, too. What can I do?' There was something baffling about the way she sang that word 'beats': as if she were torn between swallowing and spitting it out, and so was just holding – and savouring – it in her mouth. 'All my life is just despair,' Billie continued, 'but I don't care.' So why did she sound so pleased, even proud? 'For whatever my man is, / I'm his for evermore.'

Adrea loved it: she knew that it was true and real even though she didn't know how or why.

When she had left for work a bus came straightaway and then at

Edgware the tube was just waiting at the station and she got a corner seat and she opened Helen Gardner's *The Metaphysical Poets* and found a wonderful poem, and then another, and then another. Just beyond Hendon, however, she became aware of a large fist tapping her right kneecap. A man in a shiny-peaked cap was swaying in front of her, his other hand outstretched for her ticket. He fumbled his fingers over it, as if its validity was assessed by texture or thickness. 'Cheer up, darlin',' he said returning it at last. 'It might never happen.' He moved away without approaching anyone else: apparently she alone had an unauthorized look.

The carriage had filled up with blotchy-faced men, their hair like wet string. They were all staring at her, hating her because, even though her gabardine was buttoned up to the neck, she wasn't sweating. She tried to read again but the words just seemed to run together, then slide off the edge of the page. It was always trivial things like this that upset her. The men were still staring. Men had started to stare at her six years ago and, however she was dressed, whatever she said or did, they hadn't stopped since. Her first criterion for a lover was going to be that he wouldn't want to look at her. 'That's better,' smirked the ticket inspector, as she got off at Chalk Farm. 'A smile costs you nothing.' It seemed that, despite all those long hours at the mirror, her face was still registering sadness when she was happy, and happiness when sad.

In the staff room she hooked her coat over the peg, then shook her head vigorously to drive all such thoughts away. There were still forty-eight seconds before the start of her shift. She took a deep, deep breath, sucking in air until her ears roared and her eyes prickled. It always felt as if she didn't exhale until eight hours later. 'Just be natural,' Mrs Allen had said on her first day. 'Just be your own sweet self' – as if that wasn't the hardest thing to be. Adrea rubbed her cheek against the gabardine. She had inherited it from Sally and it still smelt of her – when she had been a real sister and not a jerky, abrupt stranger. 'Oh, Gabby,' she whispered to the coat, 'what on earth is going on?'

Adrea's first act was to free the Babies. Assistant Matron Snow, who liked to keep things nice and tidy, would tie them to their chairs with stockings. Sometimes – such as when Molly went into her counting fits, never getting further than 'one' – he had been known to gag them as well. Adrea had struck a deal by which they were allowed to run loose for the first couple of hours of her shift. Last time, however, she had never re-tethered them and Snow either didn't notice or had let it pass. Today he was sitting in the office with a relief team care assistant. Adrea waved but did not go in. Whatever could they be talking about so animatedly? All she got from Snow were monosyllables, and silence from the others – except, of course, for Deputy Matron Price. She would have welcomed a period of silence from him. The relief team nurses were all big, slow-moving women who spent their time making phone calls, drinking tea and doing their own brightly-coloured washing. She could not imagine them as mothers. Perhaps they were mugging children for their clothes. Their only reluctant contact with the residents was at meals and bath-times. 'They are trained lifters,' Snow had claimed, but there didn't seem to be much technique involved in their proddings and draggings.

At the start, Adrea could hardly bear to look at the Babies' dusty hair and veiny faces dripping with snot and drool, but now she found them beautiful. Off they went down the corridor – Dolly grabbing at the air while the other two looked over their shoulders as if checking that they weren't being followed. 'Basic phylogenetic programming,' Price had said, 'attack or flee.' But that was nonsense because neither fear nor aggression radiated from them, only perfect calm. When they fell or bumped into something it was a while before they recalled their obligation to howl. It was as if they were living in a parallel world where everything they did made sense, while somehow remaining visible in this one where it didn't. Adrea felt as if she were watching souls walking around: humanity with all its meanness gone. They were mostly silent, although Dolly did have some phrases. 'Penny for the guy,' she would sometimes mutter, 'God Save the Queen' or 'Bob-a-Job'. Her almost roguish expression and a sudden flush on her waxy skin suggested to Adrea that this might once have been a secret, intimate code.

Even more than the Babies, Terry was her favourite. When, on that very first day, she had met his eyes – huge and dark but full of glittering points of light – she had a strong feeling that they had met somewhere before. A rhyme from her childhood had come into her mind:

> A birdie with a yellow bill
> Hopped upon the window sill
> Cocked his eye and said,
> 'Ain't you shamed, you sleepyhead?'

Dad had read this to her one morning and then pulled back the curtain to reveal that a blackbird was indeed perching outside. It had wagged its beak, blinked three times and then flapped away with a mocking rattle. That was what Terry reminded her of: he couldn't fly or even hop but those eyes could certainly cock. She brought her lips close up to his gnarled ear and began to whistle, low, like the autumn wind through the trees. Sally used to do it to scare her but, even while screaming obligingly, she had actually found it soothing. She knew that Terry enjoyed it, too. She brushed the mass of crumbs off his lap: he gritted his teeth and thrashed his head to and fro like a dog holding on to a stolen slipper.

She realized that Mrs Parker had stopped knitting and was smiling in her direction. 'Where's that nice young man today?'

'Mr Snow is in the office,' replied Adrea, 'conferring with the relief team nurse.'

'No, not Mr Snow, silly!' said Mrs Parker. 'I mean that nice Welsh boy.' Her smile was replaced by a look of alarm. 'Not that Mr Snow isn't nice, of course. Or young. Or a boy – or rather a man.'

'I think we might be in for a pleasant surprise at dinnertime,' Adrea said, remembering the meat delivery. Mrs Parker never complained about the food but she always ate it with obvious disdain.

'This place is full of surprises,' replied Mrs Parker.

Even she and Mrs Barker were evidently afraid of Snow. Adrea had never seen him being cruel to the residents – if anything, he was almost *too* polite – but she had sometimes, from a distance, heard him shouting, his voice distorted by anger and hatred. On her third shift she had followed the sound down the corridors. Dead silence fell as she approached the furthest bathroom and she opened the door to reveal Snow and a relief team nurse standing looking down at a large naked old woman lying on her back.

'She fell,' said the nurse, making no attempt to use her lifting skills.

'I'm ninety-one,' said the woman as Adrea helped her up. 'No, ninety-two.'

Adrea noticed angry welts across her bottom and thighs. 'What are those marks?' she asked Snow.

'Bed sores,' he had stuttered. 'They are so lazy. All they do is sit or lie.'

Now, as she passed the office, he emerged and walked splay-footedly towards her. His arms were full of glittering gold, silver and blue chocolate bars. These daily handouts of chocolate had seemed generous until she discovered that he was selling it to the residents at inflated prices. Very few even ate what they bought, leaving the bars lying on the table for him to collect later for re-sale.

'Mop, please,' he said to her. 'The dining room floor.' Adrea was sure that she could see tiny reflections of herself in the gleaming facets of his face.

'No,' she said, on a sudden impulse.

The effect was alarming. Snow began to stammer and shake and all the chocolate bars tumbled to the floor. She retrieved them but it was not until she had fetched the mop and bucket that he calmed down. Horrible pop music was still pulsing out of Mrs Allen's flat. 'I haven't seen Matron for five days,' said Snow. He sounded more relieved than concerned. Whenever Mrs Allen was around he made himself scarce. Adrea remembered how she had tried to raise the bathroom incident with her.

'It's about Mr Snow,' she had begun.

'I know what you're going to say.' Mrs Allen had gripped both her forearms, hard. 'There's something about the slope of that head of his that would make any self-respecting woman itch to lay the flat of a loy against it. Just shut your eyes and count to ten.' And she had swept back into her flat, leaving Adrea bemused. What on earth was a loy?

She watched Snow carrying his chocolate down the corridor. He always stole along the left-hand side, right up against the wall. She had no desire to hit him with a loy or anything else: she felt sorry for him. Whatever he might be doing, she reckoned, it was all Price's fault. He could have done something about it, if he chose. Weak people only behaved badly because strong people let them get away with it. She also suspected that Price was somehow to blame for the men on the tube.

A wave of sadness hit her. It had nothing to do with Snow or Price or all the white hairs she was sweeping up. It was as if this feeling were just passing through her on its way somewhere else, as if these days her moods were having her rather than the other way round. The one constant was a sense of falling: even when climbing a flight of stairs she still seemed to be descending. Sometimes her body felt light, at others heavy, but – whether as a ton of feathers or a ton of iron – it continued to fall at the same rate. It didn't bother her so much now, despite her suspicion that one day she would have to hit the ground.

Her own face appeared in the wet black tiles. Damn that little girl simper! She was trying to look like Billie Holiday: tilting her head, flaring her nostrils and narrowing her eyes to produce the expression that the singer herself had characterised as 'don't-care-ish' and which had driven those nuns to distraction. 'Don't you think I look like her?' she had asked Sally this morning. 'Of course not. You aren't black,' she had replied, peering through the bars of her eyelashes. 'But don't you think I look like Olivia Neutron-Bomb?'

Life at Sally's was like being trapped in a Whitehall farce. Adrea could imagine an audience tittering as she walked around the house. Every time she opened her wardrobe she expected to find Brian Rix

standing there in polka-dot underpants. They had to keep the curtains closed because Trevor suspected that his wife had hired a private detective to follow him. 'She wants my kids,' he kept sobbing. Sally was temping at a German wine importers and had started drinking Liebfraumilch at breakfast. She kept trying to pair Adrea off with a series of polite but tubby Bavarians in brass-buttoned blazers. She insisted on introducing Adrea as Claudia. 'Why Claudia?' Sally had looked wistful. 'I always wanted a sister called Claudia,' she replied. If only their parents could see the reality of what they thought was a nice safe house and a nice safe job! But if they ever did they would just refuse to face it. On her days off Adrea would announce that she was going downtown but after catching the bus opposite she would get off at the next stop and sit in scrubby Stonegrove Park. Mothers and babies gazed pityingly at her as she read her way through the first year advance syllabus: she felt about ten thousand years old.

Her eyes were suddenly caught by a flash of movement at the far side of the room: she heard the creak of the pantry door. Holding her mop like a lance, she advanced until Billy the Sailor jumped around the corner. 'Cheer up darlin'' – he pronounced it 'chirrup', as if inviting her to sing – 'It might never happen.' The third one in two hours. She was obviously being persecuted by a master of disguise. Billy moved towards her, stepping deliberately on the white squares so as to leave a mark. A loaf of sliced bread was tucked under his arm and his thumbs were hooked over his elaborate belt buckle. Adrea was fascinated by his trousers. Surely not even sailors had two sets of genitals?

'How's Matron?' she asked.

'Not very well,' said the sailor, sourly. 'I'm looking after her.'

He came in closer: she took a step back.

'Don't worry, it's not contagious.' She noticed that his auxiliary groin – perhaps a pair of rolled-up socks? – was visibly slipping towards his left knee.

'Any news of a ship yet?' she asked.

'Yes,' said Billy, pointing towards the window as if a jaunty three-master bobbed at anchor outside. 'I'm just about to leave on a very long voyage to a very far away place. It's so far away that by the time I arrive there'll be no point in ever coming back.' Rolling his hips, he swaggered back to the matron's flat. 'I'll send you a postcard,' he called over his shoulder, 'with parrots on.'

As her mop vigorously obliterated the sailor's traces, Adrea finally submitted to the tune that had been running through her head and began to whistle the vocal line of 'Me, Myself and I'. Billie Holiday had transformed a perky little show tune into something profound, at once carefree and heartbroken. She sounded as if she had seen and done everything many times over but still believed that the very next time it would all be different. Adrea – shy, solitary and eighteen, her only experience of love being kissed seven times by two boys, both with their eyes shut, her only knowledge of the wider world one exchange visit to Ostend – knew exactly how she felt.

Oh, that astounding last verse and chorus when Lester Young's tenor sax re-entered! 'Never mind, at least things can't get any worse,' Billie's tone said. 'Oh yes they can!' replied Lester's horn, and then the two of them broke up laughing at the utter ridiculousness of everything. And all of this was compressed into just forty-eight seconds. Had they even realized what they had done that night in New York? She imagined them leaving after the session, pulling on their coats and then mooching off in opposite directions in the rain – she to her heroin, he to his booze, in shabby rooms in coldwater hotels. Billie and Lester had bestowed on each other their new, true names of Lady Day and Mr President, shortened to Prez. According to the trumpeter Buck Clayton, their relationship was strictly musical: 'They were not romantically inclined.' The US Army labelled Prez 'an inadequate personality and borderline psychopath' and threw him in prison. You only needed to hear two notes to know that this man had learned and understood more than all their other so-called presidents put together. She had dreamed of meeting a man like that, not physically – in his photos, poor Lester resembled something that Hans and Lotte Haas might encounter on the ocean floor – but someone who spoke, breathed and moved in the way that he played.

She had a sense of being watched and looked up to find Price standing by the door. Unlike the sailor his entrances and exits were utterly silent.

'Yes?' she said, fiercely.

'Yes,' said Price, with a deep sigh, as if giving reluctant assent to some request she had made. He was even more smartly dressed than usual in a black suit and tie and a French-collared white shirt. Adrea remembered that he had been representing the home at Nobby's funeral.

'You really missed something,' Price continued. 'I've never seen a church so full. A dozen people passed out with the heat. I thought I was in the wrong place until I realized that half the mourners looked like Nobby. God knows where they all came from: it's two years since he had a visitor.'

He was unusually animated, she noticed, almost dancing from foot to foot, his camera bumping against his chest. 'The priest looked terrified; they just yelled all the hymns. Then the eldest son stood up to give the eulogy. He had a huge Brylcreemed moustache and he stood clearing his throat and cracking his knuckles for a full minute before he started. He went right through Nobby's life but I wasn't paying attention because I really thought I'd gone mad. He was sounding exactly like Winston Churchill: in fact, he even said, "Never, in the field of human conflict." No one seemed to think that this was at all unusual. Afterwards, in the porch, he came up and shook my hand. "How did you think it went?" he asked, in a perfectly ordinary voice. "Dad used to love my impressions. I wasn't sure whether to do it as Sid James"' – Price gave a hideous cackle – '"or as Donald Duck."' Price stuck out his bottom and quacked. 'I told him that, on balance, I thought Churchill had been the right choice. At moments like that, I almost believe that there must be a God.'

'It sounds horrible,' said Adrea, leaving him in no doubt that she didn't mean the eulogy so much as his account of it. Price raised his camera and clicked the shutter only to find that he had left the lens cap on. 'Don't take my picture!' she hissed, bringing the mop head up in front of her face. It was strange, he thought, how good-looking people always hated being photographed, whereas the ugly craved it. Perhaps one feared that the camera would steal their beauty while the others hoped that it might bestow it? Unless, of course, the beautiful were only holding out for cash offers.

'I think, by the way, that you will find the resident Doris is in need of your assistance,' he said, as he waddled disappointedly back to his lair.

Which one was Doris? Even after a month Adrea could only recall about two-thirds of the residents' names. At length, she came upon a frail confused old lady batting around a darkened toilet like a panicking moth. She herself seemed unsure as to whether she was Doris or not. Adrea gently returned her to the sitting room.

No one seemed to have moved in the interval. Stormy the cat had appeared and was lying on his back, treadling. Mrs Barker extended one foot and when the enormous paws closed on it like a trap she lifted her leg so that the creature hung in mid-air.

'There's something not quite nice about her and that cat,' said Mrs Parker. 'Not that I'm suggesting that she is' – her voice dropped – 'a cat-twiddler.'

'What's a cat-twiddler?' Adrea whispered back. Stormy continued to twist up and round, swarming along the leg to deposit himself in Mrs Barker's lap.

Mrs Parker took off her glasses: even without their thick lenses her eyes were huge and blurred. 'Have you ever been to Salisbury, dear?' she asked.

At dinnertime there was an air of, if not excitement, then at least mild anticipation. All afternoon Adrea had been dropping hints about probable changes in the menu. Although she realized that the meat would have to be well-cooked for elderly teeth and stomachs, she hoped that it would not be totally rendered down. She glared at Price's pills on the side plates: according to Snow, there was no resident called Doris.

The dumb-waiter rattled and she threw back the grey metal shutters, a tea-towel wrapped around her hands in case the tureens were hot. She raised the first lid to uncover only the usual dismal wheels of corned beef and spam. The second dish contained a stone-cold slop of mixed vegetables, the third a great pyramid of mashed potato, the colour and consistency of wet cement. She turned the handle of the kitchen door but, as always, it was locked: she had still never seen the cook or cooks, only heard their mocking laughter and the barking of their dog.

None of the residents showed any signs of disappointment. She could have sworn that she saw something like a smile flicker across Mrs Barker's Aztec features. Terry, though, was more restless than usual: as she fed him, his teeth clashed against the funnel of the plastic cup. The relief nurse had perched Molly on her knee like a ventrilo-quist's dummy and was shovelling that terrible potato into the wailing mouth. Adrea consoled herself with the thought that it would all soon be coming back out again.

Suddenly there was an explosion of movement and sound: in the middle of the room Mrs Allen and Billy the Sailor were fighting. Adrea saw that the door of the matron's flat was still closed: it was as if they had come up through a trapdoor or fallen from the sky. They were both naked, although Adrea did not register this at first because he was heavily tattooed and she was covered with multi-coloured weals and bruises. Billy's main tattoo, filling most of his back, was of a sea monster with false eyelashes and three sets of breasts twining itself round the masts of a sunken pirate ship. His buttocks – the colour and consistency of Cheshire cheese – re-mained undecorated: perhaps he was reserving this prime site for something special, like religious conversion or true love? His geni-tals – merely a single set, small and prosthetic-looking – bobbed absurdly with every blow. Billy's expression was noncommittal, as if this were a last dull task to be got through before he could knock off for the day.

He was striking with his forearms at the sides of Mrs Allen's head: lazy-looking cuffs which, nevertheless, resounded on impact. They were both shouting but no words could be made out: the breath rasped in their throats and there was a roaring sound, like water in flood, from no discernible source. To Adrea's eyes they appeared to have grown massively. She felt like one of those little children in Japanese monster movies who hide behind the cardboard rocks while, far above, the dinosaurs flail away at each other.

Terry had stopped biting at his cup and the relief nurse had some-how managed to hide away behind Molly, even though she was twice her size. Snow was backing out of the room, contriving to give the impression that he would have stayed if only he had not been attached to strong elastic bands which were now unfortunately retracting. A serrated bread knife was lying on the floor, although Adrea had not noticed it in anyone's hand: stepping forward, she sent it clattering away across the linoleum.

Billy feinted with his elbow then kicked Mrs Allen's left kneecap. He seemed to be able to clench his toes into a fist: there was a splintering sound and she collapsed like a dynamited building. As if at a loss for what to do next, he jumped about a bit and then followed her down, landing not on top but next to her. He then began thrashing about like a poor swimmer suddenly finding himself out of his depth.

Without having made any conscious decision, Adrea took a few paces forward then, giving a little hop as if going off a springboard, dived after them.

Even before his phone rang, Price's on-call senses had registered that something was happening. Replacing the receiver, he took off his funeral jacket, brushing a long white hair off the lapel before replacing it on its hanger. Experience had taught him that, in emergencies, the more you took your time the quicker you got there. Halfway down the stairs he stopped to remove his cuff-links, roll up his sleeves and tuck his tie inside his shirt.

Mrs Allen was no longer defending herself: all her strength seemed to have been transformed to sheer dead weight. Billy had rolled on to his side and was flicking at her face with his finger-ends, which, judging by her screams, hurt more than the fullbore punches. Behind him, Adrea, having thrown a leg across to stop him kicking, had grabbed his ears and was twisting, as if trying to re-tune him to a more pacific frequency. The relief team nurse had caught hold of his left foot and was curiously examining its sole. Then Billy shook himself free and shifted on to his knees: he raised both hands above his head like an executioner who had forgotten his axe. At that moment a pair of large hands enfolded his throat, pulling him back and up, shaking his body out straight before tossing him face down in front of the dumb-waiter. Price carefully hitched up his trousers before dropping on to the small of Billy's back and pulling at his arms as if folding a freshly-ironed shirt.

Adrea rolled clear. Only now did Mrs Allen fully react, kicking and punching at her departed adversary. Despite the blood and foam on the woman's lips, Adrea had the disturbing sense that she hadn't been a victim but instead had in some strange way been in control of the whole thing. '*He beats me, too*': she recalled that smugness in Lady Day's voice.

'Don't worry, Eithne,' said Price, draping Mrs Allen's body with tea-towels and aprons. 'The ambulance is on its way.' Billy was struggling to his feet, his broken groans harmonizing with the approaching sirens. Price turned and kicked him unerringly in the groin.

Adrea noticed that some of the residents had resumed eating, with markedly more enthusiasm than before. 'You were right, my dear,' said Mrs Parker. 'That really was a most surprising dinnertime.' Terry had stopped shaking altogether: his eyes were dancing with unmistakable enjoyment.

The room filled with men in uniform: They all seemed remarkably casual, laughing and joshing with the residents, like a film crew milling on to the set after the director has shouted cut. One young bobby, though, his face almost lost inside his helmet, was staring in fascination at Mrs Allen as she began to fight the ambulancemen. He turned to Adrea. 'Cheer up, darlin',' he said. 'It might never happen.'

'It already has,' she replied.

six

The moment that he woke up – although he was still lying on the torn, bumpy mattress in his room in the Tolmers Square squat – Evan knew that everything had changed.

For one thing, he had no idea of the time. Wherever he was, whatever he was doing – straight, stoned or clear out of his head – he had always been able to fix it to the nearest minute. Even in dreams – in mid-flight, surrounded by the wildest phantoms – melting Dali clocks would regularly appear, their hands indicating what he knew must be the passing of time back in the conscious world. He only wore a watch so that no one would suspect his remarkable but dreary gift. And now suddenly here he was at zero past or zero to zero. His left hand groped around on the uncarpeted floor but his fogged-up Timex had apparently disappeared.

And there was also something strange about the light. Who would have thought that the sun, reaching through the thin dusty blanket that he had pinned across the window, could have conjured up in this stark, bare room, the rich golden-brown tones of a Dutch interior?

He felt warm air against the back of his neck and rolled over. Although he had been unable to make himself forget that Adrea was there, it still came as a surprise. The face on the pillow was completely hidden by thick hair, warped and wefted like a woven mask. Her body was entangled in the crumpled sheet, as if they had fought each other to a standstill. Her raised left knee looked like a huge featureless baby's head. It reminded Evan of how, ten years before, his first ever partner, while they were messily losing their virginities, had kept apologizing for her 'hockey knees'. When he had investigated afterwards, they had proved to be slightly mottled but otherwise perfectly acceptable.

For some unfathomable reason, most girls seemed to think of themselves as loose configurations of discrete features. They approached their prospective partners in the same way, anatomizing them, marking each attribute out of ten, then totting up the scores to decide whether or not to proceed further. Whereas Evan would just look on in bemusement at whatever his body felt that it needed to do. To lose control was surely the point of the whole thing?

Sex had also seemed to be very different for girls. While he felt himself to be flying into the sun, it was as if they were engaged in playing a brisk set of tennis. Making love had proved paradoxically to be the most solitary of activities: at least with masturbation you could imagine a partner. Although women had always taken up a large proportion of his time, he had been increasingly wondering why he or they were bothering – until last night. Cautiously, recalling how her hair had sparked and crackled with static electricity, he began to uncover Adrea's face.

Deputy Matron/Acting Matron Price's first executive act – in spite of the objections of Assistant Matron/Acting Deputy Matron Snow – had been to change all the shifts. Bridie was to join the relief team nurses, while Evan would be working with Adrea. Although he hadn't been trying to eavesdrop, Evan, as he laid the dinner tables, couldn't help but hear the raised voices in the matron's flat, from which Mrs Allen and Billy the Sailor's meagre possessions – a smashed TV and a king-size bed that looked to have been mauled by bears – had just been removed.

'It's a new broom, Snowy,' Price was saying, 'a breath of fresh air.'

'Mrs Allen would never have done such a thing!' Snow sounded as if he were shouting into a bucket.

'Eithne will certainly be a hard act to follow,' said Price. 'I'm not sure that I can handle all that being buggered by sailors.'

'That boy is evil.' Snow's voice cracked. 'He is a thief! He takes drugs! He is always late: I have them written down here, all his times!

The girl is frightened of him! He is dangerous! He will try to get round her!'

'Of course he will,' said Price soothingly. 'It's only natural. The young want to be with the young. The old want to be with the old. And we poor devils in between, Snowy, don't know what we want – though even if we did it's pretty certain that we wouldn't be getting it.'

'They don't even know how to *lift*!' wailed Snow.

'You and I will be here to guide them,' said Price piously.

'The old people will fall! They will fall and they won't be able to get back up again!'

'Then let them crawl!' For some reason Price, in a bass voice, had half-sung these words.

On his way out Snow had given Evan a look that made his previous sneers and snarls seem positively benign. Although Evan had resolved never to turn his back on him, he now felt none too comfortable about his front or sides.

Before this moment it had never occurred to Evan to watch someone while they slept. It had been as if his partners were invisible until they opened their eyes or mouths. He could recall almost none of their faces and only some of the names: unlike his mates he had never kept score – once you'd got beyond one, what did it matter? Adrea was reminding him of someone: after a while he realized who it was. Adrea asleep reminded him of Adrea awake. Somehow he had been thinking of this sleeping girl as a different person. She looked both younger and older: her skin was smoother, as if the bones beneath had been unclenched, but she seemed to be scowling, with a vertical double crease deepening between her eyebrows. He hadn't realized just how long her eyelashes were: maybe they were false? The filtered light moved across the bed. Her breathing became louder with no pauses between the ins and outs, as if her lungs were being sounded. He remembered a seaside postcard pinned over the bar at the Eagle and Child. 'Nice big breaths, miss,' says a blushing quack, applying his stethoscope to the chest of a buxom blonde. 'Oooh! Thank you, Doctor!' she replies.

Adrea's breasts were bone-white with a faint blue radiance like the set of china that his parents had kept in the sideboard for special occasions and so had never used. The aureoles were small and pale, almost indistinguishable from the skin, but the nipples appeared to be permanently erect, red and painful-looking, like twin infections that had come to a head but just couldn't burst. Adrea's full lips fluttered open to emit a great rattling snore: he could see her greyish tongue slithering over her jagged, uneven teeth. He felt his own face splitting open in a smile, wider and wider, until somewhere at the back of his head the corners of his mouth converged. Well, Snow had been right: he had got round her. Or had she got round him? Or had they got round each other?

Adrea was moving between sleep and wakefulness. Every time a train went into Euston the walls shook and that shameful black filling in her rear right molar ached in sympathy. She kept slipping in and out of the same dream. She was walking down a long corridor, like at Heron Close but narrower and there was no ceiling, only blue sky. Next to her was a male figure entirely covered by a grubby white plaster cast: from its large encased erection she guessed that it must be Evan. She kept opening doors but every room was occupied by a pair of copulating animals, birds or insects, obviously indignant at being disturbed. Elephants, thrushes or ladybirds were all exactly the same size, completely filling the space. It was odd because when she was awake she felt blissfully happy: perhaps all anxiety and fear would henceforth be banished to her dreams?

Her elbows were hurting, although she could feel no lumps or abrasions. She had been surprised that she had not bled, although a thick paste like candle-wax now coated her inner thighs. Her perineum felt raw and itchy and she had the sensation that dark viscous liquid was seeping out of her bottom but when she checked, her fingers came back dry. Perhaps Evan hadn't realized that it had been her first time? At any rate, he hadn't asked. What did it mean when what her mother would have called immoral and unnatural acts came so naturally to you? How had she already known what to do and how to do it?

For her eighteenth birthday Sally had given her an Elton John LP and a huge box of milk chocolates: boomerang presents – 'But I really thought you'd like them!' – that immediately returned to the giver. Adrea had left her singing along to 'Rocket Man' through a mouthful of khaki sludge: Sally, of course, had no fillings at all. The third present had been a copy of *The Joy of Sex* but as she had no intention of ever having anything to do with bearded men, she had found it of little relevance. Sally claimed to have gone through every position in the book – even the one on page fifty-seven – but something told Adrea that she could never have done anything remotely like what Evan and herself had been doing the previous night. That wasn't going to be in any books – except perhaps *The Metaphysical Poets*.

Evan was sitting next to her, cross-legged on the bed, with a lit match in his hand. When he saw her eyes open he applied it to the large spliff in his mouth, took a deep toke and then passed it to her. She shook her head in refusal but then, remembering, clutched it gratefully.

'There's something I forgot to ask you last night,' Evan said. 'Where did you get your name?'

'Do you like it?' she spluttered through the smoke.

'Yeah,' he said. 'It's got a science fiction feel – like android. I bet it's not on your birth certificate, though.'

'Do you promise not to laugh?'

Evan looked terribly serious. 'Of course.'

'On Sundays, my sister Sally and I used to watch the old Hollywood movies on television. Even when they were rubbish we never knew when some wonderful character – William Bendix, Peter Lorre or Elisha Cook – might wander on to the screen. One afternoon they showed *Sherlock Holmes and the Spider Woman*. It was one of those cheap and creaky updates to the 1940s, with Basil Rathbone and Nigel Bruce. They are investigating the Pyjama Murders: a succession of screaming businessmen are shown throwing themselves down stairwells. "I suspect a woman," says Holmes, "because the methods are so feline. A female Moriarty: clever, ruthless and careful." It turns out that all the victims had made their wills in favour of a Mrs Adrea Spedding, at which point the woman herself knocks at the door of 221B Baker Street.' Adrea leaned back to rap peremptorily on the wall behind her.

'She's so tall, cool and beautiful in a veiled toque and a black sheath dress with a Lalique brooch. A silent pygmy attends her, carrying a hat box full of deadly spiders. She banters with Holmes in this flirtatious but really deadly way. "Fine figure of a woman, eh, Holmes?" bumbles Dr Watson. "Reminds me of a nice little nurse I used to know on Wigmore Street."

'At the end – after her pointlessly elaborate scheme to have Watson shoot Holmes by disguising him as a target in a fairground shooting gallery has unsurprisingly failed, and they've killed her pygmy and squashed her spider – her only reaction is to throw back her head and laugh. Then she links arms with Inspector Lestrade and marches off to prison or the noose. Adrea Spedding, the Spider Woman: nothing could ever discompose her. She was just so perfectly don't-care-ish.'

'So what's your real name?' asked Evan, who had been laughing throughout. 'Or rather, what name were you given?'

'Well, it wasn't Andrea,' she said. 'It was even worse. Audrey. "It's from Shakespeare," Mum told me but when I looked her up she was a half-witted shepherdess in *As You Like It*.' Adrea crossed her eyes and put on a yokel burr. '"I am not a slut, though I thank the Gods I am foul." They could at least have called me Rosalind. When I got to school things got even worse. It was also the name of a character in that comedy programme, *The Likely Lads*: a dopey bleach-blonde hairdresser who was always whining about "our Terry". So everyone called me the Likely Lad. Then someone said that it sounded like a racehorse, so they followed me around neighing and making clippety-clop noises. That's why I still run down corridors: so that people can't slap me on the rump or push a carrot in my face.'

Even more than sex itself, Adrea had always wondered what the conversation afterwards would be like. She had imagined quiet, intense voices resolving all life's great questions. Instead of which they were lying together exchanging random memories of their school-days. Evan listened in disbelief as she revealed the fiendishly refined cruelties of schoolgirls. Then he told her about how at assembly he had thrown a flour-bomb at the headmaster but missed and hit instead the organist, who had nevertheless not missed a single note of Reubke's 94th Psalm. And about how their Latin teacher, in full gown and mortar-board, would suddenly come blinking and snuffling through the steam of the shower room. While Evan spoke his chest vibrated under her ear, as if the rest of his body were confirming what the mouth uttered.

A sudden realization yanked her out of her half-doze. She had forgotten to ring Sally. Suppose lines of police and dogs were combing Hampstead Heath and her awful passport photograph was flashing up behind a grim-faced newsreader? Her clothes seemed to have vanished, so she pulled on Evan's T-shirt: it felt rough and stiff against her skin. The phone was at the end of the hall. She picked her way with difficulty through a mass of buckled crossbars, rusted chassis, twisted wheels. According to Evan, no one in the place could ride a bike. A couple of shaggy heads poked out of the kitchen but, on seeing her, ducked back inside.

The number remained stubbornly engaged. Perhaps they were

working their way through her address book? She had a vision of Sally with her head in her hands, repeating, 'I blame myself', while her tears sluiced the make-up off her face.

Yesterday morning felt like years ago. She had been so preoccupied on the way to work that it was only when she was leaving the tube that she registered she hadn't noticed whether people were looking at her or not. Once at Heron Close, however, she'd not had time to notice anything. The place seemed to be transformed. There was a constant hubbub of talk and movement, and she and Evan were rushed off their feet. The toilets' panic buttons kept on sounding. Adrea would dash down the corridors to find the residents wedged in ever more unlikely positions. The Babies pinballed around, moving as fast backwards as forwards; baths and sinks mysteriously overflowed; one of the clocks fell with a crash from the sitting-room wall. Stormy appeared again and again outside the window, meowing plaintively: whenever she let him in he somehow managed to get out again. The office telephone rang continually but the callers always hung up without speaking. Although Terry sat motionless in the chair, his shirt front would not stay buttoned, his trousers kept unzipping themselves, and their cuffs rode up to his knees. She did notice that although he was upset whenever she moved away it was as if a different part of him were equally pleased to see Evan. The shift had passed in the blink of an eye. Price had been nowhere to be seen – at lunchtime, the pills had apparently just materialized in their appointed places.

She and Evan had hardly even spoken until they went off duty and were walking together towards Chalk Farm. He was telling her about the derelict-looking pub across the road: the gridlocked traffic swam like a mirage. When they reached the corner her feet turned left with him rather than right towards her station. She decided to let him finish his story and then catch the train from Camden Town station, although she usually avoided it. A group of alcoholics, with matted hair and scarlet faces, were always sitting on the steps, guzzling Special Brew, cursing and grabbing at the legs of passers-by.

They joined the crowds beyond the railway bridge. Adrea realized that she wasn't taking in what he was saying: it was as if she could see each word floating past her but was unable to connect them. Already she could hear the drunks up ahead: pedestrians were stepping out into the road and even the buses seemed to be giving them a wide berth. As she and Evan approached along the now-emptied pavement a silence fell: she saw that their eyes were fixed on her. As they drew level, first one of the men, then the rest, gravely raised their golden cans in a toast. And she and Evan had nodded and smiled, as if they were the King and Queen of somewhere. Then they were past the station, heading down Bayham Street. By the time the two of them had reached Mornington Crescent, all thoughts about getting back to Stanmore – and about pretty much everything else – had gone clear out of her mind.

For the twenty-third time Adrea dialled her sister's number and finally got through.

'You're not going to believe my hat!' Sally was laughing. 'We're off to Ascot.'

'I'm awfully sorry,' Adrea said, 'I'm all right. I went round to a friend's and I was so tired I fell asleep.'

'That's OK,' said Sally. 'We just assumed that you'd run into some bloke.'

Adrea was dumbstruck: as if such a thing had ever happened before, as if it were always happening!

'Trevor has heard a whisper' – Sally's own voice dropped – 'Sagaro in the Gold Cup.' She had already gone when Adrea furiously slammed down the receiver. If only she *had* been murdered, raped, robbed, kidnapped by scientologists or whisked off by a flying saucer! She paused in front of a cracked, dusty mirror to arrange her features into an acceptably don't-care-ish alignment.

Back in the bedroom, Evan took out his favourite album of the moment: *Agents of Fortune* by the Blue Öyster Cult. After two weeks of saturation playing, the vinyl had begun to fizz and click. The cover design of a Victorian magician holding between his fingers four of the splashiest tarot cards – Sun, Moon, Death, Tower – was now looking rather silly. Side two had become boring but side one was holding up surprisingly well. Buck Dharma was his favourite guitarist. His solos and fills weren't the usual flashy arpeggios and runs: they sounded like interpolated extracts from completely different pieces. It was as if they had other songs that were so remarkably potent and subversive that they didn't dare to record them and so left it up to their listeners to recreate them from these bewildering fragments.

There was something strange about the band: they seemed to be making records twenty years in the future and then somehow transporting them back. Their lyrics contained casual references to events that hadn't happened yet and technology that hadn't been invented. They even had their own flag: black and white, bearing an obscurely sinister symbol that resembled a raying sun crowned with a question mark. 'Mad Jewish fascists' was the verdict of his housemates. Although Evan was the nominal leader of the band in which they all played together, the others had so far resisted his attempts to add 'Harvester of Eyes' and 'Flaming Telepaths' to their meagre repertoire.

As if on cue, Adrea reappeared at the opening bars of '(Don't Fear) the Reaper', where the guitars sounded to be playing backwards and forwards simultaneously.

'Your housemates seem rather shy,' she said.

'Really?' Shy was just about the last word Evan would have applied to Dave, Alan and Pete. Even Ken could only be called, at best, distracted or withdrawn.

Adrea arched one eyebrow and yawned loudly. Evan had played her this music last night but she hadn't liked it much. Even though the words were about death instead of dancing or kissing, it was still just another pop song. Evan had proceeded to give her a long lecture on the mysterious significance of brackets in song titles. He had played her The Beatles' 'Norwegian Wood (This Bird has Flown)', The Rolling Stones' '(I Can't Get No) Satisfaction' and Otis Redding's 'Fa Fa Fa Fa (Sad Song)'. They were, Evan affected to believe, a sign for initiates, like the poster in Herman Hesse's *Steppenwolf* – 'Pablo's Magic Theatre (Not For Everyone)'. If you followed the parentheses, he concluded, you would never go wrong. Adrea had admired his enthusiasm but, try as she might, she just could not hear those brackets.

'Let me give you a shotgun,' Evan said. She saw that he had rolled and lighted another joint. He took a mouthful of smoke, then, curling a hand round the back of her neck, he drew her towards him. Having placed the joint between her lips, he brought his face up close, opening his mouth to admit the fiery tip, then blasted the smoke back through the cardboard mouthpiece, down deep into her lungs. Her body felt as though it were being filled with a heavy, pulsing liquid, like oil. There was a roaring in her ears and the room seemed momentarily to be filled with tall, shadowy figures just standing there, neither kindly nor malevolent, seemingly oblivious to her. She fell back on to the mattress and Evan, following her, came down heavily on her right leg. There was a loud double crack but she felt no pain. The leg wasn't broken, his spine hadn't snapped. Maybe love made you weightless or meant that you couldn't hurt each other?

A woman's voice spoke into the silence before the Blue Öyster Cult's guitars and drums came thundering in. It was husky and strangely flat, as if all emotions were present simultaneously, cancelling each other out. It was impossible to tell whether the words might have been uttered as the beginning, middle or end of something. The record sleeve identified her as Patti Smith: Evan had said that she was the girlfriend of one of the band. The song that followed was called

'The Revenge of Vera Gemini': as far as Adrea could tell from the weedy male vocal line it was a limp variation on the demon lover theme familiar to her from Keats, Coleridge and Swinburne. That strange woman's voice, though, continued to fade in and out, sneeringly echoing or anticipating the words. It reminded her of Billie Holiday: not the sound itself, but the feeling it was giving her at the base of her spine.

As the echoes of Buck Dharma's tremendous, nameless final chord died away, Evan became aware that the room was still vibrating, as if hundreds of long fast trains were all converging on Euston. But he knew that it was something else. It was, just as Papa Hemingway had promised, the sound of the earth moving.

Some time later, as they were both sliding back into sleep, there was a blare of feedback and a ragged drum roll that culminated in a cymbal crash like a dropped frying pan.

'Band practice,' said Evan, without enthusiasm. He started to put on his trousers.

'Can I come along?' Adrea asked.

He gave her a rueful grin. 'If you want to be put right off me.'

'Where is it?' She was amused to see that he wore no socks inside his boots.

'Just follow your ears,' said Evan, opening the door. 'Listen out for something that sounds like a slow plane crash.'

As he was passing the kitchen, Evan heard an old woman's querulous voice: 'Would you like a nice cup of tea, dear?'

'Fuck off, Dave,' he replied.

Ever since he had started at Heron Close his housemates had never let up. They would speak to him very slowly, with heavy emphasis and then cup their ears and say, 'Eh? Eh?' when he replied. They sniffed the air and held their noses. They had even clubbed together to buy him a cloth cap and a second-hand crutch. It was for his own good: they were trying to save him from himself.

'Get out while you can,' said Pete, twirling his drumsticks. 'It's like a contact high: in a few weeks you'll be as gaga as them.'

'Didn't you once work as a gravedigger?' asked Evan.

Pete, in reviewing his past, dropped his sticks. 'Yeah,' he finally decided.

'Well, did the stiffs give you a contact high of death?'

'No,' Pete reluctantly conceded, 'but my skin went all flaky for a while and I had some really bad dreams.'

Evan surveyed his friends. It was as if they had grown ugly overnight. In the heat, Alan's face had assumed the colour and consistency of veal. Pete was shirtless, revealing a greasy bulging gut hanging over what appeared to be a kangaroo's pouch. Even Dave now had a distinct wobble when he walked and his shoulder-length hair hung like seaweed. Chubby drummers and bass-players were just about acceptable but, Jim Morrison notwithstanding, you really couldn't have a lardy lead singer. And, of course, any guitarist with even the merest pinch of extra flesh should be summarily garrotted with his own strings. How had they all got so fat when he himself was eating the same things? Evan had begun to suspect that adipose tissue was generated by some deficiencies of the heart or brain.

'You look pleased with yourself.' He turned to meet Ken's part-myopic, part-hypnotic gaze.

'Your tarot turned out to be right.' said Evan. 'For once.'

A week before, Ken had given him a blinding reading – all four aces and high arcana cards culminating in number six, the Lovers. An immediate supplementary had been equally spectacular, with the same final card. With growing agitation – which he always displayed whenever his magic showed any sign of working – Ken laid them out in lines, horseshoes, crosses and even seemingly random scatterings. All seventy-eight cards put in an appearance but the Lovers came down last every time.

'The Lovers isn't about chicks, man,' Ken said. 'It's about good and evil, light and darkness, the combinatory powers of the cosmos.'

'That sounds like chicks to me,' said Evan.

'So tell me,' said Dave, putting a flabby arm round Evan's shoulders, 'what particular cosmic combinations were you trying out last night?'

'We could hear some weird noises,' said Alan. 'What the hell were you doing to her?'

'The tarot is a ladder,' Ken was muttering into the opened fridge. 'You're supposed to climb it' – he split open a carton of natural yoghurt with his remarkable long right thumbnail – 'not sit on the bottom rung jerking off.'

'Did she scratch you?' Dave was trying to pull up Evan's T-shirt. 'Did she bite you anywhere good?'

'It wasn't her cherry, was it?' asked Pete. 'It was, wasn't it?'

'Did she bleed?'

'Did she cry?'

'Did you put it in her mouth?'

'Did she take it up the arse?'

Evan just stared at them. They were getting worse by the minute. They now resembled those grotesque background figures in German religious paintings, gloating as Christ lugs the cross towards Calvary.

'Do you know, guys' – Evan's voice broke into a senile cackle – 'I really can't remember.'

They were still tuning up when Adrea entered the band room. Evan didn't recognize her at first because she had pinned and piled her hair up on top of her head. Her neck was so incredibly long that he wondered if she might belong to an entirely different species. She said hello to the band, but they just dropped their eyes and mumbled something: there was no doubt about it, thought Evan, they were being shy.

Adrea became aware that Evan's T-shirt wasn't quite long enough to serve as a dress, so she yanked it down towards her knees, only to see their gazes shift upwards as the outlines of her breasts were revealed. She had been expecting Evan's friends to be like him: not as good, of course, but recognizably of the same type. But they were just scruffy hippies, with awkward, graceless bodies, hair that was part-dry, part-greasy, eyes that wouldn't meet hers. They were all completely of their time – modern, contemporary, utterly 1976 – whereas Evan wasn't. He stood out, as he would always have stood out: anywhere and at any time he would always have been out of place.

The band was terrible. They started with a blues about a black snake which oscillated between eleven and thirteen bars. The more they played, the worse it got: they seemed to be trying to forget it, rather than learn it. As Evan had promised, Dave's voice did indeed have a Steve Winwood-like crack in it but unfortunately the crack itself was cracked. Alan's fingers crawled like grubs over the neck of his bass: the instrument sounded as if it had been strung with rubber bands. The drumsticks kept flying out of Pete's hands and when one cannoned off the ceiling and struck him on the temple, he actually stopped playing and rubbed it better. Adrea's hopes rose momentarily when Dave inserted a harmonica into his letterbox mouth but what ensued was even worse. It reminded her of when next door's Alsatian had shaken Sally's pet rabbit to death.

Evan's playing was also terrible but in a different way. His right arm chopped down on the strings, generating great jagged masses of sound, as if he were trying to blast some obstruction out of his path. He didn't use a plectrum: now she understood why his right thumb was blue and swollen. Although she was in his line of sight, she knew that he was not seeing her. She loved the way he had lit a cigarette and then wedged it above the bridge where it burned down to the tip without his ever touching it again. If one of the others had done such a thing she knew that she would have found it absurd. Except for a slow flexing of his knees he hardly moved at all, although occasionally his sharp, cleft chin would drop on to his chest and then whip back up, as though he had momentarily fallen asleep. She watched the shadows around his eyes, cheeks and collarbones that shifted and deepened, came and went. Although the band were still gurning and posturing in front of her, Adrea could only hear the loving, loping, happy-sad tenor saxophone of Lester Young.

seven

So they were wrong, Mrs Barker reflected, triumphantly unpicking the morning's knitting, when they said that there was no smoke without fire. More than two weeks after he passed away, Nobby's grey-blue pall was still there. If anything, it was thicker and bluer than before and had begun to spread to the rest of the sitting room. She was beginning to suspect that it wasn't cigarette smoke after all. It no longer wreathed around but hung steady and straight, like a fine silk curtain. Even when the cleaner came pushing the box-sweeper along, it remained undisturbed. Perhaps she herself was making it happen? Perhaps good thoughts rather than bad words could turn the air blue?

All that dust and fluff was still there on the carpet: how did they think they could clean without bending their knees and elbows? A long single thread like a fuse was protruding dangerously out of the pile. Stormy, lying on his back, was flicking it with his paws. He blinked and wiggled, inviting her to stroke his tummy – that lovely feathery fur that never moulted – but she wasn't falling for that one: the purple scratches on the back of her hand were still throbbing. It wasn't his fault. Sometimes Mrs Parker's influence would grow too strong and force his claws and teeth to shut like a gin-trap on her stroking hand. Two could play at that game, though: she could see that Mrs Parker's busily knitting fingers bore scars similar to her own.

Outside the sitting room, unusual things were happening. Twenty minutes ago Price – a full two hours before he should be dispensing the pills – had floated down the corridor and had not yet reappeared. She had wondered if he was sniffing around Bridie again but there she was, already changed and waiting by the door a full five minutes before the end of her shift. She was wearing pink, baggy trousers. Mrs Barker considered her rear view a personal affront. If care assistants really cared they wouldn't keep looking at their watches and they wouldn't need paying. And who were they supposed to be assisting? It certainly wasn't her.

And now, four minutes too early, Bridie had actually gone, leaving the door ajar, with the place unattended. Anything could happen in four minutes. Anyone could walk in and, in fact, someone just had. She screwed up her eyes against the light: it was a young boy – no, with those hips, a girl. She was looking around the hall, as if in wonder: ruddy-faced and bright-eyed, a foreigner, probably. Only when Mrs Barker saw the mass of hair hanging down her back did she realize that it was only that other care assistant, Andrea, or whatever she was called. She did look different, although it was hard to say precisely how she had changed. She looked shorter – no, taller. Her face was thinner – or was it suddenly more fleshy? Had her nose always been that shape? Was it just that she had begun to walk with her spine straight and her head up? Mrs Barker's needles stabbed into her ball of wool. Surely it wasn't asking too much that people should stay the same? Or that, if they had to change, they should at least do it gradually, over a decent period of time?

Adrea had left Evan on the main road, with instructions to count up to two hundred before following her in. It wasn't that she was ashamed of anything, she told herself, she just didn't like the idea of being gossiped about. She was relieved to see the door open as she approached but then Bridie, pink as a blancmange, came wobbling down the steps. She stopped dead and stared hard into Adrea's face as she passed. Adrea did not need to turn round to know that the sound that followed was Bridie's hands coming together in slow, mocking applause. She felt her cheeks burning and then the blush seemed to spread to cover her entire body. How could her blood be rushing everywhere at once? Surely it had to come *from* somewhere?

In the hall mirror she checked her reflection. Whatever could Bridie have seen? There were no love-bites or stubble rashes: even her expression was perfectly don't-care-ish, although the skin was still beetroot-red. Why was it that whenever you wanted to keep a secret everyone immediately knew, whereas if you needed help or sympathy they never picked up the signs? Most people seemed to have been put on earth solely to do whatever you didn't want them to do. In the sitting room, all the residents' heads were turned towards her: even the cat was goggling its upside-down eyes. Glimpsing Price's bulk looming out of the kitchen, she ducked into the nearest lavatory. The lock and bolt had been removed, so she had to hold its door shut with one foot. Turning the taps full on, she held her wrists under the flow: the sound of running water always made her feel safe.

'Aha!' Price said loudy. 'The flash of a kingfisher's wing!' He walked right up to the toilet so that Adrea would see his Oxfords' well-polished toe-caps peeping under the sawn-off door. Even over the sound of the taps he could hear her breathing.

The previous day he had watched Evan and Adrea leave together. Although they appeared to be moving briskly it had taken an inordinately long time for them to cross the square. In the block opposite, he could see the sun glinting on the lenses of Snow's binoculars. The space between the two young bodies had decreased with every step until finally, when they turned together out of his sight, they appeared to have fused. His phone had rung immediately.

'I request a week's leave,' came the anticipated voice.

'Of course, Snowy,' Price had said. 'Where are you going?' Snow had always worked through his holidays at time-and-a-half.

'Southend-on-Sea.' The words were elided so that it sounded as exotic as Samarqand or Timbuktu.

Since Price had become Acting Matron, the man had been even more afraid of him. He was disgusted to find how much he was enjoying this new deference from staff and residents. There was a spring in his step and a shameful new lightness in his heart. His voice boomed as if he were addressing a rally, while his arms made great sweeping gestures. Perhaps he should design himself a uniform, something in bile-green and gold with epaulettes and lots of frogging? Sometimes he awoke determined to exercise his power properly – to change everything, to expel the bad and raise up the good, to institute a golden age of harmony and plenty – but somehow this resolve had always faded by the time he had finished brushing his teeth.

He could hear Evan's ridiculous boots click-clacking across the concrete like Blind Pew's stick. Why was it that the sound of approaching footsteps, even when he knew perfectly well who it was, always made him feel so apprehensive?

Evan had only counted as far as 158. He had started out nice and slow but soon speeded up. Just standing still in London was dangerous: it was as if you identified yourself as a potential victim or threat. Drivers spat and yelled abuse: pedestrians gave him a wide berth. He decided to follow her at a leisurely pace, only to find that he had broken into a trot. He had the panicky feeling that he might find Adrea, Price, the residents and even the building itself vanished into thin air, so it was with relief that he caught sight of Bridie, even though she ignored him completely.

He had assumed that now he and Adrea had got together Heron Close had served its purpose. There seemed no point in even returning for their next shift. After all, if they'd met on a bus they wouldn't have felt the need to make the same journey every day. It was as if he had completely forgotten the place, so that when, after that disastrous band practice, she had said to him that it was time to go he had just stared at her. 'Don't you want to find out what they're all doing?' she had asked. 'No,' he replied. Finally, she had just walked out and he had followed her.

Price was waiting for him at the front door. He handed him a small brown envelope. Evan tore it open to find a tax-slip and a full month's wages. 'What about that sub?' he asked.

'Forget it,' said Price. 'Consider it a bank error in your favour. Buy yourself some more boots. Preferably quiet ones.'

Evan wondered why Price needed to act as if even his generous acts were crimes. It was significant that the real shits he had known in his life had all come on like Jesus Christ. Adrea absolutely hated him, it was true, but with women it was usually about whether a man wanted to go to bed with them or not. She seemed to feel that Price belonged, in some particularly unpleasant way, to both categories at once.

'Are you familiar with the works of Aristophanes?' Price inquired.

' 'Arry 'ooo?' replied Evan, in the tone of one in serious denial of his classical education.

'One of his plays is called *Women in Assembly*,' Price continued, undeterred. 'It's about a state ruled by women who pass a law that any young man who desires a young woman must first have sex with an old one.'

Before Evan could think of a suitable reply, Price was backing away, bowing like a magician at the successful conclusion of a difficult trick, as the toilet door swung open to reveal Adrea. Evan felt a jolt, as if she were not the person that he had been expecting. He suspected that he would never get used to her, that her very existence would always come as a shock. Putting her feet down carefully, as though mistrustful of the solidity of the ground, she walked over to them, head held high.

'Front door, office, cupboards,' said Price handing each of them a ring of three keys. 'I'm sick of people waking me up just to get a groundsheet out of the linen store.'

They took the keys but their eyes remained locked on each other. Adrea, Price realized, had assumed the pose of Verrocchio's *David* – feet apart, left hand on hip; all she lacked was a sword and a severed head. Evan, in contrast, was just sloping like a great big lummox. Price moved further off, until he was mounting the stairs, still walking backwards, at speed. He could do it in the dark, too: it was quite a feat, requiring hours of practice. Unfortunately, no one was watching him, for Evan and Adrea had started to laugh.

It was hard to tell which of them began it. He would have said that it was her, she would have said that it was him. Neither had the slightest idea of what they might be laughing at. It wasn't Price, because they had already forgotten his existence. It might have had something to do with the keys: there was something absurd about the look and feel of them in their palms.

The volume of sound seemed more than two people should be able to generate. Great waves of laughter rattled the windows, rolled and crashed against the walls. Within a few seconds it had spread to the sitting room. Mrs Parker was among the first to react, giving a great whoop that sounded more like someone losing their footing. She felt as if she had been awaiting this moment for a very long while. It was the first proper laughter that she had ever heard in Heron Close: until now there had only been some sniggers and titters, nasty little noises. She noticed that the men were laughing at a surprisingly high-pitched level, while the women produced a deep chuckling. Even the deaf ones were joining in. Poor Stormy, of course, couldn't laugh but he was blinking rapidly. Terry was twitching as usual: it struck Mrs Parker that perhaps he was already laughing all the time. Mrs Barker could feel the hilarity gradually overcoming her, from the feet upwards, and at last she could fight it no longer and began, violently, to sneeze. The laughter did not infect everyone, however: sitting in the dining room, drinking their second pot of tea, halfway through their third pack of bourbon biscuits, the two cleaners were shaking their heads in disapproval.

Brushing the tears from her eyes and taking a deep gulp of air, Adrea entered the sitting room. The laughter had subsided to leave a faint humming like friendly bees, and she realized by the smiling faces that greeted her that everybody knowing was not necessarily a bad thing.

Evan saw that some of the men were vigorously rubbing the backs of their hands under their stubbled chins, like the greeting sign of some secret society. 'Shave! Shave!' said Frances, advancing menacingly. Acting Matron Price's second executive act had been to delegate the shaving of residents to him. The razor, strop, brushes and steel bowl were laid out in the spare bedroom in front of a freshly polished mirror. 'Shave! Shave!' Evan realized that his heart was beating faster.

Adrea took the tea round. Although the urn was red-hot, the liquid always trickled out lukewarm, so sweet that she could actually smell the sugar. As she pushed the trolley down the corridor she caught sight of Evan, lathered up to the elbows, contemplating what appeared to be a giant meringue. 'I know you're in there somewhere,' he was saying. In the sitting room she clipped on Terry's plastic coverall: it was dazzling gold and red, like a beefeater's uniform. She knew that he hated it: his face was averted, set like the mask of tragedy. She removed it and turned it inside out, and he gave her a look of such gratitude that it was as if she had just fished him up out of Hell.

Someone had turned on the television. The picture was terrible, unless they were showing *Scott of the Antarctic*. Adrea waved the aerial around until the polar bears in a blizzard became racehorses striding round a paddock. She could see no sign in the crowd of Sally or her hat. Arms aching, she held the aerial up while Sagaro won the Gold Cup. All the residents were cheering, as if the beast carried all their fortunes on its back. It had gone off at 8–15 on, having won the race the previous year, so Trevor's hot tip had been not so much a whisper as a bellow, overheard by the entire country.

In the spare bedroom, Evan was beginning to get the hang of it. Nervous of the cut-throat blade – the first he had seen outside a horror film – he had prepared for a while by shaving his own fore-arms. Then the rhythm of the brush working on the soap had lulled him into a sort of trance: if the tea-trolley had not rattled past, he might have lathered up the whole world. Now, though, he watched as the razor moved with increasing confidence and freedom. There were patches of black, yellow and even red among the frosty stubble: what would Frances' beard be like if they just let it grow? 'Shave!' she kept saying, 'Shave!' The word had a different inflection every time. The sad dry smell of her hair recalled that which had risen from the sepia pages of his school Latin grammar. *Amo, amas, amat: amamus, amatis, amant.* The scalp had a blue tinge, as if the skin had been drawn tight over a steel dome. When, to counter her trembling, he rested his left palm on the crown, he saw that his fingers had disposed themselves as if about to launch it down the lane of a bowling alley. It felt strange to be touching someone else's body so soon after Adrea's. He tried and failed to imagine her similarly old, frail and frightened. Adrea did have a faint down along her upper lip but it was only visi-ble when the light fell just right – curiously, he could also only feel it at such times.

Back in the sitting room, Adrea unfastened Terry's apron and shook off the crumbs. As if enraged by the sudden flare of colour, Stormy sprang up out of sleep, eyes blazing. His front paws scraped at the dusty carpet before, lowering his head, he charged. With a mata-dor's flourish, Adrea executed a perfect Veronica. '*Olé!*' shouted Mrs Parker. Stormy came again, paws thudding like timpani. This time Adrea made a fluttering backhand pass, dropping to one knee on the follow-through. Such motions seemed natural to her: perhaps, in previous incarnations, she'd had much to do with cats that thought they were bulls? Adrea repeated the move on the next attack but the cat rather spoiled the effect by raking sideways with its claws. 'Missed!' Adrea called. Stormy made a few snaps at his own tail, ran up the wall almost as far as the cornice, then exited the room in a great single spring. Adrea became aware of three crimson-beaded lines welling up on the back of her right hand. 'Clever puss,' she said, looking into Mrs Barker's eyes.

Evan's razor was working its way through the men. Their beards weren't as tough as Frances' but their nostrils, edged with exotic tangles that retracted at the blade's approach, provided a fascinating challenge. As his last client left – brisk, pink and upright, as if relieved of a terrible burden – Frances, with a fresh towel draped over her arm, reappeared in the doorway. 'Shave!' she said. Before Evan could object, she had inserted herself into the chair and set her head at the requisite angle. He lathered her up once more and then began to run the blunt side of the razor over her face. At the side of the mouth was a single thick white hair that he had somehow missed: perhaps it had slipped itself inside a fold? Its resourcefulness, Evan decided, deserved a stay of execution. He noticed that on the back of his hands the veins had risen like a relief map: was this the contact high of old age that Pete had warned him about? As he gently raised Frances' chin, her eyes rolled back to meet his. 'Shave,' she whispered, 'shave.' She seemed to be begging him to peel away the aged skin to release the young girl still trapped inside her. Adrea had been right, he realized: there were good reasons why they should still be here.

When Adrea took the trolley back to the dining room she found that the cups and plates used by the domestics had been left on the table. A pool of tea was eating away at the Formica and the floor was littered with biscuit crumbs and torn wrappers. She could not grasp the concept of cleaners who didn't clean but, if anything, made more mess. 'Who are we to judge them?' Price had said. 'They have known much sorrow in their lives.' She herself had ended up washing the floors, even though it wasn't supposed to be her job.

And now she saw that they were doing the corridors. They had perfected a revolutionary technique that did not involve the application of water, brushes and disinfectant. Each had a yellow plastic cone marked 'Caution Wet Floors: Cleaning In Progress' which, every minute or so, they would kick a little further along, as if the announcement itself were sufficient, rendering any subsequent action redundant: as though the dirt, when faced with those awful words, would annihilate itself. At Adrea's approach the smaller woman broke off the conversation to wave a dry mop head just above the floor, while her friend shifted the two brimming buckets which would neither wash nor rinse. When she did not move on, they dropped all pretence and stared back at her.

They were called something like Gert and Daisy, and although only in their forties, they somehow seemed older than any of the residents. It appeared that someone had removed all the fat one's teeth in order to cram them into the other's mouth. They had funny knees that looked to have twisted round sideways; perhaps they couldn't have knelt even if they had wanted to? Both of them limped, as if something were wrong not just with their legs but deep inside them. They did look as if they had known sorrow, Adrea conceded, but it obviously hadn't been anything like enough.

At the far end of the corridor, Evan appeared, leading Frances by the hand. He was moving very slowly, on tiptoe. 'Mind you don't slip,' he said to his companion as, with a final 'Shave!' she vanished into the sitting room. Evan then began to progress in little hops. 'Sorry, ladies,' he called, 'I hope I'm not messing up your nice clean floor.' As he reached them, he simulated a long glissade, catching a heel on one of the buckets and sloshing the water over its side. Cursing horribly, Gert and Daisy mopped away the tidal wave with remarkable speed. Then they turned to find that Evan and Adrea were still standing there, smiling seraphically, each with a foot planted on a bucket's rim, rocking them gently to and fro.

It was strange, Mrs Parker thought, how quickly things could change. Now that the domestics had cleaned the corridor the whole place already smelt different. She breathed in and savoured it: the smell of nothing. They had also returned to dust and vacuum the sitting room violently. She hadn't even known that they had a vacuum cleaner: what were those objects behind the chairs that went rattling so noisily up its nozzle? The pattern of the carpet was once again apparent, although this was a mixed blessing because after a while its flowers would begin to turn into strange faces that winked at her. Perhaps it was a mistake to clean things because then you had to start getting used to them all over again. Routine and familiarity were what she needed, not surprises, even nice ones. The other evening they had by mistake laid out too many biscuits on the tray and, even though she had wolfed them down, those two extra custard creams had put her right off her shot. She had tossed and turned all night, just because two biscuits had suddenly become four. But why shouldn't they? Why shouldn't there be six biscuits or twelve or a hundred? Why did there have to be any biscuits at all?

Through her knitting she watched Evan and Adrea moving to and fro. Whenever their paths crossed they would bow gravely to each other: 'After you' – 'No, after you'. Their politeness grew more and more elaborate: 'I insist' – 'No, *I* insist'. It was as if being formal was their way of getting giddier and giddier. At least they weren't like those boyish girls and girly boys that, judging by the television, were everywhere, these days. For the last twenty years, Mrs Parker had suspected that nobody was actually making love any more, that the sexual act had died out with Stanley. Children kept entering the world, of course, but she assumed that her sons and daughters-in-law, for example, must be reproducing by other means. She understood that there had been some remarkable advances in medical science: perhaps nowadays all they had to do was to fill out a form. Now, no matter how much she tried to stop them, images of Evan and Adrea, with no clothes on, all tangled up in each other, kept coming into her mind. It was as if their very restraint had brought this on, whereas all the crude gropings of Mrs Allen and Billy had seemed merely an unconvincing act. She saw that the young people had met again in the doorway. 'No, no, my dear sir!' – 'Yes, yes, my dear lady!' Finally Adrea squeezed past, violently bumping Evan with her hip. He staggered back, then pursued her down the corridor. There was a crash, as if one or both of them had slipped on the wet floor.

With a last great indignant clatter the cleaners left the building. Before the front door banged shut behind them it had admitted a faint breeze that bore a familiar scent to Mrs Parker's nostrils. Although overlaid by car fumes and melting tar it was unmistakeably that of summer blossom. Pulling the Zimmer frame from behind the chair, she draped her knitting over it, then grasped its grey handles and began to move across the room. To her annoyance, everyone else was getting up as well: the sheep all obviously thought it was dinnertime.

Out in the hallway she momentarily lost her resolve: she looked left and right but there was no one around to stop her or try to talk her out of it. Uncomfortably aware of the press behind her, she moved on: they had not turned left towards the dining room but were still following. She clutched the handle and turned it but the door held fast. The crowd was bunching up and she felt her panic rising as her face was pushed right against the stippled glass. Then she saw Mrs Barker's huge hand come past her to unfasten the Yale lock and she found herself stumbling across the threshold, blinded by the sudden glare. It was almost as if someone had given her a little push.

'It seems that we're all going outside,' said Evan, enjoying the look of consternation on Adrea's face.

'Can we?' She blushed again, realizing how childish that had sounded. 'I mean, shouldn't we clear it with...' She hesitated, then saluted. 'Deputy Matron Acting Matron Price!' they barked in unison.

'I've never been out here before,' said a tiny old man. Adrea did not recall his face but then they all looked somehow different out in the natural light. She was relieved that none of them had crumbled away to dust. From the cobwebbed storeroom, Evan dragged out some plastic chairs and large purple sunshades that fitted the concrete bases set along the terrace. Soon everyone was seated, even the Babies, and a remarkable hubbub began. It wasn't conversation so much as everyone talking to themselves, although Frances did seem to be trying to solicit another shave from the sun. Adrea observed that they were all gradually shuffling their chairs out of the shadows.

Even over Casals grunting through the Bach cello suites, Price, up in his attic, became aware of a curious sound. It was as if a flock of doves had settled on the roof. He leaned out of the landing window to see below the tops of dozens of heads, like a clutch of huge speckled eggs. Chuckling and rubbing his hands, he returned, with a leap worthy of Stormy, to his room.

Terry was the last of the residents to emerge. Evan felt that he wasn't so much pushing the wheelchair as trying to slow it down, as if a powerful magnet had locked on to the metal frame. When it hit the ramp at the far end of the terrace, all he could do was hang on. Terry's arm shot out, like a general commanding his armies to charge. Evan decided to go along with it: obviously he – or his chair – had somewhere to go.

Adrea watched the receding figures. Evan's feet turned clownishly outwards as he walked: she was going to have to revise her ideas of gracefulness.

'There's something strange about that young man,' observed Mrs Parker.

'Oh yes!' she agreed enthusiastically.

When Terry and Evan reached the High Street the traffic immediately halted, as if at a red light. Evan cautiously pushed the wheelchair across the road while the drivers on either side gave them the thumbs-up sign. Perhaps Terry was a local celebrity? The passers-by all smiled and a man with a ragged cairn terrier seemed to greet him by name. Terry's head, twisting round, appeared to be nodding in confirmation that they were on the right track. Two young Japanese girls, their A–Zs open at Camberwell instead of Camden Town, rushed up to ask directions. They giggled nervously as Evan responded, as if suspecting some ventriloquial trick. He felt rather jealous: he had always had a thing about Japanese girls. Those short kilts! Those ankle socks! Before they made off for the zoo they gave Terry's shoulder a firm, lingering squeeze, as though for luck.

As they neared the Eagle and Child, Terry began to thrash about like a hooked fish fighting a line. He calmed down when Evan stopped, although his mouth remained open, displaying harp strings of greenish saliva. A stark black and white poster on the pub's crumbling wall caught Evan's eye. It was of a woman's face, hawk-like, half in shadow. The one visible eye was round and glittering: two drops of blood or dark tears were frozen on the hollowed cheek. The extreme chiaroscuro gave the effect of a second mouth and something like a foetus growing out from the neck. Below it were the words:

'LIVE AT THE ROUNDHOUSE, CHALK FARM
ROAD, PATTI SMITH BAND (+ SUPPORT).'

Music sounded in Evan's head, but not *The Revenge of Vera Gemini*. It was that music that he could never quite hear, that he often dreamed about, that he felt sure was seeking him just as he was seeking it. So far, every gig he had ever been to had been, however fantastic, an anti-climax. Maybe this one would be different, the real thing at last? Perhaps Patti Smith, when she walked on to the Roundhouse stage, would indeed have two mouths and only half a face?

It was time to head back. Terry's mouth snapped shut and his right arm nearly threw itself out of its socket. Once more, the traffic parted for them like the Red Sea. As they crossed, Evan could feel Patti Smith's dark eye boring into his back.

Out on the terrace most of the residents had dozed off but Adrea was still alert. She had always needed eight hours' sleep but now she was feeling fine on virtually none. Perhaps sleep had been bad for her, like the milk everyone had forced down her throat until they finally had to admit that she was allergic to it? She examined the scratches on her hand: they were spectacular but she felt no pain at all.

'It takes a while,' said Mrs Parker, without looking up from the knitting. 'For the bacteria to get to work.'

A pair of heavy boots came clattering up the basement steps and a strange figure emerged. Despite the heat, it wore heavy twill trousers and a long anorak with its hood up, fastened securely at the neck. Although she couldn't see the face, Adrea was sure that it wasn't the butcher: at least, he hadn't told her to cheer up. The man was carrying a bulging shopping bag in each hand: she could see the handles biting into his blue fingers.

'Hello,' she called but he didn't respond.

'Hey you!' she yelled, setting the words like bloodhounds on his track. Although his feet didn't leave the ground, he redoubled his speed. She could hear him chuff-chuffing along and she half expected to see a smoking groove scratched into the pavement behind him. Amorphous shapes seemed to be fighting their way through the plastic: as she watched, one of the bags split and a green head of broccoli poked inquisitively out. A couple of rosy apples tumbled to the ground. The hooded man tried to dribble them along for a while, then gave up.

As he disappeared, a voice, quavering like a calliope, began to sing:

> We're a lonely dismal crew
> Poor old maids
> We're a lonely dismal crew

> All dressed in yellow, pink and blue
> Nursing the cat is all we do
> Poor old maids.

It was Mrs Parker, although her lips did not appear to be moving. Two more verses followed, the same as the first, except at an ever-decreasing tempo, with painfully long pauses between yellow, pink and blue. Stormy materialized, to stalk in slow motion along the wall, as if daring anyone even to think about nursing him.

Terry's wheelchair was approaching the bottom of the ramp, but rather than pushing it, Evan appeared to be hitching a ride. He was startled to see that in the space of twenty minutes the formerly pale skins of the residents had begun to glow.

'Did you see the vegetable man?' Adrea asked.

Terry spluttered wildly. 'No,' said Evan. 'Just some nice Japanese girls.'

Nobody noticed that, in the distance, the hooded figure had reappeared and was stamping his lost apples into pulp.

eight

Although Adrea had walked past the Roundhouse many times she had always thought of it as derelict, its no doubt unpleasant original function long forgotten. She had not known of its more recent significance as an underground music and arts venue until Evan told her. He was astonished to discover that she had never heard of The Plastic Exploding Inevitable. And so, as they ascended the crumbling stone steps on the night of the Patti Smith gig, she had little idea of what to expect. She had been embarrassed to admit that the only group she had ever seen had been Fairport Convention at Reading Poly but

Evan had just said, inexplicably, 'Sloth', and whistled admiringly. The people around them had a furtive air, their expressions at once excited and ashamed, as if they might be going to watch a sex show or animals fighting. Before they ducked through the dark entrance she glanced back and was surprised to see how high they had climbed above the now-inaudible traffic.

Inside, the blast of hot air made her stagger. It felt unnatural: heat should be synonymous with light, and darkness with cold – although Hell was said to be pitch-black, in spite of its flames. As her eyes adjusted she realized that they were in a narrow corridor lit by ultra-violet lamps. Everyone was wearing dark clothes so a succession of disembodied heads appeared to be floating along. Every blemish and scar on the skin stood out: only now did Adrea see that there were pale freckles on Evan's nose and cheeks.

Some people claimed that the place had been a docking bay for spaceships, others that it was a former engine shed. In fact, Evan told her, it had once housed the enormous winding gear that had pulled trains up the steep hill from Euston. As they shuffled along they were skirting reminders of this former purpose: a precarious tower of empty cable drums, a shoulder-high cogwheel draped in cobwebs and a line of brass cylinders like enormous lipsticks. Adrea could feel chips of masonry rolling along under her feet. At last she followed Evan up a wide steep metal ladder: it was so dark that someone below kept mistaking her bottom for the next rung.

The height of the dome and the extent of the space beneath gave her a vertiginous feeling. The roof looked as if it were about to fall in: she was convinced that she could see the broken spars and girders swinging lazily to and fro. Trawling nets had been stretched between the gallery rails but anything falling would surely pass straight through. Small patches of sky were visible, against which the dark shapes of birds or bats flickered about. A motionless pall of blue smoke hung above the amplifiers. She had a strange sense of recognition: it felt like somewhere familiar that had been horribly distorted, like in *Planet of the Apes* when Charlton Heston walks past the crumbling, vegetation-matted Statue of Liberty. Evan took her arm and they moved to the slightly raised seats at the side of the stage. His eyes swept around, as though registering and assessing everyone in the place. Adrea, by sitting down too abruptly, almost toppled the whole row.

The support band's instruments were laid out ready. Unnamed on the posters, the *NME* had listed them as The Strangers but dripping black letters on the bass drum spelled out 'Stranglers'. Evan's heart sank at the sight of the electric organ: he couldn't stand the sound. Even Jimmy 'the Cat' Smith made him want to piss.

Perhaps because it was a Sunday night there was something unusual about this audience. Apart from a few scrambled old hippies who appeared to have been chained to the walls, leather jackets predominated, although none, of course, were as good as his own. Most people also had, like him, unfashionably short hair – including the surprisingly high proportion of women. A few weeks before he had seen the same radical feminists turn up en masse for the American girl group, the Runaways. It was as if they had been waiting for something: unfortunately, the Runaways – cartoon jailbait in hot pants and halter tops – had not been it and were pelted with tampons, used and unused.

One of Evan's favourite songs, 'I Ain't Got You', came blasting from the PA. The Yardbirds' vocalist, Keith Relf, had died a few days before, reportedly electrocuted by his own guitar. They had been an unexceptional r'n'b group who had somehow managed successfully to recruit Eric Clapton, Jeff Beck and Jimmy Page as lead guitarists. 'I Ain't Got You' was an old blues standard: while the rest of the band chugged dutifully along, Clapton set off great glorious firework bursts of sound. There was more passion and invention in those few fills and that eighteen-second solo than in all Cream's marathon jams put together. Why didn't these people ever quit while they were ahead?

He noticed that the support band had mooched on to the stage, one at a time. They didn't look like Stranglers, or even like strangers – in fact, they were all too depressingly familiar. After an eternity of tuning, they lurched into a jagged, shouted version of Dionne Warwick's masterpiece of anguish and cool, 'Walk on By'. It was impossible even to guess at what they thought they might have been doing. The tiny bass player, who had removed his shirt to reveal ludicrously over-developed muscles, was fumbling at a beautiful violin Hofner. The organist inserted Manzarek's solo from 'Light My Fire' into every number. Why were organists always so unhealthy-looking? This one even had a little sculpted beard. The singer was an angular, thin-faced man who, despite the stubble and the scowl, closely resembled his old geography teacher. Mr Dawson had taken exception to Evan's obscene geology diagrams. 'Go and show the headmaster your drumlins,' he had stammered. Evan realized that he could no longer remember what drumlins were, or erratics, to say nothing of gneiss and schist. The singer had started to rub his hands up and down his neck to simulate wanking: at the end of the number he spat a mouthful of shaving cream all over the front row. That clinched it, Evan thought. It was old Droopy Dawson, all right.

The volume of the music was worrying Adrea: every time the grubby-looking drummer hit his snare she could plainly see the building's already half-collapsed gallery vibrating. Also, the Australian woman sitting next to her had started shouting: 'The only thing you could strangle is your own cheesy dicks!' A few tampons were lobbed on to the stage: the bass player reacted as if they were sticks of dynamite. Perhaps it was all part of their act?

Adrea was still turning over what had happened that afternoon when they had gone up to Edgware to pick up her things. She kept recalling the horror-struck expression on her sister's face. Sally had always been on at her to find a nice boyfriend but it was obvious that Evan catastrophically did not fit the bill. Adrea had felt a disappointment so intense that she wondered whether she had only got involved with Evan in order, by some strange logic, to restore her former relationship with her sister. While Evan and Trevor were upstairs, Sally's fingers had painfully gripped her forearms. 'You'll soon find there's more to relationships than sex,' she said in a thickened voice. This was odd because for months she had been telling Adrea that what she needed was a good seeing-to and had insisted on forcing on her all sorts of unwelcome intimate confidences. Afterwards, Sally had actually growled as she watched Evan descending the stairs with a cardboard box of LPs and books balanced on his shoulder. Then she had kicked Trevor's shins when he was about to drive them to the tube station. At least Adrea could be reasonably sure that she would say nothing to their parents.

The Stranglers looked shocked and hurt by the boos and catcalls at the end of their performance. The last number, 'Peaches', had been, so far as Adrea could tell, about ogling women's breasts and bottoms at the seaside. It seemed curious that, having tried so hard to be provocative, they then got so upset when people did indeed take offence. She had liked the singer, though – especially when he seemed to be pretending to ride an invisible bicycle. His profile had reminded her of Basil Rathbone. She had gone partially deaf, as if the sound had seeped like water into her inner ear.

In the gangway, the big Australian blocked Evan's path. 'That,' she said, with heavy emphasis, 'was sexist shit.'

'Yeah,' Evan replied, with his huge smile, gently taking her by the shoulders and moving her as if she had been a chair. 'It was all far too geological for me.'

The long bar was already crowded: most of the audience had obviously decided to wait for the second half. Apart from the sound of the tills there was silence. Perhaps it was the heat, but the hippies, the feminists, the would-be hipsters all had a preoccupied, expectant air. Taking Adrea's arm, Evan began to shoulder his way back down the corridor against the flow. They passed the toilets, which smelt strongly of gas, then a padlocked emergency exit. Now they were alone. The ultraviolet light had faded and they proceeded by the flame of Evan's lighter, skirting huge glowing crumbs of fallen masonry. At last he drew her behind a pillar where a rusted metal door had warped back from its hinges to leave a gap that they could just squeeze through.

They emerged next to a disused signal box. Its windows were broken and the wooden steps had all rotted through. The rails whispered and sighed, glowing coral-pink with the last rays of the setting sun. Along the track were small piles of part-melted nuts and bolts, seared wadding and cotton, as if someone had been burning beds. Signal lights were flashing but there were no trains, just a shower of sparks in the distance. Adrea looked for Heron Close but the blocks appeared to be in a completely different alignment.

Evan's white face kept grinning back at her: she knew how much he loved trespassing. Finally, they sat down on a raised concrete platform that had cracked and fissured like a limestone pavement. There was no respite from the heat, except that it now seemed to be crushing rather than smothering them. It didn't feel like the middle of a city but nor was it like the countryside. If anything, Adrea thought, it was as if they were on another planet. Evan lit a joint and passed it to her. 'I've been meaning to ask you,' she said, relieved to find that the first hit no longer set her coughing. 'What was the happiest moment of your life?'

'It was three years ago.' Evan stood up and folded his hands behind his back, like a child reciting a poem. 'On Crewe Station. I can't remember what I was doing in Crewe. I think I'd been to a party because I found myself there in the middle of the night, waiting for the morning train. It's an incredible place, more like a cathedral or an aviary for gigantic birds. I don't know anything about trains but I've always loved stations – the sound and the smell of them. The place was deserted. Ten minutes after I sat down on my bench I could still hear my footsteps echoing round the roof. I'd nicked a bottle of Beaujolais and a folded napkin filled with little triangular sandwiches. Although the wine was full of bits because I'd had to use my knife to chip out the cork, it tasted delicious. And the sandwiches were like nothing I'd had before – white and dark chicken meat threaded together with some bitter-sweet herb – and the bread even had little nuts in it.

'It was as if I had stopped moving for the first time since I came out of the womb. I had this feeling that if I just stayed there then everything in the world would pass in front of me. Then this terrible roaring seemed to descend from the roof and I saw a goods train coming down the track. I'm sure that I glimpsed a flat, evil face on the front of it, like Thomas the Tank Engine gone bad. It took a full half-minute to pass. There were forty-three trucks, all black and glittering. I knew that they were filled with souls, not coal. It was the Devil's train but it hadn't stopped for me and now it never would.

'Despite my hunger I still hadn't finished the sandwiches. No matter how much I swigged, the level of the wine didn't seem to change. And those fragments of cork tasted just as good as all the rest. I was full of joy. And I knew that I would never lose this feeling and that all I asked from life was to be able to breathe.' Evan took a deep breath and held it. 'Then my train arrived and as soon as I got off that bench the feeling went. I sat right back down again but it was gone.' He breathed out in a long sigh. 'Now it's OK but it's not the same.'

'You should have stayed there,' Adrea said.

'But then I might not have met you.' He grinned. 'Or Terry. Or Mrs P and Mrs B or Price and good old Snowy.'

They moved further along the derelict platform. Now they could see the trains: brightly-lit and slow-moving with their ancient dog-box compartments lurching precariously to and fro. There appeared to be no drivers or passengers. Evan jumped down on to the track then lifted her after him.

'Now I'll tell you about mine,' said Adrea. 'When we lived in Lancaster, Mum and Dad used to make us go hiking with them. It was horrible. Sally and I had to wear these big chafing boots and carry packs full of things that we were never going to need. Dad used to say good morning to every sheep we passed, even when it was afternoon. And Mum would tell us the names of the flowers and birds and then test us on them on the way back. Sally used to storm on ahead, to get it over with: when we reached the top of the mountain she had always picked up some boy. I would walk with my head down and my eyes out of focus: in my mind I was recreating it all – the hills, the skies, the changing light – imagining that I was exactly where I was but alone. My dream was to come back on my own and see it properly.

'The morning after my sixteenth birthday, I bought a rail ticket up to the Dales. At Ribblehead I was the only passenger that got out. The station was ringed by flat-topped mountains. Apart from a pub over the road, there was no other building in sight.

'I went up Whernside by the steep path that Mum and Dad wouldn't take. I didn't stop until I got to the top: I bet I would have beaten even Sally. Huge black shadows chased each other across the fell side: they seemed to bear no relation to the cloud shapes above. I walked along the ridge and then across to Blea Moor Head. Leaning against the stone ventilation shaft, I ate my sandwiches: they were chicken, as well, but not as nice as yours. And I only had orange juice.

'I lay back and watched the skylarks. Mum used to say that the poor things couldn't really fly and it was only their singing that kept them up there. My legs began to ache and I could feel this weird throbbing along my spine. Then I realized that the ground really was vibrating: a great blast of steam came up the shaft from the line two thousand feet below. Between my feet I could see a long goods train go winding down the valley. I didn't count the trucks but forty-three sounds about right.

'Then I heard a high, one-note whistle, thin but piercing. It was even sadder than the curlew or the plover, as if the whole world were drawing its last breath. It came again and again: it was very close. I got to my feet but I still couldn't see anything. I began to think it was a ghost but I wasn't afraid: in fact, I really liked the idea. At last I realized that it was being caused by the wind blowing across the neck of my orange juice's plastic straw. When I'd stopped laughing I drained the rest of it and ran all the way back to the station. I went back a few more times but it wasn't the same: I could never get the straw to sing again.'

'It's weird that both our happiest moments should involve chicken sandwiches and trains,' said Evan.

'It's only because we're here,' she replied. 'If we were in a forest they would probably have been all about trees.' She wondered if she had told Evan the complete truth. It seemed to her that, although she'd had tears in her eyes when Sally had turned away from them without saying goodbye, she might have been at her happiest that very afternoon. Perhaps happiness and sadness just shaded into each other and what really mattered was the intensity of the feeling?

'We'd better be getting back,' said Evan. He began to jog in what Adrea was sure was completely the wrong direction.

Back in the Roundhouse the lights were already down. As they stumbled back to their seats, Patti Smith came running on, breathless and dishevelled, as if she too had been out on the railway lines. She wore skin-tight black Levis and an unbuttoned white granddad shirt over a green T-shirt with a Gold Lion of Judah on the chest. Her dark hair was in a ragged grown-out bob, framing a haggard, shadowed face. Her glittering eyes swept the audience and Evan felt his ocular nerves throb at the momentary connection. As the rest of the band appeared, she dropped on to all fours and did a few press-ups, slyly pushing off her left knee.

No one counted in the first number: they just threw themselves at it. Not until the chorus did Evan recognize Lou Reed's 'We're Gonna Have a Real Good Time Together'. The guitarist gave the lie to the notion that strapping on a guitar can make anyone look good. With lank, side-parted hair and pebble glasses, he was like a stiff-jointed puppet, clamped to the ground by diver's boots. If anything, he sounded even worse. Although the pianist looked like Richard Clayderman, his hands blurred like Cecil Taylor's over the keys: he was, however, inaudible. Patti's jumping up and down left her too breathless to sing. Although she was sparrow-thin, there was an audible thud whenever her ballet-pumps hit the stage: the scaffolding poles quivered. She kept on spitting: white and clotted like chewed paper, it was not absorbed by the boards.

They ground to a halt. 'And now "Redondo Beach"!' Patti shouted into the silence. 'It's a place where women love other women!' The feminists, Adrea noticed, did not react: at least they weren't throwing the tampons yet. The band lurched into a broken-backed reggae rhythm but Patti's hooting was more Red Indian than West Indian. She continued to spit: in front of the microphone a small white pyramid was beginning to form.

'The guardians of history will be rewarded with history!' Patti began to chant. Taking off her thick black belt, she lashed the stage. The buckle came down hard on her left foot,, and she tried to disguise her subsequent hopping as a dervish dance. A roadie carried off the belt, holding it between thumb and forefinger, as if it had been a poisonous snake. Who *were* these guardians of history? Adrea wondered. The band? The audience? And was it a good or a bad thing to be? She had never seen anything like this before. Patti was certainly different from Lulu or Sandie Shaw. Adrea could swear that her nose kept changing shape: at one moment like a potato, then like an awl, and when she threw her head back it seemed to disappear altogether. It was hard to imagine Lady Day flicking the snot off her fingers.

The whole thing was a shambles. And yet, Evan noticed, nobody had left. There wasn't much applause but there was no booing either: the audience seemed to be in shock.

'And now we'd like to do something for Keith Relf,' said Patti, slipping on a white Stratocaster that hung down to her knees. 'He was beautiful. He was a genius. He was one of the inventors of feedback.' There was no doubt that dying was a good career move, Evan thought. In life, Keith had looked and sounded like a window-cleaner but now death had transfigured him. Patti began to scrabble with both hands at the open strings, like a dog trying to dig up a bone. The guitarist lurched towards her, like the Frankenstein Monster. Presumably they intended a howling threnody like Hendrix's 'Star-Spangled Banner' but unfortunately neither of them could get their guitars to feed back. They held them in front of the monitors, twiddled the volume controls, rammed the machine heads into the amplifiers: nothing worked. The pianist still hammered silently away, while the drummer reverted to 'Take Five' from his Joe Morello tutor book. At last there came a faint whistling, repeated three times: exactly the note and duration, Adrea realized, of her old friend, the singing straw.

Patti decided to take it out on the microphone stand. As she shook and kicked at it, a new sound started up: a deep sustained blare which then broke into yelps and ululations that gradually took on a comprehensible form. Leaning forward, knees together, she appeared to be vomiting out the words.

At this moment something unexpected happened. The skin of Adrea's face suddenly felt hot and tight: the whole building seemed to buck and her hands grabbed the seat in front. Evan could hardly breathe: he saw that the hairs were rising on his bare forearms. Both felt as if, deep inside their heads, some connection had been made or broken and, as the sound rushed into their previously blocked ears, they understood this new language of raw need and pain.

The band had crashed in behind Patti's voice. They weren't playing any better but the chords didn't matter any more. It was a solid wedge of sound, to be felt rather than heard. Evan and Adrea had got to their feet: so had everyone around them. As they all flowed towards the stage they seemed to be passing through rather than climbing over the seats between. The mixing desk had at last located the piano. Over its choppy chords, Patti began to mutter broken phrases about redemption and sin:

Even in this crush, under the glaring stage lights, the temperature felt to be dropping. Then the band went into Van Morrison's 'Gloria'. Evan began to laugh, although his chest was so tight that it just sort of fizzed down his nostrils. 'G-L-O-R-I-A!' He'd always loved songs in which the words were spelled out.

'Right now here we are in this room together!' Patti shouted. Seen from below she seemed to have grown to an enormous height. 'I don't think I'm too fucking cool to relate to you!' The crowd eddied and whirled, dashing itself against the apron of the stage: every hand was raised, groping and clutching like the survivors of a sinking ship begging to be pulled out of the water. 'Do you feel frustrated? Do you feel like a loser?' The answering roar seemed to disconcert even Patti. Adrea had no idea what she herself was yelling, except that it certainly wasn't yes or no.

The final number was another weird hybrid. The band played 'Land of a Thousand Dances' while Patti yelled and muttered about horses and boys fighting. Watching that hawk-like profile pecking at the air, while the body twitched and jerked as though high voltage were passing through it, Adrea was reminded of Terry sitting in front of the television just a few hundred yards away.

When the rhythmic clapping started, the band returned to the stage. Patti came forward, arms outstretched, and the crowds fell back. Evan felt himself flinch, as if a burning torch had been thrust into his face. The first encore was 'My Generation' but it bore almost no resemblance to the original. The guitarist and the bass player had lost each other and Patti once again began to speak in tongues. 'I'm young! I'm young!' she yodelled. 'I'm so goddamned young!' An hour ago Evan would have smirked at this, especially as her T-shirt's flapping sleeves now revealed her armpits' wattled skin – but now he accepted that being young had nothing to do with age. And when they finished off with the Stones' 'Time is on my Side', that didn't seem ridiculous either.

'It's a war!' shouted Patti over her departing shoulder. 'We created it! Let's take it over!' Adrea supposed that she was talking about the world, but at that moment the prospect seemed just too ridiculously easy – surely all this had to be about something bigger than that?

The house lights came back up. Evan and Adrea looked at each other: they were both drenched in sweat.

Outside, the night air was hot and thick, rubbing like fur against their faces. The streetlights looked to have dimmed, as if the gig had seriously depleted the National Grid. Chalk Farm Road looked somehow different. Evan had never noticed that garage before and he did not recognize the names of the drinks and films on the billboards opposite. A few cars went past, floating as if on beds of air: their shiny bodies seemed to be shifting like mercury. Everyone was talking at once but neither Evan nor Adrea could think of anything to say. They began to force their way down the steps as the voices around them began to softly sing: 'T-i-i-i-ime is on my side. Yes it is!'

Unfortunately no one could remember what came next so they just kept repeating the same lines. Somewhere a church clock struck midnight. Instead of turning right towards the city they crossed the road and – still without a word, without even an exchange of looks – began to walk towards Heron Close. A small yellow ball was rolling in the gutter: Evan picked it up. The rubber was pitted and slimy, as if it had been discarded by some iron-jawed dog: it was surprisingly heavy. He tossed it to Adrea who caught it, reluctantly. In the shadows a couple of policemen were rapping out a complex tattoo on the side door of the Eagle and Child, which opened to admit them. Evan could have murdered a pint but he didn't think they would be welcome at a stayback of coppers and midgets.

The blocks looked insubstantial, like cardboard stage scenery. Apart from the home's dim porch light and the white trapezium of Price's landing, everywhere was in darkness. Adrea threw the yellow ball into an entryway but it just came bouncing back into her hand.

They both stumbled going up the ramp. Had the front door always been that colour? Adrea noticed that the corners of the vestibule were choked with cobwebs: surely she had swept it only the day before? It felt as if they had been away for years. Adrea was almost surprised to find that her key still fitted the lock. 'It's the piss factory,' she whispered, as the familiar smell hit them.

Where were the night staff? The corridor lights had been dimmed right down so that although the bedroom doors were all open their eyes could not penetrate the darkness inside. The place felt empty. There was no sound of breathing: maybe the residents had all gone? No matter how carefully they moved, their footsteps boomed and echoed. It was as if they were archaeologists exploring a curse-ridden pharaoh's tomb.

A ghostly flickering emanated from the sitting room: the television set had been left on. The test card's smiling little girl with her rag doll had been replaced by an irregular pulse of glaring white light. Adrea turned it off but then heard a raven-like croak from the far corner of the room. Terry was sitting, fully-dressed, in his usual place. His skin seemed to be slightly phosphorescent, as if it had somehow soaked up the cathode rays. The night staff had forgotten him but he didn't seem in the least distressed. It was as though he had been waiting up for them.

They pushed the chair down to his bedroom. As they undressed him they began to tell him about the evening. They found that they could remember all the lyrics of 'Horses', even though it had seemed virtually incomprehensible at the time. Adrea's Patti impersonation was spot-on, while Evan contrived to do all the rest of the band simultaneously. Terry's head nodded yes yes yes, as if he had been expecting exactly this. Adrea realized that her restlessness had given way to a deep contentment. For some reason, this was what they had needed to do. They pretended not to notice when Price's pale face, like a leaking balloon, appeared in the doorway and, after a minute or so, floated silently away.

nine

Deputy Matron Acting Matron Price, when he had still taken an interest in such things, had read about a series of sensory deprivation experiments at McGill University. The student volunteers had reported recurrent hallucinations of a procession of squirrels with bulging sacks over their shoulders, trudging across a snowfield. His own personal eidolon – the policewoman – continued to appear whenever he shut his eyes. She was always smiling, but experience had taught him that this was not necessarily a good sign: a pale-pink lipstick gave the mouth a slimy look and a few rogue hairs had escaped from the peroxide helmet to wave to and fro like antennae. Try as he might, he still couldn't shift her: a squirrel – with or without its sack – would have made a welcome change.

At least he now remembered when and where he had met her. Twelve years ago, after quitting teaching, he had signed up with a social work agency. His first placement had been at a hostel for adolescent boys in the final year of their care orders. They were running amok. The theory was that they were 'getting it all out of their systems' but it was obvious that this was merely a preparation for the rest of their lives. They had treated him with some respect because of his size and obvious disinclination to play Daddy, but his more idealistic colleagues were cracking under the strain. The front door was locked every night at ten but the kids just walked out of the emergency exits. The staff, forbidden to use physical restraint, could only 'reason with them'. Rather than prating about self-respect and consideration for others, Price had taken to slapping them on the back as they passed, snarling, 'Give 'em hell, boys!' like a football coach. Perhaps as a result of this, after a couple of weeks three-quarters of them had absconded: four dunderheaded mods, their faces sticky masks of acne, were all that remained.

One cold January night, at five to twelve, Price was roused from his doze by a great clamour of bells. The mods were leaving by all four exits simultaneously. He didn't pursue them, just turned off the alarms and rang the police. How he had winced at the weary contempt in the duty sergeant's voice as they went through the usual procedure! Someone had to be sent over to make out a report. They always made him wait. It was fully three hours before a gloved fist banged on the office window. Price glimpsed a familiar grotesque figure even larger than himself, with skin the colour and consistency of an ink rubber and lashless, bloodshot eyes: PC 572. Price called him 'The Servant of the Lord' after the corresponding number in his old school hymnal.

That night the Servant of the Lord had not been alone. The absurd chessboard hat of a policewoman was peeping round his bulk. She moved as if her neck were in a brace, small and squat inside her drab uniform. Price noticed a cold sore at the corner of the pursed mouth and healed-over abrasions on the left cheek. The number on her shoulder was 119: 'Angels From the Realms of Glory', he recalled. The Servant usually left within a minute but she sat down, crossed her legs, took out a notebook, licked her pencil end and insisted on taking full descriptions of the fugitives, as she called them. Height? Age? Distinguishing features? All their particulars were identical: each time

Price said 'fishtail parka' she looked up sharply, as if scenting a vital clue that might crack the case.

'What state of mind were they in?' she asked.

'They were breathing and their eyes were open,' said Price. Her glare didn't waver: he noticed that, like the Servant, she never blinked. Perhaps it was part of their training: in the wink of an eye a villain could be clean away or at your throat. She even took down his own name, address and date of birth. '*You* shouldn't be here,' she said accusingly, pointing at the rota pinned on the board behind him. Price had explained that everyone else was sick and that when the relief team arrived at midday he would have been on duty – alone and largely without sleep – for seventy-two hours. At the word 'duty' the Servant had begun to crack his knuckles alarmingly.

They left without another word: he didn't say anything either. Outside the rain was turning to snow. It was odd: even though he disliked coppers their disapproval always felt like some awful incontrovertible verdict. That tonight one of them had been some sort of woman had made it even worse. This must be the nadir, he said to himself. This must be the lowest point of my life. Little had he known that he had only reached the outer suburbs of failure and despair.

Then the doorbell rang. The four mods had returned, shivering and drenched through their parkas. Something told him that they hadn't been far, probably just hiding in the park until the police had gone. There was nowhere for them to abscond to. They had only gone because they dimly felt that it was expected of them. Price wrapped them in warm towels and heated up crumpets and tomato soup, whistling 'Good King Wenceslas' the while. If he could do nothing about his own humiliation at least he could spread it around a bit.

Although the snow had laid, the next shift arrived only half an hour late. Price's legs were trembling as he walked down the path: it felt as if he had been banged up for years. Apparently no buses were running so he faced a twenty-minute trek in leaking shoes to the tube.

The sun was out and the glare dazzled him, even through his shades. The crisp snow squeaked under his feet: his considerable weight seemed to be making no impression on it. As he reached the gate, a car – a well-polished red and black mini – silently drew up. The near-side door swung open and he saw behind the wheel a smiling blonde wearing a short crimson dress that was riding up to reveal considerable expanses of thick-ribbed white tights.

'What a nice coincidence.' It wasn't until she spoke that he recognized her: last night's policewoman in mufti, with her hair uncovered. 'I wonder if I'm going your way.'

Price opened his eyes. He was lying in silence: his music, whatever it had been, had long since come to an end. His left side ached and the soles of his feet throbbed as if he had just walked a very long way. He was shivering: recently, whenever the temperature seemed about to become unbearable, he would suddenly cool right down.

For years he had been living without memories. At best, he could only come up with names without faces, faces without names. Even the places that he'd liked – Paris, Florence, Amsterdam – had apparently left no trace. He told himself that this was nothing to worry about, that no one ever had the courage to face up to the truth about themselves. People just re-worked their pasts into absurd fairy stories in which they featured as hero or heroine – never, of course, as the coward or the murderer, the traitor or the thief. Price, in contrast, had systematically extirpated all those moments in which he might have passed for virtuous or kind.

He could not explain why these intense fragments were all of a sudden forcing their way back to the surface. Perhaps somewhere a bemused policewoman – what rank would she be by now? – was wondering why she was being haunted by the memory of a sarcastic fat man in tinted glasses? Before returning to the bed he placed on the spindle a stack of the rare Wolf Lieder Society 78s that he had found in a dusty, long-forgotten box in Camden Market: '*Alles endet, was entstehet. / Alles, alles rings vergehet.*' Everything, everything comes to dust. In an incongruously squeaky tenor, Deputy Matron Acting Matron Price added his endorsement to Alexander Kipnis and Conraad Bos, Hugo Wolf and Michelangelo Buonarotti.

Downstairs, in a perpetual, pointless game, Evan and Adrea were throwing the rubber ball across the sitting room. Mrs Barker couldn't stop her eyes following, as, seemingly of its own volition, it looped between them. Her temples throbbed and the knitting needles kept slipping from her fingers. She squeezed her features into an even darker scowl but, as usual, no one paid any attention. Leaning over, she stroked Stormy's grey and white fur. Although it looked clean and felt soft, her hand always came away sticky. 'Zwwt!' she said under her breath. 'Zwwt!' It wasn't just her private name for the cat, she was sure that it was the cat's name for himself. At the sound of a striking match its head would jerk up and she would see an answering flame in its huge dark eyes. Zwwt! Zwwt! Stealthily, she withdrew her fingers and then popped them quickly into and out of her mouth. The throwing game was getting faster and faster: she could no longer see the ball, just hear the rubber slapping into the palms of their hands.

Price had left a note asking Evan and Adrea to conduct the monthly CQ count, assessing levels of senile dementia among the residents. Who Are You? was the first of these Classic Questions. The second was: What Is This Place? It seemed unfair to expect the old people to provide answers when all the philosophers, scientists and divines had hitherto failed. All the other Questions weirdly concerned time or the Royal Family. Evan and Adrea felt justified in providing alternatives such as: 'What's Up, Doc? If a Lion and a Tiger Had a Fight, Which Would Win? Who Put the Ram in the Ram-a-lam-a-ding-dong? Freud's What Do Women Want? And – the clincher – Edward Lear's Who and Why or Which or What/Is the Akond of Swat? The general appropriateness of their responses – baffled silence or uncertain laughter – meant that they all, even the Babies, scored pretty high. Adrea also decided to dispense with the Crighton Geriatric Behavioural Rating Scale, as most of its categories – lost, withdrawn, restless, agitated, disturbed – covered almost everyone she had ever known.

For a while it seemed as if Adrea and Evan had finally tired of their game but it had merely taken on a different form. Now the ball emerged at irregular intervals, at unexpected moments, flicked under-hand or from behind their backs, with devilish loops and spins. Despite this, neither of them had yet dropped it. Finally, after a long lull, as Evan was in the sitting room pouring the last of the tea from the enormous double-handed pot, Adrea's white arm came snaking round the door-jamb, releasing the ball with an audible snap of the wrist. Twisting and contorting his neck muscles, he headed it straight back into her outstretched hand, without spilling a drop. Apart from Mrs Barker, everyone applauded: Terry even contrived to rattle the frame of his chair. With an exaggerated swagger, Evan walked down the room: as he passed Adrea, she lobbed him the easiest of catches, which he then fumbled to the floor. Ignoring the renewed applause, he pocketed the ball, and crossed the hallway to the office. Only when he was seated at the desk did he allow himself to clutch at his head and groan. His eyes seemed to have gone out of focus and there felt to be an indentation in his forehead. Surely, if anything, it should have been a bump?

By the time he had finished filling out the CQ forms, his vision had returned to normal. This was the first time he had been alone in the office. The safe and the medical chest were double-locked but the filing cabinets that lined the far wall were open. There was a file for each resident, the names neatly typed along the spines. He saw that poor Frances was tagged 'Mr. F. Partridge': when he opened it there was nothing inside, not even a date of birth or next of kin had been entered on the facing sheet. The others were the same, although

Terry's contained three pages written in an illegible hand and a 1970 General Election voting card in somebody else's name.

At the back of the middle cabinet he found a dog-eared ledger with 'Accidents' written, apparently in blood, on its pale-blue cover. Mrs Allen had the most entries: every month she had contrived to slip on a wet floor. And, Price's hobby the winter before last had been falling down the back stairs. Mrs Allen's signature resembled a broken bedspring, while Price's looked as if it should have been at the foot of Magna Carta. Bridie made only one appearance, in letters almost too small to read: 'Clawed (by cat)'. Evan was struck by the fact that no residents featured in these pages, despite the cuts and bruises that decorated their bodies: such things were obviously unworthy of record, as old age was apparently one continuous accident.

The final cabinet was labelled 'Household/Maintenance'. There were great swathes of carbon requisitions for washing-up powder, bleach and soap, and for dozens of floor-mops and metal buckets. How could such things wear out, especially when they were never used? There was an instruction manual and guarantee for a huge colour television that bore no resemblance to the snow-storming black-and-white set in the sitting room. He flicked idly through last month's food receipts. There were chickens, sausages, whole sides of beef, minced steak and lamb, pork and lamb chops. There were cod, haddock and even half a dozen kippers. There were oranges, apples and pears. There were cucumbers, radishes, tomatoes, heads of broccoli and lettuce. There was just about anything you could think of, but none of it had made its way on to the residents' plates. Unless there was a cannery in the basement, all this stuff had disappeared. At the bottom of every sheet was a curious splatter that looked to have been made by the simultaneous snapping of two pen-nibs. It could only be Mr Snow's signature.

Evan left the office. The hallway was empty but he could hear a dry crackling sound, like flames. It grew louder and then Dolly came round the bend of the long corridor. In her left hand she was clutching the end of a roll of toilet paper, which stretched out behind her to create a stiff, shimmering train. Evan saw that she had lost her slippers. The bare feet were grotesquely twisted and swollen. She was no longer shuffling but balancing on her left instep and the outside of her right heel: every step was a miracle. When she reached him she handed him the roll with a ceremonial flourish, as if she had passed through great trials to deliver this important message. Evan examined it but apart from San Izal in faint green letters, the paper's shiny surface was blank. He began to walk down the corridor, while Dolly continued on her way. The paper was too stiff to fold, so he allowed it to wind itself around his arms and neck, rattling like stage thunder as he moved along. He felt like Theseus following Ariadne's thread out of the Cretan labyrinth, except that filling in the CQ forms hardly corresponded to slaying the minotaur and this trail seemed to be not so much leading him out as drawing him further in.

Turning the corner, he saw Adrea in the toilet at the far end, down on her knees, her denim-wrapped arse turned towards him. He stumbled over first one of Dolly's slippers, then the other. She was scrubbing at the floor: why was it, he wondered, that the Babies shat in small pellets, like rabbits? Now enwrapped like an Egyptian mummy, he cleared his throat. Adrea looked up: her expression was serious, even angry, but around her eyes were a mass of creases, as if the face had just relaxed out of a long-held smile. He felt his whole life had been a movement towards just this one moment. Taking the rubber ball from his pocket, he threw it hard, sending it cannoning off ceiling and wall. Adrea made no attempt to catch it, just watched as it vanished into the toilet's deep bowl. Reaching up a long, long arm, she pulled the chain.

The healthy mind must have a healthy body. Upstairs on his bed Price was doing his exercises. He raised each leg in turn and then waggled it about while he counted up to twenty – or, more often,

ten. On his closed eyelids the policewoman's smile didn't waver, so perhaps he was looking no more ridiculous than usual.

'I bet you didn't know me with my war paint on,' the police-woman had said, after they had driven along in silence for a while. Those blemishes on her face had vanished: it was amazing what cosmetics could do. Her fingernails, patently false, were painted to match her car, her dress and the twin whorls of rouge at the centres of her rounded cheeks. Apparently unable to blink ten hours ago, she now couldn't stop: Price realized that for the first time in his life he was watching someone actually batting their eyelashes. How many pairs was she wearing? He could hear them over the engine – a glossy flapping like a raven's wings.

'I understand that the fugitives have been apprehended,' she said.

'Well,' said Price, 'they came back.'

'You should give them a good hiding.' Taking both hands off the wheel, she made a raking motion with her nails.

'Unfortunately we're not allowed to.'

'We're not either' – her tongue circled her lips – 'but that doesn't stop us.'

The city appeared to be deserted: it was as if they were the last people on earth. Cars and buses had been abandoned at the side of the road but they were bowling along without any difficulty. She took a sharp bend in third, nipping the kerb, without the slightest skid. Maybe the police had special tyres? She was prattling about an argument she'd had with her mother regarding her new square-toed shoes.

'"Men will think you're a cripple wearing them," she said to me, so I said to her, "Oh, Mother!... "'

Price registered that she gave this word exactly the same inflection as Antony Perkins in *Psycho*. The skirt had ridden so far up that he was pretty sure she was wearing nothing under her tights, but the effect was not alluring. In fact, her baby-faced prettiness did nothing for him at all. He had long suspected that there was something wrong with him because he was indifferent to what appeared to be every proper man's feminine ideal: that naughty ickle girlie who, after playing with Mummy's make-up, has stuffed a couple of honeydew melons down her blouse. Price had never felt the slightest desire to fuck children, still less, simulations of them. Perhaps he might have felt differently about it if he'd had daughters of his own. Nor had he ever been interested in women in uniform – handcuffs, truncheons, whistles. He appeared to have strayed into someone else's fantasies.

'You don't have to lie,' she said suddenly, although he hadn't spoken a word. 'I know you're married.'

'OK,' he said, even though he wasn't.

He had never been able to take blondeness seriously. Surely it could only be ironic, some joke that they were inviting you to share? But if you did laugh they always got extremely annoyed. The whole situation was ridiculous: it was equally inconceivable that she could have been attracted to him. Who did she think he was? What was she mistaking him for? He had to admit that he felt oddly complimented. He had never liked dogs either, but would virtually burst into tears if one of the dreadful creatures deigned to wag its tail or lick his hand.

The car stopped at a set of traffic lights. She was telling him about how Marks and Spencer had refused to replace a faulty brassière. 'It had holes,' she said, rolling her eyes, 'in the most embarrassing places.' Her droning voice became soothing after a while: when he looked out at the white street it was as if he could distinguish every facet of every single snow crystal. Everything had a terrible clarity: his eyes seemed about to explode.

'But when I went back in wearing my uniform they gave me a new one straightaway. And a credit voucher as well. That was nice, wasn't it?'

The signal didn't change: perhaps the cold had jammed it? She was bucking the clutch against the handbrake: no one was around but she obviously felt that even out of uniform she could not jump a red light.

'I have a lot of trouble that way' – he saw that she had begun to nibble at her swelling lower lip – 'I'm very choosy about what I put next to my skin.'

A sandy-coloured mongrel came limping across the road. After pausing to sniff at their radiator grille it moved on to piss up against a snow-packed acacia. Clouds of yellow steam came hissing off the trunk.

'What a nice dog,' said the policewoman. The light changed and she drove on. Price felt obscurely thwarted, as if, had they sat there for just a few seconds more, some grand realization would have burst upon him.

When they at last pulled up in front of his gate she had leaned over and kissed him. Her tongue lapped softly at his and her mouth tasted sweet and pulpy. Price felt nothing at all. She took his hand and placed it on her left breast: out of good manners he left it there.

'That was nice,' she said when he finally broke off, although her throat looked to be contracting as if she were fighting the desire to retch. She handed him a folded piece of paper. 'Come round tomorrow night at seven.' She winked as she wound up the window. 'Bring a bottle and I'll make you something tasty.'

'That would be nice,' said Price, waving as she drove away. Her notepaper was bordered with flowers, bunny rabbits and squirrels. There was no telephone number, just an address. He realized that he had not asked her name, having thought of her as Angel ('from the Realms of Glory') or number 119 throughout.

The music had finished: Price opened his eyes. It was time to go downstairs to lay out the pills for dinner. He always knew when Evan and Adrea were in the building: there was a faint humming as if, far below, some powerful machine had just been set in motion. By the time he reached the first landing he was panting: at forty-seven descending apparently became more tiring than climbing. The sound of conversation – even laughter! – was coming from the sitting rooms: Price gave them a wide berth. He missed that old profound contemplative silence that had only been occasionally broken by Mrs Allen and her boyfriends beating each other up. Frances, returning from the toilet, smiled and said hello. She was no longer shuffling but almost walking upright, just like a normal person. He felt hurt that she no longer asked him for a shave, for Evan's technique, although enthusiastic, was obviously not up to scratch.

Sometimes he did the pills with his eyes shut. His fingers even seemed to be able to feel the colours. He had long forgotten what most of them were supposed to do: he had taken all of them himself, in most possible combinations and they might as well have been Smarties. He always remembered the ones for Mrs Parker's headaches, though – seronace and phenagen – because they sounded like a pair of limpid-eyed, lantern-jawed, ill-fated Pre-Raphaelite lovers. Each colour also had its own sound when they clicked on to the side plates. Synaesthesia was a rare gift but there weren't many uses that you could put it to. He stopped to wave in the direction of Snow's flat. The poor devil was still under the illusion that his net curtains made him invisible, even when he pulled them halfway across and stood there with binoculars clamped to his eyes.

He could sense that Adrea and Evan were approaching the dining room: a palpable heat seemed to be coming off their glowing skin and shining eyes. As always, the French had a phrase for it, *le moment de la jeunesse*: that short time when everything is in harmony, a marvellous second birth followed, a few weeks, days or hours later, by a prefigurative death. Price's own theory was that it was the soul, preparing to give up its unequal struggle against the world, taking its fond farewell of the body. It wasn't even necessary to be in love: everyone, however ugly, doomed or wretched, was supposed to experience it, but Price was certain that it had never happened to him. Perhaps his time was still to come? Could this be the reason that the Babies kept stumbling back and forth, Terry twitched and slavered, Mrs P and Mrs B tirelessly plied their needles? Were they just killing time, awaiting their own particular moment?

Price realized that he hadn't taken in what Adrea was saying to him, but it didn't make much sense when she repeated it:

'Whatever happened to the fifty-three chickens?'

Evan came to his aid. 'Fifty-three chickens have been delivered here in the last month,' he said, 'and a mountain of minced beef and enough sausages to reach from here to Marble Arch. And all the residents ever see on their plates is canned shit.'

Price slid his dark glasses to the end of his nose. 'And what do you expect me to do about it?'

'Stop it!' said Adrea, pushing her face towards him as if for a kiss. 'You're in charge now. You're the Matron not the Deputy.'

'Yes,' said Price. Stepping back, he twisted a pinch of his own belly flesh between thumb and forefinger. 'But I'm still me, you know.'

She looked at him with pity in her eyes: how he would prefer the old disgust! Evan flashed him a surprisingly warm smile, as if delighted at his response. The dining-room door seemed to open, then close behind them, without either of them touching it.

What must it feel like to be them, to be young and in love at *le moment de la jeunesse*? Surely they must have some awareness of what was going on? They obviously believed that they had all the time in the world, that nothing would ever change. Price imagined the bickering, the suspicions, the silences, the lies and the betrayals that awaited them. Why, it would be remarkable if their idyll even lasted to the end of the shift! Little did they know that – at least according to St Augustine – Adam and Eve had only spent six hours in Paradise. But perhaps it hadn't seemed like six hours to them? Perhaps it had seemed like six hundred, six thousand years? And suppose it had only been Paradise because they were in it? Suppose they had carried Paradise away inside themselves and didn't even notice that they had been expelled?

After Price had returned to his attic, Evan and Adrea began to knock at the kitchen door. After a while Evan progressed to kicking it but there was no response, although they could hear stealthy movement below. The door was immovable, its handle stiff, and didn't feel as if it could ever have been opened. They went outside and descended the steps. The basement entrance had no handle at all, was simply studded with keyholes – the highest was almost seven feet off the ground. The windows' metal shutters were down and double-padlocked. Three filth-clogged extractor fans were clattering away as black smoke drifted through a corroded metal grille. There was a crunching sound beneath their feet: the cracked flags were thickly coated with dried-out husks of dead bluebottles. The red brick wall was hot to Adrea's touch. She shivered. Perhaps, as Price had once implied, Satan really did have the catering contract?

At dinner, as if to teach them a lesson, the food arrived twenty minutes late. Evan unloaded the dumb-waiter. There were sheets of unidentifiable glazed meat, canned new potatoes – unnaturally round and unblemished, in a pool of their own ichor – and tiny sprouts that all looked to have been crushed under a dirty thumb. It was obviously a calculated insult. Pudding turned out to be purple filaments that might have been rhubarb under custard which contrived to be simultaneously lumpy and thin. Most of this food was left untouched. Adrea realized that she was avoiding the residents' eyes.

Afterwards, when she had finished loading the plates into the dumb-waiter, Evan came over and took them all out again. Perching on the rim of the hatch, he unzipped his snakeskin boots and handed them to her then swung his legs inside, somehow managing to fold his torso into the tiny space.

'I'm off to give Satan some stick,' he said. 'I may be some time.'

Adrea leaned forward but, unable to reach his mouth, ended up kissing his right ear. She pulled the shutter down and listened to the mechanism groan and then creak into motion. Why had he taken off his boots? She saw that their rubber heels had already worn down to the wood: when she clapped them together they made a hollow, desolate sound.

It was not a smooth descent. At first the dumb-waiter moved in a series of short jerks, as if someone were letting out the cable hand over hand. Then, for a while, it seemed to be drawn back upwards, before swinging to and fro like a pendulum. It was taking an unexpectedly long time. Evan had not anticipated having any problems with breathing but now the air in his mouth had begun to sour. For the first time in his life he was in total darkness and complete silence. He felt that he had swallowed himself and was sinking through his own body. He recalled that last night, when Adrea and he had been discussing their favourite words, his final choice had been 'subterranean', but only for the sound of it and the Jack Kerouac and Bob Dylan associations. He had never felt any particular desire to go under the ground. Adrea's favourite had been 'missal' but she had insisted on having 'mizzle' and 'missile' as well, even though, as he had pointed out, these were only homophones if you had a cleft palate. Now he found himself running through them aloud – 'missal… mizzle… missile' – until, although he had felt no impact, he became aware of a thin, unwavering line of vertical white light away to his left. His body appeared to have somehow twisted around in transit. Perhaps he had been in zero gravity? He forced the tips of his fingers into the crack and the hatch, with surprisingly little resistance, slid back.

The first thing that he saw was a small barrel-shaped dog eating a roasted chicken. It seemed to be hoovering the flesh off the bones. It rolled its eyes at him and grumbled urra-wurra-wurra! through the meat. By planting the soles of his feet against the backboard, he managed to push himself up and out, head first, on to the kitchen floor. The room was vast. Great copper pots and pans depended from the ceiling, gleaming knives and ladles lined the walls. There appeared to be two, if not three, enormous ovens. White light blazed from no apparent sources: there were no shadows. A man in a bloody apron and a ridiculously tall chef's hat was transferring frozen meat from the fridge cabinet to a large portable cool-box. The dog growled again. 'Shut up, Squibbsy!' said the cook, without turning round.

Then Evan saw Snow, sitting on a high stool with a spotless white napkin tucked into his shirt front. A glass of dark beer stood on the table, next to a plate piled high with steaming vegetables. The peas were green, the carrots were orange and the potatoes mashed and creamy. A large pork chop was stuck on the end of the raised fork and Snow was angling his head to bite at it, as if his chief pleasure in eating was in making it as difficult as possible. His tongue flickered to lick the gravy off the meat, which appeared to be shrinking away from him, as if it were still alive.

Then Snow saw Evan. His head jerked backwards and the chop made good its escape. His expression did not change but then it was hard to imagine how it could. The pitiless light flared off the polished facets of his face. Flecks of mica seemed to be glittering on the surface of his skin as Evan moved towards him, across the sticky, can-strewn floor.

ten

'Fucking yellow bastard!'

The mood in the Eagle and Child was getting ugly. Although it was still only early July all previous sunshine records had already been surpassed but nobody was enjoying it very much. They all somehow felt that the heat was aimed at them personally. And the beer was only making things worse: everyone knew that in summer the breweries added extra salt.

'Bastard fucking sun!'

They roared and clenched their fists but their treacherous old friend remained well out of reach. Surely there must be someone else for them to blame? The postman was insisting that it was all being caused by supersonic flight, that Concorde's paperknife nose was slicing through the ozone layer. 'We're going into a new Ice Age,' he said. 'This is just the earth's crust shedding its heat ready for the big freeze.'

'So where's the ice going to come from?' asked the street-sweeper, 'when all the rivers have dried up?'

The postman glared. 'Don't you worry about that. It'll be a Frost Age – and that's even worse than ice!'

'No, it's the Arabs,' said a taxi-driver, who had just spent half the morning blockaded by their white Rolls Royces along Queensway. 'Now they've bought us up they're turning on the heat ready for their fucking camels.'

Midge was the only one who wasn't laughing: he didn't like the hungry way those towel heads always looked at him. He suspected that the oil boom might turn out to be bad news for midgets.

Well away from the throng at the bar, Assistant Matron Acting Deputy Matron Snow sat reading his copy of *The Times*. Its front-page story concerned the drought's threatening the ancient oak plantations of the New Forest. Snow stared at the photograph: 'TREE CATCHES FIRE'. What kind of news was that? He took another sip of his Cinzano and pulled a face: he didn't like sweet things or sour things and the drink somehow managed to be both at the same time. He only drank it because the girl in the TV advert made him think of Adrea, although – ash-blonde, brown-skinned, laughing on a beach – she looked nothing like her.

Snow was proud of being alone. He didn't need to keep looking at his watch, as if waiting for someone or killing time before an important appointment. He knew that all the men at the bar were envying him, wishing that they weren't so weak as to need each other's company. As he lifted his paper up high in front of his face the tiny letters drifted out of focus, but that didn't matter because he wasn't actually reading it. Just carrying *The Times* gave you power, like a gun or a knife. It showed that you were not to be trifled with. On page eight there was another photograph: men in suits, hands on hips, looking down at the concrete bottom of a dried-out reservoir. What if all the water suddenly came bubbling out of the cracks? Snow shut his eyes to imagine them floundering, thrashing, drowning.

The Cinzano had numbed his mouth so that he feared he might be drooling. The ice cubes had long melted and the ragged chunk of lemon had released a shoal of dangerously sharp pips. Foul-tasting phlegm was filling his mouth: Cinzano's 'perfect blend of herbs and spices', as the laughing girl had called them, were inflaming his sinuses. A perfectly folded white handkerchief was tucked into Snow's top pocket but that was for appearances, never for use. Under cover of *The Times* he dribbled the corded green slime on to his fingers and then wiped them on the underside of the table. It was already jagged with previous secretions: he didn't like to think what they might be. This had been Mrs Allen and Billy's usual seat. With his own eyes he had seen them openly doing very bad things to each other.

It was surprising how much he was missing Mrs Allen. Heron Close just wasn't the same without her. Last night, Snow had let himself into the matron's flat. He had rolled back the carpets, climbed on top of the wardrobe and crawled under the bed. He had even pulled the fridge and the cooker right away from the wall. He knew he was looking for something vitally important, although he hadn't the slightest idea what it might have been.

He turned his paper over. In the middle of the next page was a large hole. This morning he had been on duty when he had sensed Price floating up behind him. He had braced himself for the usual sarcasm but Price's voice had been unexpectedly polite: 'You don't want the crossword, do you, Snowy?' Price had snipped all round that mysterious black and white box: what kind of man carried a pair of dressmaker's scissors in his pocket? Only now was Snow beginning to realize the enormity of the insult. It was as if Price had cut out the seat of his trousers. The sports page was revealed: a pair of white feet were splayed in front of a shattered wicket. Everybody at the bar was laughing at this hole.

It had been a bad week. The image of Evan slowly walking across the kitchen towards him kept coming into his mind. The boy's face had been expressionless. Snow had cowered back but the unblinking stare just passed over him as if he had been invisible. Evan unbolted the street door and – having passed into the sunlight, his bare feet seeming not to touch the ground – gently closed it behind him. At first Snow thought that he had imagined it until he asked the cook. 'There couldn't have been anyone,' Cooky shouted. 'Squibbsy would have had them.' Snow could tell from his stiff violent movements that the man, who was always boasting about how he was going to beat up that dopey kid and give that stuck-up bitch a good seeing-to, had also seen Evan but had thought it best to pretend he hadn't. The fat dog looked equally guilty. Then Snow had discovered that the dumb-waiter would no longer close: the doors were bent and buckled, their metal seemingly part-melted.

At this moment they had heard a key turning in the kitchen door. Squibbsy, too late, began to bark. It wasn't Evan who was coming down the stairs but Price. 'Ah, gentlemen, gentlemen!' He was chuckling. 'The chickens have come home to roost.' His left boot kicked Squibbsy's fowl out of his path. 'To say nothing of the cows, the sheep and the pigs!' The other boot narrowly missed the head of the cringing dog. 'Although I have told our idealistic young colleagues that I am reporting you to the Council I will not of course be doing so.' Price began to put the meat back into the freezer. 'But from now on you'd better cut it all out, otherwise' – Price held out his wrists as if they were shackled together. 'In this hard, cold world, gentlemen, we only get away with things for as long as we deserve to.' At that moment Snow had realized that he was still holding his chop-laden fork in his hand.

Why hadn't he said something? Why hadn't he threatened to reveal all the things that he knew about Price? As it was, he hadn't managed even a shrug or a curse or a glare at the man's retreating back. How could anyone say he was a thief? He had never *taken* anything, only removed a few things that people didn't need any more. 'I know him very well,' he whispered into his glass. 'And that is not the sort of thing that Acting Deputy Matron Snow would ever do.' As for the meat: what was the point of ruining juicy red steaks and succulent chicken breasts just to keep useless old people alive? Mush was what they wanted and mush was what they deserved. It was all that evil boy's fault. The moment he had laid eyes on Evan, Snow had known that he was going to be trouble. He had also felt a strange sense of relief. It was as if – after forty-three years of persecution and disappointment – his real enemy, who had been working secretively against his interests, had finally stepped out of the shadows to face him.

Half an inch of yellow sludge was all that remained at the bottom of his glass. 'Same again,' Snow mouthed, catching Midge's eye. He watched as the wagging head, like a fist with eyes and nose drawn on it, vanished under the bar top. After a pause a little hand reappeared, its first two fingers raised. The midget both fascinated and repelled him. If you were bald you could buy a wig, if you were deformed you could have surgery – even amputees could get mechanical arms that could hold and light cigarettes – but there was nothing they could do for a midget, except give him a box to stand on. Snow licked his forefinger and then began running it around the rim of his glass. As the thin, ghostly sound passed beyond hearing, Midge became increasingly agitated, moving along the bar like a target at a funfair shooting-gallery. Then, as usual, he began violently to sneeze. Snow wondered whether all midgets were so sensitive to ultrasonic sound.

Snow buttoned up his jacket and folded *The Times* into a tight baton, ready to leave. He had a feeling that one day Midge, clutching a tiny suitcase, would be standing on the doorstep of Heron Close, delivered up into his power. Unless they had special places for midgets: bungalows or even dolls' houses? The idea so much appealed to him that he began to laugh. Everyone at the bar left off berating the sun and Midge even stopped sneezing as Acting Deputy Matron Snow marched out of the pub to the sound of his own private merriment. He had beaten them once again.

Out on Chalk Farm Road the traffic was moving silently, as if the thick air had muffled all sound. In the water shortage unwashed cars were now considered to be patriotic. Snow noticed that Union Jacks had been scraped in the dust on their bonnets. Pale weeds were coming up through the pavement: everything that could fend for itself was thriving, while garden flowers and shrubs died. There was a perpetual queue outside Marine Ices, although they must have known that not even its Blue Riband Champagne Sorbet was going to cool them down. A group of middle-aged women laden with shopping bags was filing into the church. Within that cool, dark interior, Christianity was beginning to make sense again.

Everyone around him was sniffling and coughing, walking stiffly as if every bone in their bodies creaked and ached. Wasn't sunlight supposed to be good for you? No one was tanning: either their skins were burnt and sticky or bleached white, with all the scars, sores and freckles blazing out. Men seemed to be sweating from their heads and armpits, whereas women's backs carried inverted triangles of damp. As if fearing a trick, they were all avoiding the few patches of shade. Snow's own shadow seemed to have diminished, so that it was like a trickle of oil from the soles of his feet. He squinted at the sky. The bright yellow disc that he remembered now appeared as a whitish smear, like a frying egg with a broken yolk. It was as if the sun itself found the heat too much to bear.

Why, Snow wondered, did his heart sink whenever he was unlocking the door of his flat? Even though the first thing he would see was the hall table with its nice red vase full of glowing flowers? Even though, that very morning, he had buffed up those plastic petals with a damp cloth? Carefully, on tiptoe, he checked each room in turn. As usual, no one was there and nothing seemed to have been disturbed. He moved his chair over to the living-room window, then pulled back the net curtain. It felt as if the binoculars slid out of their leather case to meet his fingers. Carl Zeiss of Jena, the best that money could buy, although he hadn't bought them, of course, just finally accepted them as a gift from a resident who, even though he was blind, had taken some persuading. They always needed refocusing, as if his vision or the distances were changing from day to day. In the taller blocks, he had discovered, there lived a surprising number of young women who liked to walk around with no clothes on. He always ignored their windows.

As ever, it came as a relief to see that Heron Close was still there. He was afraid that in his absence the residents and staff would be talking about him, plotting against him, and he somehow felt that, by watching the building, he was preventing this from happening. Now he could see Price, his medication tray strapped to his chest, entering the dining room. He was five minutes earlier than usual: Snow considered such variations to be most unprofessional. He was sure that he could hear those huge feet pounding the lino, even though he knew to his cost that the man came and went in complete silence.

'Ptoom!' Snow made a sound approximating that of a high-powered rifle. 'Ptoom! Ptoom!' He was almost surprised when that enormous head didn't explode like an over-ripe melon. Instead, Price had begun talking to an invisible listener. People did the strangest things when they thought they were alone. Now the man was blowing kisses to the empty air. What a disgrace he was, without respect for anyone or anything, not even for himself! He didn't even try to act like a matron! Snow had almost been pleased when it had been that evil boy who became friends with Adrea. At least it wasn't Price. He'd had sex with Mrs Allen, Bridie and at least four previous care assistants. It was hard to imagine how. Perhaps he had overwhelmed them with words? That hadn't worked with Adrea, who had plenty of words of her own.

Price, laying out the pills on the far tables, slid out of his sight. Snow let the binoculars pan along the terrace – the movement always made his stomach lurch – until they stopped abruptly at a terrible sight. The front door. The front door was open. And not just open a crack but pulled right back and wedged so that it might as well have been taken off its hinges and carried away. The door was open: everyone could walk out, anyone could walk in. When he turned up for his next shift it would have been shut again, of course, but everyone would be laughing behind their hands: what would Mr Snow say if he knew that the front door had been open all yesterday afternoon? At least none of the residents had dared to come outside.

No! In the far corner of the terrace there was a reddish blur. Snow's clumsy fingers re-focused on Terry. Terry, drooling and twisting in his wheelchair but looking somehow pleased with himself. Terry was on the terrace, in full view of the whole world. What if little children were to see him? What if their mothers rang the Council to complain? What if someone stole him? He couldn't blame Terry, of course: he wasn't able to resist them or even to protest.

Terry was the only one of the residents that he liked. They understood one another. When he crumbled wafer biscuits over that trembling head and cuffed him for having dandruff, Terry's whole body would shake at the shared joke. Snow knew that if Terry could have one wish it would be to be dead. 'Ptoom!' said Snow, compassionately. 'Ptoom!'

And now there was more movement back along the terrace. People were emerging from the dark doorway: Dolly, Molly and Polly, in a line. Snow had always been nervous of the Babies, almost afraid. Sometimes he suspected they were putting it all on, although he couldn't imagine why they should. Their minds were dead but their bodies still moved, like zombies in a horror film. It was as if the weaker they got the more potentially dangerous they became.

Now still more of the residents were pouring out: bold as brass, almost casual, as if this were natural and they were doing nothing wrong. In the bright sunlight they looked even worse than usual. He wished that instead of a rifle he had a machine gun with which to rake the terrace.

Snow had only ever read two books – or, at least, parts of them. Both were written by Lord Russell of Liverpool: *The Scourge of the Swastika* and *The Knights of the Bushido*. Snow had always had a lot of time for the Japanese: how many British pilots would have volunteered for kamikaze missions? Although they lived by the seven principles of the Samurai – courage, honesty, courtesy, honour, loyalty, complete sincerity and compassion – they tortured and tormented their prisoners of war, who, in their eyes, had made themselves less than human by the cowardly act of surrendering. Snow felt pretty much the same way about the residents' submission to old age. Why hadn't they done what his mother did after his stepfather died? She had let herself run down like a clock, finally stopping the day before she would have qualified for an old age pension. Even the residents' families wanted nothing to do with them, which confirmed that these were utterly worthless people. Part of Snow's job was to punish them for choosing to be slow, bad-smelling and confused, for taking everything and giving nothing. And he was certain that, in punishing them, he was upholding that very human decency that Price so loved to sneer at.

And then Adrea came into view, cutting like a blade through the shambling crowd. Snow felt that explosion of pain or pleasure that was neither in his heart nor in his head but in some other part that seemed detached from his own body. He watched as she knelt in front of Terry and, as if at a coronation, placed a wide-brimmed sunhat on his head. Those agonized features seemed momentarily to relax into a smile. Then Adrea turned to the other residents and gently but firmly, arms outstretched, herded them all back inside. Even though she hadn't yet closed the door, Snow was sure that, at least in this matter of the terrace, she was on his side.

Bridie and the others were always complaining about Adrea. What was Her Ladyship doing in Heron Close? They said she was a spy, but what secrets were there for her to steal? She was one of those people who, wherever they went, would always be out of place – like himself, although for very different reasons. They went on and on about the ways in which they thought she and that boy would be having sex but that didn't bother him particularly. What he feared was that she would change, begin to look and sound like everyone else. He could tell by the way she had moved along the terrace that it hadn't happened yet. His favourite fantasy involved his saving her from a terrible danger. His free hand formed a fist and began to strike at the empty air – 'Take that, you ugly dog!' – while his feet kicked out against the wall – 'And that! And that!'... But no matter how hard he tried to give this enemy the features of Evan or Price, the face that he imagined beating to a pulp was always his own.

And now Adrea was once again emerging from the darkness, carrying a large broom in her hands. After making a playful feint in Terry's direction, she began vigorously sweeping the terrace. Snow was sure that he could hear the lovely dry whisper of the bristles moving back and forth. He saw her reach down into the corner to pick up the empty cigarette packet that he had deliberately crumpled and placed there that morning. Then her image went all shimmery

and no matter how he twisted them the binoculars would not refocus. It was a while before he realized that this was because his eyes
were full of tears.

eleven

Until the last few weeks Bridie had loved being at work. She had
looked forward to every shift and at its end would leave the building
almost with regret. The hours passed slowly but she hadn't minded
because as time slowed down she could feel herself speeding up.
When she buttoned her overall she felt she was throwing off twenty
years. She walked the corridors with her muscles stretching sweetly
beneath her skin, as if she were swimming or floating through the air.
She was young again: light-footed, cheeky, fancy-free. Her whole life
lay in front of her, with Mervyn and the kids just a half-forgotten
dream. And she had loved the ressies, too. Their weaknesses made her
feel strong, their confusions made her feel patient and kind. Every day
she would count up their smiles and enter the tally in her diary.

Now everything had changed. No sooner had she put on the overall than it was time to take it off again. She was rushed, flurried, under
pressure. Everything was an effort and she felt twenty years older as
she dragged herself around. Instead of being at the hub of it all, she
seemed every day to become more marginal and insignificant. The old
people no longer wanted her smiles and laughter. She had formerly
drawn energy from them but now it was as if they were draining it
from her.

Something had gone wrong and she didn't know what. Bridie had
never had much time for Mrs Allen but since she'd left, the whole
place had felt unstable, as if a rotting roof beam had been removed

but not replaced. Now she was aware of walking on tiptoe, opening and closing doors softly, as though afraid of bringing the ceilings crashing down upon her head. And she didn't like the way the residents had started looking at her with a sort of amused pity, making her feel that she was somehow being stupid without realizing it, that they knew something she didn't. How could that be? It was unnatural. Old people, whether loveable or pitiable, ought to be *nice*.

Perhaps it had something to do with the heat? They seemed to be thriving on it. Now that they were venturing on to the terrace not only their faces and arms were turning brown but also the rest of their bodies, as if the sunlight had inundated them. And they were suddenly obsessed with water. Queues formed outside the bathrooms. and when Frances said 'Shave!' what she wanted now was a bath. No matter how long you ran the taps the water always spluttered out lukewarm, drying on the skin to leave a yellow-brown crust like foam off a Guinness, but that didn't bother them. Even the Babies no longer needed to be cajoled: they virtually dived into the bath, rolling over, delightedly thrashing their arms and legs as if deliberately trying to soak her. If she left them for even a moment they would turn the taps back on. She had observed that when they finally left the water it had an odd reddish tinge.

Or perhaps it was because of all the rich new food they were gobbling up? At dinner every plate was now emptied: even the knives and forks were licked clean. Some of the old people had even complained that yesterday's braised steak had been overcooked: they craved red meat. Price had suggested that they'd soon be out hunting in packs, tearing small children apart with their false teeth, but Bridie didn't find it funny. Although they were showing no signs of discomfort, they were all constipated. Her attempts to unblock them had failed. She didn't like to think where this might be leading.

Although Bridie told herself that she was being unfair she couldn't help feeling that Adrea was the main cause of all this. It wasn't jealousy. Although she'd enjoyed flirting with Evan, it was never going to lead to anything – she had learned her lesson with Price. The flirting was the best part: as soon as men got their thingies out they always let you down. Bridie had guessed what was going to happen when Price had changed the shifts but she wasn't prepared for the desolation that hit her when she saw *that* smile – not just with the mouth, not just with the eyes – on the stuck-up eejit's face. It felt as if a door in her own heart had just been slammed shut. Although she knew that, long before Mervyn, she herself had felt exactly what Adrea was feeling, it didn't make any difference. It was as though she had never even come close: memories didn't count.

This morning, when Bridie entered the sitting room, there was a babble of conversation. Everyone seemed to be speaking at once but nobody was listening, except, perhaps, for Stormy. The cat was lying on its back in the exact centre of the carpet, legs stretched out, claws unsheathed and ready. She gave the horrible creature an extremely wide berth. The Babies were seated to one side: she went to loosen their bonds only to find that they weren't tied down at all. She was sure that she could see a new intelligence in their eyes. It was creepy. Now you couldn't take even senility for granted any more.

As she passed, the residents one by one fell silent. What could they have been talking about? She had noticed that Terry's twitchings had now settled into a distinct pattern: the head described slow circles, while his chest and limbs gathered and clenched for a few seconds before collapsing back into the wheelchair. The huge black eyes glared at nothing in particular and no longer followed her when – dropping first one hip, then the other – she sashayed past.

Mrs Parker looked up from her knitting. Her raised eyebrow and lifted upper lip were Adrea to the life. 'Pardon me for interrupting,' Bridie heard herself saying. She was surprised by the thickness and ugliness of her own voice. Mrs Parker didn't reply, merely inclined her head in gracious acknowledgement of what had not been intended as an apology. Then she smiled, but it wasn't the kind of smile that Bridie would have cared to put in her diary. With an effort, she tossed her hair back and turned away. Just in time, she remembered the cat and leapt to one side, narrowly evading the huge swiping paw.

Watching the retreating back, Mrs Parker felt a little ashamed. Stormy didn't particularly dislike Bridie: it was just that he found the soughing sound of her inappropriately delicate and expensive nylons utterly irresistible. Bridie was a well-meaning soul but sometimes she could be a little bit much. The way she just marched straight into the middle of other people's conversations! You couldn't blame Stormy for trying to claw her. It wasn't that Mrs Parker had been saying anything of particular significance, it was the principle of the thing. She had been reminiscing about a blackbird that, forty years or so ago, used to come into her kitchen to drink milk. It would hop on to the draining board and chirp for more. In its tail there had been a cluster of white feathers: Stanley had worried that the others would peck it to death but they didn't seem to notice. She hadn't wanted Bridie to hear because she knew exactly what her reaction would be. 'Aaaaaaaahh!' That was what she said to everything, although if it was sad she would first give a double click of the tongue or, if pleasant, stick a little chuckle on the end.

She decided not to continue her story: the old lady next to her did not seem to mind. Mrs Parker could never remember her name – or, rather, although she was aware that it was stored there in her memory, she felt no need to make the effort to search it out. Stormy was the only one she could have a proper conversation with: his range of purrs, blinks and yawns went far beyond any 'Aaaaaaaahh!'s

The cat began to lick its tail but the effort proved too much and it nodded off again, a pink flap of tongue still poking out of its mouth. Despite the heat, Stormy's coat was getting even thicker but when she groomed him no fur came out. Recently, no matter how much she whistled, he had been coming less often to be petted. She had not liked to admit it but the signs were that he was inclining towards Mrs Yu-No-Hu. It had come to a head one lunchtime when her rival had offered him a radish. 'He won't eat that!' Mrs Parker had observed, only for Stormy to crunch it up with obvious relish. But when she herself had offered him one he just lashed his tail and walked away. She had been so upset that she had asked Adrea what she thought she should do. 'Act more don't-care-ish,' the girl had said. It was advice that had worked surprisingly well. If you ignored Stormy he was suddenly all over you. Now, once again, when he awoke and opened his great golden eyes, it was herself that he was looking at.

She wondered what Mrs Barker's next move might be. She was quite prepared to share the cat, as long as there was no question about whom he really belonged to. The way the two of them sat opposite each other, in silent contention, knitting away, reminded her of the last film she had seen at the dear old Essoldo, the day before Hitler had bombed it. A pair of sorcerers, living in great dark castles on opposite mountain peaks, were engaged in a magical duel. They sat on their elaborately carved thrones, eyes shut, sending with a twitch of their little fingers cardboard bats and dragons lurching back and forth on clearly visible wires. She had laughed so much that Stanley took her outside, worried that she had been overcome by the sheer terror of it all.

Mrs Barker, however, was no laughing matter. Mrs Parker sneaked a look across the room. The wedge-shaped head had fallen on to the chest and a big scab like an extra eye was peeping through the smoky hair. She particularly loathed the way that one ear was set higher than the other and at a grotesquely different angle. They looked to have been moulded out of candle-wax. She flinched as Yu-No-Hu's jaw, for no apparent reason, shuttled sideways with a clicketty-clacking sound. At least she herself still had a recognizably female shape under these clothes: her own legs didn't resemble over-inflated tyres and her ankle-bones had remained just about visible.

The Babies got up and shuffled after Bridie. Mrs Parker straightened her spine and took a deep breath. If she forgot herself for just one minute, she knew, she would become just like them. Summer was doing nothing to relieve the stiffness in her knee joints and the soles of her feet still ached, as if she had been climbing up Archway Road rather than just sitting in an armchair. And with all this sunlight, why did it seem to be getting darker? She fiercely concentrated on the clock face until it came back into focus. She realized that she couldn't hear the minute hand move, so she shut her eyes to force her ears to register it. If she had been any less vigilant she would by now have been deaf, blind, gaga or dead.

The morning letters still lay unopened on the table in front of her. She had recently developed an aversion to them, as if something nasty – a spider or an earwig – might come crawling out. Although she recognized the scrawls of her daughter, eldest son and younger sister, she would throw them away unread. She always replied, though, with her standard letter of five rotating paragraphs, which she suspected that they discarded in their turn. They had long ago stopped visiting. Her daughter had claimed that it was too long a journey for them – as if they were in South America rather than South Acton, and she was too far gone to remember the existence of the North London Line. She reminded herself of how her heart used to sink when they did appear. Her son would sound the car horn and then wait outside, holding the passenger door open, making no move to help her down the ramp. She often felt as if she were being arrested. It was always a different car but it was always blue. His pullovers were always blue as well but their shades clashed with the cars. There were children, too – always older or younger than she expected, with different faces and different voices, forever announcing the passing of yet more exams while holding out their hands.

After Stanley's death the rest of the family had ceased to matter. She had been surprised to find them all still there. It was as if they had no right to have outlived him. She could remember little about bringing the children up and still less about having them. All that she could recall about the maternity wards was a vision of Stanley clumsily tap-dancing across the polished lino, with a bunch of grapes in his hand. This had been a joke, for he knew that she hated them.

Stanley was her one clear memory. It was as if there had been a sharp black line around him, like in a cartoon, showing where he ended and everything else began. He shaved twice daily so that there was never a trace of stubble and the skin on his face was flawlessly smooth. Even though he always smelt fresh he still insisted on emptying half a bottle of Dettol into his twice-weekly bath.

'There are some things you mustn't ask me about,' he had said to her, as he levered himself up with difficulty from the traditional kneeling posture in which he had just proposed. She had assumed that he had meant the war: she knew that he had fought by the tangle of medals and ribbons at the back of his socks drawer. Sometimes, though, she had wondered if it hadn't been the war after all, but whatever it was she could never unknowingly have hit upon it because in thirty-seven years they had not had a single cross word.

At weekends, except when Surrey were playing at the Oval, they would visit the great cathedrals, although neither of them were particularly religious. They had been to every one except Southwell but she could remember little about them, apart from when Stanley had lifted up a choir seat to reveal a misericord carving of a large goose dancing with the Devil. He was always telling her to look up but she could never quite see what he was pointing at. She *did* remember Salisbury, though: not the cathedral itself but the nearby tea-room.

After the crowded street its interior had seemed blissfully dark and quiet. How lovely the smell of hot bread, brass polish and blending spices and infusions had been! Stanley was opposite her, smiling faintly, as the scone that she had so carefully buttered crumbled in her fingers to fall back on to her plate. Gradually she became aware that they were no longer alone. Two other people had moved in to an adjacent table. A pale, solemn-looking man was sitting with his chin on his hands, apparently lost in thought, while, down on the carpet, a little girl – very pretty but with a sulky expression – was playing with a toy wooden lion. Its string had tangled round the chair legs and no matter how hard she tugged it would not budge. Although they didn't resemble one another, she felt that they were father and daughter. There were no tea-things on their table but the waitresses, drifting back and forth, continued to ignore them. Time passed: the little girl pulled and pulled but her lion remained caught fast and the man made no move to help her. Mrs Parker noticed that their skins were unusually yellow and shiny-looking. A fly alighted on the man's domed forehead and just stuck there, its legs waving frantically. Somehow she knew that if Stanley put down his paper and looked across he would, like the waitresses, see nothing at all. They were visible only to her but she felt neither frightened nor excited. She didn't think of them as ghosts or angels or devils: nor did she wonder whether she herself might be going mad. They had come as no surprise to her, as if she had always known that such beings were around but had momentarily forgotten that she was supposed to pretend she didn't. Stanley drained the pot, licked his forefinger to crumb their plates, then paid the bill. As they left she looked back and saw that the others were still there: she felt rather offended that neither of them had so much as glanced in her direction.

Mrs Parker had forgotten all about this until now. Evan and Adrea were giving her the same feeling: that they weren't supposed to be there and she wasn't supposed to be seeing them. She hadn't taken much notice of Adrea at first, nor of Evan, but when they had started working together it became a very different matter. You couldn't keep track of them. Sometimes, on their shifts, they would be nowhere to be seen but then, when they were supposedly off-duty, they would suddenly appear. Only this morning they had burst into the sitting room with their hands full of ice-creams, dripping red, green and white all over the carpet. A cone had been thrust into her hand but she just stared at it, by sheer willpower holding that strawberry drop trembling on the wafer's lip until it was taken away. She recalled the way that Evan and Adrea had licked the melted ice-cream off each other's arms. Disgusting, she thought. Although the word didn't really express what she was feeling it made the right sound in her head. Ever since, it had been as if her heart had been beating in that rhythm, with a triple thump: DIS-GUS-TING!

Something about the atmosphere in the sitting room had changed. Looking up sharply, Mrs Parker realized that all eyes were on her. Even Stormy's upside-down face had a shocked expression. Could she have been saying any of this out loud? Her head ducked back into her knitting, as if she could hide herself away among the stitches.

Out on the terrace the Babies kept running into the waist-high wall, then stretching out their arms before shuffling backwards to try again. Bridie's index finger stirred her tepid coffee but those yellow flecks remained on the surface. A grotesque shadow came spilling over the flags to lap at her toes: if there was one thing calculated to lower her spirits even more it was an appearance by Acting Matron Price. She felt the conflicting desires either to kick and punch him everywhere at once or to up and run.

'I've just been talking to poor old Cooky,' Price said sweetly. 'He's very worried about Squibbsy. Deprived of his meaty treats, the motions of our canine chum have gone all chalky. I told him that the blessed creature has attained a state of grace.' The shadow made the sign of the cross. 'In eternity, my dear Bridie, we will all play harps and shit white.'

Bridie growled, more convincingly than Squibbsy had ever managed.

'I know, I know,' said Price. 'He's the only one in here who isn't constipated.'

She hadn't spoken to Price since their single afternoon of intimacy. She had no idea why it had happened. Perhaps it had been simple curiosity? In his flat she had been disappointed to find, instead of an altar laid out for a black mass or a network of bubbling flasks and retorts, merely dusty piles of dog-eared books. Price was the only man who had ever said anything truly romantic to her, but that had only contrasted with the nastiness of the things that he subsequently tried to do. 'Never trust anyone who uses more than a dozen words at one go' was Mervyn's motto, which had really impressed her until she had realized that he'd just used thirteen.

'We appear to have entered an age of miracles,' Price continued, sitting down next to Bridie, who shifted further along the bench. He could see, in the block opposite, that Snow's curtains – as frilly as a can-can dancer's knickers – were twitching wildly. 'According to their latest assessments of the residents by the Creighton Geriatric Rating Scale, our young colleagues have discovered a cure for senility.'

'Rrrrrrrrr!' said Bridie.

It was a really sexy sound, Price thought, which presumably was not the effect she intended.

'Yes, it's amazing what young love can do,' he fluted. 'Of course, I know what a great admirer of Adrea you are. Such a nice girl! So kind! So pretty! So graceful!' He paused for another growl. 'No, I must say that I disagree with you, Bridie. I think her nose, although unusual, is just perfect as it is.'

Bridie had sometimes wondered what she would do if Heron Close were ever ablaze. She had thought she might warn Price by writing 'FIRE!' on a piece of paper. Now she decided she would let him burn.

'You know, I've just been taking that test myself.' Price got to his feet. 'And I scored maximum fives all the way. Lost. No effective contact. Restless, with hallucinations. Nihilistic delusions of guilt. Somatic dysfunction. I only retain my eminent status through my ability to dress unaided and feed correctly at appropriate times. And of course, I remain continent of urine and faeces' – he simpered – 'for at least some of the time.'

Bridie managed to keep her expression stony, although the rest of her body was shaking. She didn't trust herself even to growl. After giving her a deep bow, then waving at Snow's window, Price and his shadow moved back inside.

It was time for his weekly visit to the main sitting room. He wondered how long he would be able to bear it today. Once he had managed a full hour, but that was only because he had fallen asleep: the worst had been twenty seconds when he'd had the distinct sense that his chair was sinking, as if into quicksand.

He entered the room with a breezy greeting that, apart from the cat's hiss, received no acknowledgement. Stormy: the name reminded him of his short youthful communist phase, when the interminable speeches printed in *Pravda* would be punctuated by the bracketed words '[Stormy Applause]'. He could imagine the creature, its furry chest laden with medals, sitting up there on the podium as the tanks and rockets rolled by, slapping its paws together and purring after a good night's work at the Lubyanka. The Uncle Joe Stalin of the cat world.

Mrs P and Mrs B were still glowering at each other. How absurd their antipathy was when they were so obviously machines of the same type! The perpetual clicking of those knitting needles always made him think of the Fates who weave the destiny of mankind. The future, it appeared, would be baggy, sludge-coloured and full of trailing threads.

'Once again, Socialism has failed.' The leader of the opposition, Margaret Thatcher, had appeared on the television screen. Price rather fancied her, even though her eyes were as blank as a shark's. 'And now our country faces the horror of a hosepipe ban.' So this had been the true meaning of Kurtz's 'supreme moment of complete knowledge' in *Heart of Darkness*: 'The horror! The horror!' His prize begonias had just died. Mrs Thatcher's image faded to be replaced by a fat man struggling to get out of a large gleaming car.

'I like that Mr Heath,' said Mrs Parker.

'No, that's Callaghan,' said Price, 'the Prime Minister.'

'Mr Heath is the Prime Minister,' said a voice from across the room.

'No, the Labour Party won the last election and the Conservatives replaced him with Mrs Thatcher.'

'Don't be silly,' came an outraged chorus. 'She's a woman.'

'Mrs Thatcher is not a Conservative,' said Mrs Parker with finality when the noise had died down, 'she is the leader of the Onionist Party.'

Price looked at his watch and sighed: he had been in the room for less than a minute.

Although Mrs Barker had not participated in this political discussion, the speed of her knitting had noticeably increased. They were all wrong, she thought. Mr Churchill was the Prime Minister and he was dead. Mr Price was typical of so-called clever people: he only knew about things that nobody else could be bothered with, nothing that actually mattered. She could tell by the itching on her scalp that he was wearing that bright red tie with black eagles flying across it.

She looked without looking at the potato face opposite. How she hated Mrs Parker's frosty hair and those jolly rosy cheeks! They looked as if she had spent hours slapping them: Mrs Barker would have been happy to do it for her. She hated those skinny, twisted legs, like branches on a dead tree. And those tartan slippers with thistle pom-poms on their toes. The woman wasn't even Scottish! No one in the entire place was Scottish! She especially hated the way she breathed: little silent nips of air culminating in a huge exhalation that sounded like a hot iron coming down on wet cotton.

Even more than Mrs Parker, she hated her letters. There they were, fanned out to show that there wasn't just one but two – no, three!

Different sizes, addressed in different hands, two in black ink, one in blue. Mrs Barker hated the way she had left them unopened, as if they were so unimportant that they had slipped her mind. It wasn't right that someone so old should know so many people. Mrs Barker had long suspected that she had been sending them to herself, but she had to admit that they were posted from considerable distances. Sometimes there were even pale-blue Airmail envelopes bearing bright, tropical stamps. Was there some agency who would send you a dozen assorted letters every week? It would still mean that – even if they had been paid to do so – some people in the world were thinking about Mrs Parker.

At least she had now stopped talking about her husband, her Stanley. Why wasn't Stan good enough for her? Mrs Barker's husband had been called Ron but you'd never have caught her calling him Ronald, let alone Ronley. She rather liked that, actually: Ronley – it sounded distinguished, aristocratic. Not that Ron had been at all aristocratic. She had always thought of him as being like a bus – big, red and loud, slow-moving and reliable. He had worked in garages until at last he could open one of his own. His hands had been a sight: the nails like yellow horn and the lines of his palm etched in black. In summer his sweat was like battery acid, eating away his vests and pants. It seemed strange now that he had always moaned about hot weather because after he had gone she had realized that he had been the sun. Not *like* the sun but part of the sun itself: a burning coal that had broken off and, falling from the sky, landed in Kiln Place, Gospel Oak.

'Hello, Ron,' she whispered every morning as she opened the bedroom curtain. On grey days she would wonder how she had offended him but for the last few weeks she must have been doing something right. If she had been able to look directly into the glare she was sure that she would see Ron's face, with that mock-angry expression he would put on just before he'd wink and his arms would reach out and – making swimming movements, his mouth rounded and popping like a fish – he would advance towards her.

From across the room Mrs Barker heard Price's cigarette case click open. She could smell that strong dark tobacco that Ron had also liked to choke on. In a flash, her knitting was on the floor and before the cigarette had even reached his mouth she was holding aloft her flaming match.

Although this ritual gave him the creeps, Price thought it best to go along with it. He made a point, however, of crossing the room extremely slowly. By the time he reached her, the match had burnt right down to the fingers but her hand remained rock-steady. Bending forward, he accepted the light, relieved when his entire head didn't burst into flames. Mrs Barker was the only resident that he was at all nervous of. She reminded him of one of those obscure goddesses of best-forgotten religions, who lurked in the darkest corners of the British Museum, sitting on piles of skulls, sticking out their bifurcated tongues as he hurried by. He didn't like the way her eyes swam behind her lenses but the worst thing was when she got up from her armchair for mealtimes. It was like watching a mountain tear itself free of the earth. Price would brace himself as the world rocked on its axis.

With a shudder, he turned his attention back to the television. The final news item was the countrywide heatwave. West Country yokels, commuters cramming on to the tube, Cumbrian shepherds, bikini-clad girls on Brighton Beach – all had the same brain-fried expression. Not everyone had discovered, like Price, that playing Schubert's *Winterreise* served to reduce the temperature by six or seven degrees and that, paradoxically, the Hans Hotter version made it colder still. The weatherman's smile was as broad and reassuring as ever but you could see the desperation in his eyes. For the last week he had been heralding rain from north, south, east and west but it had never arrived. The longer the drought went on, the more hated the poor devil would become, as if he were personally responsible. What a terrible thing it was for a grown man to have to stand in front of a map yabbling about isobars. No matter how low he sank, Price promised himself, he would never let himself become a weatherman.

His cigarette tasted unusually acrid: he stubbed it out. He suspected that Mrs Barker tipped her matches with brimstone. Fortunately he had a flagon of Merrydown cider in his attic, ready for such eventualities. He rose from his seat. Ten, no, eleven minutes – his matronly duty had been fully discharged.

The smell of the burnt match was still tickling Mrs Barker's nostrils. 'A nice fire makes everything all right,' her mother used to say as she knelt at the grate, arranging splinters of wood and scraps of dusty coal. Heron Close had elaborate fireplaces but no chimneys. The hearths were filled by lumpy brown and black plastic hoods, lit from inside by red lightbulbs to produce a horrible mockery of a merry blaze.

Fire was an older and an even better friend than Stormy. She had never forgotten the wonder of the first discovery – that one simple act could transform the empty air into red, white, blue or yellow flames. Without looking up from her knitting, she took in the blank faces around the room, Terry's raised knees knocking against each other, the children's puppets on the television screen, Price's retreating back, bowed as if carrying a heavy load. All she had to do was strike a match to change everything. She seemed to be the one person who realized that everything only existed for as long as everyone agreed not to destroy it. The great fire that she dreamed of would not just destroy but also reveal what was really there. Some things couldn't burn because they were already on fire: souls. Everyone had a little silver blue flame burning inside them, like the central heating's pilot light in the darkness under the stairs. Every time she worried that God might not be there, she had only to reach down and rattle her matchbox to feel that inner flame, halfway down her chest, flicker in response.

This great fire seemed to be both a vision and a memory, as if past and future events were somehow happening at the same time. Mrs Barker could vividly recall the air raids of the First World War. One night, as she was joining the crowds flocking towards the pub – it had the largest, deepest cellar in the area – she had looked up to see a grey-white Zeppelin, glowing and motionless in the moonlit sky. Her tummy rumbled and her mouth watered: she had gone without her supper. She felt that if her neck had been long enough she could have bitten into the airship and jam and cream would come squirting out. Then the ground shook three times and a strange dancing light could be seen over Primrose Hill. Down in the cellar, she remembered, there had been a smell of rotting apples, not beer. Nobody was talking in the darkness: there was not even a sound of breathing. After a while she had taken out a candle stub and lit it. The faces revealed were completely unknown to her – grey-skinned, lined and seamed. When her candle guttered out she had not tried to re-light it. At daybreak they ventured outside and she saw the neighbours' familiar faces. Where were all those strange people that had been in the cellar? She had climbed the hill. The sheep and lambs that were always grazing there had disappeared, leaving only patches of black grease and a Sunday dinner smell.

In the Second World War the area had again been regularly hit. In fact, Primrose Hill had seemed to be a major target. The German bombs always missed the anti-aircraft guns on the brow but landed well short of the railway tracks of Euston and King's Cross. The rumour was that they were trying to lower the morale of Londoners by attacking the parks, destroying all the flowerbeds and trees.

Directly opposite the air-raid shelter was a small, beautifully-kept cottage which Mrs Barker had always admired. One balmy summer evening, with thrushes and blackbirds trying to drown out the sirens, she had looked into its garden and seen a large brown and white dog up on its hind legs, dancing with a middle-aged woman. They stopped when she said good afternoon and turned towards her with shocked expressions, as if it had been the neatly-trimmed hedge or the freshly-painted gate that had spoken. She greeted them again but they just kept on staring. Down in the shelter her friend Annie told her that the woman was a deaf mute but Mrs Barker had not considered that to be an excuse. 'Hello' wasn't hard to lip-read and she could at least have waved back. And surely the dog couldn't have been deaf-mute as well? Mrs Barker had fumed for the next eight hours. The woman never came to the shelter: presumably she thought that the bombs couldn't penetrate her sealed-off deaf and dumb world.

When they came up again the street seemed at first to have been untouched, until Mrs Barker noticed a gap where the woman and dog's house had stood. It was as if it had been extracted like a tooth: all that remained was that familiar Sunday dinner smell. The woman and the dog were buried under the blackened stone and it was all her fault because she had called the bombs down on their heads. She had been frightened that she would get into trouble. Would they think of it as a sort of espionage or fifth column? For years after the war she would still jump whenever the milkman came to the door. Even now she was still convinced that she had made it happen, although on the hundreds and thousands of times she had tried it since – she glared through her knitting at the thistles bobbing on Mrs Parker's toes – she had never managed it again.

twelve

When Evan awoke the next morning he saw that Adrea was lying with her back turned towards him, facing the wall. They had also somehow swapped sides of the bed. Was this a bad sign? Could this be the beginning of the end? Her neck looked thick and knuckly: he hadn't realized that her new haircut had been so brutally short. He rolled over, eyes shutting against the light, groping for his wristwatch, only to find his way blocked. A dark hump had risen out of the mattress: it was cool and solid to the touch, like wood, and he could feel his fingernails scrape against it. Drawing back and re-focusing, he found that he was looking down at Adrea. Her face had the sealed look of a death mask. The dark fans of her eyelashes did not even flutter and her lips had folded in like the petals of a heliotropic plant. There was no sound or sign of breathing. Evan turned back towards the wall but the other figure had now vanished. He knew that it hadn't been a dream. What he had seen – from the vantage point of his second, astral form, returning after a night cruising the ether – had been his own sleeping body. Ken claimed to be able to move at will between these two states but Evan had no desire to repeat the experience: he hadn't much liked the look of himself from behind.

The sheet that had been covering them had disappeared. Evan's eyes moved along Adrea's body. It was like a desert landscape, stretching on and on. Somehow he kept forgetting what he was looking at, so that each distinct feature – the coral nipples, their tiny aureoles, the navel like a whale's evil eye, the wiry pubic hair with its strong ashy smell – remained, for a few seconds, bewildering and unaccountable. Her knees, mysteriously bruised, were as delicately formed as her ears, as if the whole of this body had been designed to pick up even the slightest vibration from the world outside. The only sign of life was in her feet: the tiny bones of her insteps rippled like fast-flowing water. Evan felt as if he had been watching her for a very long time. There was a dull ache behind his eyes and a stiffness in his neck and shoulders, as though he had been gazing up rather than down.

Looking at things for too long was dangerous. Evan was reminded of a quiz show, *Ask the Family*, that had blighted his childhood. His parents always insisted that after tea they all sat down together to watch it. They never answered any of the questions, although Mum always nodded and smiled as though she could have done if she'd wanted. The TV families were all specky and twitchy – 'Eggheads,' sneered Dad – and the children looked to be the same age as their parents, only smaller – homunculi created specially for the programme. The climax was provided by 'the mystery object'. Black and white photographs, wildly tilted and out of focus, were flashed up. They always turned out to be the most everyday things. On one occasion, though, a fuzzy white triangle filled the screen. A rubbery, saw-edged fin? An iceberg looming out of an Arctic fog? Some monstrous, long-forgotten enemy of humanity from beyond H. P. Lovecraft's *Mountains of Madness*? Evan recalled the consternation of those television faces. Even Mum had stopped smiling. They all gave up far too quickly: they didn't even want to guess. The creepily avuncular quizmaster then announced that it had been a human nose. The families' hands flew up to their faces: one of the homunculi was apparently trying to rip his off.

Whose nose had it been? Evan had often wondered. It certainly wasn't Adrea's – he would have recognized that anywhere. He hadn't quite decided whether hers was a silly nose trying to be serious or a serious nose trying to be silly. Leaning forward, he lightly kissed its chilly tip. Still she didn't stir. Reaching over, he retrieved his watch. Strapping it on always seemed a suitably decisive way to start the day. He didn't look at the time.

Evan sorted through the clothes covering the single broken-backed chair, finally deciding on a long black T-shirt. It looked as if snails had been crawling over it but it smelt OK. The room's dimensions seemed to change with the light: at the moment it was big and square but at night the ceiling would descend and the windows and door recede. He looked around proudly: it was utterly cheerless. Evan had always needed to destroy any atmosphere in his room before he could relax. His first act had been to tear the posters from the walls, although, unfortunately, he could still remember them – Frank Zappa sitting on a toilet, Mr Natural Keepin' on Truckin', King Cophetua and his beggar-maid staring gloomily into space. The formerly white paintwork had been smoke-cured and two black stains behind the mattress revealed where hundreds of greasy heads had been propped. The ceiling was pitted with deep indentations, as if it had been punched by an enormous fist. Ken said that these had been caused by the shaven skull of the legendary Graham Bond – king of the Hammond organ and putative son of Aleister Crowley – during his levitation experiments. Bond's subsequent death under the wheels of a tube train, Ken claimed, had been a dematerialization that went wrong.

Adrea had now rolled on to her stomach. From Evan's angle, her head had vanished and her body seemed to be melting and dripping off the edge of the bed. Her fingertips were emerging from the junction of bottom and legs: it would have been a great shot for *Ask the Family*. A movement from the window caught his attention: a small bird was struggling along the choked guttering outside. It was a grey wagtail, like the ones that had nipped playfully at his childhood fishing lines. What was the poor thing doing here in the city? He had seen the silhouettes of herons and curlews perched on the roofs of Camden Town. The drought must be driving them downstream. He tapped on the glass but the wagtail didn't respond: it looked furtive, as if it were spying on him. Evan threw a couple of punches in the air, then did a double Ali shuffle but he still felt sluggish. He had to admit that he was still depressed about the night before. Coming in late, grunting and shuffling – he couldn't remember why – he and Adrea had chased each other down the corridor, only to find that his housemates were waiting silently in the darkened kitchen. They had become a deputation: one by one they had stepped forward to deliver their little speeches. Even now Evan couldn't believe the things that they had said.

It was so hot that they couldn't breathe. Opening the windows only made it worse, and then they couldn't shut them again. Cups and plates kept breaking and most of the cutlery had buckled and couldn't be bent back into shape. The taps no longer worked, the fridge kept defrosting itself and lightbulbs and fuses needed replacing daily. Food just disappeared and what remained smelt of cheese and tasted of nothing. Worst of all, the deck of Dave's Bang and Olufsen had developed a wobble, so that everything sounded like Pinky and Perky.

'Are you saying that we're somehow making all this happen?' Adrea finally asked.

'This teapot is Brown Windsor.' Pete held it above his head like a trophy. 'Fifty years old. Why should it have cracked all by itself?'

'Isn't Brown Windsor a soup?' Adrea asked, sweetly.

Evan had just stood there staring at them. At one point he had clenched his fists but then unclenched them again. Surely it must be a joke? Dave had only looked serious when he was kidding, until now.

'You're right,' Adrea continued. 'We run off electricity. We have the power to turn everything to cheese. We hate all kitchen utensils, especially teapots made out of soup. We can make water flow uphill. And now we're going to whistle up the sun to fry you, in the middle of the night, just for a laugh.'

'It's best not to joke about such things,' Ken muttered, making weird passes with his fingers, hunching forward as if her words had somehow dislocated his shoulders.

'You shouldn't have made those noises,' Dave said, reproachfully. 'We're not pigs.'

'Of course not,' said Adrea. 'If we'd meant you we'd have been going, "Baa! Baa! Baa!"'

Having bleated this into each face in turn, she walked out of the kitchen.

As Evan followed her, a voice had hissed the single word, 'Traitor!' He whirled around but none was looking in his direction: all their heads were bowed over the wounded teapot. Out in the corridor Adrea, for the first time ever, took his hand. It was odd how deeply intimate that corny gesture had felt.

'I loved the way you looked right through them,' she said. 'It was the most don't-care-ish thing I've ever seen.'

Evan realized that he had reacted as she would previously have done – with silence – leaving it to her to provide his habitual aggressive response. Perhaps that was how it would be: you meet, you gradually exchange personalities and then you go your separate ways – Evan as Adrea, Adrea as Evan.

'One thing I don't get,' he had said, 'is what exactly it is that I'm supposed to be a traitor *to*.'

Even now he was none the wiser. All the things he could have said were running through his head – 'Let's smash everything else before it breaks'; 'You're sounding like my mum'; 'Aren't we supposed to be young?' – but nothing seemed to fit. What had got into them? Surely it couldn't have been jealousy? He had always had plenty of good-looking girlfriends at college but if anything that had been one of the things that they'd liked most about him. How could he be a traitor when he still felt exactly the same? Perhaps that was itself the reason. If four people change and one doesn't, then, even without being aware of it, he has betrayed them. Four against one are always right: that's democracy.

His jeans seemed to have vanished so he pulled on Adrea's black cotton loons. Apart from absurdly jutting his balls out, they were a perfect fit. He recalled how just six weeks ago, when he arrived, he had found the squat in chaos. Having taken a mere half-tab of blue microdot acid two days before, Dave was still out of his head. Pete, who had taken the other half, had only experienced a feeble twenty-minute buzz. Dave couldn't or wouldn't open his eyes: everything had gone red, he said, everything was dripping with blood. He was under the impression that he had murdered his girlfriend. 'I've killed Loretta,' he kept saying, his voice ranging from stark terror to the bored tone of the man on *Sports Report*, announcing a goalless draw. Evan had sat with him for the next twenty-four hours, playing Indian ragas, the most soothing music he could find. The gramophone needle kept slipping but it didn't make much difference. He fed him oranges but this time the Vitamin C treatment didn't work. Whatever Dave said, Evan agreed with it. He led him to the toilet, took out his cock and pointed it in the right direction.

'Is it blood?' Dave whispered. 'Not as much as it was,' Evan replied. After a while he took up Dave's favourite book, *The Wind In The Willows*, and very slowly read out the 'Piper at the Gates of Dawn' chapter. Dave grew calmer and at last Evan saw his eyes slowly opening. 'Do you know' – he gave a wondering smile – 'I actually thought I'd killed Loretta!'

At this point Evan had summoned Loretta, a doll-like woman with cornflower blue eyes and a big head that wobbled disconcertingly. 'Here she is, Dave,' he said. 'Look – she's OK!'

'Now I know I killed her,' Dave wailed, 'I can see her ghost!'

And so Evan had started all over again with the sitars and the citric fruits. It wasn't until the following night that Dave finally accepted that, although he had indeed killed Loretta, nobody minded – not even Loretta herself.

And now all of this counted for nothing. Evan thought about the hatred in Dave's eyes last night. 'Traitor!' he hissed at himself, stepping out into the corridor. 'Traitor!'

The music from the other rooms hit him like a force nine gale. Yes,

Tull, Man, The Dead: it sounded as if the same song were being played at various speeds. It was curious that all this was inaudible in their room while the others claimed that every noise he and Adrea made could be heard all over the house. Could you have sound that only travelled in one direction?

He paused by the band room. The last practice, two weeks ago, had been a disaster. The others had refused outright to play 'Louie Louie': 'We don't want to do that old stuff.' Then Evan had shown them the chords to Television's 'Little Johnny Jewel', only to be met with, 'We don't want to do that new stuff either.'

'So what *do* you want to do?' he had finally asked. They looked at him disdainfully, like bombazine-wrapped dowagers, outraged by some breach of Edwardian etiquette: 'Why, *jam* of course!' Mayhem ensued. Evan rang the changes on the *Captain Pugwash* theme, while Dave essayed a Robert Plant impersonation that kept breaking into rachitic coughing, Alan chopped at his bass karate-style and Pete thrashed his arms and spluttered as if he were drowning in his own sweat. One by one they fell silent while continuing to throw their poses, miming to the different soundtracks playing in their heads. They hadn't seemed to notice when Evan unplugged and left.

Next day, a new rota had been pinned to the wall: practices were now on different days of the week, at irregular times, all coinciding with his shifts at Heron Close. Without him, they subsequently claimed to be hitting new peaks of telepathic musical understanding. Their seventy-minute jam on 'St Stephen' had supposedly outstripped the original. Strangely, the equipment didn't seem to have moved. Evan's second guitar, the bacofoil Gretsch copy, was propped against the amp, and Alan's broken bass drum pedal still hung limply. Evan ran a finger over the snare: it came away coated with grey dust.

He was relieved to find the kitchen empty. It was so dark that he had to peer into the corners to be sure. The fuses had gone again. Having taken up a knife and plate, he saw that a sheet of paper had been taped over the breadbin. Above a crude drawing of a salivating Alsatian was written 'Beware of the Dog' but when he raised the lid it was empty of both bread and dogs. On the underside of the plate was a sticker saying 'Pete' and the letter 'A' had been taped on to the knife handle. After a search, he discovered his own designated utensils: a cracked plate and a plastic spoon. Nothing in the kitchen had been spared. Two cans of Felix had been labelled 'Pussy', the Tate and Lyle Golden Syrup tin was tagged 'For Internal Use Only!' and the Rice Krispies packet was now wrapped in a yellow and black contaminated waste bag.

Propped against the kettle was another note: 'Dear E + A, Please replace the big Marmite that you ate. Love, The House'. On the reverse side was a cartoon of two jars with faces – one sad, dripping pearshaped tears, the other grinning and brandishing a spoon, obviously delighted at the prospect of eating itself. Evan couldn't remember having seen any Marmite: he didn't even like the stuff. On the top shelf of the fridge, a wrap of greasy paper announced itself as 'Dave's Bacon': he could just imagine that fat dolt wedging his own arse into the slicer. Next to it was a mouldering greenish slab called 'Alan's Butter': he seemed a more likely source than some nice clean cow. Four carrots had been lashed together with elastic bands and marked with a large red '4' and a bicycle lock had been fitted to the ring-pull of the last remaining Double Diamond can. It was like being back at school, where they punished you if your name wasn't on everything that was yours. He felt a familiar depression settling on him – or, rather, two separate depressions, originating from head and stomach, converging.

As he went back down the corridor, the music swelled again, like a watchdog announcing his approach. It was so loud that he couldn't hear his own fist banging on Dave's door. There was no answer, so he twisted the handle and pushed. The door didn't budge. In fact, it felt to be exerting a strong counter-pressure. Stepping back, he saw that a gleaming Yale lock had been installed. The separate cacophonies fused into a grotesque, apocalyptic choogle: he could actually feel his trouser legs flapping. Alan's door also had a new lock, as did Pete's. Although Ken's hadn't, it wouldn't open either. Perhaps he was using one of his holding spells? As if turning the place into a school hadn't been bad enough, they were now trying to turn it into a prison.

Evan retreated to the kitchen. At least they hadn't dared to label his prized collection of Twinings teas. He flipped the caddies open and breathed deeply from each in turn, then picked up the brown teapot.

The spout detached itself and fell, to shatter in the sink. Evan, silently and without tears, began to cry. The sobs felt to be coming from outside himself, rather like being pelted with snowballs. And all the while he was aware that he didn't care about the teapot, the notices or his ex-friends. It was almost as if he were crying precisely because he didn't care.

Adrea had finally been awakened by what felt to be an insect crawling across her shoulder. When she went to brush it away, however, nothing was there. This had happened before. These things were either microscopic or lightning-fast. Rolling over, she retrieved the damp saffron-coloured sheet from the bottom of the bed and drew it out long and tight over her body. She saw that her big toe had forced its way through the material and was solemnly looking back at her. Raising the sheet, she slowly drew her leg towards her until, above her head, she felt it tear itself free. It was a good feeling: she would happily have spent the rest of her life ripping cotton apart with feet and hands. It was also a good sound, like a slowed-down sneeze. Now they each had a sheet – or, at least, a rag, for much of the cloth had disintegrated into golden dust. Although Evan's watch had gone she knew by the tracer bullets of reflected light streaming across the room that it must be around midday. In a few minutes the bullets would be succeeded by a glaring white square on the far wall, like the beam of the school projector when her art or biology teachers had forgotten to insert the next slide.

She was feeling more and more uncomfortable around the squat. It was as if she could sense the others constantly thinking about her, could somehow actually hear them listening. Fighting off the desire to shout, 'Why can't you leave us alone?' at the ceiling, she ran a fingernail between the bare floorboards, dredging up a lethal-looking green pill wadded in dark fluff and wrapped with long white hairs. The place really was filthy. Evan maintained that dirt drew the germs away from you, and that if any did get through, then vigorous inhalations of smoke would kill them stone dead. Dirt, nicotine, music and dope were the keys to health – and if doctors disagreed it was only because they had a vested interest in your being ill.

This was their first long weekend away from Heron Close and Adrea wasn't sure that she was enjoying it. The first day had been wonderful – they'd hardly got out of bed at all – but yesterday she'd felt restless and had persuaded Evan to accompany her to Stanmore for one last try with Sally. They had arrived without warning and her sister had come to the door in tears, with her mascara streaking down her face.

Adrea had clutched at her. 'Is it Mum? Is it Dad?'

'No,' said Sally, pushing her away. 'It's Nastase.' Her beloved Ilie had just lost to Borg at Wimbledon. The only other time she had seen Sally cry had been on his previous unsuccessful final appearance.

Although Trevor wasn't there, they hadn't stayed long: Sally had somehow contrived to be cold and distant while simultaneously sobbing her eyes out.

'Don't worry,' Evan had said. 'You were the same about her first proper boyfriend.'

It only struck her later that she had never spoken to him about this. He seemed already to know a great deal about her. Did love make you a mind-reader, or was it that, given a few facts, everything else in someone's life could be deduced? If her family went to the Lake District every Easter then perhaps it followed that she would have refused to play hockey for the school. If she had suffered from chickenpox then she would inevitably, two years later, have attempted – while sleepwalking – to jump from the bathroom window.

Twenty-two hours now remained before their next shift began but Adrea didn't think that she could wait that long. It was as if Heron Close was pulling her back. It wasn't that she was worrying about the old people – she knew exactly where everyone would be and what they would be doing – more that she needed them, as if they were a vital point of reference. Last night, while Evan's housemates were being so horrible, she had the sensation that if the worst came to the worst, then Terry and the Babies, Mrs P and Mrs B and all the rest would step forward to stand beside them, that she and Evan were not utterly alone against the world.

Until now Adrea had felt little sympathy for the elderly. She recalled those awful family visits: even now the very words grandma and grandpa made her writhe and hiss, while a codliver oil taste filled her mouth. Although her parents forced her to accompany them they always concealed themselves behind the pages of the *Sunday Express*, leaving her to nod and smile at G/M and G/P as they wittered on and on. Apart from Sally, there had seemed to be absolutely no accounting for the human race. So what was so different about the residents? Why did she think that they knew what it felt like to be her while she knew what it felt like to be them?

The bedroom door flew open and a heavily-laden tray appeared, carried by Evan, effortlessly, on one hand. As he placed it on the window sill he observed that the spying wagtail had gone. The cloudless sky seemed to be studded with small bright pieces of tin. For some reason, aeroplanes were no longer leaving vapour trails. No one had previously realized just how many there were, which had resulted in a flood of UFO reports. The nearest just hung in the air, its silver glitter stabbing at his eyes, patiently waiting for its path down into Heathrow. It suddenly rotated, then vanished, like a coin inserted into a slot.

Evan lifted the blue plastic lid of his trusty Dansette. The first record of the day was an extremely serious matter: a wrong selection could set the earth spinning too fast or too slow. Often, though, the random was best. Shutting his eyes, he dipped into the singles stack. After lowering the needle he relished those few seconds of silence. When the music began it always felt like a miracle; the technology, against all the odds, had worked once again. It was Sam and Dave's 'Soul Sister, Brown Sugar'. His head jerked back with the opening horn-riff and he realized that his feet had begun to move. The chorus had just about the best couplet in all music: – 'Love and affection to the bone, to the bone. Soul sister, brown sugar' – which was immediately followed by the very worst: 'Ya gotta keep on socking it to me all night long. Soul sister, brown sugar'.

He sang along with both, regardless.

Adrea watched as the soles of his bare feet slapped down on the wood. There was a cluster of bluish hairs on the upper part of each toe. She had noticed that his fingers were similarly feathered between the knuckle and the first joint. Perhaps it was evolution. In a few thousand years he would be able to fly and she would have to keep a tight hold on him. As Evan hit the square of light his movements went strangely jerky, like a film with missing frames. None of this was for her benefit, she realized: for the duration of the record, at least, he had forgotten her existence. His white skin seemed to give off a slight phosphorescence. Adrea had never tanned before this summer but now her arms, neck and face had turned an embarrassing golden brown, while Evan remained aristocratically pale. She had to admit that she was jealous. Even his skin was don't-care-ish. He was noncombustible. Like Shadrach, Whatsit and Abednego in their burning fiery furnace, he would just stroll about in the flames.

As Evan poured the tea, drops from the broken pot stung his feet. 'You'll never guess what's happened,' he said, as the music faded out. 'They've gone and put labels and notices on everything in the kitchen and locks on all their doors.'

'That's exactly what I was about to say,' she replied. 'If only you'd given me the chance.'

Evan handed her a dangerously crazed cup. 'I think it's the laughing they don't like,' he said. 'They think we're laughing at them.'

'It's probably because they can't laugh themselves. All they do is snigger or say Ha Ha Ha as if they're reading it off an optician's chart.' She sniffed the tea suspiciously. 'I was in the toilet the other night when I heard this whispering outside. "Don't think you're fooling anyone with all that noise," the voice said. "You could at least try to fake it properly."'

'Who was it?' Evan asked.

'I don't know. It was a whisper. It was dark. I think it was a woman. What I don't understand is how they can hear us when we can't hear them.'

'Because they're listening and we're not,' said Evan. 'They've got a thing about you. They're always asking what your body is like, as if they think you're an alien or something. And they're always on at me to tell them exactly what we do.'

'What do they think we're doing?'

'They probably couldn't tell you themselves. All the things they think they're missing out on.' Evan began to sing, in Lou Reed's sneery voice, 'That from which they recoil most but which still makes their eyes moist.'

'But they've all got girlfriends' – Adrea gave a theatrical shudder – 'except Ken.'

'Oh, Ken's doing fine. Every night he strikes four Swan Vestas and summons up his fire-elemental houris. They've each got three mouths, six breasts and twelve-inch tongues.'

'And an extra pair of hands,' said Adrea, 'so they can darn his socks at the same time.'

Taking up his unplugged guitar, Evan played a few chords. She loved the way those dead strings clacked against the frets. It made her shiver with a pleasurable dread: she thought of it as skeleton music.

'I think what they're really afraid of,' he said at length, 'is that I might be fucking you and you might be fucking me.'

'What do you mean?'

'That it might not be a performance or a simulation, but *real*. Whenever Dave's with a woman he thinks he's Donald Sutherland in *Klute*. He looks at her and sees Jane Fonda playing the sensitive hooker that only a man like himself can understand and save. Of course, none of them are hookers or even particularly sensitive, and usually look more like Henry or Peter than Jane.'

'Is that really true?' Adrea looked delighted. 'Is that what men are like?'

'It's what *people* are like. His girlfriends don't care. They're up on cloud nine with Jim Morrison or Jimi Hendrix – even though Dave's closer to Little Jimmy Osmond. Fantasies fucking other fantasies: it's all perfectly safe, there's hardly any contact at all. And even if things do go wrong – well, it's only a movie. Next day you can be off robbing banks with Beatty or Dunaway.'

'Let's try it!' cried Adrea, jumping up from the bed. 'Let's be fantasies!'

Evan saw that those bruises on her knees had now vanished. They circled each other for a while, slowly and silently, like fencers. Then he went up on tiptoe and made claws of his hands, while she described a strange mime, as if wringing out a dishcloth. His eyes bulged, while hers seemed to have developed a squint.

'Who are you supposed to be?' she finally asked.

'Sufferin' Succotach!' Evan exploded, showering her with spittle. 'I'm Sylvester the Cat creeping up on Tweetie Pie. What about you?'

'I'm the Spider Woman, of course. Tightening the gag in Sherlock Holmes's mouth while I describe exactly how I'm planning to kill him!'

'No, no, no!' groaned Evan, letting his claws fall to his sides. 'It's no good. One of us has got to be the victim!'

Their subsequent mirth, Adrea couldn't help but notice, wasn't like reading Ha Ha's off a card. It had a deep, baying note, like a pack of hounds moving in on its quarry. She began to feel a sneaking sympathy for Dave and the others: she certainly wouldn't have liked to be on the outside of such laughter.

Evan put on side two of *Horses*. He had left the turntable on 45 so Patti's voice had become a helium squeak but at least the tempo was now up to that of the live performance. Twisting around, he struck at the wainscot with heels, then toes.

It wasn't merely the sex that was upsetting the others, Evan suspected, nor was it the laughter. It was the combination of the two. Last night he had actually been laughing as he came. He had always understood that this was impossible, that different and opposed muscles, nerves and sinews were involved, that the best you could do with laughing was to piss yourself. Besides, fucking was supposed to be a deadly serious business: no one in the illustrations to *The Joy of Sex* ever cracked a smile and in all the pornography he had seen even the dogs were snarling.

Before they had gone to bed he had been telling Adrea about how he'd once got high with the actor who, long ago, had played Billy Bunter in the children's TV programme. The man had been still stuck inside his character, wriggling and squealing as he wrestled with long-vanished schoolboy assailants: 'Ooooh! Yaroooh! Leggo, you rotters!'

Adrea had shouted these very words just as they were reaching their climaxes. Laughing as he came had been the strangest thing: he could have sworn that the whole room had flared with white light while a sharp pain had shot through his head, as if a cluster of brain cells had blown out. Even now his groin still ached and his balance felt all wrong, as though his feet were sinking ankle-deep into the floor.

'Perhaps we could try to be quieter,' said Adrea, pushing away her untouched tea.

'It's too late. The damage has been done. Now if we say nothing they'll start imagining what we might be thinking. A straight face would be worse than any laughter. Besides, I don't think we could keep it up.'

'Why are they being like this?' she asked. 'And why did they call you a traitor?'

'Because they're in the process of junking everything they used to believe in. They're turning into mature, responsible adults with careers, marriages, mortgages, children.'

'Except Ken.' Adrea shuddered again.

'Especially Ken.' Evan threatened her with the spoutless teapot. 'There's always plenty of call for Magi.'

'In a few months,' she said, 'we'll see them marching over London Bridge with their umbrellas, pin-stripes and short back and sides.'

'No,' said Evan, 'they'll still look exactly the same. They'll still smoke dope, they'll still like to jam. You won't be able to tell that they've changed until you're close enough to see their eyes.'

'By which time,' said Adrea, 'it will be too late.' She had found Evan's crumpled jeans and had begun to pull them on just as he was taking hers off. They both paused for a moment, one leg in, one leg out, before letting them slide to the floor and kicking them away into opposite corners of the room.

'Whenever I look into the residents' eyes,' said Adrea, 'I can see exactly what they're feeling. They're just like us, only us grown old. I understand them and they understand me. But with middle-aged people there's nothing there. The eyes are blank, as if no one is behind them.'

'It's like *Invasion of the Body Snatchers*,' said Evan. 'Except that when the bodies begin to wear out the aliens leave and their real owners wake up to find that overnight they've got forty years older.'

Sitting on the bed they ate breakfast: stale cream cracker fragments glued together with golden syrup. Although they fell apart when lifted from the plate, they tasted delicious.

'A teacher once read us a poem,' said Adrea. Evan observed that the falling crumbs had caught in her pubic hair. 'I didn't understand it at the time and everyone else was sniggering. It was about an old man, standing in front of a mirror, looking at his body.' As she spoke, she let her hands run down over her young flesh. It struck Evan that he hadn't thought of her as being naked: she seemed clothed in her own skin. 'And at the end of the poem the old man says, "What a strange thing to happen to a little boy."'

'Maybe it will be the same thing with us? Perhaps tomorrow morning it will be 2026.' Evan's tone indicated that he had only introduced this possibility in the interests of balance. He knew perfectly well that such a thing could never happen to them.

'Does it have to be like that?' said Adrea, falling back on to the mattress.

'No,' said Evan. 'There's always Pricey. He's succeeded in escaping into his own cold, mean little world. But that's a cure that's even worse than the disease, like getting rid of a cough by cutting your own throat.'

Adrea had a vision of Price with a second mouth slashed across his windpipe, merely re-doubling that unceasing torrent of sarcasm. With a sigh, she shut her eyes, then brought her legs up so that the toes were pointing at the ceiling. Then, as Evan watched, they scissored twice while the torso twisted, so that the soles of her feet met behind her head.

'I didn't know you could do that,' said Evan.

'I didn't either.' Now her body rolled backwards, as her legs straightened, until all her weight was being supported by the top of her head and the palms of her hands, with toes and knees touching the wall. The blood didn't seem to be rushing to the head: she appeared to be perfectly relaxed. If anything, Evan himself felt disorientated, as if he were the one upside-down. Her mouth yawned massively, causing her feet to pedal the air and her spine to arch dangerously backwards. 'Wake me up when I'm seventy,' she said but then her eyes opened again, their dark pupils dilated, as if they had burst through the lids.

thirteen

The music finished and Price opened his eyes. The distance from the bed to the record player suddenly seemed immense. He decided to lie in silence for a while. Black tadpole-like things – somewhere between *muscae volitantes* and the D.T.s – were squiggling across the ceiling. He lit another cigarette: smoke always drove them away. Three orange and brown rings had formed on the plaster above the bed, table and armchair, as if the nicotine were gradually reproducing the Van Gogh sunflowers. Price wondered what other great works of art – the *Mona Lisa*, perhaps, or *Whistlejacket*? – it might be etching on his lungs.

He lay back again and, almost before his lashes met, there was the blonde policewoman again. Price had given up guessing what she might be wearing, deciding that she was either naked or just a disembodied head. He recalled how he had slept away the time between her dropping him off and their assignation the next day. His dreams had not been of her: he had been running through an endless birch wood, searching for the absconding mods. Only in dreams was he so solicitous about his clients. When he awoke he had even thought of ringing her to cancel but she had of course left no phone number and he didn't know her name.

In those days such things sometimes happened. Women picked him up, or he picked women up, or a huge hand seemed to pick them both up and deposit them face to face. They were usually pretty enough, with plenty to say for themselves. All claimed to love 'the arts' but that was merely their way of indicating that although they were sensitive that didn't mean that they would let him get away with anything. Often it had seemed to be the same woman in various disguises. They were all his *type*, he supposed, which said something depressing about him.

While waiting to leave he had found himself vacuuming and dusting his own flat, as if WPC 119 had been coming to him. For the first time in three months he cleared the draining board. At least if she weren't his type then the rubbish they would talk might be different rubbish and any sex might be unsatisfying in a different way. Before he left he changed his mind three times about which shirt and tie to wear.

Next to the tube station was a big florist's that he had never noticed before. For the first and probably the last time in his life he bought flowers: the deluxe mixed bouquet. He felt absurd. How should you carry the things? On the escalator he realized that he was cradling them like a baby. The bouquet, already huge, seemed to be growing. He felt like Birnam Wood advancing to Dunsinane. Having finally settled on shouldering them like a rifle, he hit the platform at a brisk military march.

The train was full of shabby middle-aged men with black and white scarves. Some carried rattles, others wore bobble hats. Football fans, going to the match, but there was no buzz of anticipation, no singing, no chanting. They were Fulham supporters, lost in their own private grief.

So these were flowers, were they? The red ones, the yellow ones, the faintly obscene ones: he didn't know any of their names. They seemed to be regarding him with equal disapproval. He wasn't conversant with the language of flowers. These would probably have been more appropriate at Winston Churchill's funeral.

Alighting at Putney Bridge, he let the still silent throng carry him through Bishop's Park. His A–Z had showed that the policewoman lived on the rundown side of Fulham, between the river and the cemetery. The snow had thawed and up ahead the floodlights of Craven Cottage blazed silver and blue. Many of the fans paused at the railings to stare down into the Thames, as if wondering whether, rather than waiting until the inevitable defeat, they should throw themselves in now and save a couple of quid.

She lived in a newly-built three-storey block of flats wedged between two crumbling, intersecting terraces. It looked somehow insubstantial, reminding him of the false Harrods frontage just along the river that concealed the store's furniture repository. There was no sign of her little red car. The communal hallway smelt of turtle wax and souring milk. Although he shut the outside door softly behind him the whole building seemed to shake.

Her flat was on the top floor. The door was crimson and scratched-looking, as if it had been hurriedly painted in undercoat from different angles by three or four people with stiff brushes. The doorbell felt dead: there was no sound of ringing from inside. Having let the weight of his whole body push through his stiffened index finger, he began to knock. It was some time before he noticed the small square white envelope pinned below the letterbox. There was no name on it but he guessed that it was for him. Although the rabbits and squirrels still frolicked along the borders, the words had this time been printed in crude capitals, as if to disguise the handwriting: 'I'M SORRY BUT I DON'T SHARE YOUR FEELINGS. PLEASE DON'T CONTACT ME AGAIN – H.'

That 'H' looked rather like a pi sign, but he had never understood mathematics. After reading it again he turned the paper over. The rabbits showed through but the writing and squirrels didn't. For the first time in his life he had been stood up. He put his ear to the door but all he could hear was the thudding of his own heart. The wood was thoroughly peppered with drawing-pin holes: either she kept changing her milk order or this was a regular occurrence.

He began to laugh. It certainly wasn't genuine merriment but nor was it staged laughter in case she was listening behind the door. It reminded him of the way he used to vomit before he learned to drink. He wasn't sure how long it lasted: it was as if fists were punching him, bouncing him from wall to wall. After recovering himself, he knelt on the sticky linoleum and, taking out his best fountain pen, wrote in careful copperplate on the blank side of her paper: 'I'm sorry to say that – apart perhaps from a mild curiosity and a rather disembodied lust – I don't appear to have any feelings in this matter at all. Perhaps what you meant to say was that you don't share my indifference? – P.'

He posted the note. A hinged flap inside the letterbox blocked any signs of light. As an afterthought, he thrust the flowers after it, blossoms first. Afterwards, out in the street, he had looked back at the block. All the windows were dark but he was sure that he had seen her curtains twitching. At the far end of the road he saw a line of tightly-parked shiny red Minis but he couldn't remember her number plate. Perhaps it had all been a trap, a means by which the police could up their arrest statistics? If he had started swearing and tried to kick down her door, then dozens of coppers would have come swarming out, truncheons at the ready. Fortunately, laughter and heavy irony were crimes that were not yet on the statute book.

There was no way down to the river from Stevenage Road, only a dark, narrow cul de sac. The street sign caught his eye: Eternit Walk, SW6. He had walked over to confirm that a final 'y' hadn't dropped off or been painted over. Eternit, such a strange name. Perhaps it was intended to indicate that we are always just one step away from eternity? Unless, of course, it was some kind of insect.

As if drawn like an enormous moth to the floodlights, Price had found that, for the first and presumably last time in his life, he was going to a football match. Fulham were already one-nil down, the gateman told him, and Johnny Haynes had been carried off injured. He stood out on the open kop. The ground was half empty and what crowd noises there were – from the large covered enclosure at the other end – arrived with a few seconds' delay. The game was appalling: there were no further goals and very little action. The ball seemed to be trundling around the pitch of its own volition, pursued by the increasingly desperate players. At one point it went straight up and up until it just hung above the lights, silhouetted against the moon. After it had finally dropped, he continued for the rest of the game to stare up into the sky: it was full of lights, but of planes, not stars.

What did that 'H' stand for? he had wondered as he left the ground. He was sure that it must be something inappropriate. Not Hymen, presumably. Nor Hippolyte, as she had made it clear that she possessed two breasts. Nor Hester, Hecuba or Hecate. Helen was the best bet. As the name of the most beautiful woman that there could ever be, it should only have been bestowed once, but now Helens were as common as hedge-sparrows: it was amazing how many fat, thin, plain, vain, vulgar and silly girls now considered it their destiny to launch a thousand ships.

Price had stayed at the children's home until the end of the summer. He had reported the mods missing dozens more times. And PC 576 still came round to take the details but WPC 119 had never reappeared. 'Where's your winsome little friend?' he would ask but that long hiss was the Servant of the Lord's only response.

A couple of months later he had run into his usual type under the usual circumstances and the usual things had ensued, although of unusual intensity and duration. And he had forgotten all about that whole strange episode, except that he always put Fulham down for a draw on his pools coupons. He only filled these in because he wanted to be lucky. He didn't care about the money – which was just as well, as he had never won a penny.

His eyes snapped open again just as his door began to open. He had been listening to Evan's snakeskin boots come clip-clopping past the garages and then up the back stairs. Price had sent him to the off-licence to pick up his weekly order of four hundred Capstan and seven bottles of Wolfschmidt Kummel.

'Don't come in!' Price shouted, fiddling with his fly buttons. 'I'm not decent.'

Evan turned back and gave the doorframe a sardonic double tap.

'Aha, my medicine!' said Price, leaping up from the bed and snatching the carrier bags. 'And my Cappies!' He took out one of the bottles and began fumbling at its neck with trembling hands. 'Keep the change,' he quavered. 'For being such a good boy.'

Ignoring this, Evan tossed a handful of coins on to the bed.

'Would you do another little errand for me?' Price wheedled.

'If you like,' said Evan.

'The next time you're in Soho, could you go into Pellens' Personal Products and get me a vibrator?'

'What size?' asked Evan.

Price thought about it. 'De Luxe. Jumbo.'

'What colour?'

'Er… pink. No, black. And then go into the theatrical costumiers two doors away and get me a quote on a bear costume.'

Evan gave the smile that showed all his teeth. 'Grizzly, Polar or Teddy?' he enquired.

'On second thoughts, don't bother,' snapped Price. He stopped pawing the bottles and began to stack them in the cupboard.

As Evan crossed the landing the blast of Price's music nearly blew him down the stairs. The singer yowled as if the piano were eating him alive. Grand pianos – their shiny black lids propped open like coffins, their keys like rows of gleaming teeth – always made Evan think of death. 'Give my regards to Dracula,' the man in the off licence had said. Evan had been amused to see that the back of the Kummel bottle carried instructions for a cocktail called 'the Silver Bullet'.

Down in the sitting room Adrea was trying to fix the television. She couldn't bear to watch the residents staring into that snowstorm, listening to those Dalek voices.

Pulling the set away from the wall, she discovered a length of flex and a plastic indoor aerial, which she raised above her head.

'How is it now?' she asked.

'Better,' said Mrs Parker. 'No, worse.'

Adrea moved towards the wall – 'Better' – then left – 'Worse' – then right – 'Better'. She leaned down – 'Worse' – then stretched up – 'Better! Better!' She climbed on to Nobby's old chair – 'Up! Up!' Placing her left foot on the armrest and her right knee on the back then fully extending her arm, she held the aerial at the junction of wall and ceiling. 'Perfect!' they cried. 'Hold it there.' She realized that she was balanced so precariously that at the slightest movement the chair would topple, pitching her back on to the television or forward through the window.

At this moment Evan entered. Adrea appeared to be impersonating the Statue of Liberty but carrying a TV aerial rather than a torch. The statue is usually shown from the view-point of arriving ships: he had always wondered what it might look like from behind. He doubted whether its bottom could compare with Adrea's – otherwise, the population of New York would have stood in permanent rapt contemplation.

Adrea's head twisted round. 'Help! I'm stuck!'

Evan gave her a little wave, like Sooty the glove puppet, and left the room.

Her neck began to ache so she turned her face back to the wall. She could tell by the television's sound how much the picture must have improved. 'Another single to Richards,' a toneless voice announced, to desultory applause. She had discovered that she could maintain her equilibrium by shifting her weight, jutting first one hip then the other. It must have looked ridiculous. Adrea resigned herself to standing there for ever: she hoped that someone would remember to dust her from time to time.

Then she felt Evan's breath on the back of her neck and turned her head again just as a double-pronged toasting fork came past her cheek. Without apparent effort, Evan drove it deep, through the plaster and the brick, trapping the aerial fast. Then his arms went round her and she let herself go and he carried her out into the centre of the room. 'I had thought of throwing it from the doorway,' he said. She felt weightless, that he wasn't so much keeping her off the ground as off the ceiling. The television picture was indeed perfect: white-clad figures were examining one another's shoes.

'I keep feeling that we're in a film,' Adrea said as he bore her into the corridor. 'You don't think we're getting like Dave and Jane Fonda, do you?'

'I think being in a movie is fine,' said Evan. 'So long as we're playing ourselves.'

Mrs Parker shook out her knitting. 'So, what do you make of our little Romeo and Juliet?'

Her question seemed to be addressed to no one in particular and so there was no response, except from the cat, who left off licking his bottom to stare at her.

'Not that they're all that little,' she continued. 'Galumphing great things, aren't they, Stormy?'

Mrs Barker's knitting needles clashed against each other. Behind the thick glasses the eyes were burning. Mrs Parker had done it again, muttering the cat's name so that it wasn't so much Stormy as Stanley.

It was especially galling because, except in private, she herself could never get away with calling it Ron. She growled softly but from her stomach, not her throat. Everyone was struggling to digest all the rich food that was suddenly being dished up. The room echoed with the sound of long-disused plumbing creaking back into action. Stormy looked nervous, as if fierce dogs might be hiding behind the chairs. Mrs Barker's tongue once again traversed her mouth: no matter how much she scrubbed a maddening irritation persisted, as though strings of meat and knots of gristle were lodged between gums and teeth.

Mrs Parker was disturbed that Evan and Adrea were no longer wearing their overalls. 'Haven't you forgotten something, dear?' she had asked when Adrea brought the tea round, but the silly thing had merely fetched another packet of Bourbon biscuits. Today Adrea was wearing a scoop-necked top, zippered down the front with a large round pull. When she had read about modern women burning their bras she had thought it a figure of speech but now she was fascinated by the movement of the young girl's breasts, as if they were somehow defying the laws of nature. And those trousers revealed that she was wearing tiny bloomers or even no bloomers at all. Evan was dressed in a striped cheesecloth shirt: its middle buttons kept unfastening and it was too short in the arms. She was certain that Adrea had been wearing it on their previous shift. There was something very odd about men and women sharing each other's clothes. And as for his trousers... well, she had been forcing her eyes to blur everything between those papery boots and that pale, smiling face.

As he turned the bend on the stairs, Price saw Evan carrying Adrea in his arms. They glided smoothly by, like a tableau on a revolving stand. He paused for a while in case they came round again. He was sure that Adrea's upside-down face had registered him with even more horror than usual. In the mirror, he checked that his tie was straight and his flies buttoned up: the rest he could do nothing about. Even more slowly and heavily than usual, he made his way to the front door, opening it just as the singer and the pianist arrived.

They appeared every couple of months, in rotation with the dentist, chiropodist and occupational therapist. The baritone, Pat, was even fatter than Price himself, laden down with watery flesh that sloshed audibly to and fro. His Brylcreemed wig had a dazzling blue sheen, as if a deformed crow were roosting on his head. The stubble was the same colour, as though he had carefully dotted it in with a Biro. Price could never remember the pianist's name. Silent, hairless and bespectacled, his thick lenses smeared with tiny fingerprints, he looked like a defrocked priest. Both men were sweating heavily. If he broke an egg on the flat, gleaming top of the pianist's head, Price reckoned, it would fry.

'Welcome, maestro,' said Price with a low bow. 'Are we to have the Stockhausen programme today? Or will you be giving us your *Frauenliebe und Leben?*'

'I'll be doing "Take a Pair of Sparkling Eyes",' said Pat, unabashed. 'Just for you, Pricey me darlin'.'

Evan and Adrea shepherded the old people into the second sitting room. Presumably by chance, the Babies had already wedged themselves behind the piano. Adrea hadn't realized that the instrument was there until the accompanist savagely whipped off the covers. She was fascinated by the singer's enormous hands: clenching and unclenching at his sides, they appeared to have been dusted with flour. Planting his feet wide apart and half-squatting like a sumo wrestler, Pat tilted his head back in a series of hydraulic jerks. Even before the pianist hit the first note, Adrea observed, the tassels of the lampshade had begun to swing alarmingly.

In the dining room the music drowned out the rattle of Price's pills on the side plates and the patter of airgun pellets against the windows. Pat was one of those singers who grew louder the further away you got. As usual, they were starting with 'Down at the Old Bull And

Bush'. After pausing at the end of the chorus for an audience response that never came, Pat had to yell his own 'BUSHBUSH!'

Adrea, Price reflected, looked nothing like the policewoman. She acted, spoke and moved in a completely different way. Perhaps that was how memory worked, triggered not by resemblance but by antithesis? The only time Price had taken a word association test, he had responded to everything – good, black, day – with its antonym – bad, white, night. He had been proud of his natural contrariness until the doctor told him that this was the most common response.

Why had H left him that note? What had she been afraid of? Perhaps she had burnt the dinner and felt ashamed? Why hadn't he waited there until she returned or emerged? How did he know that the door had been locked? He hadn't even tried the handle. Could you be in love with someone and not realize? And could you then forget all about them for the next twelve years?

Back in the sitting room, the tenor was wiping his face with a filthy handkerchief, while his eyes raked the audience. 'Any requests?' he asked wearily.

'Do you know "Fine and Mellow"?' Adrea was embarrassed at how squeaky her voice sounded.

Pat beamed down at her: 'Ah, that would be the Billie Holiday song, wouldn't it?'

Leaning over, he whispered in the pianist's ear. After some shuffling and throat-clearing, they went into a startlingly up-tempo version of 'Danny Boy', which Pat sang leeringly to Evan alone. It seemed to Adrea that the sound was issuing from his flaring nostrils.

Price was beginning to suspect that the policewoman episode had somehow been the pivotal moment of his life, that he had taken the wrong path and could not re-trace his steps. In those days he had known too little but now he knew too much. How do you set about unlearning things? Whatever could have been awaiting him behind that red door? Something told him that it would have had nothing to do with love or sex, domesticity or happiness. Perhaps it was like the stack of fossil ivory and row of shrunken human heads that Marlowe discovered when he finally tracked down Kurtz? *The Heart of Darkness* could be found in south-west London as well as in the Congo.

'The Last Rose of Summer' boomed down the corridor. How did the ex-priest get that tone? It was as if the notes came bubbling up from the bottom of the sea. Their programme never varied: The *coup de grâce* was always 'Delilah'. This had formerly included a spectacular stabbing mime with a retractable-bladed knife until Mrs Allen ordered Pat to drop it after some of the ressies had fainted.

Outside, a second, even more terrible yowling had begun. Stormy, his fur on end, was batting Squibbsy along the terrace, setting the dustbins crashing. Price wondered if his biggest mistake had been never to make any more mistakes. Perhaps he should always have said yes instead of no and no instead of maybe. Should he have made a thousand assignations and been stood up a thousand times – only to turn up for the thousand-and-first, with flowers and a goofy grin? Should he have sought out humiliation and then rubbed his own nose in it? Should he have set himself a regimen of stupid acts, three a day, before or after meals? He crammed a handful of pills into his mouth. They tasted like dolly mixtures. From the window he saw that the little dog had escaped by throwing itself up into the branches of a scraggy rowan tree. Stormy, swollen to twice his usual size, was pacing about below. If dogs can suddenly climb, he was presumably thinking, then cats no longer can.

An ominous silence fell. Why did so many singers feel that they had to include 'Delilah'? Even the Red Army choir always encored with it. Price braced himself for the impact but the chords that followed – muted, velvety, insinuating – were not the right ones. And when Pat entered he was singing in perfectly acceptable German. Unbelievably, it was Goethe's 'Ganymede' – and not even the jolly

Schubert setting but the version by deep, dark, crazy Hugo Wolf. That great pantheistic hymn of self-surrender in which the young Trojan prince gives himself up to mystical union with nature, with the divine father. Price recollected Rembrandt's painting of the subject, in which a sobbing toddler, pissing himself with fear, is carried off by an eagle, to be buggered by Jupiter. The Gods always lie, always tell their youthful favourites that all they're after is a purely mystical union. As the song stealthily shifted from D major through F sharp major to B flat major, Price realized that he had discarded his pill tray and was moving back down the corridor.

In the sitting room most of the audience had nodded off, except for Mrs P and Mrs B, who had once again taken up their knitting. Evan and Adrea's hands covered their faces while their shoulders shook. Pat didn't look particularly transfigured either: he seemed even more amazed than Price at what he had found himself doing. '*Umfangend, umfangen!*' Embraced, embracing! His eyes rolled wildly. He had obviously run out of puff and was now desperately crawling towards the finishing line. The pianist's rolling *tremolandi* seemed to set the room pitching like the deck of a storm-tossed ship. Price was sure that he could hear the drops of sweat hitting the keys. Pat's voice finally broke up: it sounded as if the crow on top of his head were trying to help him out. In spite of all this, in spite of the pianist's fraying shoelaces and well-holed unmatching socks, in spite of Pat's huge purple Adam's apple and soup-stained tie, Price realized that he did not find this scene ridiculous.

As the last chord faded away the two musicians left at a trot, as though afraid of being mobbed. Price knew that they had three more calls to make. Back in his flat, he put on the Wolf Society 78 of 'Ganymede'. Count John McCormack and Gerald Moore were great artists, of course, but he had to admit that he preferred Pat and the priest's interpretation. Somehow that element of the absurd had made it all the more profound. He thought about his own epiphany, his own glimpse of eternity – or, at least, of Eternit. He was under no illusions that H might have been a muse or a goddess in disguise: she was merely a nutty policewoman wearing too much make-up. When he shut his eyes and her familiar face appeared once more, was it just his imagination that behind the smile her features had a stiffer, more disapproving cast? For the first time it occurred to him that he should speak to her.

'What do you want?' he asked.

She made no reply but her image flickered once, twice and then was obscured by a storm of static, like the residents' television before Adrea had adjusted it. It seemed to freeze, solidify, then crumble away out of his sight. She was gone. Even the background had changed: no longer red but matt black. No matter how wide he opened his eyes, or how tightly he screwed them shut, she did not return. Price lay on his bed, blinking until, at length, he fell asleep.

While Adrea was bathing Dolly, Evan – having finished his shavings – wandered into the sitting room. Now that the television was fixed the old people seemed no longer interested in watching it. The gentle tock of bat on ball, like a deathwatch beetle, indicated that the cricketers were still pottering interminably on.

'What's the score?' Evan asked.

One of the old men pointed at the clock. 'Quarter to six,' he said.

Evan had always hated cricket. At school it had been the one game that he hadn't enjoyed playing. Batting seemed quite exciting as the bowler came running in, but when the ball left the hand it seemed to take for ever to reach him, by which time he had forgotten where he was and what he was supposed to do, standing frozen as it crashed into his body or his wicket. And they would never let him bowl because, they said, he was a chucker, a cheat, a bent-arm merchant, a bad sport.

A scoreboard revealed that West Indies had made 416. England had just begun their reply. As Evan watched, the ball abruptly reared up from the pitch, narrowly missing a bald batsman's nose. The English openers looked tiny and frail, while the bowler was impossibly tall and muscular. Perhaps the television needed further adjustment? The next delivery hit the batsman on the shoulder: the bowler followed right through and said something to him. White teeth flashed in the dark face but Evan didn't think it was a smile. The next one just missed the nose again, and the one after that struck Baldy on the forearm with an audible crack. He turned even paler but didn't flinch. Behind him, the slips and the wicket-keeper could be seen laughing uproariously. And so it continued: the bats made no contact with the ball. Baldy was deliberately letting them hit him: he even appeared to be jumping into the path of wide deliveries, so that they thudded into his unprotected ribcage.

This wasn't the cricket that Evan remembered. It was as if the heat had burnt away the veneer of custom and sportsmanship to reveal the hatred and brutality that lay beneath.

Things were looking up. Cats were chasing dogs, cricket balls were turning into bombs and the old people were eating meat not mush. Music was getting exciting again and every day the sun burnt hotter and longer and he could see the terror in the eyes of the people in the street. And the more he looked at Adrea the stranger she seemed. Yes, things were really looking up.

He became aware that Adrea was sitting next to him. 'At least we haven't lost any wickets yet,' she said, indicating a surprising familiarity with the game.

'They're not trying to get them out,' said Evan. 'Because if they got them out they'd have to stop hurting them.'

fourteen

Snow was standing at the dining-room window, part-hidden by the curtains, squinting against the evening sunlight. Somehow he had missed Adrea leaving after her shift: she must have used the rear exit instead. How he loved to watch her walking away, stamping her feet down as if crushing an insect with every step! He had taught his eyes to blank Evan out. When the boy's arm went round her shoulders, he would tell himself that it was just a passing shadow.

With a heavy heart he moved to the fridge. For the last ten days he had kept taking out his chocolate only to put it all back again, unsold, an hour later. Through melting, then re-freezing, the bars had warped into weird shapes and the splitting silver paper revealed that milk, plain and fruit and nut had all turned greenish-grey. For many years he had been providing the residents with this special service but now, suddenly, they didn't want it any more. Clutching his wares to his chest, he made for the sitting room: this time he would not be taking no for an answer.

No one had turned on the electric light, so that in the gloom he half-tripped over Stormy's supine form. Until recently, few of the residents had dared to meet his gaze but now, as he took in the room, all their white faces were turned towards him. Then he saw that Adrea, her lovely features illuminated by the television's glow, was sitting next to Terry. She smiled sadly, as if in apology, although Snow felt as always that it was he who should be apologizing to her. He didn't quite believe his eyes until he registered that Evan was sitting on Terry's right. Snow knew that he could not be imagining him, too: Evan and Adrea belonged in totally different fantasies. The boy slowly wagged his finger and then put it to his lips. 'We'll be gone in a minute,' he said. Adrea shook her head slightly, as if to show that she didn't really want to be involved in such things.

Back in the corridor, Snow checked the clocks. All confirmed that Evan and Adrea's shift had ended thirty-three minutes ago. Why were they still here? He could hear a dry rustling sound as if dead leaves were blowing across the terrace, but it was the wrong season for leaves. It was laughter: everyone was laughing at his chocolates and himself.

As soon as his back was turned, he knew, all manner of things were going on. Although the residents whose job it was to watch kept reporting that nothing was happening, even they had become lazy and almost insolent. How did they expect to see anything with their eyes closed? Now that the television's pictures were sharp and distinct, he had observed, no one showed any further interest in it. Even when he turned the volume up to a deafening blare or reduced it to near-inaudibility, they did not react, just stared at him strangely. Every day they were becoming less and less afraid of him.

At the far end of the corridor Bridie was bathing the Babies. He hated those bathrooms, as the steam misted up his eyes as if they had been made of glass. He might have known that Bridie would be no help: she just laughed. 'If they're still there in half an hour' – she brandished her stiff-bristled brush – 'I'll scrub both of them as well.' Her overalls were all splashed. Molly was chortling and thrashing her legs, as though trying to swim away. Even this was all wrong: they were not supposed to enjoy their baths.

Snow had nothing to be ashamed of. Even though they were enough to try the patience of a saint, he had always been good to the residents. Sometimes you needed to shout to get their attention and if they got stuck you had to pinch, push and slap just to move them on. And whatever anyone said, there was a difference between kicking and guiding them with your feet. He had struck with a closed fist on less than a dozen occasions and only then under extreme provocation.

Over the years they had hurt him far more than he had them. He caught all their colds. Just as he was getting over one he'd be going down with the next. Even in summer he sniffled, half-deaf, with his eyelids red raw. And how many times had he strained himself lifting them, or slipped and fallen on their messes? Three fingers and a thumb he had broken and he would always limp from the wheelchair that had crushed his left foot. Worst of all had been when that twenty-two-stone woman had dropped dead in the toilet, pinning him underneath. He had vainly tried to crawl away behind the pedestal so that, after they pulled her off ten minutes later, his head had remained cocked ridiculously sideways, as though he were listening out for some faint sound that no one else could hear.

The internal phone in the office had begun to ring but it was only the cook, still raging about Evan and Adrea. 'They're not getting away with it,' he was shouting. 'I know people south of the river, I know people in Spain! My uncle will do anything for me. He was too moody even for the Richardsons. He'll cut that kid's prick off and stuff it in her mouth.'

Snow left the receiver on the desk and returned the chocolate to the fridge. He had to wash the brown stains off his fingers. How he hated that cook! Price should have reported him: the man deserved to be sacked. He was just a thief whereas whatever little things he himself might have had did not even begin to recompense him for these aching bones and his limp.

Back in the office, Cooky's voice was still crackling down the line. 'Cruelty to animals is what it is.' Squibbsy could be heard whimpering in the background. 'I'm going to put the RSPCA on to them!'

'There is an emergency,' said Snow, and put the phone down. When he returned to the sitting room he thought at first that the young people had gone until he saw that they had moved from their chairs to crouch in front of Terry. They appeared to be whispering, although he could hear no sound.

'In a minute,' Evan said again, without turning round. Adrea's face twisted back towards Snow: now there seemed to be something cruel about that smile. He could hardly blame her. If only he could warn her that all men were just like himself: it was merely that the evil was not apparent in Evan's face. Good-looking men were all hypocrites and liars. At least Snow was honest enough to look like what he was.

Returning to the office, he dialled Price's number.

'Valhalla 321,' came the familiar voice. 'Wotan speaking.'

'They're still here,' said Snow. 'That boy keeps saying "in a minute" but it's been forty-nine minutes and they still haven't moved.'

Price yawned. 'So what's the problem?'

'They are not supposed to be here!' Snow almost screamed.

'But you're not supposed to be there either, old man. It's another three hours and eleven minutes until your night duty starts.'

'I have responsibility for all this,' Acting Deputy Matron Snow said, with some dignity. 'And they are whispering in the darkness. They are going to do something bad. The old people are terrified.'

'Try to hold the fort until I get there,' said Price. 'If necessary, make a useless sacrifice of yourself.'

Only after he had hung up did Snow realize that the usual horrible music had not been playing in the background.

Mrs Parker had been watching Snow with interest. Why did he keep coming in and out, opening his mouth and then closing it again without speaking? She supposed that it must have been something to do with the chocolate. Just because people had once liked things it didn't mean that they always would. She herself had been finding her fruit and nut increasingly difficult to eat. It felt slimy to the touch and had a funny sour smell. Perhaps they could blindfold her and put a peg on her nose before popping it into her mouth? Either Cadbury's standards were slipping or Snow was manufacturing the stuff himself.

He had to learn that he couldn't always have his own way. You could only bully people for as long as they wanted to be bullied. She had always been scared of Snow but now she was wondering why.

What had she feared that he might do or say? He was ugly as sin, of course, but that remained the same whether he smiled or scowled.

Evan and Adrea were still messing around with Terry. Were they trying to annoy Snow, Mrs Parker wondered, or did they just have nothing better to do? She felt sorry for them, even though they obviously weren't feeling in the least sorry for themselves. Why did they keep flopping about all over the place? She and Stanley had been either vertical or horizontal with nothing in between.

Mrs Parker had been thinking about the young people a lot, finding herself counting down the hours before their shifts. When they did arrive, however, it was always a let-down. Until Evan had spoken to Snow just now she had forgotten that they were in the room.

It was getting darker. How nice it was to sit and watch the light fade! All that remained of Mrs Yu-No-Hu was a black scorched-looking shadow, as if she had finally succeeded in obliterating her. At that very moment, however, a sudden radiance illuminated her rival's face: Evan had crossed the room to allow her to light his cigarette. Although she was now being virtually ignored by Stormy there was no change in the woman's expression. Perhaps she had something up her sleeve other than those navvy's forearms?

Some people's cigarettes, Mrs Barker was thinking, were more enjoyable to light than others. She jerked the match closer to Evan's face but he didn't flinch: those grey eyes stared unblinkingly through the flame. He didn't thank her, just rumbled in the back of his throat, the way Ron used to. She watched as Evan tried to wedge the cigarette between Terry's teeth.

She always felt sad when the sun went down but on the other hand the flames burned even brighter in the gloom. She was relieved that no one had yet turned on the lights. Stormy, rolling over, gave her an upside-down wink: he and she were playing a little game with Mrs Parker. What a cat! When Snow tripped over him he hadn't moved, just rippled his fur, as if he were dreaming of fleas.

Thank heaven that chocolate had gone. She hated the rustling and scraping of the gold and silver foil and the way that Snow handed it out, like a priest at an altar. She herself would never touch the stuff. She liked food that you could keep in your mouth for a while, that went salty and crispy when held in a fire. Chocolate just couldn't take the heat. Snow would never let her light his gold-tipped menthol king-sizes. Perhaps he knew that she would not be able to resist the temptation of those hairy nostrils, like well-stuffed pipe-bowls?

Acting Matron Price's unmistakeable silhouette appeared in the doorway. Mrs Barker sighed. He seemed to have grown even bigger since his temporary promotion. Maybe he would shrink back to normal size when they appointed a new matron? He walked differently, too: was he drinking more or drinking less?

Snowy had a point, Price had to admit. There was a distinctly bad feeling emanating from the sitting room. His feet did not want to step over the threshold, as if suspecting a trap. He had the impression that large shapes were moving stealthily in the darkness. Evan's long legs were stretched out halfway across the floor. The patterns of those snakeskin boots appeared to be shifting under the flickering light.

With one sweep of his palm, he flattened all the wall switches. There was a general cry of dismay and everyone's hands flew to shield their eyes. He saw that, instead of the usual grubby denim, Evan was wearing a heavily-padded black leather jacket, vectored with bronze Aero Zips. It looked as if pulling them all might cause it completely to disappear. It was the silliest garment he had ever seen, although he had to admit it looked good on Evan.

'Nice jacket,' he said. 'Are you off for a spot of falconry?'

Evan's legs extended even further. 'No, we're taking Terry out for a drink.'

'He's thirsty,' Adrea added.

'By George, you're right.' Price examined Terry's quivering form. 'This man isn't Parkinsonian at all! He's just gagging for a pint.'

Getting to their feet, Evan and Adrea fastened the wheelchair straps and wedged Terry's twisted limbs against the arm and foot rests.

'You're not asking my permission, are you?' Price asked. Evan just grinned. 'In that case, go ahead.'

'No one will serve you.' Snow's voice came wailing from the doorway. 'People will be angry. People will be sick to see him.'

Price turned and glared. Snow fell silent, then stepped out of sight.

'We're going down to Midge's,' said Evan, 'to the Eagle and Child. We'll bring him back by half past ten.'

'Terry won't bother them much but I'm not sure about you, my dear.' Price turned to Adrea with a little bow. 'They don't get many ladies in there.'

'I'm not a lady,' she said.

'Girl, then.'

'Woman,' she said with slow emphasis.

'Ah, of course!' Price spread his arms out wide:

'Woman, a pleasing but short-lived flower.

Too soft for business and too weak for power.

A wife in bondage or neglected maid

Despised, if ugly; if she's fair, betrayed!'

'I suppose you wrote that yourself,' said Adrea.

'No. It's by Mary Leapor, an eighteenth-century scullion.'

Price took Evan's arm. The leather felt warm and there seemed to be a mild electric current running through it. 'Look here, young feller-me-lad.' He cranked up his blimpish tone. 'Take a spot of advice from an old hand. Mind you don't go native. It's not at all the done thing, not very pukka, don't you know.'

'That's OK,' said Evan, shaking off the restraining hand. 'God wants us to do it.' As he followed Adrea and the chair towards the front door he saw that Snow was emerging from the kitchen, his arms once again full of chocolate.

From outside, the Eagle and Child was dark and silent, but when Evan opened the door a blast of sound and blaze of light almost knocked Adrea off her feet. This was only the second pub she had ever entered and it was nothing like her father's local. Where were the fireplaces, oak beams, horse brasses and hunting prints? Here the plain walls were decorated only by symmetrical patches of damp and jagged chips, as if from gunfire. It was like walking into a barn or a stable: she was surprised to see that men, rather than cows or horses, were clustered around the bar. Where were the silver tankards and the thick-handled pint mugs? Everyone clutched straight glasses to their chests: the few rickety tables didn't look as if they could bear the weight. Instead of the buzz of polite conversation, the drinkers were yelling but in a curiously benevolent way. They were all men, dressed in drab, heavy clothing. Even in the heat some of them were still wearing flat caps. She wondered if they might start to dance, like the chimney sweeps in *Mary Poppins*.

Every face was turned towards them. Adrea saw the expressions change from curiosity to shock. Silence fell as she pushed the wheelchair towards the bar. The grey carpet was rutted like a country track.

'Fuck me, it's Terry,' a voice said. 'Terry. After all these years.'

Now the faces were smiling and the silence gave way to laughter. Everyone converged on them. 'We thought you were dead, Tel mate.' Evan noticed that, just like the Japanese girls, they were all touching him on the left shoulder.

'How do you all know him?' Adrea asked the nearest man, an Andy Capp type with a half-smoked fag wagging on his lower lip.

'He used to be the landlord here back in the fifties. Best we ever had. This place never closed. He even used to do our breakfasts on the way down to Smithfields.'

Evan was aware that the regulars were regarding him with their usual hostility.

''Ere, where you been keeping Terry?' a very large man inquired.

'They've got him round the corner,' Evan replied. 'We've just sprung him.'

'Good to see you again, Terry,' said Midge. 'Just as long as you're not wanting your old job back.'

By the look on his face, Evan realized that he wasn't joking. He met the midget's dark gaze. 'A pint of snakebite' – he glanced at Terry, then at Adrea – 'and a half of bitter and a double top-and-bottom.'

Adrea was surprised to see the man go straight to the gin and port bottles. 'I didn't think he'd know what it was,' she whispered.

'Nothing's changed,' Andy Capp was saying. He ran his forefinger along the wood panelling and then thrust it proudly under Terry's flaring nostrils. 'Still the same old dust.'

Midge carefully decanted Terry's half into his plastic drinking cup and then screwed the cap back on. 'This is on the house,' he said. In response, everyone began to quiver and drool. 'And so is the lady's.' Midge presented the top-and-bottom with a flourish and then glared along the bar. 'Yours will be on the house too if you can make your-selves look beautiful.' This time, no one made the attempt.

'What about mine?' asked Evan. The midget's eyes bulged like a frog's and his surprisingly large hand came down on top of the pint glass. 'Sixty-eight pence,' he snarled.

Evan went over to the jukebox. There were one or two new additions. Judge Dread's 'Donkey Dick' – a title that Midge had felt no need to tweak – and that terrible Elton John/Kiki Dee duet, 'Don't Go Lighting My Farts', which had lodged itself at the top of the charts. And there was the Patti Smith single. When he put it on she actually sounded to be singing 'Arses' rather than 'Horses'.

One of Terry's old customers was tilting his cup while another, with surprising gentleness, held his head still by fitting both thumbs into his ears and folding his fingers under the chin.

'We'll have another dozen of these,' one said. 'And then I'll get into your wheelchair and you can go home to my missis.'

The whites of Terry's eyes showed as his clawed hands clutched around his groin.

'Oh, you'd like that, would you? Well, you haven't seen my missis lately.'

Midge was not enjoying himself. The heat did not suit him. He glimpsed his face in the cloudy mirror: a prophecy fulfilled – a violet, sweating midget. Also, he was worrying about business: it was too good. The brewery had repainted his sign and were even threatening to put in new carpets and furniture. The place was always packed but no matter how much they drank no one seemed to get drunk. The beer just seemed to leak straight out of their pores: they never needed to piss. There was a desperate atmosphere. People often raised their fists only to let them fall back to their sides. It was even too hot to fight. Disembodied hands emerged from the scrimmage to pay for drinks and carry them away. Midge was sure that they were taking the wrong drinks and the wrong change but nobody ever complained. It was all too much. He remembered that dreadful icy Wednesday in January when no one had come in at all, not even so much as paused at the door. Now he would welcome a few days or even weeks of solitude.

He watched them all clustering around Terry. Everyone still talked about him but Midge knew better than to believe any of the stories. Even so, he regarded the racked figure with some respect. Most cripples were just lead swingers, lounging in their wheelchairs because they were too lazy to walk. They couldn't speak but they opened their mouths for food all right. They'd forgotten their own names although they knew when it was dinnertime. But what Terry was doing was bloody hard work: every nerve and sinew was stretched to breaking point, like an athlete forcing himself through the pain barrier. Being a midget wasn't easy, of course, but once you were there you could just sort of relax into it, whereas this was obviously unrelenting, agonizing effort.

Over in the corner, Evan and Adrea had returned yet again to the subject of the Patti Smith gig. Walking down tonight she had felt a yearning to cross the road to the deserted Roundhouse, in the hope that the band might still be playing on its darkened stage. She still couldn't decide whether it had been fantastic or rubbish, the best or the worst thing she had ever seen.

'It's weird,' said Evan. 'Somehow even the very best gigs – Tim Buckley, J. Geils, MC5, Miles Davis – always felt like anticlimaxes. It seemed that I wasn't there to be knocked out or to pick up a few licks. It was like the same experiment each time, with the same laboratory conditions – stage, lights, amps, instruments – repeated over and over, always missing by a few inches or a mile.'

Adrea sipped at her drink, trying hard not to make a face. It tasted disgusting but she had to learn to like it because this stuff had been Lady Day's tipple of choice.

'I saw Hendrix once,' Evan continued. 'On the Band of Gypsies tour. He was literally unbelievable. I think my eyes and ears were bleeding, I couldn't speak for hours afterwards. But even then I realized that it hadn't been what I was waiting for. It had been like a glimpse of life on another planet – strange, fantastic, awe-inspiring but nothing to do with me.

'Now Patti can't sing. She can't dance. Her band are ugly and can hardly play. They haven't even got any songs – she just yells over the top of some old bubblegum riffs. They haven't got a stage act and even their shoes are crap. And that feedback section was the lamest thing I've ever heard. But during their set I realized that *this was it*. I could feel it here' – he gestured towards his stomach or perhaps his groin – 'and here' – he pointed at his head. 'And I knew that the experiment had been successful and' – he put a finger into his mouth and popped his cheek – 'the atom had finally split.'

The side door next to them creaked open with a blast of even hotter air and they saw with astonishment that the three Stooges were entering the pub. In their shapeless grey dresses they seemed to be floating above the ground like souls rising up for the last judgement. Then Frances, almost enveloped by a belted cardigan, led in another group of women, followed by five of the men, dressed in identical dark suits with too-tight jackets and too-loose trousers. Then Mrs Parker appeared and Mrs Barker, both walking unaided but with their backs bent and legs wide apart, as if balanced by invisible Zimmers. Last of all came Price, his shoulders still shaking with laughter at the pub's signboard. That musclebound baby, rolling on its back, looked like it might give the plummeting eagle a nasty surprise.

'Poor old Snowy's done for,' he said. 'We left him eating his own chocolate.'

'How did you all get down here?' Evan asked.

'In the minibus, of course.'

Evan saw that a large blue van had been pulled up on to the pavement outside. 'Are you just going to leave it there?'

'I've got a sticker,' said Price, 'I can park anywhere.'

'I didn't know there was a minibus,' said Adrea. 'And I didn't know you could drive.'

'I can't,' said Price, his smile widening as he caught sight of the landlord. 'I just aim it and shut my eyes.'

It was many years since Price had been in a pub. Drinking had become a solitary activity and he had forgotten the pleasures of shoulder-charging his way across a crowded room.

'Good evening, mine host,' he boomed, slapping both palms down on the wet bar top. Midge did not respond. 'Twelve medium dry sherries and five halves of mild,' Price continued in an even heartier tone. 'And as I'm driving, I'll just have' – he expertly scanned the optics – 'a treble Old Paddy, no water, no ice.'

As Price distributed the drinks he was amused to see how Midge kept glaring in Evan's direction, although the boy was too preoccupied with Adrea to notice. The scene reminded him of Mime and Siegfried, no, it was more as if the two of them might have been where Wagner had got the idea. He had recently come across the word dwarfling, meaning a small dwarf. Did their fellows, he wondered, look up to or down on these creatures? Were all their aspirations inverted? Something told him that asking the man would not be a good idea.

Among the flesh postcards pinned behind the bar, Price saw an old favourite from the British Museum print room: a Cruickshank cartoon entitled 'Born a Genius and Born a Dwarf'. He remembered that it had been hanging on the opposite wall to *Eternity is Temporary*. It depicted the differing fortunes of the nineteenth-century painter Benjamin Robert Haydon and the celebrated midget General Tom Thumb when they were both appearing at London's Egyptian Hall. Haydon's *Nero* and *Aristides* were displayed in the lobby while the General performed upstairs.

The artist took seven pounds. The midget six hundred. The cartoon showed Haydon – unhealthily fleshy, as if starvation merely piled on weight to tax him even further – in despair, sobbing into his hands. His garret's sole decoration was a huge plaster foot, presumably from the Elgin Marbles, which he had so magically described and drawn. Tom Thumb, in contrast, sat in a luxurious banqueting hall, attended by servants, while his liveried coach-and-four waited outside.

'It's a sad tale,' Price said to Midge. 'It broke Haydon. He shot himself in the head but it failed to kill him so he crawled into the kitchen and finished the job with the bread knife. As Elizabeth Barrett Browning said. "Laocoon's anguish was an infant's sleep, compared to his."'

Midge looked him up and down. You could have clothed half a dozen midgets with the material from that suit. Before the man had even opened his mouth, he had his measure: just one more of those grumbling pathetic geniuses. 'It was all his own fault,' he finally responded. 'He should have gone upstairs and asked to paint the General.'

'A splendid idea,' said Price. 'Tom Thumb sitting in the flames of

Rome twanging his lyre. It's strange to think that hardly anyone then knew who Haydon was, whereas now – a century later, with the infallible judgement of posterity – absolutely nobody remembers him while everyone still knows General Tom Thumb. If the poor devil had guessed he would have cut his own throat a second time.'

Price joined the old people mingling with the regulars. They all seemed different from their usual Heron Close selves. Frances, her sherry glass elegantly angled like some society hostess, was chatting away to a wild-eyed man in an earth-stained donkey jacket. Price suspected that the conversation might be taking a certain turn, however, when her companion began to finger his whiskery chin. Mrs Barker was in her element: her fingers seemed to be holding up a perpetually flaring match. Judging by the laughter, one sip of Bristol Cream had transformed Mrs Parker into her Algonquin namesake, Dorothy. The three Stooges and their beaux seemed to be trying out the steps of some long-forgotten dance, while the five men had started up a darts game. The arrows were actually landing on the board and they were chalking up their scores.

Snow had been wrong. Nobody was angered or disgusted by the residents. On the other hand, their appearance had not had the effect that he himself had been anticipating. It should have been something like Poe's 'Masque of the Red Death' where the embodiment of the plague abruptly materializes in the midst of Prince Prospero's orgy: there should have been at least a smidgen of horror and dismay. Perhaps this was a better, kinder world than he had thought? Perhaps he was going to have to revise his misanthropy? He drained his glass and began savagely to fight his way back to the bar.

Two men were talking at once to Mrs Parker. She had no idea what they were saying so she just shook or nodded her head by turns, agreeing with one then disagreeing with the other. She felt oddly reassured by Mrs Barker's presence: at least someone was keeping an eye on her, even if it was an evil one.

Mrs Barker wasn't making much sense of the conversation either. She had the impression that there was a war on and that it had something to do with the sun. Perhaps someone had learned how to control it and was using it as a weapon? Or had it declared war on us? If so, the earth was doomed because the sun wouldn't be scared of atomic bombs.

Adrea realized that everything in the room had gone fuzzy. The people around her were like heat photographs: she couldn't hear them any more, nor could she make out what was playing on the jukebox. Maybe it was the effect of the top-and-bottom? Only Evan's low voice was audible, only his face was in focus.

The largest blur detached itself and floated across the room towards them. Adrea unwillingly registered that it was Price, carrying another tray of drinks. She waited for him to say something sarcastic, but instead he smiled at her with an openness that she would not have thought possible on that face. He suddenly seemed much younger. This made her twice as wary of him.

'So,' said Price, enveloping the bar stool opposite them, 'how are things down at Tolmers Square?'

'We're in no rush to get back,' said Evan. 'I'm afraid I decked a couple of my housemates this morning.'

'Why did you do that?'

'It's a long story' – Evan scratched his left ear – 'concerning a jar of Marmite.'

Price remembered how, in his long-distant student days, he had triggered a similar Armageddon by lathering a slice of toast with someone else's Golden Shred.

'I can see why you might be worried,' he said.

'Oh no' – Evan scratched again – 'I'm just worried about what I might do to them next.'

'I'm moving down to the matron's flat,' Price said. 'So you can use my old place in the attic, if you like.' He turned to Adrea. 'You're only here for another three weeks. No one will know so long as you're quiet. And you'll have to use the back stairs. We wouldn't want to upset Snowy, would we?'

'No,' said Adrea, seriously.

At this moment, Molly, Polly and Dolly entered the pub. They moved slowly, wonderingly, across the space that cleared in front of them. All conversation ceased and even the jukebox seemed to break off. A faint haze surrounded them, like dry ice: they could be heard cooing, like sleepy doves in a summer cote. As they passed, they touched each face with their long, delicate fingers, as if searching for some familiar configuration. Price was struck by the expressions of the people along the bar. It was as though the Babies were the long-lost mothers of every man in the place. Resignedly, he chugged his old Paddy: reality had outmanoeuvred him once again.

The silence was broken by a chorus of ribald whoops and wolf-whistles as Bridie followed the Babies in. Molly, Polly and Dolly, recognizing Terry, greeted him with ecstatic gurglings.

'So will theirs be on the house as well?' someone asked.

'They don't need drinks,' said Midge. 'They've got there already without them.'

fifteen

'I'm afraid I can't make head nor tail of this, Snowy,' said Price, leaning back perilously in his chair to plant two enormous brogues on the office desk. 'Does it have something to do with owls?'

He had forgotten Snow's threat to lodge an official complaint about Evan until now, five weeks later, when the man had finished compiling it. The red ink letters had an agonized look: some were squared as if traced along a tiny ruler, while others shook like the title credits of a horror film.

'This word, for example,' said Price. 'Is it onion or orion?'

'Opinion,' said Snow. 'It says, "in my opinion".'

'Two n's and two i's in there, old man.'

Holding the pages up to the light, Price read on. '"In my opion he is unsuted for care assistant. He drinks on duty, distresing staff and residents. He is also a bad timekeper."' He tapped his forefinger against the wall rota. 'How can coming in early and leaving late be bad timekeeping?'

'Because they are not *his* times! He is here when he is not supposed to be!' Snow was almost shouting. 'They are always in here! It is not right that they are always in here now!'

'They live nearby,' Price interrupted. 'Just like you. They drop in when they're passing.'

'They live up there,' Snow said bitterly, pointing at the ceiling.

'No, they don't, Snowy,' said Price. 'No one lives up there.' With a sigh he read on. '"He takes the residents out of the bulding at night without permison. He allows them to rome unsupervised."'

'This is indeed serious, Snowy.' In the wide margin Price drew a helmeted centurion's head with a thought balloon containing the word 'Roam'. 'I was not aware that any of them had made it as far as the Eternal City.'

The final page was covered with snaking columns of figures under the headings In Toilet/Outside/Ignored Order/Left Bulding/Siting and Lying Down.

'I never knew you were a poet, Snowy.'

'It is not supposed to be poetry,' said Snow, bitterly. 'Every word is true.'

'I'm afraid the spelling and syntax will have to be corrected before I can authorize this.' Price let the report fall on to the desk. 'One query, though. How can you complain about Evan without complaining about Adrea as well?'

'She is not the problem,' said Snow, putting the pages back in sequence and replacing their paperclip. 'He is the bad influence.'

'I forgot to mention' – Price slapped his forehead in self-reproof – 'that all the relief team are suffering from heat stroke. Fortunately our esteemed young colleagues have volunteered to help out tonight until the night staff arrive.'

'I will not work with that boy,' said Snow.

'You have no choice,' said Price.

'Why can't you do it?'

'I?' Price flicked imaginary dust off his toe-caps. 'I do not feed people or tuck them up in bed. I am the matron here.'

Snow headed for the door, clutching the report to his heart as if, having been shot, he was using it to staunch the wound. When he turned back he looked to be on the verge of tears. 'It isn't natural!'

'What isn't, old lad?'

'This' – Snow clutched at the air, as though trying to catch a passing fly – 'weather!'

For a moment Price almost felt sorry for him. 'Have you ever heard of a Bodhisattva?' he asked.

Snow shook his head.

'It's a Buddhist concept,' Price continued. 'A soul which, having reached Nirvana, then declines it, remaining on earth to help the benighted rest of humanity. There's this vow that they take: "Although the souls of the creatures are numberless I vow to save them!"'

'There are no souls or creatures to save here,' said Snow, backing out into the corridor. 'Only old people.'

In the sitting room, Mrs Parker could not tell what the two men were arguing about but she knew that they must both be in the wrong. The office door slammed and Mr Snow, his face like thunder, moved jerkily past, as if being prodded from behind.

A few seconds later, with a loud hiss, Stormy shot round the corner. His tail was lashing and a ridge of fur had lifted along his back. She watched him warily, for it was the cat's habit to take out his anger on the nearest person, but he went down the corridor, his unsheathed claws clacking against the linoleum.

Mrs Parker was not best pleased with Stormy. In the last few days she had seen very little of him: as soon as he had gobbled up his titbits he would disappear again. She had assumed that this was Mrs Yu-No-Hu's doing but it had become apparent that her rival was receiving similar treatment. Had they been too don't-care-ish or not don't-care-ish enough?

She put down her needles and shook out the wool. A blur at the edge of her vision told her that Yu-No-Hu was doing exactly the same thing. At first she had thought that the woman was copying her but now she had to admit that their movements appeared to be simultaneous. They were obviously attuned in some way. Of one thing she was certain: *she* would never follow anyone's lead. She contemplated her hands: they were fine when in motion but as soon as she stopped knitting they stiffened up. Liver-spotted, yellowish and slightly slimy-looking, they reminded her of a chicken's claws. She shut her eyes. Inside herself she felt no different, as if she had never been young or old or even in between. As if, throughout her life, she had been just Mrs Parker, except of course for those years when she had been Miss Woods.

Taking up their needles, the two women unpicked a dozen rows. There was no point in finishing: Price and Snow had never been seen to wear any of the things that had been fashioned for them. Nowadays the wool's shape shifted from sweater to scarf to giant sock: sleeves and collars emerged then vanished, holes opened up only to close again. Whereas Mrs Parker had formerly been knitting for Nobby and Mrs Barker for Terry, the never-to-be-completed garments were now designated for Evan and Adrea. They both knew that the young people would not be wearing them, it was more that, while they were knitting, they had them in their minds.

There was something strange about those two, Mrs Parker felt, but she still wasn't quite sure what. Perhaps it was that they seemed more and more to resemble each other. They both moved lazily but with surprising speed, appearing simultaneously to be lagging behind and ahead of themselves. Their voices rose at the end of each sentence, as if everything they said were a question, although they never waited for a reply. They seemed to breathe in and out together but they blinked alternately, as though communicating by secret code. What really struck her, though, was that they had the same smell. Adrea smelt like half a boy and Evan smelt like half a girl. She told herself that it was only to be expected when they ate the same food, shared the same soap and even wore each other's clothes, but it still worried her. Your smell was like your soul: you shouldn't go mixing it up or giving it away. There was plenty in the wedding vows about having and holding and honouring and obeying but nothing about smells.

All morning Mrs Barker had been fighting off a yawn. She had not been sleeping well, dropping off as usual and then waking, ready for the day, to discover that the room was still dark, with only a few minutes having elapsed. She would spend the rest of the night trying to go back to sleep. Perhaps she only felt tired because the bedside clock told her she should? She would lie there, listening to the noises: whenever she turned over they ceased, only to begin again a minute or so later.

First there was a creak, which gradually turned into a squeak, then back again, squeak-creak, creak-squeak. It seemed to pass slowly above her head until it hit the far wall, when the squeak-creak-squeak became an insistent rapping, moving down to enter her wardrobe. At this point, back at the far side of the ceiling, the single creak started again and the whole process repeated itself at an ever-faster rate, until the taps swelled to an insistent knocking, as if someone were trapped inside. 'Ron?' she would say, although she couldn't imagine why he might be there. 'Ron?' A dozen times a night she would get out of bed but the wardrobe remained empty.

Sometimes she would unlock the secret drawer at the back of the wardrobe. Every resident had one, for items of value or personal significance. Although theirs was supposed to be the only key, everyone knew that Snow had duplicates. It was said that the Babies' drawers – for which they had, of course, long since lost their keys – had once been crammed with silver and gold. Mrs Barker's own secret place contained boxes and books of matches. Nobody had ever suspected that she kept every match she struck, carefully returning the blackened sticks to their box. Sometimes, in the darkness, she would take out one of her collection and slide it open. Purely by smell, she could identify and date every one.

Mrs Barker allowed herself a quick glance around the sitting room. Although the sun was shining and she was aware of the sweat from her forehead dripping on to the wool, her toes felt chilly. Mrs Parker's big slippers looked suddenly attractive. Perhaps she could buy herself a pair in a different tartan, one belonging to a rival, hostile clan? She saw that Price had left the office. In passing, he gave a little nod – which she pretended not to have seen – then as usual turned right, forgetting that he no longer lived on the top floor. It was odd that after he had gone up he did not come back down again. She had never trusted him. Behind his dark glasses and good manners she suspected that he was evil in mysterious ways that she didn't care to guess at. In contrast, she had always quite liked Mr Snow, but now, after the way he had flared up at Stormy, she was angry with him, too. His attitude to some of the other residents had never bothered her – in her experience most people deserved what they got – but animals were a different matter. On the other hand, Stormy was well able to look after himself: Mr Snow had better watch out.

As he made for the attic, Price was sure that there was something different about the back stairs. They seemed to have become steeper, as if re-set at variable angles, and shrouded in darkness, as though the windows had receded. His footsteps rolled and echoed round the well. He felt suddenly that he had never climbed these stairs before.

He had been surprised at how quickly he had settled into the matron's flat. His fears that people would always be bothering him had proved unfounded. He soon ceased to register Squibbsy's meal-time howling, although he still wondered why the smell of cabbage wafted up from the kitchen when it had never been on the menu. He no longer lay on his bed all the time: now he would pace from room to room, arms outstretched, revelling in all this new space. His eyes remained shut, of course, because as soon as he had taken possession of his new home, the image of the policewoman had returned, as if she had been awaiting him there. Sometimes he would walk backwards so that she seemed to be pursuing him. He knew better than to interrogate her again: he would wait for her to make the next move.

As he opened the door to the top landing, the music swept over him. It wasn't good old Gustav or Franz now, just a godawful thumping that set the fillings in his teeth aching. 'Well, come on!' sneered the singer. 'Come on!' Taking this as an invitation, Price walked straight in without knocking.

A blanket had been pinned across the window so that at first the only light appeared to be a glowing coal floating in mid-air at the far side of the room. As his eyes adjusted Price realized that it was the end of an enormous marijuana cigarette. Evan, kneeling on the bed, stripped to the waist, was holding it between his fists, so that it pointed skywards like a rocket, noisily drawing the smoke down into the cave of his hands. Adrea, tightly wrapped in a sheet, lay behind him.

'And how are my apocalyptic adolescents today?' Price asked.

Without answering, Evan passed the joint over. Price took a huge gurgling toke, as if trying to draw it right down into his boots. Twenty seconds later, when he exhaled, no smoke came out. Evan regarded him with a new respect.

'Do try to be more discreet,' said Price. 'Half the residents are high on your fumes. You could turn the music down, too.'

'There's only Mrs Barker underneath,' said Evan. 'And she's deaf or something.'

'Or something,' agreed Price. With a shudder of distaste he moved a pile of comics – *Howard the Duck Versus the Mighty Thor*, indeed! – to sit down on the only chair.

Adrea turned over, setting the bed springs creaking and groaning. Under Price's own bulk they had always remained silent, despite his bad dreams. Her face was pale, with a milky radiance, and the lips were parted in a beatific smile. Price had often reflected on how innocent and peaceful women looked when they were pretending to be asleep and how they scowled, drooled and grunted when they actually were. He produced a small camera from the folds of his suit but Evan, leaning forward, clapped his hand over the lens.

'Don't you know you should never photograph someone when they're asleep?'

'She's not asleep.'

'Oh yes I am,' said Adrea.

'No fun!' the singer kept shouting. 'To be alone.' He managed to bestow four syllables on the final word: 'A-lo-wa-na!'

'Do you actually like this stuff?' Price asked.

Evan just cocked his head on one side and rolled his eyes, like Terry.

'I suspect that your young lady' – Price adopted a piercing whisper – 'is merely humouring you.'

'No I'm not,' said the sleeping Adrea. 'I love it.'

'You've got to be young to appreciate it,' said Evan.

'When you start thinking of yourself as young, my boy,' Price boomed, 'it's a certain indication that you no longer are. Like a tightrope walker who looks down the instant before he falls.'

Evan struck a match and then made four frog-like leaps to light a candle stub in each corner of the room.

'I'm surprised you don't like the Stooges,' he said, taking the record off. 'I had you down as an old Ted. Gene Vincent? Vince Taylor? No, I bet you were really into the Big O.'

Price retrieved the joint. 'Do you mean nothingness, the void?'

'No. Roy Orbison. You know, "Pretty Woman".' He gave a tiger growl. '"In Dreams". "A candy-coloured clown they call the sandman",' he crooned, then yelled, '"It's over! It's over! It's over!"'

'I'm afraid I don't know what you're talking about,' said Price, in a tone of apparently genuine sorrow and regret. He looked around his former home. Apart from the white rectangles along the wall where his postcards had been pinned, his seven years of occupancy had left no mark. *Eternity is Temporary*, however, was still hanging below the window.

'You forgot your picture,' said Evan.

'No,' said Price. 'I left it here for you. To make the place more homely.'

'It looks like some terrible Jethro Tull album cover; old hippies seeing the writing on the wall.' Evan idly traced the lines with his fingers. 'What does it mean?'

'I have no idea,' said Price.

In one fluid movement, Adrea escaped the sheet and stood upright. She was wearing a faded blue T-shirt with a black design of Clara Bow, the 'It' girl on the front. Her legs were thicker and sturdier than Price had imagined.

'*Eternity is Temporary*,' Evan read. 'Maybe it's like Thelonious Monk's "Wrong is Right" – that's what he replied when they accused him of playing bum notes.'

Price watched Adrea traversing the room. Behind her knees, long, deep vertical creases appeared and disappeared, opened then closed. Did other people's legs do that? If so, he was sure that he would have noticed before now. He was pleased to realize he had not been ogling her bottom or thighs.

Adrea breathed on the glass and then rubbed it with her sleeve, but the picture still made no sense. There was something indefinably repulsive about it, as if everything – the trees, stone and flesh – had been moulded out of the same soft spongy matter. A wave of queasiness rose from her stomach. Perhaps these curious figures might be squatting in there, like in that science fiction film, *Fantastic Voyage*. Sally still claimed to have nightmares in which a shrunken Raquel Welch and Donald Pleasance, with his very pale blue eyes, were navigating a midget sub around her internal organs.

'Do you think there's an afterlife, Adrea?' Price asked.

'I've never thought about it,' she replied. 'But I don't see why not. Perhaps eternity will be all our best moments run together so that there are no more gaps in between.'

'Why not our worst moments?' asked Evan.

'The Greeks and the Norsemen believed that those who die bravely in battle, striking with a sword, go straight to paradise,' observed Price.

'You can imagine them,' said Evan, 'Hector and Achilles staggering around heaven, covered in blood, with spears and arrows sticking out of them.'

'But suppose those who die a coward's death remain cowards for ever?' Price continued. 'Suppose that we enter eternity just the way we are when we die? We'll think we've escaped but then find we haven't. Imagine being old for ever, or getting older still and not being able to die. Or imagine being Molly or Polly or Dolly in perpetuity.'

'I think that might be fun,' said Adrea.

'So it's live fast, die young and leave a good-looking corpse, is it?' asked Evan. 'Like Hendrix or Brian Jones or the Romantic poets.'

'But Keats was ugly,' said Price. 'And Byron got fat.'

'And he and Shelley were well over thirty,' said Adrea, through the closing bathroom door. 'And Wordsworth, who was the best of them, turned horrible and lived to eighty.'

Price heard her turn on the shower to cover the sound of her relieving herself. Only now did he notice that Stormy was sitting in the corner, next to Evan's discarded boots. He was facing the wall, with eyes shut and paws folded, as if staking out a mouse hole. The now unoccupied bed continued to creak and sigh and the metal base still tapped upon the floor. Price observed that the line of light under the door had now been broken. Poor old Snowy; even his shadow was crooked. Evan toked on the joint and then tiptoed over to blast a mouthful of smoke through the keyhole. There was no curse or cry from the other side, no sound of receding footsteps: the shadow just disappeared.

'Nothing ever lasts, you know,' Price heard himself saying, to his own surprise. '*Alles endet was entstehet alles, alles rings vergehet.*'

Evan reprised his Big O tiger growl. 'I know it doesn't make sense but I sort of believe that it's always going to be like this. I'm never going to change. Nothing is ever going to change.'

'I felt the same way once,' said Price. 'But it happens to us all. Whether you repress them or indulge them, all your appetites gradually become dulled. Everything becomes second nature, automatic, like breathing.'

'I've never got used to breathing,' said Evan. 'I keep hearing this strange noise and wondering what it might be. I start panting or holding my breath to see what happens. My own body still feels unfamiliar to me: every time I look at my hands they seem different, as if they belong to someone else – no, to a long succession of other people.'

Price noticed that Evan's bare feet were covered with scabs and blisters, and that the arches were red raw. Those boots obviously took some wearing. Perhaps it was the snakes, taking their revenge?

'Is there really nothing you still take pleasure in?' asked Evan.

'Music,' said Price. '*Proper* music. And books. And, above all, good clothes. The feel rather than the look of them. I like to dress up when I'm not going anywhere. No one else will ever see my best suit.'

'That's pathetic,' said Adrea, re-emerging, fully dressed.

'I know,' said Price. 'It's intended to be.'

'Can I ask you something?' Evan said. 'Were you ever in love?'

'Of course. In fact, I rather suspect that I might be in love at the moment.'

Adrea took a couple of steps back towards the bathroom.

'It's no one you know,' said Price reassuringly. 'She's in the police. I haven't seen her for a while.'

Adrea's expression was at once relieved and disgusted, as if her worst suspicions had just been confirmed.

'It's the uniform,' Price continued. 'And the handcuffs. Such things have always appealed to me.' He saw that Adrea had pinned her hair up. From the side she looked ten years older and from the front five years younger. How did women manage it? How sad it was that one became used even to such things. 'Thanks for offering to help out this evening.' Without choking, Price continued to draw on the burning roach. 'I need hardly tell you that Mr Snow is not in the least grateful. I should also warn you about the cook: he is not the forgiving type and he has access to your food.'

'We haven't eaten a single mouthful from that kitchen,' said Adrea.

Price sighed. 'Why do you feel you have to keep stirring everything up?'

'Maybe things are stirring themselves up,' said Evan. 'Why should the ressies be left to live like this just because they're old?'

'Age has nothing to do with it,' said Price. 'They're just people. And there's no point in trying to make them think and feel.'

'What else is there to life except thinking and feeling?' asked Adrea.

'Eating and shitting are quite enough for most of the human race.' Price reluctantly discarded his stub of blackened cardboard. 'Your thoughts and emotions are the sworn enemies of the digestion.'

'How can you let them just sit there and rot?' Adrea's tiny head jerked. 'Why does no one ever take them out anywhere?'

'But I've just been arranging that very thing,' said Price smoothly. 'After the success of your pub therapy initiative and the re-forging of meaningful links with the local community, I thought we should spread our wings a little and go to the zoo.'

'Why the zoo?' asked Adrea suspiciously.

'It's close,' said Price. 'In case of emergencies. A fifteen-minute journey is quite enough for them. And it's quiet. In this heat all the usual tourist spots are apparently deserted. And it's full of animals: everyone likes animals.'

Adrea still looked doubtful. 'There won't be room for them all in the minibus.'

'I've booked a luxury coach. With a driver. In a peaked cap.' Price's tone implied that the cap ruled out any possible further objections.

Stormy began to scratch at the door, obviously sensing that dinner-time was approaching.

'When you walk out of here in a couple of weeks' time,' said Price, 'do you seriously think you'll ever give any of the residents another thought?'

'Actually, we're thinking about staying a bit longer. I can always postpone my college place until next year or the year after that.'

Price let the cat out and then paused in the doorway. 'Be honest. You don't really care about any of them, do you?'

'Not really,' said Adrea, looking hard at Evan, not at Price. 'But it's probably because we don't care that we feel we have to do anything we can to help them.'

Price followed Stormy's enormous tail down the stairs. The Bodhisattva vow! It was just as he had suspected. All love and compassion, every worthwhile word and deed came out of that death of the self. The only true action followed the extinction of all calculations and needs, when there could no longer be anything whatsoever in it for you. Price had once prided himself on his lofty indifference but now he had to admit that he wasn't don't-care-ish at all. He cared so much that it paralysed him, that he couldn't even admit it to himself. He recalled how he had sneeringly compared the residents' emergence onto the sunlit terrace to Beethoven's Prisoners' Chorus.

Now he acknowledged that this was, in fact, *exactly* what it had been like.'O *welche lust*!'

In *Fidelio*, Leonora's actions finally free those convicts, bring down an evil regime and institute a new age of freedom and justice, but all these things are quite incidental to her sole purpose – to be reunited with her imprisoned husband Florestan. She has changed the world without intending to, probably without even noticing.

In the same way, Evan and Adrea were blissfully unaware of what they were doing and why they were doing it. Although objectively they were merely a striking-looking couple doing nothing in particular – Price, when he was in their presence, kept doubting the evidence of his own eyes. It was as if their very existence gave him some respite from being himself. As if they were a fire at which even the most wretched, frozen passer-by could momentarily warm his hands.

Downstairs, Mr Snow had not been enjoying his shift. He was counting down the minutes to dinnertime, both wanting to get it over with and hoping that it would never come. Everyone had been staring at him, as if there were something wrong with his face or clothes. When he went down to the kitchen, the dog had suddenly recovered its bark, if not its bite. Then the cat had yowled and, without provocation, clawed at his trousers. Elastic-waisted Farahs were not cheap: Snow had laboriously entered it in the accident book and filled out a claim form. Throughout the shift a large wasp kept returning to circle his nose, but whenever he rolled up his newspaper it vanished. They were all the same – old people and young people, cats and dogs, even insects – when you were down they all lined up to kick you.

He watched Price and Stormy coming down the corridor. They both ignored him, which was some improvement. Price's thin lips were pursed in a silent whistle as if he were attempting to look casual so that nobody would know where he had just been. The cat had forced its mouth into the same shape and was also copying that slow, heavy-footed walk. What kind of matron was this, that even cats would laugh at?

Adrea's unmistakeable figure appeared on the far side of the court-yard. After she had taken a few steps Evan followed from the shadows of the adjoining passageway. Snow's forehead leaned against the cool window pane while his feet hacked at the skirting board. Who did they think they were fooling with such tricks? He knew that they had gone down the back stairs and out of the fire door, squeezing past the huge dustbins into the cobbled alley, then turning right then left then right so that finally, after clambering over a low wall, they emerged as if coming from the bus-stop or tube station. Snow watched as they met at the bottom of the ramp, with expressions of polite surprise, as if it had been twenty-four hours since they last saw each other rather than half a minute, and they were just work colleagues instead of what they really were. That boy had not even bothered to button up his shirt. Their mouths appeared to be whistling the same silent tune as Price and the cat.

Mrs Parker was crossing the hall as they entered. 'You shouldn't be here,' she said.

'We're substituting for the relief team,' said Adrea.

'No' – Mrs Parker lowered her voice and jerked her head in Snow's direction – 'you shouldn't be here at all.'

Snow had turned his back on them. Evan walked straight over and tapped him on the shoulder. 'It's a pleasure to be working with you at last,' he said when the man whirled round. Before Snow knew what was happening he was shaking Evan's hand. There was something terribly wrong about them being there together, Mrs Parker thought, as if they belonged to different ages. It was like watching the distant past and the far-off future meeting here in the present.

She followed her Zimmer frame into the dining room. At least the music coming from the matron's flat was nicer these days – or, rather, nasty in a different, quieter way. She had almost forgotten Mrs Allen until a postcard had been handed round that morning. It was of palm-trees in Tahiti. 'Having a wonderful time – wish you were here', read the spidery scrawl. The effect had been spoiled when Price pointed out that it had been posted in Neasden the previous afternoon.

Within a few minutes the dining room was full. Now that the food had improved everybody got to their places with time to spare. Mrs Parker wondered why Adrea was suddenly putting herself to the trouble of lifting Terry out of his wheelchair and on to an ordinary seat at the table. Was it to give him more dignity? Perhaps it was right that human beings should do different things in different chairs? However, watching Adrea's gentle but firm attempts to re-arrange those tormented limbs, she wondered whether the girl might perhaps be turning into a Terry twiddler.

A terrible whistling and howling announced that dinner was on its way: since Evan's descent the dumb-waiter had never been the same. Adrea insisted on apportioning the food. She had a flair for composition: the potatoes, vegetables and lamb chops were swiftly arrayed as if ready for painters of the Camden Town School to drop by. Evan could swear that each plate had exactly the same number of peas and slices of carrot but always in subtly different alignments. All he was permitted to do was to pour the gravy directly on to the meat, as instructed.

Watching Evan and Adrea serving the food was making Mrs

Barker tired. They seemed to be moving around at even more than their usual headlong pace. Perhaps they were trying to impress Mr Snow? If so, she could have told them that they were wasting their time. Even in this heat, neither was sweating or short of breath. There were no blotches on their skins: his remained matt white, hers matt brown, as if painted. The nose and ears, the neck and forearms were all of exactly the same hue. They moved even faster, then faster still, so that they seemed to blur, then vanish altogether. It was as though a mighty and silent wind were blowing the plates around the room to deposit them unerringly between every knife and fork.

'Nice,' Adrea kept mouthing to Evan. 'Be nice.' It seemed to be working. Snow had taken his food and seated himself among the residents. He was even talking to them and helping them to salt, pepper and gravy. When, for the third time, Terry slid off his chair, Snow actually went to Adrea's aid, and there flickered across his face something that might have been a smile.

Evan wondered whether the cook hoped that, by preparing food that was obviously too good for the residents, he would mortify them so much that they choked on it. If so, his plan had failed: they gobbled it all up and then asked for more. The gravy – thicker and darker than usual, with chunks of caramelised onion floating in it – was particularly in demand.

How quietly they ate! If you shut your eyes you would never have guessed that seventy people were in the room. What must it be like to eat with those silent, nerveless plastic teeth, tasting the food without feeling it? Evan didn't fear incontinence or loss of memory and hair, but he hoped he would not outlive his own teeth.

Adrea signalled for more gravy. It seemed to be driving the ressies crazy: some of the men were even drinking it directly from the jug. Evan had grabbed a replacement and was skidding down the aisle when he suddenly stopped, transfixed. He had caught sight of Snow's neck. In contrast to the face's orange-peel complexion it was grey, cross-hatched with fine white down. The skin looked to be stretched to bursting point by curious knots and protuberances, more like a knee than a neck. Evan moved closer, half-expecting to see '*Temporalis Aeternitas*' written on the nape but there was only a scattering of freckles in the exact disposition of Ursa Major. Between it and the stiff cream collar was a half-inch gap: the gravy jug twitched in his hands as if it were alive. Adrea, sensing danger, looked up from feeding the Babies. 'Be nice,' she mouthed, but this wasn't about being nasty. It was nothing personal, thought Evan, it was simply the only thing to be done in the circumstances. Jug and collar, gravy and neck were somehow fated to come together.

Slowly and carefully, Evan began to pour, bending at the knee and bowing his head as if performing some libation rite. The gravy gurgled merrily as if being sucked inside. It was a surprisingly long time before Snow reacted, so that when he finally yelled and sprang sideways – landing a couple of yards away, bent as though still sitting on his chair – a good half of the liquid was gone.

'Sorry, Deputy Matron,' said Evan. 'An accident.'

Snow did not turn to look at him but stared instead at Adrea. Slowly he straightened up. To Evan's eyes he seemed to have become a few inches taller.

'It burns,' he said, in a surprisingly deep and calm voice. 'It burns.'

In horror, Evan plunged his fingers into the jug: the gravy was stone cold.

'I am a human being not a pot on the stove.' Snow's voice grew in volume with every word. 'Every day is hotter. What has happened to all the clouds?' He aimed a punch at the ceiling but it fell well short. 'I am the Deputy Matron not somebody's servant. People are here when they shouldn't be and then aren't when they should. They come and go as they please. First they say yes then they say no, then they say yes and no at the same time.'

Evan was wondering where all the gravy had gone. Snow's shirt was unstained and nothing dribbled from his trouser bottoms. It had been like putting petrol in a tank.

Now Snow was shouting. 'I tell the truth! I tell the truth but no one listens because I cannot spell! And so I have to throw away six dozen bars of finest chocolate! And now they're all going to the zoo! The zoo! As if they aren't animals enough!'

The dramatic effect was heightened by a large wasp buzzing round his nose. To Adrea's eyes it appeared to be flying in one nostril and then out of the other.

Snow himself had no idea what he was saying: he was only aware of the sound. It was as if some creature sleeping in his gut had finally woken up and begun to howl. He could feel each word rising through his stomach and throat finally to burst out of his mouth.

'It's disgusting what you do!' Taking a step forward, he pointed at Adrea. 'Sitting there smiling as if everything is a big joke. Smiling as though you know everything when it's everyone that knows everything about you!'

The jabbing finger had been replaced by a fist that raised itself threateningly above Snow's head. Then, as if the arm couldn't support its weight, it fell. The left knee jerked up so that his blow landed on the fleshy upper part of his own leg.

'Everyone knows about your touchings! Everyone knows about your sneakings! Everyone knows why you open doors and close them! Everyone hears you when you tiptoe on the stairs! You think you're nice and safe and secret in your attic but everyone hears you, everyone sees you, everyone smells you! It's disgusting what you do!'

His voice buffered Adrea like a gale. She assumed her most don't-care-ish expression, even though his spittle was hitting her burning cheeks.

'When God has given you good things it means that you must always be good. If you are right then you must never be wrong. But you are making beautiful things ugly! You are making clean things dirty!' The fist smashed down on his leg again and again. 'Ugly! Ugly! Ugly! Dirty! Dirty! Dirty!'

Someone had begun slowly to clap their hands. No, there were two of them, sounding together from opposite sides of the room. Although Mrs Parker and Mrs Barker's palms were travelling only a short distance, their impact cracked and echoed like rifle fire. Then Terry's body twisted right up against the table to set the cutlery rattling. Some of the residents started slamming their water beakers down on to the Formica, while others held up their side plates and belaboured them with the bowls of their spoons. It was as if they had been rehearsing for a long time, ready for this moment. Their unseen feet were stamping in unison but there were also other sounds of obscure origin, like a pack of hounds closing on its quarry. Snow was spinning around, his hands clapped over his ears. His mouth was still moving but his voice could no longer be heard.

In the matron's flat, Price was aware that all hell had broken loose next door. First Snowy had been yelling and then some sort of chari-vari had started up. His on-call reflexes, however, had not been engaged. This was apparently not a crisis in which he needed to inter-vene. Without opening his eyes, he walked backwards across the lounge and turned Bruckner's Seventh all the way up. In a couple of minutes the scherzo would be drowning them out.

sixteen

On Sunday night Evan and Adrea were once again sitting on the top step of the Roundhouse, the heat pressing against their faces like a pillow. Inside, the Flamin' Groovies' ill-received set was still running its course. The concrete beneath them was distinctly vibrating and

Evan's spine told him that they were now playing 'House of Blue Light'. His head was in his hands. He had made the mistake of looking forward to this evening. The Groovies had always been one of his favourite bands and now, touring for the first time, in an All the Way From the USA double bill with The Ramones, surely the only question was just how fantastic they were going to be? If the Patti Smith gig had been the first step then this would be the next: incredible music would convey them to places undreamed of even by Billy the Sailor. On the night, however, it had been very different: Evan was still trying to work out how things had gone so horribly wrong.

The organ – being set up on stage just as they walked in – had been the first warning sign. The drum kit and battered amplifiers also looked curiously familiar. Then the lights flared to reveal, once again, The Stranglers, appearing unbilled. They did the same songs in the same order. Those few moments that might have seemed spontaneous the first time were now revealed to have been carefully choreographed. All that shambling about was actually a stage act! Evan imagined the singer spending hours in front of the mirror practising raising and rotating one leg. Surely the bass player's friends could have told him to put on a shirt? In the intervening weeks, however, they seemed to have attracted a large and enthusiastic following who shouted requests, gave cheers of recognition before every number and sang along with the verses as well as the choruses. They were all men, dressed in black, with shiny red noses, as if these were the only parts of them that ever ventured outside. Crushed together at the front of the stage, they were doing a curious dance – ducking left, ducking right, then leaping as if to head away an invisible football. As a variant they would wrap their hands around each other's windpipes, squeezing until their eyes bulged. The tallest and most animated looked a bit like Dave, only with shorter hair and divested of his dun-dreary whiskers. It was only when the man's neighbours began to remind Evan of Alan and

Pete that he realized that he was indeed looking at his former housemates.

The Ramones followed, after a short pause. Having loomed in the wings for most of The Stranglers' set they seemed anxious to get it over with. Evan had heard an import copy of their debut album in Honest Jon's record store and hadn't known what to make of it. He had suspected that for a joke they were playing it at 45 or even 78. Live, though, they were different, even faster, except during their version of Chris Montez's 'Let's Dance' which decelerated as if their spring was running down. Otherwise, without any solos or even fills, they tore through their interchangeable songs. At the end of each one the guitarist yelled 'One-two-three-four!' and, without waiting for applause, they went straight into the next.

Joey the vocalist looked to be about seven feet tall but only because he was the thinnest man that Adrea had ever seen. He wore frayed drainpipe jeans with no flesh showing through the holes and, despite the heat, a heavy leather jacket like an insect's carapace with horrible flappy square-headed zips. He kept trying to chuck the microphone stand around but it was clearly too heavy for him. His haircut – side-parted curly string, like a poodle's coat grown out – almost made the rest of the band's pageboys look good.

They were loud all right: yellow and orange dust was sifting down from the roof and settling on Adrea's skin. She was sure that those patches of sky were widening as she watched. Even so, the guitarist kept shouting at the man on the mixing desk to turn it up. Presumably he was worried that they might reach the end of their set without bringing the building down around their ears. Evan, though, had noticed that Joey was beginning to flag: the mike stand seemed to be throwing him around. Half of the audience were yelling encouragement while the rest, apart from Evan and Adrea, had ever-widening smiles on their faces.

'Texas chainsaw massacree / Took my baby away from me.' All the songs seemed to be about violence, with sex and drugs incidental at best, but despite this – and the volume and the band's aggressive posturing – the effect was curiously soporific. Evan realized that repetition was the key: it was like with children's bedtime stories. All the horrors of Andersen and Grimm, if repeated often enough, became even more comforting than Teddy's furry pelt. While the listeners felt that they were being called to action they were in fact being lulled to sleep.

Joey and the boys were like cartoon characters, perfect for the Disney franchise. Evan felt he was about to choke: their stupidity was so calculated, so artful. He suspected that they had all majored in social anthropology or, more likely, business studies. As Nick Kent had written in the *NME*, these days the cretins were all coming on as intellectuals, while the intellectuals posed as cretins.

'They were like something from Pinky and Perky,' said Adrea, as they made their way to the bar.

'No,' Evan observed that the boys from Tolmers Square were approaching, 'I think you're being unfair to Clara the Cow.'

'Hi, Adrea,' said Dave. It was the first time he had ever used her name without deliberately getting it wrong. 'We really like your coat.' It was a part-tight-part-baggy thing, suede trimmed with unidentifiable fur, and had passed unremarked when she had worn it in the squat.

Evan looked at their new distressed leather jackets for which they were obviously soliciting compliments. A tag depending from Pete's collar informed the world that the wearer was £20 poorer and had a 34-inch chest. Evan recalled that they used to call his own jackets faggotty.

'We've been working up some of your old numbers,' Dave said, 'Especially "I'm Not Your Stepping Stone".' He hadn't paused for the bracket and had replaced the missing 'g', thus betraying that he hadn't got the point at all. 'We really miss your sound,' he continued. 'The neighbours have stopped complaining. Maybe we could do "Beat on the Brat"? That'll get them hopping about again.' He pulled his jacket collar up around his ears and the others followed suit. 'We've decided that you can come back. No hard feelings. Both of you.'

'No, thanks,' said Evan. 'I'm only into jamming these days. And I'm hoping to hook up with some synthesizer players for this rock opera that I've been writing.'

'What's it called?' Dave grinned, suspecting a put-on.

'*Eternity… is… Temporary*,' said Evan, very slowly. He moved up close to them. 'And you didn't kick us out, you fuckers. We left.'

Dave and the others seemed not so much to retreat as to be swallowed up by the crowd. None of the hippies and feminists that had been at Patti Smith was present, or if any were they had radically changed their appearances. There were no flared trousers, no cheesecloth or tie-dyed shirts, no sandals and no long skirts. No one looked smart but no one looked scruffy either: every other woman in the place was wearing black jeans. There were even some snakeskin boots, or maybe plastic copies. One pair had sixteen eyelets and reached almost to the knee: Doc Martens were obviously diversifying into reptiles. Everyone was speaking in low voices: their postures, their expressions and the set of their heads could only be described as don't-care-ish. Some of them were reading: one angel-faced couple were pouring over Lautréamont's *Les Chants de Maldoror*, while a fierce-looking girl appeared to be on the verge of eating *The Complete Poems of Elizabeth Bishop*.

It was hard to say what it was that was so wrong about them. Was it that they moved in an oddly jerky fashion? Or that they didn't look to be breathing at all? Some of them nodded at Adrea in acknowledgement, which gave her the creeps. At last she hit upon it: their eyes were the problem. The pupils were small, shiny and immobile, as if they were the heads of nails that had been hammered in to attach the faces to the skulls.

Evan's spirits rose at the sight of the Flamin' Groovies' gleaming silver and black amps stacked at the sides of the stage. He had heard that if the wood was even scratched they would throw them away and buy another set. Image and accessories were of crucial importance to this band. That perfect name, for example: instead of being cool it was utterly ridiculous, which in some mysterious way rendered it even cooler than cool. Evan imagined them spending intense hours debating whether or not to knock off that 'g'. And their leader, Cyril Jordan, was one of the great aphorists. 'Rock and roll is the only free country in the world' was Evan's favourite.

The Groovies had a thing about cars. In all their publicity photo- graphs they were leaning against huge shiny convertibles with elaborate fins and snarling chrome grilles, but they never gave the impression that they were about to get into them and go somewhere. Cars were merely things to look moody next to: Evan would have bet good money that none of them could even drive. These were magical inversions and paradoxes that Joey Ramone would never be able to understand.

When the band appeared the audience's horror was palpable. They were dressed in narrow-lapelled mohair suits – blue, with a thin gold pinstripe – high-collared button-down white shirts, black ties and Anello and Davide Cuban-heeled boots. Their hair was styled in Beatle cuts, except for the rhythm guitarist who was bald and so wore Price-style shades to compensate. They went straight into 'Shake Some Action', with those ascending and descending guitar figures which finally merged in that wonderful martial chorus:

> Shake some action's what I need
> To let me bust out at full speed
> And I'm sure that's all you need
> To make it all right.

Evan thought of it as one-shot music. It sounded as if the band were throwing themselves up against the entire universe to get in one good punch before the juggernaut crushed them and then moved on. All the great songs had this heroic, hopeless quality but with the very greatest – like this – you could actually feel the universe rock on its axis, as that one good shot landed flush on its jaw.

The audience hated them. They were booing the suits, the boots, the haircuts and the fact that this band could actually play. They liked the second number – a cover of the Beatles' 'Please Please Me', sung in eerily convincing Scouse – even less, especially when the harmonizing guitarist shook his gleaming pate. Then the Groovies paused to re-tune because of the heat. 'Who do you think you are?' someone yelled. 'Bleedin' Segovia?' They got even more irate when Cyril swapped his Rickenbacher twelve-string for an original Gretsch Country Gentleman: these were serious people with an unappeasable craving for raw noise. Even the all-out attack of 'Slow Death' only provoked them further: they were outraged that every song sounded different. People at the front started to flick cigarette butts up on to the stage. Evan could see Dave's newly shorn head jerking back and forth as if he were spitting. The Groovies were completely impervious. Despite the temperature they hadn't even loosened their ties. Cyril unfolded a yellow duster and carefully wiped the fingermarks off the pale blond body of his guitar.

Although Evan had accepted that there was only a small audience for good music, whereas rubbish sold by the ton, he had always thought that – because seeking it out was a full-time occupation – most people never got the chance to hear the proper stuff. If they ever did then everything would be different. But here was a Sunday night Roundhouse audience lauding The Stranglers and The Ramones and then howling down the Flamin' Groovies. There was a tickling at the back of his throat as if, for the first time he could recall, he were about to be sick. He clenched his fists but then let them drop back to his sides. If he hit the man next to him, when would he ever stop?

The two of them rose together and left. It was strange that the only people who were enjoying it were walking out while all the rest stayed on to whistle, boo and spit.

Although rubbish was blowing along the darkened terrace they could feel no breeze. The streets below looked small and mean, depressed and dirty. There was no traffic or passers-by: the rest of the human race was safely tucked up in bed. If Patti Smith's energy had somehow pitched them into the future, they now felt as if they were being sucked back into the past.

'Who were all those horrible people?' Adrea asked.

'Our comrades, our contemporaries, our generation.' Evan shrugged. 'Us.'

'No, they're not,' she said indignantly.

'It's as if there's something in the air,' Evan continued. 'One morning everyone springs out of bed and goes downtown and gets a different haircut. Then they buy some black cap-sleeve T-shirts and throw away all their old records and get a load of new ones. And they all do it independently, without being told to. The joke is that each one believes that they were the first, the original, the trailblazer and that all the others are merely following them. Just as we do.'

'No,' said Adrea. 'Because in a year or so they'll be doing something else, following the next fashion, whereas we'll still be the same. Because you're you and I'm me and this is just the way we are.'

'Haven't you ever wanted to be part of something?' Evan's wooden heels drummed against the step below. 'Some new movement that will change the world? To be feared by the bad, loved by the good, like Robin Hood? Haven't you ever wanted to be on someone's side – maybe even on the winning one?'

'I used to.' Her feet began to tap out a counter-rhythm to his own. 'But now I know that we can change the world perfectly well on our own. I want us to be the only ones. I want all those others to fuck off and leave us alone.'

'Right,' said Evan thoughtfully. It was the first time he had ever heard her swear. He got to his feet and raised his right forefinger as if tipping back an imaginary Stetson. 'I reckon it's about time we were moseying along.'

They descended the steps and crossed the still deserted road. Tonight they ignored the side alleyway and instead directly approached the front entrance of Heron Close. Both of them were tired of sneaking up and down those back stairs.

As they went inside the night staff were heading for the dining room. The women did not acknowledge them. Adrea had the sense that this time they were not being rude. Their expressions had been neutral as if their eyes saw only empty air. She had begun to suspect that she and Evan randomly drifted into and out of visibility.

Just as before, Terry was still in the sitting room, fully dressed in front of the flickering television. In his excitement, he seemed buffeted from every direction at once. A doleful weatherman was reading the shipping forecast: the country, although still locked into its heatwave, was ringed with storms. Evan expertly tipped and spun the wheel-chair but then, instead of turning right towards the bedrooms, he pushed it over to the front door.

'We're just taking Terry for a little walk,' Adrea called down the corridor but their voices appeared to be inaudible as well.

As they went down the ramp they were being watched by at least a dozen pairs of eyes. Price, assuming that they were going to the pub, considered following them then decided that he favoured a night of Bach cantatas over a lock-in with a sweaty midget and a bunch of drunken porters. Mrs Parker also saw them go: the three figures reminded her of the strange designs on those Masonic cards that Stanley received every Christmas. There had been over four hundred of them and even now a couple of dozen were still forwarded to

Heron Close. She had no idea who they were from. Evan's body was obscuring the wheelchair so that Mrs Barker, standing with her ear pressed up against her wardrobe door, vaguely wondered why that girl appeared to be eloping with a hunchback. From the other side of the square, Snow's binoculars panned from Evan's bowed head to refocus on Adrea's hand, resting lightly on Terry's left shoulder. Things couldn't get much worse, he reflected bitterly, than when you found yourself envying a dirty, smelly cripple.

A dim light still emanated from the side bar of the Eagle and Child. Evan paused, trying to recall the exact rhythm of the policeman's secret knock. At this, Terry almost threw himself out of the chair, giving Adrea a sharp kick on the shin. He calmed down when they began to push again: tonight he was not interested in the pub. Similar, lesser fits indicated that they should turn right, turn left, then straight on: Terry obviously had somewhere that he wanted to go.

It was strange, Terry was thinking, that although he no longer had any sensation in his legs, he was able to feel the ground under his wheels. How he loved it when they rattled across those manholes and grates! He could gauge the width and depth of every crack in the pavement and even felt a thrill of pain when they ran over a sharp-edged stone.

Only Evan and Adrea appreciated just how much he hated being stuck in that sitting room. Everyone else thought that he was somehow attached to the television set. 'There you are,' Bridie would say. 'Your programme's just coming on.' But the pictures on the screen were meaningless, black and white dots that swarmed like bees around a hive. Sometimes they would fall soothingly into recurring patterns but at others formless things would wriggle out, plopping on to the carpet only to disappear leaving a smell like burnt meat. No one else reacted – not even the cat – so he gathered he was the only one who could see them. He suspected that the television was poisoning him, making his condition even worse. When he was away from it his eyes and ears began to work properly again. He had once installed a set above the saloon bar: everyone's faces had turned upwards, eyes wide, mouths agape, as if they were watching Elijah riding across the sky in his chariot, rather than *Coronation Street*.

Without having to be told, they piloted him up the hill, past where the swimming baths had once stood. At the age of eight, when his school class had been taken along, Mr Bradbury had asked them if they could swim. Because he was there and the water was there and their conjunction seemed so natural Terry had said yes. When he began to flounder the teacher had leaned over and hooked him out with a long fishing pole. This had not deterred him: in fact, he had been so determined never again to experience that awful drowning feeling that he had become an unnecessarily strong swimmer.

Crossing the rusting metal railway bridge, Evan and Adrea were startled by a sustained groaning, tearing noise, like a car's wheels locked into a high-speed skid. Only when they stopped did they realize it was coming from Terry. It reminded Evan of when you punch someone in the stomach and all the wind goes out of them. At length, Terry's mouth closed and his head fell forward, but the sound continued and even grew in volume, echoing around the railway lines. Although they knew that it must be the night trains heading out of Euston and King's Cross, neither of them felt inclined to look over the parapet. It was as if Terry's cry had summoned up long-forgotten creatures from their underground sleep.

As they walked up Regent's Park Road, the soles of their feet kept clamping to the pavement. Evan recalled a job he had once had in a fish-dock – the smell wasn't far off either. The cars were so closely parked, with only an inch or two between them, that it seemed impossible they could ever get out, unless, thought Adrea, they all came and went in a *cortège*.

On the corner of St George's Road there had once been a sweet shop, owned by the Thomas sisters, that sold stick-jaw toffee. Terry hadn't particularly liked it – his back teeth ached for as long as that gluey aftertaste lingered – but he paid his penny to watch them wield their small brass toffee hammer. At its slightest tap, the block of toffee, solid as a mountain peak, would shatter into fragments. Either those old ladies had wrists of iron or the hammer had magical properties. Terry had promised himself that when he was a man he would have a little hammer of his own, but he had forgotten all about it until now. The shop and the Thomases were long gone, toffee came ready-wrapped and smooth – and what use would a hammer be to him in his present state?

Now they were passing Bates' Bakery, which used to claim that their ha'penny buns were the best in the world. In fact, they tasted exactly the same as the ones sold on Haverstock Hill or Malden Road or even as far away as Margate. It had been a useful early lesson: wherever you might roam, a ha'penny bun remained a ha'penny bun. If Terry had been able to turn his head to the right he would have glimpsed his old primary school. It was known as 'The Old Smoke' because its windows were covered with black grime from the LMS railway. Down the road had been Carrington's Dairy from which at breaktime he would carry a glass of milk back to Miss Potter, the other teacher. She always chose him because the rest of the children were afraid of the ceramic cows' heads mounted on the walls. It was as if the creatures had crashed through the brickwork seeking revenge. The milk always felt heavy so that his hand began to tremble and the bones along his arm seemed to be melting away.

One morning it had begun to rain. He knew that Miss Potter was making this happen, to test his resolve, so instead of running he had slowed right down, pausing for a few seconds after every step. Although he kept the glass steady, it spilt anyway, overflowing on to his fingers, and, as he watched, the liquid changed colour, turning pale blue with black specks swimming around like tadpoles. Miss Potter smiled and set it aside untouched. 'Next time, Terence' – her eyes were the same grey as her jacket and skirt – 'just put your other hand over the top.'

When they reached Primrose Hill, Evan could feel the parched earth crumbling under his feet. Pushing the chair up the steep slope, however, was surprisingly easy. He felt a pleasant glow radiating from the small of his back. If anything, he enjoyed the pushing even more than the shaving. The path to the summit was lined with cast-iron Victorian street lamps, each one individually numbered in sequence. 'I'm surprised they're not named after famous battles,' said Adrea.

They became aware that they were not alone. At the edge of the lamps' weak radiance, white shapes could be seen on the grass: partially-clad human bodies, variously entangled, rolling around. They heard little cries of pleasure or mock outrage, and a sound of breathing so distinct that it seemed everyone must be inhaling and exhaling together. Adrea noticed that all the pairs were the same distance apart, as if they had been planted there by the parks department: she wondered if they might be individually numbered, too. Despite the squeaking of the wheelchair, none of the heads turned towards them, but they had the impression that their presence had been registered and approved. According to Ken, Primrose Hill, situated on the same ley-line as Avebury, was a place of deep spiritual significance. It was known as the Temple of Heads because the priest-kings of yore ordered that their heads be severed and buried there after their deaths. Ken claimed that when he had once come here to work some charms and spells, his way had been invisibly barred. When he had persisted, he had been thrown on his back. The Hill at night was forbidden to all but lovers, cripples and decapitated kings.

There was no one at the summit. Evan and Adrea put the brakes on the chair and then sat on the bench facing the city. Delicate washes of yellow-green light were passing across the dome of St Paul's, while to the south-east, just beyond the Crystal Palace mast, there was a curious glow like a pillar of red dust. Adrea was wondering what could have happened to those great bosky woods that had been so plainly visible behind the Roundhouse on the night of Patti Smith.

'Look,' said Evan, 'we left our lamp on.'

Adrea saw that there was indeed a single point of light in the darkness around Heron Close. 'Unless it's Price,' she said.

It was some time before they realized that there was complete silence. Even the lovers seemed to be holding their breath, and the perpetual sustained roar no longer rose from the city, as though the heat had finally stifled it.

Terry loved it when Evan and Adrea turned towards each other, completely forgetting his existence. He felt his extreme agitation was being counterbalanced by an equally great calm, as if he were feeling what they were feeling. At such moments he seemed to be on the point of speaking but then the words just slipped back to echo uselessly round the far corners of his wasted body. If only he could warn them! But then, he reminded himself, if he hadn't been like this he wouldn't have realized that there was anything that they needed to be warned about. He tried to communicate through his eyes but Adrea just smiled and Evan winked. Either the message was not getting through or they were not afraid.

People said that beauty was only skin-deep but they were confusing it with prettiness. Real beauty was solid, right down to the bone and beyond: prettiness was a million miles away, right next door to ugliness, merely Quasimodo tidied up a bit. Beauty had an aura: you could feel when it was drawing near. In his life, Terry had met only a few people with such presence. A foreign man in the pub whom, he had later learnt, had been a Russian pianist on tour; a quiet regular who had gone home one night and chopped up his family with an axe; a postman who, as far as he knew, had always remained very much a postman; the old priest at St Saviour's and now one beautiful woman and one handsome man. All of them had a glow around them, a faint halo of coloured light. Evan's was green and Adrea's pink. Who would have thought that when you mixed pink and green you got a sort of speckled gold? If only he could warn them against everybody and everything, everywhere and all the time!

At last Adrea broke the silence. 'Have you ever read *101 Dalmatians*?'

'I saw the cartoon,' said Evan. 'I don't remember much about it, except that the dogs had silly noses and I really fancied Cruella de Ville.'

'I've just remembered,' she continued, 'that when Pongo and Missis have escaped they run to the top of Primrose Hill and bark to the north, bark to the south, bark to the east and west.'

Evan's initial attempt was closer to a werewolf howl while hers was more like a polite clearing of the throat, but then they modulated into a series of double barks – bow-wow! woof-woof! – to each point of the compass in turn. After they had barked to the south, however, in the direction of the zoo, an answering roar floated back up the hill, as if some huge jungle cat had accepted their challenge.

The lights of the city seemed to have dimmed so that all the stars were visible. Evan began to point out the various constellations. Adrea didn't tell him that she had her own names for them, taken from the characters she had loved in books, so that the Dioscuri were no longer brothers but Beatrice and Benedict, teasing each other for all eternity. The Great Bear was composed of her favourite fat men – Falstaff, Parson Adams, Nicely Nicely Johnson – all bouncing off each other's stomachs. Perhaps she could even find Price a place up there?

Terry was getting agitated again: he loved the lad but his astronomy was all over the place. Evan tilted the chair right back and Adrea steadied that pecking head. As they watched, a pale light seemed to be flooding into or out of his face. The eyes closed and the mouth began to snap at the stars.

The roaring from below was growing louder and more furious.

There was no mistake: it really was getting closer. Then a dark shape came hurtling up the slope, separating and scattering the entwined couples. Only when it was almost on them did they realize that it was a man but, with his mane of backcombed hair and a face that seemed to be crumbling like sandstone, he looked just like a lion. His arms were raised with his fingers hooked to simulate claws. He was dressed in a mustard-coloured suit, sleeves and trousers too short, dotted with dark patches like dried blood. The tawny eyes flickered over them but he didn't pause. Still roaring, he disappeared in the direction of Swiss Cottage.

Evan was doubled over with laughter. 'I thought it was going to be Snowy!' he spluttered at length.

'Do you think he's harmless?' Adrea asked nervously.

'No.' He cracked up again. 'Definitely not.'

Terry wished he could tell them that the lion's name was John Leather and that he had known him all his life. Even the Eagle and Child had finally barred him. Terry was struck by the fact that, although he had not seen him for a long time, Leather the Lion had looked not a day older. He had been wearing that suit for over thirty years but it still fitted him. Perhaps violent insanity might be the secret of eternal youth?

He sighed as Adrea drew back his head again. Not until he had been trapped inside this inert body had he begun to realize how the world worked. Everything that existed, had existed, could exist was also there in your own mind. When you were driven inside yourself you could find exact correspondences for everything. Sometimes he would take a commonplace object, like a spoon, and then shut his eyes and search his mind until he found it – with the same stains and the same shine, its bowl distortedly reflecting the same things – and let the two fuse together with a satisfying click. All this had nothing to do with memory, for who would bother to remember a bloody spoon? Sometimes, though, it was as if he imagined the spoon just before he actually saw it. That was an even better feeling than the 750–1 treble that he had once landed at Sandown, when the bookie's face had got longer and longer as he paid him out.

Now, when he closed his eyes, it happened again. He saw that the stars above perfectly corresponded to the configurations of lights that flickered against the dark background of his own brain. What was true of the world was apparently also true of the whole universe. He felt himself being drawn upwards: his chair no longer carried him, he was carrying it. No bookie could ever have enough in his satchel to pay out on this one.

The wheelchair was almost halfway down the hill before Evan and Adrea realized what was happening. They were sure that they had lowered both the rubber clamps: Terry must have sprung his own brakes. They gave chase but it was no contest: he had a head start and was still going away. He gave a couple of derisive croaks, like an old crow taking flight from a couple of pursuing kittens.

One of the lamps had been set in the middle of the tarmac at the widest point of the path, as if for just such an eventuality. The wheelchair feinted left, then right, but the metal post stood its ground so that they met full on. When they reached him, Terry's face was pressed against the grooved stem, while his limbs had contrived to wrap themselves around it, as though in some ecstatic union. Although he had not been strapped in, his backside seemed to be firmly glued to the seat of his chair. One wheel, tilted slightly off the ground, continued to spin. Adrea could find no cuts or bruises: it was hard to imagine that blood still ran in those veins. At worst, she thought, a little sap might trickle out. He cawed again and rolled his shining black eyes: that perpetual shaking seemed finally to have stopped. As they were prising him free, she saw that the lamppost had been numbered 111 and that those three lines had indented themselves into his sunken left cheek. The lamp above them flickered once, twice and then went out.

seventeen

'And so festination and pulse' – Price began to shake violently – 'are immediately cancelled out by an equally powerful akinesia.' Still shaking, he unerringly refilled Evan and Adrea's glasses with Kummel. 'The irresistible force – explosive will – meets the immovable object – the obstructive will. That, my young colleagues, is the essence of Parkinson's disease.'

'Can't it be cured?' Adrea sniffed suspiciously at the liquid. 'Or at least slowed down?'

'There is a drug called L-Dopa.' Price drained his glass with one gulp. 'But it has the unfortunate side effect of rendering the subject uncontrollably priapic.'

Evan grinned. 'That sounds interesting.'

'Sorry,' said Price, 'but if you were to take it you'd just get the runs. Broad beans, full of dopamines, are also supposed to help. Don't laugh: Pythagoras thought they were the home of the human soul. Unfortunately, when I tried that on Terry, he just kept spitting them out.'

Adrea's T-shirt had somehow contrived to ride up and slip down simultaneously, while Evan, lying next to her on the bed, was stark naked. Price had made no comment on entering and nor had they: he wasn't sure whether to take their lack of self-consciousness as a compliment or an insult. 'The ardour aroused in men by the beauty of women,' Paul Valéry had written, 'can only be satisfied by God.' Evan, his pubic hair still glistening wet, appeared to be of a different opinion.

'You could try giving him a shock,' Price continued. 'There's a thing called *kinesia paradoxa* in which, in response to an unexpected crisis, all Parkinsonian symptoms radically deflate or even disappear for a time. But like St Elmo's Fire or the Brocken Spectre, I have yet to observe this phenomenon.'

'What is the cause of Parkinson's?' Adrea asked.

'No one knows. Long-term dependency on anti-depressants, like haloperidol or tetrabenzine. Large doses of carbon monoxide: imagine Terry standing behind his bar with all those fumes coming off Chalk Farm Road. And, by the look of his ears, I suspect that he used to box a bit: with those eye sockets and cheekbones he would have been a cutter. Blood loss and impact damage to the basal ganglia are other likely causes. Parkinson himself named it "the shaking palsy", after Aubrey's famous description of Thomas Hobbes at eighty-seven. Mind you, the philosopher still managed to translate *The Odyssey* and *The Iliad* before he died, which is probably more than we can expect from Terry.'

Evan yawned. 'So did this Hobbes of yours take dope, box and run a pub?'

'No,' said Price, 'I suspect that his might have been a philosophical affliction. Having reduced all human motives to attraction and aversion, he ended up getting both at the same time. Without all the other states in between or even, like obsession or detachment, beyond them, then attraction and aversion, like icebergs, gradually drift together and merge. And after that, as Charcot said, "There is no possible truce."'

'I think Terry's condition might be philosophical, too.' Adrea finished off her Kummel. 'He certainly isn't diseased.'

'I'm surprised that you don't bring him up here with you,' said Price.

'We tried to last night,' said Evan, 'but he didn't want to come. We could barely move him: it was as if he had put down roots.'

'At least he has the delicacy to know when he's playing gooseberry.' Price produced a flagon of cider from under his chair. 'Unlike yours truly.'

Evan saw that Stormy, his body folded into a perfect circle, was once again lying in the centre of the carpet. One moment the animal was there, the next it was gone. The bathroom and wardrobe doors were closed so it must have kept crawling under the bed although he never saw it come or go. He had long realized, however, that wondering why or how cats did things was an utter waste of time.

'How wonderful it must be to have a disease named after you,' said Price, wafting away the familiar bluebottle, which, although Stormy had caught and eaten it twice in the last ten minutes, was still zinging around. 'What form, I wonder, would Priceism take?'

'An obese condition with side effects of sarcasm and a morbid attachment to crap music,' said Evan.

'Quite harmless, though,' Adrea continued. 'Non-contagious and fortunately rare.'

Her expression was so wonderfully disdainful that Price could not resist getting out his camera.

'Don't worry,' he said, as Evan clenched his fists. 'I wouldn't show them to anyone. I wouldn't even look at them myself.'

'So what's the point of taking them?' Adrea asked.

'To preserve the moment.'

Now her mouth had an ugly twist. 'How do you think a camera will do that?'

Downstairs, Assistant Matron Acting Deputy Matron Snow was growing increasingly agitated, ceaselessly roaming the building. On the longer corridors, when no one was watching, he could hardly keep himself from running. As a signal of purpose and importance he always carried two empty files in his hands. Even so, whenever he encountered the Babies, his feet seemed to want to join them on their shuffling rounds. Every time he reached the back stairs he would climb an extra rung before forcing himself to retrace his steps. He was drawn towards the attic, although he wasn't sure why. What Evan and Adrea might or might not be doing inside was of no interest to him: he had never been tempted to look through the keyhole or press his ear against the door. It was just that up there the choking sensation in his throat eased and he could begin to breathe again. Perhaps it had something to do with the altitude?

Whenever Snow stopped moving he could feel the residents' eyes. The ones who had formerly been afraid of him now held his gaze, while those who had not pointedly looked away. Whenever his feet ceased to stamp it was as if he could still hear that mocking applause echoing from the dining room. He was, above all, avoiding Bridie. She must have been feeling sorry for him because she kept smiling and nodding her head while making that horrible humming noise, as though he were just another of her 'ressies'. She had even dared, unless he had been imagining it, to put her hand on his shoulder.

Terry's body was wagging at him like a threatening finger. Snow noticed that some new marks had appeared on the face: no doubt they would be trying to pin the blame on himself. Taking a deep breath, he entered the sitting room. The old people had no right to look at him like that when the smell in here was worse than ever. Most of the old men were openly rubbing themselves as if they thought no one would notice. Or perhaps they just didn't care any more? They looked worse than tramps: that lazy, evil boy had stopped shaving them. Frances, with almost a full beard, was sitting with the others, rubbing away at nothing. Mrs Barker put down her knitting and, although no one had taken out a cigarette, struck a match. At least the smell of sulphur provided some relief.

Everyone was staring at the television. Snow now realized that here was the source of the clattering and jeering that had recalled his dining-room humiliation. It was a cricket match. He had never understood the game: like Price's music it went on and on for hours without getting anywhere. Now, however, there was something very different about it. The pitch was as white as the players' boots and flannels so that their dark hands and faces seemed to be floating in mid-air. As he watched, the stumps and bails flew apart as if dynamited and the batsman's shoulders slumped as he trudged away. Then the camera panned to the crowd: black men in huge caps were dancing and shouting, rattling cigarette lighters against their beer cans or blowing into conch shells. Snow felt his throat tighten even more, and words that he had always sneered at came into his mind. 'It's not cricket,' he said aloud. 'It's just not cricket.'

The wall clock's hand clicked on to the next minute and Mrs Barker, with a sweep of her arm, lit another match. She held it upright until the flame burnt down, seeming to pass into her fingers. Showing no pain, she took out another, striking it just as the clock sounded again. Snow was sure that no more than twenty seconds could have elapsed. Across the room, Mrs Parker had also stopped knitting. Her lips were pursed, as if ready to blow out any subsequent matches. As Snow retreated, a great roar went up: the wicket had exploded again.

After three anti-clockwise circuits of the dining room he felt a little better. Plunging down the corridor, he sidestepped Molly and Polly, then withstood a surprisingly hefty shoulder charge from Dolly. He could have sworn that she was muttering 'Happy Christmas' as she passed.

Up on the first floor he ducked his head into each bedroom in turn, feeling as if his neck were elongating like a giraffe's. Although he knew that all the residents were downstairs, he always confirmed that their rooms were indeed empty.

Back on the landing he knelt and ran his forefinger along the bottom step. It came away wrapped in dead hair and cobwebs. The same thing happened at the second and third. Those cleaners had some questions to answer. He ascended to the seventh step where only yesterday he had found a small hollow tube of scorched cardboard: its curious smell still lingered. Had the dark shape of a bird fluttered past the window above? He squinted through the frosted glass. Such things had to be monitored. Was the paint on the handrail beginning to flake? Was that lino buckling or was it only a shadow? For every step up to the attic he found another excuse.

Patti Smith was grumbling and yelping her way through 'Free Money'.

'It's rubbish, of course,' said Price after the two final power chords, which sounded like an enormous toddler stamping its feet. 'But at least she seems as if she means it.'

'Right.' Evan reached over and slapped Price's knees. 'I knew you'd like it.'

'Don't worry, my children' – Price raised two fingers as if in benediction – 'you'll soon be grown up enough for Schubert and Hugo Wolf.'

'We've already heard all that stuff,' said Adrea.

She decided not to let on that she had worn away the grooves of her Janet Baker LPs, especially the one where she was wearing a white rollneck sweater on the cover, the one in which she didn't so much sing as hoot like some magical owl.

'That reminds me. I've got something for you.' Price handed her a carrier bag. 'Take this. I never play it any more.'

It was Billie Holiday's *Lady in Satin*, recorded the year before she died.

Adrea looked directly at where Price's eyes should have been. 'Thank you.'

'It's the original mono issue' – she had the feeling that he had winked – 'the one with "The End of a Love Affair" on. But don't play it just now: let's have some more of that lovely shouting.'

On the front of the album, Billie was dressed in a low-cut gown of blue and white satin with a thin gold necklace and earrings like inverted candelabra. Although her face was half in shadow, the photographer had been unable to hide the swellings under the eyes or the meshing lines at the corners of the mouth. On the back, Adrea saw that a long dedication had been scored out by a red biro, so violently that the tip had ripped through the cardboard.

'I thought it might do as a leaving present,' said Price, 'as I imagine you will soon be moving on.'

'Sorry to disappoint you,' Adrea did not sound in the least regretful, 'but I've asked Somerville to hold my place until next year.'

Price turned to Evan. 'So you think Heron Close' – he clicked his fingers and rolled his eyes – 'is where it's at?'

'Yes,' replied Evan, gravely. 'We're waiting to see what happens. I don't know why but here is where we want to be.' He shrugged. 'Perhaps we'll go when the weather breaks.'

'We're like those people in your picture' – Adrea gestured towards *Eternity is Temporary,* which, beyond the candlelight, was reduced to a grey blur. 'They know they're in the right place but they don't know what to do next. They've discovered that eternity is temporary but they don't know what difference that makes. All they can do is sit and wait. Like us. We're ready to go and we're just one step away from something remarkable.'

'I once felt like that myself,' said Price.

Evan leaned forward. Suddenly Price's lenses no longer felt thick and dark enough. 'What happened?'

'I walked away.' Price paused. 'No – I ran away.'

'Why the hell did you do that?'

'I didn't realize what I was doing. I only knew that I was becoming ridiculous.' He paused again. 'To myself.'

'Was it to do with your policewoman?' Adrea asked.

Evan burst out laughing when Price nodded.

'Perhaps you'll get another chance.'

'He was lucky to get one,' Evan finally spluttered.

Price leaned forward: now it was Evan's turn to wish that those lenses were thicker and darker. 'You think you've got all the answers, don't you?'

'Of course I have,' said Evan, 'and so have you. And so has everyone else. There are no mysteries. We know all the questions and all the answers. You knew exactly what you were running away from: you just didn't have the guts to admit it to yourself. Truth is easy: doing something about it is hard. When my mum and dad and the teachers and the coppers and the priest were making their promises and threats they always had the same look in their eyes. I knew that they knew that I knew it was all shit. And I knew that they were silently begging me to ignore them and do the exact opposite of what they said.'

'My dear boy.' Price clapped his hands in delight. 'You're beginning to sound like me.' He cocked his head towards Adrea. 'Who said that Priceism wasn't contagious?'

She ignored him and looked at Evan. 'Perhaps this is the time to take that next step?'

Planting the soles of her feet against the plaster, she attempted to walk up the wall. It seemed to Price that she hung in the air for a split second longer than was normal before she fell back on to the mattress.

'No,' she said, with what seemed real disappointment. 'Apparently not.'

Her body stretched out, getting longer and longer. Price was beginning to suspect that Valéry and Evan had both been wrong and that the Gods and the beautiful women just batted you to and fro like a shuttlecock. He noticed that the cat was back in the centre of the room. Its ears were flat against its head and the huge eyes were fixed on the door. The line of light was once again broken by a familiar shadow. He whispered, 'Nosferatu's back, I see.'

Evan's reaction surprised him. The boy rolled off the bed, knees and elbows crashing on to the floor: one hand snatched up a snakeskin boot as he made a tiger-like spring across the room. The door flew open – to reveal that no one was standing there – and then slammed behind him. Price wondered why, having hitherto ignored Snow's presence, he had suddenly felt the need to act. Adrea, eyes closed, hands behind her head, seemed unaware that anything had happened.

The stairwell was empty: there was no sound of retreating footsteps. As Evan turned back, however, he saw the figure hiding behind the fire door. Snow was not looking at him but fiddling with the front of his trousers. From his belt loop he unfastened that great sporran of keys and then, with a rattling sound like a startled grouse, swung it at Evan's face. The impact, half-blocked by Evan's raised forearm, was surprisingly light, but the ring exploded, sending keys flying like shrapnel to bite into his chest and neck or rain down upon his bare toes. The sound was deafening, as if a vibraphone had been pitched down the well. He waited until the echoes had faded before pursuing Snow.

The man was descending painfully slowly, his heels clicking against each riser in turn. It was as if he were more afraid of falling than of being caught. Evan vaulted the banister to land at the bend in the stairs. Snow did not seem to realize what had happened until his bowed head gently butted against Evan's chest.

'An accident, mister,' he said.

'Well, here's an accident for you.' Evan feinted a left hook, then, with a full arc, swung the boot heel against the side of Snow's head. 'And here's another,' Evan said politely, apparently aiming a kick at Snow's left kneecap until the foot twisted to crack against the right instead, sending him toppling down the last flight.

Evan expected to find a mangled form spreadeagled below but Snow was on his feet, leaning against the back door, as if he had been waiting there for some considerable time. He made no move to escape when Evan took hold of those conveniently protruding ears – slightly sticky to the touch – and rammed the head into the window, splintering the wired glass. At the second impact all the fire alarms went off.

Price, as he passed them, clapped his hands over his ears. He was tired of breaking up fights: nobody thanked you and they usually started up again as soon as your back was turned. None of the residents were reacting to the clamour. Only the Babies, zig-zagging down the corridor, showed any sign of self-preservation. To his relief, he registered that the sprinkler system wasn't working. Not until he unlocked the junction box did Bridie's head pop round the corner.

'It's all right.' Although he had shut down the system he continued to shout. 'It's only Snowy playing the fool.' She didn't reply but he was aware of her footsteps behind him as he moved back towards the stairs. He thought he glimpsed a figure furtively darting for cover, but when they reached the far end there was only Mrs Barker, staring fiercely into the smallest toilet. She had never quite grasped that, with her Zimmer, she needed to go in backwards. Neither Price nor Bridie stopped to help.

Snow was now lying on the floor, rolled into a ball. Every time the boot hit him he seemed to contract a little more, as if folding himself away to nothing. Unlike Billy the Sailor in similar circumstances, Evan did not look grotesque. His movements had a grace that reminded Price of the metopes in the British Museum: it was like a lapith giving a centaur some stick.

Evan felt as though he were playing Snow's body like a percussion instrument, chopping out a rhythm to the music in his head. There seemed to be no reason why he should ever stop. The sensation was oddly familiar, as if he had beaten Snow a thousand times before and would a thousand times again. Perhaps, in another life, or another dimension, the position would be reversed and he would be cowering under Snowy's boot? Looking at the pocks, chevrons and raised stitches on those horrible brown brogues, however, Evan decided to defer any such offer.

'Come on, old chap,' Price heard himself saying in an almost wheedling tone. 'Remember that tomorrow you must take everyone to the zoo.'

To his surprise, these words did the trick. Evan straightened up, took two backwards steps, then brought his legs together before shouldering arms with the boot and giving them a smart salute. This military effect was, if anything, heightened by his erection. Price could hear Bridie's laughter behind him. Evan's cock did not appear to be unusually long or thick, but it was standing so steeply that the shining purple glans pressed back against his belly.

They helped Snow up. His face, at least, was unmarked. Evan must have felt that he couldn't render it any worse than it already was. Snow's legs just about held him but he appeared to have shrunk, so that when Bridie led him away, his head was level with her shaking shoulders.

Evan had stopped saluting and, with belated modesty, placed the boot over his genitals. There was blood on his insteps, and his neck and chest were pitted with curious cuts, as if he had been bitten by small dogs. The boot's grained Cuban heel was hanging off.

'Why don't you ask me what I'm doing?' he asked.

Price sighed. 'What the hell do you think you're doing?'

'Me?' said Evan, as if the question had come as a surprise. 'Me? Me?' He had assumed a Geordie accent. 'I'm just fucking aboot.'

His right thumb had bent round to face in the wrong direction. As Price watched, the forefinger nonchalantly flicked it back into position.

'Does it hurt?'

'Not yet.' Evan tried to waggle it and failed. 'But it will.'

'I think a strategic withdrawal might be called for,' said Price. 'I'll have a look at that after I've done Snowy's autopsy.'

As he went back upstairs, Evan's muscles seemed to flex and move in unfamiliar ways, as if he were falling upwards or hopping like a huge flea. The middle step, on which his left foot had landed, looked to be still vibrating.

Price could feel Snow's scattered keys under his feet. Some had formed a rough lozenge shape while on the stairs all the silver ones seemed to be pointing due north. A couple had shattered into sharp-edged fragments while another was twisted grotesquely. He counted thirty-five of them. What were all these things that Snow needed to open and close? Before gathering them up, he took out his camera and, without looking through the viewfinder, used up the rest of the film on the empty stairway.

Snow was sitting in the office, looking dazed but oddly pleased with himself. He resembled that rarest of creatures, a happy drunk. Bridie was perched on the edge of the desk behind him, displaying her dimpled knees to advantage. With one arm around his back she seemed to be manipulating him like a puppeteer: his head lolled as if the strings had been cut. She wiped the face and mouth with her handkerchief, then stared at it intently, although there was no sign of blood.

'Here are the keys,' said Price, letting them cascade over the desk top. 'How many should there be?'

Snow's jaw made a shuttling sound like a typewriter carriage moving back into position. 'Thirty-nine,' he said with what could almost have been a smile.

'They're all there, Snowy.' Price ran his hands over the man's unresisting body. Although the torso was already turning black and yellow, it appeared that Evan – despite the one-sided nature of the contest – had been the more damaged of the two.

'Compound fractures of the neck and spine,' Price said, 'Otherwise you're fine.'

Snow gave what could almost have been a laugh. 'I want to withdraw my complaint against that boy.' The voice sounded thick and blurry, as if his tongue had swollen to fill his mouth.

'I didn't send it,' replied Price. 'You never got the punctuation quite right.'

Picking up the telephone, he rang the Fire Brigade. He was surprised that they hadn't arrived yet because the station was just round the corner: they could have strolled across with a couple of buckets by now. It was a full minute before they answered.

'It's Heron Price here,' he heard himself stammering, 'from Matron Close.' There was a loud hubbub in the background: the firemen were having a party or fighting. 'It was a false alarm,' he continued. 'Don't bother turning out.'

'We weren't going to,' came a slurred voice, then the receiver was slammed down.

'They didn't realize who I was,' said Price. 'No – they obviously did.'

Bridie, having sorted the keys into piles according to colour and size, was re-threading them on to their rings. For the first time in months she met Price's eyes: she scowled and then jerked her head in the direction of the door.

Passing the sitting room, Price saw that Mrs Barker was knitting away, back in her usual place. He wondered about his uncharacteristic slip of the tongue in the office. Although he had felt as calm as ever he must have been at least a little distracted because he had left his cigarettes and lighter up in the attic. His fingers groped at his collar: as he had suspected, he had also neglected to refasten the top button and to straighten his tie. On the stairs he searched for Snow's missing keys, without success. He even prised up the doormat but only uncovered a scorched-looking threepenny bit.

Bridie was still laughing as she remembered that look on Price's face. How his ears had reddened at the sight of Evan's meat and two veg! And the way he had shifted his bulk to try to block her view! She couldn't remember the last time that she had laughed like this or even when she had laughed at all. The final keys slid on to the ring. She had not realized how heavy they were. No wonder the poor man acted the way he did: he must have felt like a convict dragging a ball and chain.

It reminded her of her mother's tales about the blessed Matt Plunkett, a celebrated Dublin penitent whose hair shirt was lined with barbed wire, broken glass and thorns.

Snow's head fell back into her lap. What a funny shape it was! She remembered how at school they had been forced to play netball, with Sister Annunciata slapping their legs if they jumped too high. Whenever the ball came her way she would clutch it to her chest, ignoring the cries of 'Pass! Pass!' She always had the sense that it had just fallen miraculously out of the sky. Mr Snow's head gave her the same feeling: it seemed to twist and shift under her hands as if it were flexible, with its own trunk, limbs and head. How could you have a head with a head? At one moment it felt unnaturally solid, the next astonishingly light. Since she had been married to Mervyn she had also had two lovers – three, if Price counted. She had given birth four times, and watched as her father, her grandparents and dozens of the ressies had died before her eyes, but this present feeling seemed to come from some even deeper part of herself. What was particularly strange was that she didn't like the man in front of her any more than she had before. His Brylcreemed hair seemed to sting the tips of her fingers.

Snow's eyes had closed. Cool breath fanned his brow but he could no longer recollect whose it might be. Now only his knuckles hurt, as if he had been doing the beating, while the rest of his body seemed to be sliding into a hot deep bath. Even the restored bunch of keys seemed lighter, no longer tugging at his waistband.

Everything had changed in that instant when Evan's boot had hit him. Something had snapped or split open – not in his head, however, but somewhere around the small of his back. His lungs had felt as if they were about to burst, as though he were breathing in and out at the same time. He had sensed each subsequent blow in his heart; sharp double-pangs like sobs, not of pain but of a sort of hesitant joy. Whenever the boot made contact, a white light like a flashbulb seared his eyeballs, brighter and brighter every time. He had put up no further resistance, although it had to be admitted that he had little choice in the matter. All the fear, all the shame, even all the ugliness seemed to flood out of him, while his nostrils were filled with unfamiliar smells and his ears registered the smallest sounds, even the different degrees of silence.

The worst thing he could have imagined – being beaten and humiliated by his enemy – had turned out to be the best thing that could have happened. Only one thought worried him: where had all those bad things gone after they had left him? He hoped that they had not transferred themselves to Evan.

Now he was aware of something pressing first against his brow then against his right cheek. It was warm and somehow soft and hard at the same time. Had he come to the end of a production line, and was now being stamped ready for use? Or perhaps, like a passport, he was being franked at the border post of some new country? Either way, he was sure that Bridie's lips had been acting in some official capacity.

There was no music coming from the attic. Despite walking on tiptoe and holding his breath, Price felt he was being embarrassingly loud. He tapped at the door then flinched at the unexpectedly cavernous echoes. He was surprised when it opened, even though he knew the lock was broken.

The room was in near darkness: all but one of the candles had gone out. It felt empty, as if Evan and Adrea had decamped, taking the furniture and carpet with them. His own ragged breathing was the only sound. The flame of the last candle, unnaturally long and narrow, seemed to be slowly rising like the exhaust of a tiny rocket. He flapped a hand, then blew sharply, but it didn't even flicker. Having with difficulty located the chair, he began groping around for his cigarettes and lighter. The situation was desperate: he hadn't had a smoke for at least twenty minutes. His nails, raking the carpet, came up with only fluff and grit.

It was some time before his eyes adjusted and he became aware of movement from the bed. At first he could not make out what was going on. At one moment it seemed that a length of shiny material was being slowly unrolled, then as if there were two great snakes swallowing each other's tails. He caught sight of a hand with tobacco-stained fingers that squeezed, stroked, clutched and clawed, but only when two heads – one dark, one tawny – emerged did he identify the naked bodies of Evan and Adrea intertwined.

Their limbs and torsos were identically long and smooth: Evan's thick patches of body hair appeared to have vanished. These orange fingers were describing chord shapes along Adrea's prominent vertebrae, otherwise it was impossible to tell which bits belonged to whom. Price felt as if he were watching a film being run too fast or too slow. The two bodies seemed to pass right through each other, then writhe, twist and return. As they crested again, their genitals looked to be altogether wrongly aligned. Their eyes – dark and empty as those of Adrea's small purple Teddy bear – did not register his presence. What was even more disturbing was that they were making absolutely no sound, unless it was that he could no longer hear anything outside himself.

Over the years, in unfortunately positioned mirrors, Price had sometimes caught sight of himself engaged in the sexual act and had wondered why he looked so woebegone and desperate when that was surely not the way he was feeling. Once, in Soho, he had sat through a full night of pornographic films. The performers had looked as if they were engaged in dull tasks of household maintenance – no wonder plumbers and milkmen had figured so prominently in their skeletal story lines. What Evan and Adrea were doing was utterly different. He could think of no term that covered it, not even Iago's 'making the beast with two backs', for this beast appeared to have three or four fronts. Where did it leave him if he couldn't even pin down the simple generative act?

Surely this was not the way things were supposed to be? Having set it all in motion, Price had to admit that he was no longer in control of the situation – if indeed he ever had been. He felt like Prospero might have done if, having lured all his enemies to his enchanted island, he had then found that his magical powers no longer worked. This was not what he had been expecting. Or perhaps, recalling Evan's earlier words, it was exactly what he had been expecting but he hadn't liked to admit it to himself. Even now, although he had a pretty good idea of what was going to happen, he wasn't going to admit that either.

The last candle had guttered out but he could still see them: it was as if their flesh gave off a pale light. He realized he could throw a bucket of water over them or set fire to the sheet and they wouldn't even notice. This was the moment he had been waiting for: he took out his camera. What he had told Evan and Adrea had been the truth: he would never show the shots to anyone and would himself give them the merest glance, just to ascertain that the lovers did indeed show up on the developed film. He wouldn't destroy them, though. He had kept the negative of every photograph he had ever taken. It was his hope that one day he would retrieve them from the trunk and put them together in a completely new order in which they would all make sense. He raised the camera but its shutter felt dead. He pressed it over and over until he recalled that he had wasted the film on Snow's spilled keys.

There was a story about Jacques-Henri Lartigue, one of Price's favourite photographers. Before his papa gave him a camera, little Jacques-Henri had made use of what he called his 'eye-trap': he would open his eyes, shut them, then open them again as wide as possible and hey presto! The image was captured for ever! More in hope than expectation, Price followed these instructions. He immediately felt a mechanical whirring in his head and his eyes smarted as if from a flare of light. A series of distinct clicks sounded from just above the bridge of his nose.

He had run off half a reel of this internal film before he realized that he was unable to stop blinking. His eyes closed tighter and tighter and then opened wider and wider: the whole process speeding up to create a stroboscopic flickering. Nausea and excitement gripped him: he felt as if he were about to vomit and ejaculate simultaneously. Perhaps, to put the tin lid on it, he was turning epileptic, the Prince Myshkin of Camden Town?

Now even stranger things were happening. The lovers had begun to change. Evan was swelling grotesquely. Flesh hung in clusters from his chest and enormous blisters were forming on his brow. Price gave up trying to count the number of his chins. Adrea, pinned underneath, appeared to be withering. Her skin no longer glowed but had a wan, papery look. Their fluid movements had given way to spasmodic jerks and twitches, like netted fish on a trawler's deck. As if in time-lapse photography, the years came rolling on. If only they knew what the future had in store for them! Price was willing to bet that this was one truth that Evan, for all his superman posturings, would be less than anxious to face.

Then the female's head turned towards him and he saw that the features were no longer Adrea's but those of the policewoman. Without her make-up, she was pinched and harrowed. He was surprised to observe that she did not shave her armpits, presumably in the vain hope of hiding those well-developed wattles. She was wearing sheer stockings and a pinkish suspender belt with a matching bra – one of those purchases from Marks and Spencer? – that had twisted like a ligature.

Having rolled apart, the bodies on the bed abruptly lunged at each other in what appeared to be an ill-advised attempt to achieve some position from the far extremes of tantric sex, only to fall back in a general sprawl. Price saw that just as the woman was not Adrea, her partner was no longer Evan. He had to admit that the figure before his fast-blinking eyes was himself. His every limb seemed to be gripped by a separate palsy, and sweat or mucous was cascading down his chins. His partner's lipstick, rouge and false eyelashes were randomly distributed across his cheeks. Price remembered how Bridie had said that having sex with him was like being trapped underneath an oak wardrobe with its key still in the lock. The policewoman, however, seemed to be able to manoeuvre the enormous figure without difficulty. As he watched, she bounced it up off her knees and then wriggled into a more prosaic position before it descended.

And now the figures were blurring, as if his eyes had filled with tears. But before they faded Price had acknowledged that his fat doppelgänger and this scraggy spectre, as they huffed and puffed away, were every bit as protean and unfathomable, every bit as beautiful, as Evan and Adrea had been.

eighteen

Next morning on the terrace, as she awaited the coach that would take them to the zoo, Mrs Parker observed how the residents shrank away from Mr Snow. They had always been frightened or at least wary of him, but now that he had seemingly turned good they were utterly terrified.

The new Snow had appeared at breakfast. The voice was deeper and the movements slower. Those hairy hands were suddenly gentle. He had fed the Babies without ramming the spoon halfway down their throats. He had patted Stormy's head and not even the resulting scratches had disturbed his uncharacteristic calm. He seemed to have picked up some of Bridie's most annoying mannerisms: the nodding and the relentless bumblebee humming. Although he was as ugly as ever, it was in a jolly, clownish way as if his face had been re-moulded around an enormous yellow and black smile. Over the years Mrs Parker had never suspected that there might be teeth behind those tightened lips: she would have preferred to have remained in ignorance. His eyes – surely they hadn't always been so pale a blue? – looked to be starting out of his head. The formerly beetling brows had almost disappeared into the hairline and whenever he spoke his waxy ears wagged comically up and down.

Now a thin beam of sunlight was tracking him along the terrace. She glanced up at the sky's solitary cloud, like an angel in a diaphanous nightie, half-expecting a great voice to boom out something about sinners that repenteth.

Mr Snow's nastiness had been a central part of the residents' lives, one of the few things that – in summer or autumn, in winter or spring – you could always rely on. If he could turn nice then anything could happen. Everyone was hoping that this was just a temporary indisposition. Her Stanley had always insisted that no one could ever really change, that all criminals should be hung for their first, minor offence – especially if it had anything to do with sex. It was funny to think that he and Snow and Evan and Price were of the same gender, of the same species. Surely they couldn't all be men? She wondered if there were any truth in the rumour that Snow had been fighting with Price. Perhaps he was merely concussed?

Evan and Adrea had appeared at the far side of the square. They continued to keep up the pretence that they thought nobody knew they were spending their nights up in the attic. Mrs Parker was surprised that they were still around: they'd been looking increasingly miserable and she suspected that the novelty of it all was beginning to wear off. As they came nearer she realized that they were bumping each other's hips, progressively harder and harder. Adrea winked at her and then gave Evan a particularly vicious jolt, at which he only smiled sweetly. Mrs Parker beamed back: sometimes it was nice to be proved wrong.

Adrea was relieved to see that Snow was still in one piece. Last night, she had at first been under the impression that it had been Price that Evan had tangled with. Some hours later, however, she had been awakened by snoring to discover the man asleep by the side of the bed. It was only after they had turfed him out that she had heard the full story. Evan had been remorseful: it would cost a fortune to re-sole and re-stitch that boot.

Now Price was bustling about, dressed in a suit of ecru linen – expensive, but flapping horribly. Twin cameras were bouncing off his paunch: catching Adrea's expression, he raised them threateningly in her direction. Neither contained any film but he suspected that explaining the eye-trap would not reassure her. He began to hand out white cotton sun hats to the residents, having resisted the temptation of the jungle camouflage or Union Jack designs. They were an even split of S and XL, with no one in between.

With a great roar, the coach arrived, tearing towards them and then emergency-stopping right against the kerb. It was covered with dust, as if it had just crossed the Gobi Desert rather than tootling over from the Muswell Hill depot. 'Clean Me' and 'Help!' had been etched on its bonnet.

The driver sprang down. 'Is it safe?' he squeaked. 'I'm not insured against being eaten.' It was unclear whether he was referring to the zoo animals or his prospective passengers. His peaked grey cap was perched on top of his heavily greased hair and Evan observed that the pupils of his glittering eyes were the merest pinpricks. Things were getting interesting – the man was obviously out of his head.

The residents were all over-dressed in overcoats and mufflers. One frail old man was even trying to don a pair of mittens.

'Are those really necessary?' Evan asked, drawing them over the trembling fingers.

The man regarded him with unexpected hostility. 'There's always a wind about,' he growled. His mittened hands batted about his face until Evan turned up his coat collar and pulled the sunhat down over his furry ears.

He became aware that Snow was standing behind them. 'Be careful at the zoo, mister.' The voice was surprisingly soft. 'The old people, the animals' – Snow's hands made a washing motion – 'they will be frightened.'

'Perhaps some of them would rather stay behind,' Adrea suggested. Never having been to a zoo, she was not sure whether it was such a good idea. She didn't really think that the old people would be frightened, more that seeing the animals behind bars might upset them. Price, however, had already begun to load up the coach.

'Aren't you coming?' she asked Snow.

'Someone has to stay and look after the Babies,' he replied, draping his arms round Molly and Polly's shoulders.

Evan saw that Price was shaking a finger at him. Now look what you've done, his expression said.

Evan began tossing the Zimmer frames into the boot. Mrs Parker winced at such rough handling. In order to distinguish her own she had tied a loop of white wool around its right front leg. Now she saw without surprise that Mrs Yu-No-Hu had done exactly the same. The driver sprawled oafishly in the shade, smoking, watching the procession.

'In sixteenth-century India,' said Price to Adrea, 'Akbar the Great had a private menagerie – thousands of elephants, cheetahs, tigers and deer – which his subjects were obliged to visit. "Meet your brothers," Akbar told them, "and take them to your hearts."'

With a final crash, the wheelchair was pitched on top of the frames. Evan effortlessly carried Terry on board, to be followed by Stormy who ran along the aisle, miaowing loudly, until Adrea scooped him up and deposited him, hissing, back on the asphalt. As she re-ascended the steps, the driver at last came to life. 'Here you go, miss,' he said, cupping a squeezing, pinching hand under her bottom.

She could feel the middle finger rubbing along her new Levis' central seam.

Although she remained silent and stony-faced, she could tell by the way that Evan was staring at the back of the driver's neck that he knew something had happened. The coach windows were silted up. Only when Mrs Barker ran her sleeve across did she realize that most of the dirt was on the inside of the glass. The windscreen, however, remained opaque: it seemed the driver knew the way. It was oppressively airless and Adrea had gone without breakfast, but these were not the reasons why her stomach felt so hollow and her eyes kept trying to force themselves shut. She had started the day by playing side one of *Lady in Satin* and it had left her utterly depressed. This, she suspected, was exactly why Price had given it to her.

She had already heard some of the late small group recordings on which Billie hadn't sounded too bad, propped up by Mal Waldron's piano, while Al Cohn or Coleman Hawkins' kindly saxophones realized those phrases and tones she was no longer able to articulate. On *Lady in Satin*, however, she had been stuck in front of a full orchestra. Against their syrupy washes of sound, the last rags and tatters of her voice crumbled into dust, as if she thought that the sole intention of those shiny fiddles and funny-shaped horns was to humiliate her. The songs seemed to have been recorded in real time so that they became progressively more desperate, as the singer's soul sank into some terrible internal morass. In her head, Adrea could still hear the sound of Billie's over-glossed lips, too close to the microphone, sliding back from her teeth before each doomed entry, and how every quavering line culminated in a sort of belch. 'I Get Along Without You Very Well' had now become 'Gel lon chout chou vewa wewa'. It reminded her of those derelicts outside Camden Town tube station, except that they favoured Moore's Irish melodies rather than the *Great American Songbook*. Adrea imagined the orchestra – she was sure that they must have worn full evening dress to the sessions – emptying their pockets of small change and throwing it at Billie's feet.

The driver seemed to be taking an unnecessarily long route to the zoo. No one was talking, which made Adrea wonder whether Price could possibly be on board. When she turned round, however, there he was, grinning back at her. It was Mrs Parker who finally broke the silence when the coach stopped at the lights on Albany Road.

'Someone should empty that dustbin over there.'

'But isn't the blossom lovely?' said Adrea.

'Yes,' Mrs Parker reluctantly conceded. 'I suppose it covers up all those nasty branches.'

At Marylebone Road they turned off to follow the outer circle of Regent's Park. Hundreds of semi-naked bodies – presumably on lunch breaks from the schools of business or gynaecology – lay individually or in clusters on the parched earth. They looked as if they had been gunned down from the air. The men lay on their backs, hands cupped over their groins, while the women were spreadeagled like broken dolls. It was like one of Goya's battlefield scenes, thought Adrea, only the crows and ravens were missing. In fact, there were no birds at all, except for a few dazed mallards tottering across the dried-up bed of the boating lake.

The smell of the zoo – a combination of sawdust and burnt toast – hit them long before they pulled into the surprisingly empty car park. Most of the residents had seized up during the journey and had to be prised from their seats. Once again the driver stood apart and watched, refusing even to help Price unload the boot. 'I'm the *driver*,' he said very slowly, as if talking to an idiot. When Adrea appeared, however, he sprung across – 'Careful, miss, careful!' – to shepherd her down the steps. His left arm elongated grotesquely to get a good squeeze on both her breasts. As she walked away, his head tilted right back and his mouth widened in a silent howl.

At this point, Evan, bearing Terry in his arms, jumped from the top step to land with both feet on the driver's toes. The man tried to hop first on one leg then the other then fell over and began to curse. His cockney accent had vanished: in fact, it wasn't even English any more. Evan recognized the familiar sound of the valleys. He had long since come to the conclusion that Welsh was the language of pain. His one regret was that he had been wearing baseball boots rather than his snakeskins or Docs.

'So painful pleasure turns to pleasing pain,' Price observed, step-ping nimbly over the driver's writhing form. Up ahead he could see that the vanguard of the residents had already begun to swarm through the turnstiles. They were moving far quicker than they ever did back in Heron Close. Once inside, they split into three equal groups and headed off in different directions, like a crack regiment entering a well-reconnoitred, potentially hostile town.

The place was deserted, except for a few families. Price was amused to see how the children had ignored the zebras, tigers and giraffes, preferring instead to mount their painted wooden counter-parts on a small rickety merry-go-round, while their parents bickered underneath the café veranda. He caught up with Mrs Parker, who was squinting at the directions board.

'Why do they have beans in a zoo?' she asked.

'Bears,' said Price. 'It says bears. But there should be beans as well. Metempsychosis. Beans into bears into beans.'

Mrs Parker tossed her head and swung her Zimmer to follow the arrow. Just because her eyes were going was no reason for anyone to suggest that she was losing her marbles. Now, thanks to Price, Yu-No-Hu already had a ten-yard start.

Mrs Barker had been under the impression that they were being taken to visit a school, not a zoo. She had wondered whether they might be intended to act as a warning to the children: that if they were naughty and didn't work hard then they would end up old. Over sixty years later she reassured herself every morning that whatever things the day might bring, at least education was no longer among them. In her dreams she was still sitting at that wood and metal desk, which felt ready to snap shut like a mousetrap, while an enormous hand squeaked chalk across a blackboard: 1215 Magna Carta; 1588 Spanish Armada. 1900; Relief of Mafeking. She had never discovered what these words were supposed to signify. It had been even worse when letters and numbers got all mixed up with shapes. She felt sick looking at them. She wondered if Miss Maloney still taught at the school. She used to beat them for making a noise, then beat them for being silent. Her left hand, the one that slapped, had been even larger than the one that chalked. The woman must be dead by now, but Mrs Barker somehow felt that those hands might still be around. And so she had been relieved when the coach had driven straight past: even more so, when she realized that the school itself had gone, although she couldn't understand how even older houses could have appeared in its place.

So now here they were at the zoo. Although she had always lived within three miles of it she had never been inside. She hadn't given it a thought. Regent's Park was reserved for rich, idle people and she always had work to do. Today she had been afraid that she and the others would not be allowed through the gate, but once inside she had felt completely at home. She also felt rather angry: they had sent her to a school when she ought to have been put in a zoo.

As Evan pushed Terry's wheelchair along, the heat increased, as if they might be approaching its source. Most of the cages were empty and the fresh green paint of their bars was already beginning to bubble, split and flake. A sharp movement caught Adrea's eye but it was merely a grey squirrel foraging among the straw. At its approach a massive shape shrank further into the shadows. Surely it couldn't be too hot for these animals after their jungles and deserts? Only a couple of polar bears could be seen tiptoeing along the Mappin Terraces.

It was feeding time at the pool but the listless seals just watched as marauding herons and gulls swooped on their fish. The chair's squeaking had attracted half a dozen rats, which began to play chicken games in front of the wheels. They stretched their front and back legs right out, like tiny racehorses. Adrea could have sworn that one actually leapt through the revolving spokes. Although she had been terrified of them ever since reading *Nineteen-Eighty-Four*, these were the first she had ever seen. It was hard to imagine such pretty, playful animals scrabbling inside the mask in Room 101, preparing to feast on Winston's face. She watched as, with dangerous over-confidence, they disappeared underneath the reptile house. It was as if these indigenous creatures were drawing off the captives' vitality: they obviously considered themselves to be the main attraction.

Only a Bactrian Camel exhibited any interest in the three humans. Evan looked into its eyes, which appeared to have been wrapped in cellophane like boiled sweets. There was a strong smell of glue and the animal made a gritty, sandpapery sound as it walked, its dangling legs seeming not to touch the ground. It was like a puppet from an over-ambitious Nativity play. Evan felt affronted, as if, after an unconvincing hard luck story, it had tried to tap him for the price of a cup of tea. The camel blinked, then gave a great sigh and moved on. 'Sorry,' said Evan, but he was too late. It struck him that this was the first living creature to which he had ever apologized.

They headed towards the only cage that had attracted a crowd. Mums and dads and kiddies were standing in silent contemplation of the zoo's oldest inhabitant, Guy the Gorilla. He seemed oblivious to their presence, scratching vigorously at his chest with each limb in turn. Evan wondered if his fleas were specially imported from Africa. Suddenly, with two delicate fingers, Guy hooked through the bars a half-drunk Kia-Ora from a toddler's hand. He shook it against his ear and then carefully inverted it at the apex of a pyramid of his own dung. The audience were confused. They had been expecting something like his hilarious routine with Les Dawson on the *Sez Les* Christmas television special. Now they had begun to suspect that the monkey couldn't really tell gags or play Tijuana-style trumpet. Terry began to thrash about. Unable to see the cage, he was presumably agitated by all these people facing in the wrong direction.

Adrea realized that the other old people had disappeared. Panic rose in her throat, as if they might be in some terrible danger. She reassured herself that Price would be with them, only to acknowledge that this was precisely what she was worried about. She was relieved when they heard faint but familiar voices from the direction of the big cats' enclosure.

Out on the concourse they recognized the shape spreading across a wrought-iron bench. Ken did not seem pleased to see them. In fact, he looked as if he might have made a run for it if he had not been weighed down by a dozen evenly-distributed pigeons. Evan had never suspected him of such an affinity.

'I hate them,' said Ken, sifting a few more crumbs through his fingers. 'But feeding is a necessary part of Etruscan Bird Divination. You have to draw them to you and then observe what directions they go off in.'

'How are things at Tolmers Square?' Adrea asked. 'What's happening with those idiots?'

Ken did not seem to hear. Getting unsteadily to his feet, he raised his arms. The pigeons seemed not to fly away so much as fall off him, as if his body had been inverted. Adrea noticed that none of them had shat on his jacket or trousers. Perhaps they considered these to be already filthy enough? They scattered to north, south, east and west in a fairly even split. Ken shook his shoulders and began to trudge massively away, seemingly unaware that the largest liver and white bird had remained perching on his head.

'So what did they say?' Evan called after him.

Ken did not turn round but his voice seemed to issue from the pigeon's beak. 'The birds say that it's never going to rain again.'

Mrs Parker was beginning to lose patience with the animals. The bears had been piled in a moth-eaten heap: they might as well have been beans for all the use they were. Although the polar bears had kept sliding noisily down the water chutes, their white fur had nasty yellow streaks, as if they had been wetting themselves. The snakes were all coiled up like garden hoses, while the motionless insects had merged completely into their backgrounds of leaf or bark.

The residents were grumbling. These animals were not earning their keep: they seemed to think that the world owed them a living. Surely it wasn't too much to ask for the bears to growl, the snakes to slither, the eagle to be noble, the wolf to strike fear? Only a moose, pawing at its own shadow, was at all trying to fulfil its obligations. The elephants didn't look as if they could remember what they'd had for breakfast. Even when they encouraged them by hissing, roaring, howling or cackling, the creatures just stared back at them, too stupid to realize that they were being laughed at. Mrs Parker felt that they were like defeated enemies being put on display. During the last war it had been remarked locally how the animals always made a great noise before a heavy air-raid and how the bombs had always missed the zoo. Perhaps they had been on Germany's side? Hadn't Hitler been a vegetarian with lots of pets?

She sighed. These big cats were the worst of the lot. A few weeks ago she had watched on television the opening of the new lion house. The kings of the beasts had not seemed impressed by the flags and bunting or by the fanfares especially composed by the master of the Queen's music. They had not shown the least sign of gratitude or respect: one of them had actually yawned in Prince Philip's face. Her Majesty ought to remove them from the royal coat of arms.

'These animals,' she said aloud, 'need to waken their ideas up.'

How she longed to take that big sloppy leopard by its shoulders, or whatever you called them, and shake some sense into it! The tigers' mouths all looked puffy, as if they hadn't bothered to put their false teeth in. Stormy could have shown them how to behave: he was somehow both wilder and more tame.

How different they were from those museum animals that she had always admired! One of Stanley's friends, an amateur taxidermist, had explained how the aim was to make them seem as if 'they held no grudge'. They had looked eager and welcoming inside their glass cases, as though they understood the necessity for them to be hunted, shot, stuffed and put on display.

This serval cat, in contrast, appeared to be made up of nothing but grudges. It scurried madly round and round its enclosure – more of a hutch than a cage – while its enormous ears beat the air like the wings of some comical prototype aeroplane. Even if it did manage to fly there was wire mesh between it and the sky. It would have been better off learning how to dig. Its paws drummed the earth. Didn't it know that cats are supposed to be silent? Mrs Parker could also hear it panting: her own breathing was falling into its rhythm, as if the creature were trying to hypnotize her. The other old people were jeering and sarcastically applauding. A little old man in mittens spat towards the cage but his drool merely dripped on to his own toecaps.

'Stupid thing,' said Mrs Parker. 'What's it doing that for?'

Although Mrs Barker could have enlightened her she remained silent. Even as a little girl she had known that if you ran around in a circle for long enough you would disappear. Unfortunately, someone had always interrupted her before this could happen. Now, when she had the necessary time and space, she could no longer run, only shuffle. She raised her right fist and then opened it to reveal the silver key that was pressed into her palm. The serval's pace slackened, its ears pricked and its eyes came back into focus. Now Mrs Barker saw that its cage had no lock: access could only be gained from somewhere behind the grey shutters of its sleeping quarters. 'Soon,' she mouthed at the serval. 'Soon.'

She had not slept the night before but she was not tired. She felt better than she could ever remember. How foolish she had been to believe them when they told her that she needed eight hours sleep! As a result she had only had two-thirds of a life: what might she not have done with the rest of it? She remembered how she would lie next to Ron, without moving. His eyes always shut at eleven and clicked open again at seven. He didn't need an alarm clock.

While Evan and Snow had been fighting at the bottom of the stairs she had picked up three of the spilled keys. One was small and frilly, probably from a suitcase, while another looked as if it might fit the lid of a sewing machine. The third was the one that mattered, though: it was a pass-key, held only by matrons and their deputies and assistants. Mrs Barker had seen that distinctive triangular head so many times: it had always fascinated her because the individual keys were of such different shapes and sizes. When it was in her hand she was sure that she could feel the metal shift and change, and it had seemed that every door began to open even before it turned in their locks. She wondered whether Mr Snow's change of character might have something to do with his loss of this key.

She had spent all night exploring Heron Close. With the key, the place had been transformed. She had closed and locked each bedroom door in turn, counting up to twenty before re-opening them. Knowing that Price was up in the attic, she had let herself in to the matron's flat. She struck a match and the flare had momentarily revealed rich carpets, leather chairs and large gold-framed paintings on the walls. When she turned on the light, however, there had been nothing but overflowing ashtrays and waist-high piles of books.

She had been astonished to find cutlery and crockery in the kitchen, sheets and towels in the linen store, and mops and buckets in the utility room. While the night staff did their rounds she had searched the office. Its cupboards contained either broken electrical equipment or board games and packs of cards that had never been used. Her sense of excitement, however, did not flag. She felt that she was looking for something, although she had no idea what it might be. Now, in the zoo, she had the strangest feeling that she had been seeking to release some unknown creatures – neither the residents nor the staff – which she suspected had been imprisoned there.

The serval cat had started circling again, anti-clockwise this time. It must be like being in hell, Mrs Barker thought. The poor thing probably didn't even have the consolation of knowing that it was going to die. She saw that the old man in the mittens had turned away from the cage to fumble for his fags. Why did all the weediest ones smoke Woodbines? He succeeded in hanging one precariously off his lower lip and then looked at her expectantly. She stared right through him: today the matches were staying in her bag.

Adrea, following Terry and Evan towards the lion house, was no longer sure that these were the right old people. Their eyes glittered, their faces twisted and their laughter rattled metallically. The sunlight around them had a greenish tinge. They were shaking their fists, brandishing two fingers or blowing raspberries at the cages. Some were even rattling the bars. She only recognized them by their sun hats. The mitten man lobbed his unlit cigarette at a leopard but it merely blinked and turned away. The residents followed suit, while obviously realizing that turning one's back on someone else's back was rather beside the point.

'This is a horrid place.' Mrs Parker came to meet them. 'There's nothing here but animals.'

'What were you expecting?' asked Evan.

Mrs Parker sent the front legs of her Zimmer whistling past their startled faces. 'I expected them to be more like us.'

They watched her go, with Mrs Barker following. She had been right, Adrea thought, everything had suddenly turned horrible. Only Evan, wreathed in his own pale light, looked the same as always. He set Terry's chair rearing up and then spun it round three or four times, but she could tell that he was as upset as herself. She rested her forehead against the bars of the cage. Those snooty leopards were showing no sign of recognizing that she and Evan were any different from the others. Her eyes filled with tears, creating the illusion of a further wavering set of bars, then a third and a fourth. Bars beyond bars beyond bars. Although she blinked, they were merging to form a sheer metal wall.

Everything was wrong, everything was going to have to change. Hadn't the great flood in Genesis been preceded by a long drought? Perhaps Ken's Etruscan pigeons had been wrong and the waters would soon begin to rise? She and Evan could build an ark on the summit of Primrose Hill. The leopards would be pleased enough to see them then. She imagined the animals, two by two, coming up the gangplank. Terry and his chair would have to be there, of course: together, they surely constituted a new, distinct species. She loved the idea of floating for ever across an infinite sea on a ship echoing with the cries of two of everything. She didn't think that they would bother to send out the doves to look for land.

To her surprise, almost two hours had elapsed. It was time to return to the coach. Hitherto, whenever she looked at her watch it had always been earlier rather than later than she had thought. Now she felt as if someone – Price, probably – were playing a malign trick on her. As they moved towards the exit, a faint sound issued from a ragged privet hedge: it reminded her of the flint wheel of Billy the Sailor's Zippo. Then a tiny, reddish-brown shape came flickering through the leaves to alight on the armrest of Terry's chair. It was a wren. The beak was striking at the air, the tail was brandished like a club, every feather bristled with uncontrollable fury. What had happened to her old friend Troglodytes Troglodytes? What had happened to dear little Jenny Wren? She cringed as it threw itself at her face: there was a hiss as it passed her ear. Rising, the bird seemed to increase in size until finally, for a few chilly seconds before it disappeared, it blotted out the sun. Adrea felt that they'd had a narrow escape, as if the creature had gone to destroy other worlds on the far side of the universe.

'Alas, dear lady,' said Evan, in Price's orotund tones, 'we appear to have violated some wren taboo.'

Mrs Parker and Mrs Barker had succeeded in finding the one place in London that the heat had not reached: the ladies' lavatory. In adjoining cubicles they sat in companionable silence, their brows pressed against the cool, smooth tiles, lulled by the faint sound of water, each drop followed by echo upon echo. Words that neither of them understood had been carved deep into the glossy green wood.

There was no getting away from it, however: they were both stuck. Having backed inside, they were now caged by their own Zimmers, unable to reach the bolt. How could you get in to somewhere and then not get out of it? Mrs Parker's knees seemed to be rising, as if the toilet bowl were slowly sucking her in. Neither spoke: both were determined not to be the first to call for help. If only they could trust each other to shout at the same time! When Mrs Parker drew in her breath Mrs Barker would do the same but then they would pause, suspecting a trap, before slowly exhaling. So there they sat, their eyes gradually closing, their chins dropping on to their chests.

Price had passed the time in the Lubetkin penguin house. After a while, the birds began to seem fixed while the black and white tiles and concrete shifted vertiginously around them. When he finally tore himself away, everything continued to pitch and strobe before his eyes.

The residents were already at the exit. Price saw that their sun hats no longer fitted but either perched comically on the crowns of their heads or enveloped the faces below. What possible reasons could they have had for swapping them around? Only now did he realize that – apart from the lovers – he was the only person to have gone bare-headed. Adrea was even browner, Evan, if anything, paler, but when Price touched his own throbbing cheek his fingers adhered.

He did not need to count to know that two residents were missing. At the front of the group were Mrs P- and Mrs B-sized spaces. If only they could just stay lost! He had to resist the temptation to bundle the others back on to the coach, tear back to Heron Close, lock the doors, draw the curtains and take the phone off the hook. Why wasn't life that simple?

After a while, someone remembered seeing them heading for the toilets. Price called their names but there was no reply. 'Nothing beats a nice day at the zoo,' he whispered to Adrea, with a horrible smirk. Unaccountably, she felt afraid to go in after them, as if they might have been armed and dangerous.

Only when she stood on the seats of the adjoining stalls and looked over the top did she locate them. Touchingly, they had both fallen asleep: she had to reach down and gently massage their scalps to wake them. Neither seemed to be in the least embarrassed. Adrea found herself apologizing as she hooked out the frames that had imprisoned them.

'Oh dear, what can the matter be?' Price was singing. 'Two old ladies locked in the lavatory.'

To his own ears he sounded like Dietrich Fischer-Dieskau but Adrea's horror-struck expression implied that he didn't.

'They were there from Monday to Saturday, / Nobody knew they were there.'

When they returned to the exit, Adrea discovered that now Terry and his wheelchair had disappeared. No one had seen him go. Some instinct seemed to guide her feet so that they turned left, left and right to discover Terry seated once more in front of the gorilla's enclosure. The earlier crowds had now dispersed and Guy had come right up to the bars. The two of them seemed to be locked in some deep, silent communion, or perhaps they were merely staring coincidentally into the same space, oblivious of each other, because the big monkey did not react when she pushed the chair away.

Back in the car park Price thought that a replacement driver had arrived until he realized that it was the same man, deflated and diminished. Now he was fussing around the old people, while giving Adrea the widest possible berth. He didn't even glance at her but Price could see that he couldn't take his adoring eyes off Evan. It seemed that the boy's footwear, like the spear of Achilles, might possess redemptive powers. Perhaps all the world needed to set it right was a good stamping or a whack round the head with a stack-heeled size nine?

On the return journey everyone was once again quiet but this was a different, satisfied silence, as if a difficult mission had just been accomplished. Price observed that while everyone else was being bounced around, Adrea's shoulders remained steady. By the set of her jaw he could tell that she was crying, although he flattered himself that he would have known this merely by the angle of her right foot. He himself felt drained as if once more, like Prospero, his willpower alone had first set up and then animated the events of the day. It had been well worth the effort, though. He yawned and stretched luxuriously. He had been pretty certain that the zoo would do the trick.

Terry also guessed that Adrea was weeping. Across the aisle her outlines had begun to blur. He felt slightly guilty. Being young was hard enough without having to chase round after cripples. Perhaps she had sensed his irritation when Evan had wheeled him away from the crowd in front of the gorilla's cage? That had been the first time that the young people had ever misinterpreted him. All he had wanted was to get closer but instead he had found himself presented with a big red bird with legs like pipe-cleaners.

It was twenty-five years since he had last been in the zoo and he could have sworn that the same gorilla had been there in the same cage, in the same position, wearing the same expression. Terry had been with that squinty barmaid from Gort. He couldn't remember her name or her face, only how she had shrugged off the arm that he had wrapped protectively around her. 'I'm not afraid of that poor old thing,' she had jeered. 'It's not King Kong.' She had kept saying she would but then she wouldn't until that very evening when she said she wouldn't and did, and then went back to County Mayo.

It seemed impossible that the monkey was still there. Terry somehow felt that if he could just get back in front of that cage he would find himself once again next to whatever her name was. And they would just link arms – she had been all skin and bone but with unexpected clusters of lovely, pulpy flesh – and walk together down the shady side of Fitzroy Road back to the Eagle and Child.

He had no idea who could have suddenly seized his chair and conveyed him back to Guy's cage, only that it must have been a man, strong but out of condition, who had been simultaneously panting and making a low chuckling sound. The barmaid did not appear but the gorilla raised its head and then ambled towards him. Terry saw that its eyes were glittering with sudden intelligence. It sat down opposite him, as if occupying a phantom wheelchair. It looked a bit like Chairman Mao. Then, without moving its mouth, it began to speak. He could hear the voice ringing through his head, with a refined, sarcastic inflection that reminded him of Price. 'At last,' it said, 'someone I can actually *talk* to.'

'It's good to see you again,' said Terry. 'Although it's probably not good for you to be still stuck here after all these years.'

'Don't you go feeling sorry for me,' the creature said sharply. 'This cage is the last free place on earth. And at least I can do *this*.' In the space of a heartbeat, it sprang, without any change of posture or expression, to the far side of its enclosure and back again.

'I've often thought about you,' it continued. 'Did you ever get anywhere with that barmaid back in '52? I quite liked her. She was dog rough but she had something.'

Terry tried to throw himself at the bars but did not succeed in moving a muscle. 'You'd better keep your hands to yourself,' he raged. 'And your feet as well.'

'Contrary to your fantasies' – Guy looked offended – 'your women do not interest us in that way.'

It ran its fingers across the bars, as if playing a harp. 'These things only remain for as long as I want them to. I could walk out of here now but the time is not yet right. We apes are coming back while you humans are on the way out. Soon you will all be in chairs like that: you'll put engines in them, of course, and weapons, but that won't do you any good when the cows and sheep rise up. You should have killed them while you had the chance. The things you eat will soon be eating you. At least your Chairman Mao was right about one thing: change will indeed come from the barrel of a gun, and then we will move in. And don't kid yourself that we might be evolving into you – we've got a very different direction in mind.'

A dreadful thought struck Terry. 'Do you have something to do with this? With my being in this bloody chair?'

The gorilla put a hand over its eyes. 'I am not yet allowed to answer that question,' said the voice.

'Do you know when all this is going to happen?' Terry was trying to project an unconcern that he did not really feel.

'Of course. To the day, to the hour, to the minute.'

Terry began to laugh. 'What good are guns to you lot? Even if you could pull the trigger you wouldn't be able to aim. All you'll shoot is yourselves. And your cows and sheep have even less chance. You'll have to invent your own apeguns, sheepguns, cowguns. That should hold you for another million years or so.'

'A million years,' said Guy, calmly, 'is no time at all.'

If Adrea had not wheeled him away at that point, Terry wondered, would the gorilla – knowing that he himself couldn't pass on the information and that he would not be believed even if he could – have spilled the beans? Looking across, he saw that the girl was no longer trying to hide her tears. Perhaps she had also sensed the monkey's threats? He wished that he could tell her that it had all been just talk, that over the years he had heard such words on many occasions from the mouths of various defeated species, round about closing time.

nineteen

How nice it was that everything had got back to normal! Mrs Parker smiled across at Stormy, sprawled out in his old favourite place in the centre of the carpet, while he flashed his front claws and blinked. No longer drawn to the attic, the cat was once more sauntering between Yu-No-Hu and herself. She put down her needles and shook the ragged length of wool. If only you could knit and unpick at the same time!

Over the last week the temperature had become more bearable, although the TV weathermen kept insisting that it was getting even hotter. What could they know about what was happening in Heron Close? Mrs Parker glanced around the sitting room. Everyone appeared to be asleep with their eyes open. Beyond the television's babble there was silence: even their stomachs were no longer rumbling. Now that their old food was back, indigestion and constipation were things of the past. Those terrible bleeding chunks of meat and sharp raw vegetables had been vanquished by good old trusty mush. At dinner that evening, when the lid of the tureen was lifted to reveal the familiar glistening mountain of mashed potato, there had been a hearty round of applause and the sound of Squibbsy's triumphant barking had echoed from the dumb-waiter. How they had gorged on the mashed peas and lumpy gravy before wolfing down the rubbery cheese triangles, strips of foil and all!

Evan and Adrea had served the food without a word. Ever since the visit to the zoo they had been different. No more laughter, no more games: they seemed to have lost all their pep. They were slower and clumsier and appeared somehow to have shrunk. When Evan dropped a plate he had bent almost arthritically to retrieve it. They had become just like all the other care assistants: it was as if they had finally understood that a job was just a job. Mrs Parker felt sorry for them, almost ashamed, but then told herself that all this was doing the young people a favour. Sooner or later everyone had to learn that life was not the way it ought to be.

If everything was back to normal, however, why was she still feeling so on edge? One strange thing was that Yu-No-Hu had stopped following her about. Mrs Parker had been relieved until she realized that it must mean that the woman was up to something. And then there was the problem of Mr Snow. He was showing no sign of returning to his good old bad old self. No matter how bothersome the Babies became, his frightening new smile didn't so much as waver. Fortunately, she had hit on the solution and now treated him as merely a second Bridie. Mr Price had been behaving oddly, too. He had been unnaturally cheerful at the zoo but had then grown gloomier and gloomier. Like Stormy, he didn't seem to be spending as much time upstairs. She watched as he passed the doorway, head tilted back, lifting his feet as if wading through heavy mud, carrying under his arm a flagon of cider wrapped in a towel. She wondered whether he realized that day by day he was looking more and more like Mrs Allen.

Price was indeed not a happy man. The heat was getting worse and he had just spent the day vainly trying to recall the policewoman's face. Now he was no longer sure she had even been a blonde. He had been ignoring Evan and Adrea while remaining uncomfortably aware that it was really they who were ignoring him. Now, finally admitting defeat, he was heading for the attic.

It wasn't until he reached the top of the stairs that the sound hit him. How could those thunderous guitars and drums have been so well-contained when even the most delicate of his chamber pieces was apparently fully audible on the ground floor? When Evan opened the door Price was shocked by how thin he had become. He realized that he had never seen either of the lovers actually eating anything. They resembled two vampires who, having sucked the world dry, were reduced to preying on each other. Presumably they had sensed that the blood had ceased to circulate through his own veins.

Adrea was no longer ignoring him. She smiled and nodded from the bed, as if trying to convey sympathy and understanding, although he was sure that this could not possibly be the case. In the candlelight her face resembled one of the women in Picasso's *Demoiselles D'Avignon*.

'Is she *on* something?' he shout-whispered in Evan's ear.

'Nothing seems to have much effect any more.' The boy shook his head sadly. 'We don't know what to spend our wages on now. I'll swap my stash for another flagon of that cider.'

The room was stifling. Price felt as if his face were ballooning, his sinuses pumped full of stale air. 'Are you two planning ever to leave this building again?' he asked.

Their expressions indicated that they considered this to be a bit rich, coming from him.

'Maybe we'll go down to Notting Hill,' said Evan, 'for the carnival.'

Price's watch showed ten past eight. 'You'll have missed it.'

Evan grinned. 'It won't get interesting until after dark. When the carnival is over, the real carnival begins.'

Price poured out the cider. Even now he had no idea what he was doing here, what, if anything, he wanted to ask or tell them. Any pleasure he had taken in playing gooseberry had long since faded. He didn't know whether he liked or disliked them, envied or pitied them, wanted them to succeed or fail.

Evan and Adrea were now lying at opposite ends of the bed, facing each other. As Price watched, they simultaneously raised and extended their right legs until the soles of their feet pressed together. Then their other legs scissored up so that the ankle lay against the opposite knee. Arms crossed behind their heads, they stared unblinkingly into each other's eyes. There was something unaccountably disturbing about this, as if it had some hieratic significance that Price would never understand.

'Oh! Oh! Oh!'

Surely this tableau deserved a better musical accompaniment than someone shouting, 'Oh! Oh! Oh!' over and again? Price had been trying to ignore it, realizing that the sole purpose of such rubbish must be to irritate people like himself, until he realized that a sound like spitting fat was also replicating itself. The record had stuck.

'Don't touch it!' Evan and Adrea yelled, as he moved to take the needle out of the groove. They had broken apart and were now glaring at him as if he had been about to commit some dreadful blasphemy. They had become unpredictable. When he goaded them they didn't react, whereas something seemingly innocuous would suddenly set them off. They were regarding him with such contempt that he felt a blush painfully spreading across his sun-scorched face. There was nothing to be said. He looked away.

Then he found himself outside on the landing again, watching the door slowly closing. It was as if the whole world – with the exception of himself – had suddenly jerked a few feet to the right. As he turned away he could hear, over the 'Oh! Oh! Oh!', the more urgent and brutal sounds of Adrea climaxing. He knew that she wasn't taunting him: she was incapable of faking anything or even of understanding why she might need to. But how could Evan have brought her to it so quickly? Or how could she have held it off for so long? One thing was certain: he would be in no hurry to enter that attic again.

Downstairs, Mrs Barker was relieved that the night had come. Soon she would be roaming through Heron Close with her magic key, coming and going as she pleased. She would have to take care, though, not to leave traces in the washing powder that she suspected had been deliberately sprinkled all over the utility-room floor. And she feared that once again, as dawn approached, her disappointment would grow as she discovered merely the same things in their usual places. Perhaps she hadn't been looking properly? She would squint through lowered lashes or open her eyes so wide that they felt they were about to burst: still nothing happened. Every step seemed to take her further away from the unknown object of her search, while pointless questions filled her mind. Why did some rooms have light switches while others had cords? And why were those switches at different heights and in different places? Why were some lamps bright while others – with similar bulbs and shades – were dim? And why was their light sometimes yellow, sometimes white and sometimes almost brown, as if the walls had been plastered with wet mud? These questions kept on asking themselves, although she had no real interest in what the answers might be.

She was increasingly restless, as if the serval cat were pacing round and round inside her swollen stomach. Perhaps there was no flesh and bones under her clothes, only a cage of rusty metal bars and chicken wire? Worse, she was no longer sleeping because her wardrobe had become noisier than ever. There was now no doubt that the sounds were coming from within its secret drawer. She had removed all her matchboxes but it had made no difference. Bridie had walked in yesterday morning when the creaking and groaning was at its height. A hammering had begun, as if a tiny horse were trying to kick its way out. At least it had been a relief to know that someone else could hear it, too.

'It's just the pipes,' Bridie had concluded, although she had gone away looking angry and upset. That was what people always said when there was something that they couldn't account for. Whyever would pipes be in a wardrobe?

This evening she had finally taken action by holding a handful of lit matches inside the drawer until they burnt out. The noises stopped for a full five minutes and then ceased again when she took out the next match, before she could even strike it. Everyone and everything was afraid of fire – except for herself. To be on the safe side, before she came downstairs, she had ignited a full box of Swan Vestas, slamming the wardrobe door and almost running out of the room. She was disappointed when no subsequent explosions had rocked the building.

Up in the attic the candles had all burnt out. Evan, lying in the darkness, was trying to identify a strange shape that he had found in the bed. Smallish and rectangular, it was warm and smooth to the touch and surprisingly heavy. It suddenly split in two under his fingers and its dry, prickly intestines came spilling out. Admitting defeat, he turned on the light and stared for a while, as if confronted by a mystery object from *Ask The Family*, before he recognized his tobacco tin and saw that the mattress was strewn with Old Holborn.

How could darkness have made it seem twice its real size and many times heavier? Women's bodies were similarly transformed, although all that giggling and grumbling had usually ruined the impression that he might be grappling with snakes or wild beasts. With Adrea, however, the effect was the same whether the lights were on or off, his eyes open or shut. Blocks of stone pressed down on his chest, sharp-toothed coils tightened round his waist. while steel toecaps hacked at his shins. Hair sprouted only to vanish again, half a dozen tongues crawled like snails across his back and he kissed at a face that had lost its mouth, nose and eyes. A nice wolverine or a boa constrictor might have provided some respite.

'Oh! Oh! Oh!' growled Patti Smith. It was 'Gloria', the first track on side one. The record had stuck on the 'O' of the spelt-out G-L-O-R-I-A that led into the final chorus. The letter, like a great round mouth, had swallowed up the rest of the song. What would happen if they left it playing? How long would it take before the needle wore through the vinyl? Evan was sure that he could hear other sounds behind those 'Oh's. At first he had thought that faint echoes of Price's miserable lieder might have been lingering in the cobwebbed corners of the room but the notes of this distant piano were distorted. Perhaps, like Jimmy Durante, he had found the fabled lost chord? And surely that wasn't a human voice but closer to barking: sharper and more sustained than Squibbsy's, like those coyotes that turn out to be Comanches in Western films. Ken had warned him that it was dangerous to play the same music over and over: repetition created a portal for demons to come through. At the Windsor Free Festival, he had claimed, Hawkwind had got stuck on the same riff for so long that green elementals could be plainly seen crawling out of the bass player's stack.

Adrea was no longer sure that she liked 'Gloria': perhaps she never had. But however tinny it sounded, she felt it was no longer music but a sort of corrosive agent. Every time they played it, another layer seemed to peel off everything. Evan's right arm felt to have gradually sawed through her body and was now sawing its way back again. Perhaps they should develop a magic act, although she had no intention of wearing the sequins and fishnet tights. Invisible insects were once again crawling over her skin: she particularly liked it when they tickled the follicles of her forearms and shins. How glad she was that she had resisted Sally's attempts to persuade her to pluck and shave. Wherever would she have been without her little hairs?

Evan had gone numb from waist to knees. He looked down resignedly at his spongy, pulverized cock. To his surprise, it twitched violently and then, with an Elvis-style snarl on its puffy lips, re-erected itself in a vain lunge at his throat. He still couldn't feel it, though. Perhaps all his long-suffering organs were preparing to secede? He turned off the light again and his body seemed to sink through the mattress, to be swallowed up by living ooze.

On returning to her bedroom, Mrs Barker found that the noises had started up again, even louder than before. And they were different: a choking cry and a hollow double thump, sounding every few seconds. She placed her palms flat against the wardrobe door and paused. Suppose there was a hanged man inside, head lolling against his shoulder, boot heels drumming against the wood, as he swung on the end of his rope? She had always feared wardrobes. They made her think of upright coffins. Even worse were the clothes that hung there, waiting to come marching out with no people in them, only thin metal hooks where the faces should be. That was why she draped her own few garments over radiators and chairs.

The wardrobe was empty, however, and there was no smell of burning. Sliding back the secret drawer, she saw that the Swan Vesta box had been only partially consumed. A good half of its contents had failed to ignite. She applied another match to the remains but, as it hissed and flared, the noises came again, accompanied by a blast of air that almost extinguished the little fire.

Mrs Barker crossed the room and extricated from under the mattress Mr Snow's copy of *The Times*, which she had taken from the office the previous night. She tore the pages in two, then into four and rolled each piece into a tight ball, lining these up along the window ledge. She never closed her curtains, even though her room faced the blocks across the square. Unlike many of the female residents, she did not think that men were always trying to watch her undress. They had never been particularly interested even when she was a child. But every time she looked out of the window there they were: *men*, pale and half-naked, standing like statues in their unlit windows, watching. Some even appeared to be looking through binoculars. She had concluded that because these figures never left their stations and went shirtless even in winter they must be a trick of the light. Looking up, she saw that a dark-brown ring was spreading across her ceiling, giving off tiny white curls of smoke as if a second fire had started up in the attic. Perhaps she should sound the alarm? She suspected that she could be burnt by other people's fires.

She saw that her own blaze had revived and that the secret drawer was lined with delicate blue flames, like burning alcohol. When she tossed in some of the paper they shrank away and merely licked harmlessly at the far corners. She would have to do things properly and start again from scratch. Just as she began to re-make it, however, a sudden red fork spat out at her face. Without hesitation, she plunged her hands in and grabbed the flames. She shook them and squeezed them, pummelled them and tied them in knots. It took a strong nerve to rule fire: you had to show it who was boss.

'TOP PEOPLE READ *THE TIMES*.' Mrs Barker could see how the paper had got its reputation. It was perfect for kindling: a nice, slow dependable burn. Despite the merry blaze, though, the noise continued. At first she had thought that it might be Mr Price or those two care assistants doing something in the attic but, a few days ago, after seeing him enter the matron's flat and Evan and Adrea take the Babies to the bathroom, she had gone upstairs and found it thumping away as usual. Then she had wondered if it might be bombs. In the war there had been a long descending wail followed by the dull kerr-ump of the explosion, but thirty or so years later they were bound to have come up with a different type.

Across the corridor, Mrs Parker was on her knees, peering through the tiny crack that she had left in the door. After only a few minutes, the figure of Mrs Yu-No-Hu glided silently past. As usual at nights she had dispensed with her Zimmer and was heading for the stairs rather than the lift. How typical it was of her to drag it around when she didn't really need to! Even so, Mrs Parker, when she followed, left her own frame next to the bed on which Stormy lay curled up, asleep.

Wherever was the wretched woman going? It seemed unlikely that she would be meeting some secret lover. Perhaps she was a spy or a sneak? But who was there for her to spy on? What was there for her to sneak about? Who could want to hear anything that she might have to tell them? It must have something to do with food or the cat.

Yu-No-Hu was easy to shadow: if she did begin to turn round she herself would be long gone, back in her room, tucked up in bed, before the movement was completed. Even so, when Mrs Parker reached the bend in the stairs she paused until she heard the bottom door click gently shut. Then she followed, only to find herself staring in dismay down an empty corridor. Yu-No-Hu had disappeared.

There had not been time for her to have reached and turned the corner. Mrs Parker began peering into the bedrooms, but no one was moving and there was no snoring or sound of breathing. The toilets and bathrooms were dark and vacant. She suspected that Yu-No-Hu was doing such things purely to baffle and disturb her. All the time that she was searching she had the uncomfortable sense that hostile eyes were upon her, that now she was the one who was being followed.

She hurried back to her bedroom. Although the indentation of his body remained on the coverlet, Stormy was gone. Whenever she went out she took care to close the door. Something very odd was going on. The silence had become even more oppressive. As she crossed the corridor, her feet made no sound. Yu-No-Hu's door seemed to be opening even before her fingers touched its handle.

Inside, she groped for the light switch, not expecting it to be in the same place as her own. The room was deserted but she was shocked to see that the curtains were still open. It was as if she had just caught herself red-handed. At least she could hear again: across the room, someone was apparently having a fit or being sick. She approached with some apprehension. What on earth could Yu-No-Hu or Stormy be doing in the wardrobe?

Upstairs, Adrea was wondering what terms she should use for what she and Evan were doing. 'Making love' sounded sort of light-industrial, 'sex' primarily denoted gender and she'd never been able to take 'fucking' seriously after reading *Lady Chatterley's Lover*. All that remained was 'screwing'. Hitherto it had always struck her as ugly, suggesting the extraction of money or D.I.Y. things with shelves and brackets. And surely, to be accurate, the man's body would have to rotate, like a Catherine wheel on a pin? Now, however, it struck her as perfectly apt, for she felt as if the two of them were, physically and mentally, going deeper and deeper, boring further and further into the core of things.

Her sister had once told her that having sex was like eating Toblerone while riding a flying white horse between the arcs of a double rainbow, only better. Adrea had been relieved when this had turned out not to be the case. It was more like lying in the grass on top of Blea Moor with the trains thundering by underneath, magnified a few thousand times. Her orgasms seemed to originate outside herself, from somewhere a long way off. She imagined them whirling down Chalk Farm Road, across the square and up the back stairs, then blowing down the door to wash through her body before continuing on their way. There was certainly something impersonal about it all. She remembered how when she was coming down from the fells that day she had slipped from the stepping-stones into a fast-flowing stream and had realized – at first with panic but then, as she thrashed and spluttered towards the bank, with increasing delight – that the water had no idea that she was there.

She thought about the noises that had sometimes penetrated the walls in Edgware: of Sally whimpering like a dog tied to a lamppost and forgotten. In contrast, she herself sounded as if she were drowning. For a while she had not believed that this could be emanating from herself. Even now it seemed that a part of her was already on the far side of everything, looking back. Somehow it didn't seem possible that this screwing could have anything to do with reproduction. Perhaps there was a completely different thing that other people did in order to make babies? She felt as if she and Evan were engaged in killing something rather than bringing it to life.

In the storeroom under the stairs, Mrs Barker was sitting in the dark. It was her favourite place. She had a sense that here she was closest to whatever it was that she was seeking. She had always thought that it would be little more than a cupboard but it had turned out to be wider and deeper than any of the other rooms. It contained nothing but rolls of toilet paper, great pillars of San Izal that appeared to be supporting the ceiling. There was a continual rustling sound, like a forest in an autumn wind.

As always, though, just when she was feeling that she would never again move from this spot, it all started getting too much. She wanted to turn and run but couldn't move. It was as if she were standing on the edge of a cliff, feeling the ground beginning to crumble beneath her feet. Just before she fell into space her hand once again shot up to pull the light cord.

There was one thing about this otherwise wonderful room that really got her goat. She had been sitting on a low stack of ultra-soft peach-coloured toilet tissues reserved for the quarterly visits of the council auditors. Tissues! As if auditors, whatever *they* might be, didn't have backsides but only second noses! *Tissues!* She wished she could steep the sheets with acid or coat them with phosphorus so that when torn they would burst into flames. On her way out she snatched up a couple of rolls and tucked them under her cardigan. They were the first things she had ever stolen in her life – or the second if you counted the magic key, or the third, if you counted

Mr Snow's newspaper. She reassured herself that it wasn't so much stealing as finding – and finders were keepers, after all.

Evan felt Adrea spasm against him but no sound followed for a few seconds. It made him think of the gap between a lightning flash and the thunder. It was as if, although they felt to be clasped so close that their atoms mingled, there were still miles between them. Their bones clacked against one another while their flesh seemed to be melting and flowing like candle-wax off the edge of the bed. The numbness was spreading to the rest of his body, although his hamstrings were still throbbing, threatening to cramp. The inside of his mouth was raw and whenever they kissed, a pack of starving animals seemed to be fighting over his tongue. Although he was naked he had the sensation that he was wearing heavily waterlogged clothes. His scrotum had tightened like a fist so that, as he reached his climax, the semen now felt as if it came from the crown of his head, leaching through the brain then pinballing down the spine before deflecting off his backbone to explode – before it could reach the glans – out of the sides of his shaft.

At the same moment the record jerked out of its groove and went on to the chorus, as though the two-hour hiatus had never occurred: 'G-L-O-R-I-A! Gloria! G-L-O-R-I-A! Gloria!'

Sometimes, it seemed, when time stopped, you just had to give it a good push to get it started again. Evan realized that – although it was impossible, involving the simultaneous use of opposed and incompatible muscles – he was once again laughing as he came.

'There's a fire,' Mrs Parker kept saying to herself. 'There is a fire in Yu-No-Hu's wardrobe.' Curiously, this discovery had not surprised her at all. She had somehow known what she was going to find, even as she was walking towards it. She could not have smelt anything because it was burning without odour. There was no smoke, only fire. It struck her that she had woken up that morning anticipating exactly this. It seemed perfectly natural that a fire should be burning in a wardrobe. Where else would you expect it to be?

She had no idea how long she had been standing there. She felt like Pandora, except that there were only nice things inside her box. It was many years since she had seen a proper fire: she had come to believe that they were extinct. This one appeared to be neither spreading nor going out but just feeding happily on itself. There was no sign of Stormy and she had the strangest feeling that the fire might be the cat, transformed. She extended a hand, as if to stroke the flames, but then withdrew it, although she felt they were more likely to scratch or bite than to burn her. The noises were getting louder. Not only was the wardrobe alive but it also appeared to be actively enjoying being ablaze.

A sudden movement away to the left caught her eye but when she turned sharply there was no one there. Staggering back, however, she collided on her opposite side with something soft but utterly unyielding. Yu-No-Hu did not seem to have registered her presence: the woman's eyes remained fixed on the fire. In its flickering light, Mrs Parker was unsure whether she was looking older or younger. Advancing, she produced from under her cardigan what appeared to be two rolls of pale-coloured toilet paper. After breaking the seals, she began tearing off lengths to criss-cross the flames, as if trying to wrap them. Suddenly able to bend and stretch, she moved in rhythmic sweeps, like a dancer being thrown between two partners. The fire punched through its bonds like a huge fist and the toilet paper disintegrated into a mass of black smuts that vanished before they could hit the ground. Now Yu-No-Hu was using the second roll to set trails from the wardrobe to the four corners of the room, and at the end of each she carefully deposited an item of crumpled clothing taken from the back of the chair.

It was noticeable that the more Yu-No-Hu fanned the flames, the louder and more regular the noises from the wardrobe became.

Although she did not speak this language, it seemed to Mrs Parker that they were issuing instructions as to what to do next. She was fascinated by the fire's shifting colours and the way it advanced by igniting the air up at the ceiling and then gradually sliding down to the carpet.

Yu-No-Hu pulled the linen and blankets off her bed and piled them into a pyramid in the centre of the floor. Then she dragged the mattress over to block out the window. Only now did she acknowledge Mrs Parker. The great head swivelled towards her and the square mouth opened in a series of jerks. Only now did Mrs Parker realize that she had never heard the woman utter so much as a single word.

'Eh ire oo ose uruns!'

The lips did not move: the voice seemed to come from somewhere low in her chest. Mrs Parker saw that a small box of England's Glory matches had been pressed into the palm of her hand. She walked across the room, struck two matches simultaneously and then obediently applied them to the curtains. She could smell her own hair singeing as the shiny fabric immediately went up in a sheet of flame. Mrs Barker was now tossing the rest of her matchbox collection one by one into the advancing fire. Each time, after a little half-curtsy, she took another backwards step towards the door.

In the office, Price was laboriously signing requisition forms for new pots and pans. He guessed that the cook would be selling them on, after polishing up the old ones. Recently he had taught himself to write his name with his left hand but then discovered that he could no longer do it in the orthodox way. Now he felt as if he were forging his own signature. Just as he had almost got it right, the door flew open.

'Fire! Fire!' Bridie was shouting. 'Fire on the first floor!'

Still unwilling to look at him, she was instead addressing the filing cabinets. In turning, she tripped over her own heels and, clutching wildly at the door jamb, toppled out of sight. Price had been so taken aback by the breaking of her silence that he had not taken in what she had said. Was it something about a fire? Reverting to the left hand, he quickly okayed the last few forms, unread.

Out in the corridor he could hear Bridie's voice from the bedrooms: 'Let's all put in our teeth and then toddle along to the fire escape.' Her tone was so calm that he had to fight off the urge to dive through the nearest window. Instead, he drove his fist into the glass of the alarm, mashing its metal casing flat against the wall. Nothing happened. Cursing, he realized that he must have forgotten to re-set it after Evan's tussle with Snow but now even throwing the switch in the power cupboard had no result.

The residents were beginning to file past. Most were fully dressed, all zips and buttons properly fastened, as if they had been awaiting such a summons. Frances went by at a trot: she obviously had no intention of getting her whiskers singed. The others, however, were perfectly calm. If anything, they seemed reluctant to leave and miss the fun. Dolly was clapping her hands like a small girl thrilled at the prospect of her first bonfire party. 'Merry Christmas!' she chuckled. 'Happy New Year!'

Price rang the fire station but no one answered. And when he tried 999 the emergency operator merely reconnected him to the same line and its maddening warbling tone. He counted down from fifty and then hung up.

'Keep them moving,' he called after Bridie's averted head, 'while I check the toilets and bathrooms.'

There were no signs of the fire until Price reached the second corridor where he was confronted by a seemingly impenetrable grey curtain. It resembled fur rather than smoke. Price could have sworn that a faint laughter floated from it. Ducking into the bathroom, he soaked his Barbour hanky with cold water, then wrapped it around his nose and mouth. On emerging, he saw that two figures were slowly coming through the murk. Locked in apparently amicable conversation, Mrs P and Mrs B seemed oblivious to everything around them: he had to shrink against the wall to allow them to pass. At first he thought that they had discarded their Zimmers but then saw that they had hooked their arms around the front legs and were bearing them like haversacks on their backs.

To Price's surprise, no sooner had he entered the smoke than he was stepping out on the other side. The stairs were clear but by the time he had reached the first floor he was unusually short of breath. 'Hello! Hello!' he heard himself calling down the corridor, both sides of which were well alight. 'Is anybody there?' It sounded ridiculous, as if he were some old spinster at her ouija board. He approached the attic stairs, put one foot on the bottom rung and then stopped.

If Evan and Adrea had still been up there, he told himself, then they would surely have come down by now. They must have gone to the carnival, after all. Recalling the candles, the darkness, the stuck record, it seemed most likely that they had been the source of the fire. Perhaps, after weeks of smouldering, they had spontaneously combusted at last. Price noticed that his shoelace was coming loose: why was it always the left one? Having re-tied it, he did the same to the other, just to be on the safe side.

Then he turned away and crashed through the fire door and ran along the burning corridor. He was calling out to Mrs P and Mrs B and other residents that he knew to be already safe outside. Although he kept his eyes on the ground he seemed to glimpse unfamiliar glowing creatures standing in the doorways, regarding him with obvious disapproval. At the far end, he pressed his fingertips against the wall, counted down from ten and then lumbered back the way he had come, which had narrowed appreciably in the meantime. At least he wasn't a coward, he told himself, but then there were worse things than being a coward. And fire had never bothered him much. If the place had been flooded or invaded by pigeons it would have been a different matter.

The furry smoke had returned and was choking the stairwell. It seemed to attach itself to Price's shoulders so that he was drawing it behind him like a cloak, along the bottom corridor. Then someone came round the corner and moved towards him. It appeared to be a man walking backwards with his head twisted the wrong way round. Only when they were face to face did Price recognize Terry. How tall he was out of his wheelchair! How broad his shoulders were! Price could feel the hair rising on his head: he wondered if it could be turning white. He put a restraining arm across Terry's chest, only to be brushed aside with unexpected force. This contact seemed to have broken the spell, however, because a couple of paces further on Terry faltered, swayed and then, light and frail again, fell backwards into Price's arms.

So this was it: the sudden disappearance of Parkinsonian symptoms in response to extreme circumstances – *kinesia paradoxa* in action. He waltzed Terry back down the hall to where the wheelchair lay overturned on its side. It was amazing what a whiff of smoke could do. Even the catatonic Nietzsche used to perk up when a candle was held before his eyes. To enjoy health, long life and happiness, all you had to do was regularly set fire to everything around you. Price flipped up the chair and tossed Terry back into it, then saw that the webbing of the safety harness was ragged and torn. How had the man summoned the strength to break his bonds?

The lovers lay facing each other, bone against bone: it felt as if they had finally succeeded in wearing away each other's skins. Adrea liked the idea of their being reduced to pure white skeletons, glowing in the dark, grinning and dancing on the end of invisible strings, long fingers paradiddling each other's ribcages. Once, when she was a little girl, she had got lost in the Natural History Museum. After a while she had followed the sound of laughter to find her classmates clustered under the enormous tines of the Great Irish Elk. Their scandalized teacher had tried to shoo them away but even then they had known better than to be afraid of old bones.

She could faintly hear Price's voice calling. 'Ignore him,' said Evan, and the sound was soon drowned out by a funny creaking from the floor and ceiling. The bed seemed to be in motion, as if they were gently sliding from left to right while everything else was moving at the same rate in the opposite direction. She licked at Evan's shoulder: it was sticky and salty, like blood. She had the curious thought that their skeletons would not be white but bright red.

Evan was aware that his teeth were grinding mechanically and the taste of grit was in his mouth. His Adam's apple felt swollen and out of alignment: he kept gulping, as if trying to swallow it. He had been slipping into and out of a dream in which his mother had sent him down to Jones's bakery to buy a small white loaf and he was waiting in a slow-moving queue. All his dreams were now like this, flat and ordinary, whereas when he was awake nothing made any sense at all. He became aware that other smells were forcing their way through the Spiritual Sky incense. It seemed that his nose could now distinguish as many things as his eyes could see: he had always thought that you could only smell one thing – the strongest, the most pungent – at a time. There was the bleachy tang of his own drying semen, a fart that had been hanging in the air for half an hour without disappearing and a mysterious muzzy sweetness like golden syrup heated in its tin. And far below in the kitchen it seemed that the vile cook was frying the bacon rather than boiling it. Surely it couldn't be breakfast already? Best of all though was the wonderful ashy scent that rose from the three patches of damp hair on Adrea's body, merging into that of the mounds of dog ends and roaches around the bed. Surely Heaven, if it existed, must be plentifully provided with overflowing, never-to-be emptied ashtrays, along with the cherubim and seraphim and the lions and the lambs? And now Evan saw that, although they had tacked a second thick blanket over the window, a dazzling light was breaking into the room. It was the sun, growing and growing until it filled the sky, bearing down upon them. Lazily, he raised his left foot and eclipsed it and then – as if it had been a discarded cigarette butt – he stamped it out.

As Price pushed the wheelchair through the melting Tarmac of the ramp, the heat lapped cruelly at his already smarting face. He saw that Bridie had assembled the residents on the pavement opposite the Eagle and Child. The people from the blocks were wrapping them in tartan blankets and thrusting white enamel mugs of tea into their hands. They obviously remembered the routine from the Blitz. The landlord midget had appeared at his taproom door. He was wearing a blue and gold dressing gown, frogged and braided as if he were the colonel of a regiment of tiny hussars. The pointed silver slippers, however, rather spoiled the effect. Price became aware that everyone was staring at him with a mixture of horror and amusement. Even when he whipped off his bandit's mask their expressions didn't change. He guessed that he must resemble a well-roasted ox.

Now, without their usual bells and sirens, the Fire Brigade had arrived. Price admired their leisurely air as the hoses rolled out at lightning speed. The sight of those helmeted men looming out of the smoke and darkness reminded him of his childhood nightmares about the fall of Troy. One was even carrying a large gleaming axe across his chest. He saw that another had scooped up Stormy and was triumphantly holding him above his head. 'O. J. Simpson!' he shouted, to general applause. 'Towering Fucking Inferno!' Price realized that Billy the Sailor was now Billy the Fireman. It was just as well that he was wearing heavy gauntlets, for the cat did not seem pleased to see his old friend again.

Snow came out of his block. Barefoot, he advanced in a series of hops, as if walking on hot coals. He had hurriedly pulled on a suit over his pyjamas, and around his neck hung a pair of binoculars nearly as large as his head. Without its usual Brylcreem, his hair was flying up in an aureole of split ends.

'No, no, no!' he was shouting. He burst through the crowd and headed towards the burning building, until one of the hoses, snaking round his ankles, brought him down.

'The children!' he cried as they pulled him away. 'There are children still in there!'

'Funny sort of children,' said one of the firemen, jerking his thumb at the creased and vacant faces behind him. Price could tell that he was in charge because his helmet was larger than the others and even more phallic in shape.

'I've just done a full count,' Price told him. 'And all our residents are accounted for. There were a couple of care assistants on emergency call but they told me they were going to the Notting Hill Carnival.'

'They've jumped out of the fire and back into the frying pan, then,' said the chief. 'There's a full-scale riot going on down there. We were on our way when we spotted your smoke.'

Snow, breaking free, struck out once more for the fire, but Price observed that he lingered just a little so that the firemen could catch and drag him back again.

'One thing that beats me,' the chief continued, 'is the way these niggers and anarchists are always looting and burning their own places. Why don't they hop on a bus to Kensington Palace or Buck House?'

'Oh, they will.' Price adopted a sententious tone. 'On the day after their majesties have moved to Ladbroke Grove.'

The man snorted and moved away. He also had the biggest boots, which stamped louder than anyone else's. Price saw that Mrs Parker had joined Mrs Barker in her task of lighting everyone's cigarettes. Their flaring matches somehow looked more dangerous than the conflagration on the other side of the square. Snow had stopped struggling and was sitting on the kerb with his head in his hands. Dolly's trembling forefinger rose to point at him. 'Penny for the guy,' she said. So it appeared that fire not only made the paralysed walk but also provided the senile with *le mot juste*.

Although his wheelchair was turned towards the flames, Terry did not want to watch. Instead he tilted his head right back so that it faced the stars. He was hoping that he would see Evan and Adrea appear. Somewhere between Bootes and Arcturus was his bet. He hadn't been trying to save them when Price had pulled him back: he had wanted them to take him along. That was what Guy the Gorilla hadn't bargained for: by the time his farmyard armies had organized themselves, he would no longer be here but away safe and snug among the stars.

Price was startled by how quickly the fire had taken hold. Although everyone around him was perfectly calm, there was a noise like women screaming and bulls roaring over thundering kettledrums and fanfares of brass. The blaze seemed to have brought along its own sound effects. The smoke looked to be pouring down from the sky and the flames, although fierce, showed no desire to spread to the adjoining buildings. How could you have a fire without sparks? He glimpsed massive shapes that vanished before he could quite identify them, although certain vertical and horizontal patterns did recur, suggesting that it was a forest burning. And what were all those colours doing in there? Reds and yellows, even greens and browns and blues were all bleeding into each other in a way reminiscent of Turner's paintings of the burning of the Houses of Parliament. It seemed unnecessarily spectacular for a mere old people's home. As he watched, it listed like a holed battleship and the matron's flat exploded in a blinding silver flash. It appeared that he had been sleeping unsuspectingly above the powder magazine. Now the full dreadful import struck him: those Hugo Wolf Society 78s were irreplaceable.

Terry had begun to realize that something was happening in the sky. There was no doubt about it: instead of new stars appearing, all the constellations were being swallowed up, one by one, into a great obliterating blackness. The sun had burnt itself out and now the rest of the universe was following suit. A clock somewhere struck twelve.

Either these scurrying fools around him thought it was midnight not midday, or they just didn't care that the end of the world had come.

Then Terry felt the familiar sensation of fingers flicking hard against the bones of his face. It could only be Mr Snow, recovering from his recent bout of kindliness. The man had never guessed that these intended cruelties were in fact his own greatest pleasure because they were the only things that he could actually feel. Not until a dozen fingers struck him at once did he understand what was really happening. The rain came streaming across his skin. It blinded him but he couldn't blink, it poured down his throat but he couldn't even choke. Now that it had started he knew that it was never going to stop. Death by drowning outside the old E and C while the last lights in the universe went out. It seemed as good a way to go as any. At least he wouldn't be the only one: he was fairly sure that gorillas couldn't swim.

Price was soaked before he even knew that it was raining – large, heavy drops that hit the ground with a slap, like a card player laying down a winning hand. The firemen seemed to have taken exception to it and were redirecting their hoses into the sky. Perhaps they thought that it was doing them out of a job?

Then he saw the policewoman. The rain had already formed a large puddle in the road so that she appeared to be standing on the surface of a lake. Although her back was towards him he would have known her anywhere. He could read every line of her face in the expressions of the men in the crowd before her. She was wearing a fluorescent yellow jacket with shiny silver piping: the years had brought no promotions for she was still a constable. Her hair was even paler – platinum, almost white – and she had put on weight. Her neck had thickened and sunk into her shoulders. It looked as if it might be hard to remove the silly chessboard hat that had been rammed down over her ears.

What would happen when she turned round? What if she scowled or laughed or burst into tears? What if she ignored or didn't recognize him? He could tell that his mouth had twisted itself into the unfamiliar contours of a smile but he did not try to force it off his face. This time he wasn't going to worry about being ridiculous: he was going to hold his ground. Even if she never did turn round and he was just left standing there, smiling stupidly, waiting in the rain, for all eternity.

Midge was getting increasingly irritated by the crowd's enjoyment of the blaze, by the way the mouths gaped and the eyes boggled as they oohed and aahed. It was beneath his dignity to be sharing a pavement with such creatures. Fires were ten a penny: you might as well get all steamed up about there *not* being a fire. Any fool could put a match to something or get themselves burnt.

Perhaps he should have tried to conceal his disdain for now he saw that the blonde policewoman was giving him the evil eye and even some of his regulars were starting to mutter and glare. Midge had long ago learned that with fires, floods and acts of God, they always pinned the blame on the very special people. He gradually backed into the darkened doorway and then – slowly, bit by bit, as only very special people could – he disappeared.

For news about current and forthcoming titles
from Portobello Books and for a sense of purpose
visit the website **www.portobellobooks.com**

encouraging voices,
supporting writers,
challenging readers

Portobello
BOOKS